GOD HELP THE CHILD

God Help the Child

TONI MORRISON

Chatto & Windus

LONDON

1 3 5 7 9 10 8 6 4 2

Chatto & Windus, an imprint of Vintage,
20 Vauxhall Bridge Road,
London SW1V 2SA

Chatto & Windus is part of the Penguin Random House
group of companies whose addresses can be found at
global.penguinrandomhouse.com.

Copyright © Toni Morrison 2015

First published by Chatto & Windus in 2015

www.vintage-books.co.uk

A CIP catalogue record for this book is available from the British Library

ISBN 9780701186050

Grateful acknowledgement is made to SA music LLC and Hal Leonard
Corporation for permission to reprint an excerpt from 'Stormy Weather',
lyrics by Ted Koehler and music by Harold Arlen,
copyright © 1933, copyright renewed © 1961 by Fred Ahlert Music Group
and Ted Koehler Music Co.

Printed and bound by Clays Ltd, St Ives plc

Penguin Random House is committed to a sustainable future for our
business, our readers and our planet. This book is made from Forest
Stewardship Council® certified paper.

For You

Suffer little children to come unto me,
and forbid them not

LUKE 18:16

PART I

⚜

Sweetness

It's not my fault. So you can't blame me. I didn't do it and have no idea how it happened. It didn't take more than an hour after they pulled her out from between my legs to realize something was wrong. Really wrong. She was so black she scared me. Midnight black, Sudanese black. I'm light-skinned, with good hair, what we call high yellow, and so is Lula Ann's father. Ain't nobody in my family anywhere near that color. Tar is the closest I can think of yet her hair don't go with the skin. It's different—straight but curly like those naked tribes in Australia. You might think she's a throwback, but throwback to what? You should've seen my grandmother; she passed for white and never said another word to any one of her children. Any letter she got from my mother or my aunts she sent right back, unopened. Finally they got the message of no message and let her be. Almost all mulatto types and quadroons did that back in the day— if they had the right kind of hair, that is. Can you imagine how many white folks have Negro blood running and hiding in their veins? Guess. Twenty percent, I heard. My own mother, Lula Mae, could have passed easy, but she chose not to. She told me the price she paid for that decision. When she and my father went to the courthouse to get married there were two Bibles and they had to put their hands on the one reserved for Negroes. The other one was for white people's hands. The Bible! Can you beat it? My mother was housekeeper for a rich white couple. They ate every meal she cooked and insisted she scrub their backs while they sat in the tub and God knows what other intimate things they made her do, but no touching of the same Bible.

Some of you probably think it's a bad thing to group ourselves according to skin color—the lighter, the better—in social clubs, neighborhoods, churches, sororities, even colored schools. But how else can we hold on to a little dignity? How else can you avoid being spit on in a drugstore, shoving elbows at the bus stop, walking in the gutter to let whites have the whole sidewalk, charged a nickel at the grocer's for a paper bag that's free to white shoppers? Let alone all the name-calling. I heard about all of that and much, much more. But because of my mother's skin color, she wasn't stopped from trying on hats in the department stores or using their ladies' room. And my father could try on shoes in the front part of the shoestore, not in a back room. Neither one would let themselves drink from a "colored only" fountain even if they were dying of thirst.

I hate to say it, but from the very beginning in the maternity ward the baby, Lula Ann, embarrassed me. Her birth skin was pale like all babies', even African ones, but it changed fast. I thought I was going crazy when she turned blue-black right before my eyes. I know I went crazy for a minute because once—just for a few seconds—I held a blanket over her face and pressed. But I couldn't do that, no matter how much I wished she hadn't been born with that terrible color. I even thought of giving her away to an orphanage someplace. And I was scared to be one of those mothers who put their babies on church steps. Recently I heard about a couple in Germany, white as snow, who had a dark-skinned baby nobody could explain. Twins, I believe—one white, one colored. But I don't know if it's true. All I know is that for me, nursing her was like having a pickaninny sucking my teat. I went to bottle-feeding soon as I got home.

My husband, Louis, is a porter and when he got back off the rails he looked at me like I really was crazy and looked at her like she was from the planet Jupiter. He wasn't a cussing man so when he said, "Goddamn! What the hell is this?" I knew we were in trouble. That's what did it—what caused the fights between me and him. It broke our marriage to pieces. We had three good years together but when she was born he blamed me and treated Lula Ann like she was a stranger—more than that, an enemy.

He never touched her. I never did convince him that I ain't never, ever fooled around with another man. He was dead sure I was lying. We argued and argued till I told him her blackness must be from his own family—not mine. That's when it got worse, so bad he just up and left and I had to look for another, cheaper place to live. I knew enough not to take her with me when I applied to landlords so I left her with a teenage cousin to babysit. I did the best I could and didn't take her outside much anyway because when I pushed her in the baby carriage, friends or strangers would lean down and peek in to say something nice and then give a start or jump back before frowning. That hurt. I could have been the babysitter if our skin colors were reversed. It was hard enough just being a colored woman—even a high-yellow one—trying to rent in a decent part of the city. Back in the nineties when Lula Ann was born, the law was against discriminating in who you could rent to, but not many landlords paid attention to it. They made up reasons to keep you out. But I got lucky with Mr. Leigh. I know he upped the rent seven dollars from what he advertised, and he has a fit if you a minute late with the money.

I told her to call me "Sweetness" instead of "Mother" or "Mama." It was safer. Being that black and having what I think are too-thick lips calling me "Mama" would confuse people. Besides, she has funny-colored eyes, crow-black with a blue tint, something witchy about them too.

So it was just us two for a long while and I don't have to tell you how hard it is being an abandoned wife. I guess

Louis felt a little bit bad after leaving us like that because a few months later on he found out where I moved to and started sending me money once a month, though I never asked him to and didn't go to court to get it. His fifty-dollar money orders and my night job at the hospital got me and Lula Ann off welfare. Which was a good thing. I wish they would stop calling it welfare and go back to the word they used when my mother was a girl. Then it was called "Relief." Sounds much better, like it's just a short-term breather while you get yourself together. Besides, those welfare clerks are mean as spit. When finally I got work and didn't need them anymore, I was making more money than they ever did. I guess meanness filled out their skimpy paychecks, which is why they treated us like beggars. More so when they looked at Lula Ann and back at me—like I was cheating or something. Things got better but I still had to be careful. Very careful in how I raised her. I had to be strict, very strict. Lula Ann needed to learn how to behave, how to keep her head down and not to make trouble. I don't care how many times she changes her name. Her color is a cross she will always carry. But it's not my fault. It's not my fault. It's not my fault. It's not.

Bride

I'm scared. Something bad is happening to me. I feel like I'm melting away. I can't explain it to you but I do know when it started. It began after he said, "You not the woman I want."

"Neither am I."

I still don't know why I said that. It just popped out of my mouth. But when he heard my sassy answer he shot me a hateful look before putting on his jeans. Then he grabbed his boots and T-shirt and when I heard the door slam I wondered for a split second if he was not just ending our silly argument, but ending us, our relationship. Couldn't be. Any minute I would hear the key turn, the front door click open and close. But I didn't hear anything the whole night. Nothing at all. What? I'm not exciting enough? Or pretty enough? I can't have thoughts of my own? Do things he doesn't approve of? By morning soon as I woke up I was furious. Glad he was gone because clearly he was just using me since I had money and a crotch. I was so angry, if you had seen me you would have thought I had spent those six months with him in a holding cell without arraignment or a lawyer, and suddenly the judge called the whole thing off—dismissed the case or refused to hear it at all. Anyway I refused to whine, wail or accuse. He said one thing; I agreed. Fuck him. Besides, our affair wasn't all that spectacular—not even the mildly dangerous sex I used to let myself enjoy. Well, anyway it was nothing like those double-page spreads in fashion magazines, you know, couples standing half naked in surf, looking so fierce and downright mean, their sexuality like lightning and the sky going dark to show off the shine of their skin. I love those ads. But our affair didn't even measure up to any old R-&-B song—some tune with a beat arranged to generate fever. It wasn't even the sugary lyrics of a thirties blues song: "Baby, baby, why you treat me so? I do anything you say, go anywhere you want me to go." Why I kept comparing us to magazine spreads and music I can't say, but it tickled me to settle on "I Wanna Dance with Somebody."

It was raining the next day. Bullet taps on the windows followed by crystal lines of water. I avoided the temptation to glance through the panes at the sidewalk beneath my condo. Besides, I knew what was out there—nasty-looking palm trees lining the road, benches in that tacky little park, few if any pedestrians, a sliver of sea far beyond. I fought giving in to any wish that he was coming back. When a tiny ripple of missing him surfaced, I beat it back. Around noon I opened a bottle of Pinot Grigio and sank into the

sofa, its suede and silk cushions as comfy as any arms.
Almost. Because I have to admit he is one beautiful man,
flawless even, except for a tiny scar on his upper lip and
an ugly one on his shoulder—an orange-red blob with a
tail. Otherwise, head to toe, he is one gorgeous man. I'm
not so bad myself, so imagine how we looked as a couple.
After a glass or two of the wine I was a little buzzed, and
decided to call my friend Brooklyn, tell her all about it.
How he hit me harder than a fist with six words: You not
the woman I want. How they rattled me so I agreed with
them. So stupid. But then I changed my mind about calling
her. You know how it is. Nothing new. Just he walked out
and I don't know why. Besides, too much was happening
at the office for me to bother my best friend and colleague
with gossip about another breakup. Especially now. I'm
regional manager now and that's like being a captain so I
have to maintain the right relationship with the crew. Our
company, Sylvia, Inc., is a small cosmetics business, but it's
beginning to blossom and make waves, finally, and shed its
frumpy past. It used to be Sylph Corsets for Discriminating
Women back in the forties, but changed its name and ownership to Sylvia Apparel, then to Sylvia, Inc., before going
flat-out hip with six cool cosmetics lines, one of which is
mine. I named it YOU, GIRL: Cosmetics for Your Personal Millennium. It's for girls and women of all complex-
ions from ebony to lemonade to milk. And it's mine, all
mine—the idea, the brand, the campaign.

Wiggling my toes under the silk cushion I couldn't help smiling at the lipstick smile on my wineglass, thinking, "How about that, Lula Ann? Did you ever believe you would grow up to be this hot, or this successful?" Maybe *she* was the woman he wanted. But Lula Ann Bridewell is no longer available and she was never a woman. Lula Ann was a sixteen-year-old-me who dropped that dumb countryfied name as soon as I left high school. I was Ann Bride for two years until I interviewed for a sales job at Sylvia, Inc., and, on a hunch, shortened my name to Bride, with nothing anybody needs to say before or after that one memorable syllable. Customers and reps like it, but he ignored it. He called me "baby" most of the time. "Hey, baby"; "Come on, baby." And sometimes "You my girl," accent on the *my*. The only time he said "woman" was the day he split.

The more white wine the more I thought good riddance. No more dallying with a mystery man with no visible means of support. An ex-felon if ever there was one, though he laughed when I teased him about how he spent his time when I was at the office: Idle? Roaming? Or meeting someone? He said his Saturday afternoon trips downtown were not reports to a probation officer or drug rehab counselor. Yet he never told me what they were. I told him every single thing about myself; he confided nothing, so I just made stuff up with TV plots: he was an informant with a new identity, a disbarred lawyer. Whatever. I didn't really care.

Actually the timing of his leaving was perfect for me. With him gone out of my life and out of my apartment I could concentrate on the launch of YOU, GIRL and, equally important, keep a promise I'd made to myself long before I met him—we fought about it the night he said "You not the woman. . . ." According to prisoninfo.org/paroleboard/calendar, it was time. I'd been planning this trip for a year, choosing carefully what a parolee would need: I saved up five thousand dollars in cash over the years, and bought a three-thousand-dollar Continental Airlines gift certificate. I put a promotional box of YOU, GIRL into a brand-new Louis Vuitton shopping bag, all of which could take her anywhere. Comfort her, anyway; help her forget and take the edge off bad luck, hopelessness and boredom. Well, maybe not boredom, no prison is a convent. He didn't understand why I was so set on going and the night when we quarreled about my promise, he ran off. I guess I threatened his ego by doing some Good Samaritan thing not directed at him. Selfish bastard. I paid the rent, not him, and the maid too. When we went to clubs and concerts we rode in my beautiful Jaguar or in cars I hired. I bought him beautiful shirts—although he never wore them—and did all the shopping. Besides, a promise is a promise, especially if it's to oneself.

It was when I got dressed for the drive I noticed the first peculiar thing. Every bit of my pubic hair was gone. Not gone as in shaved or waxed, but gone as in erased, as in never having been there in the first place. It scared me, so I threaded through the hair on my head to see if it was shedding, but it was as thick and slippery as it had always been. Allergy? Skin disease, maybe? It worried me but there was no time to do more than be anxious and plan to see a dermatologist. I had to be on my way to make it on time.

I suppose other people might like the scenery bordering this highway but it's so thick with lanes, exits, parallel roads, overpasses, cautionary signals and signs it's like being forced to read a newspaper while driving. Annoying. Along with amber alerts, silver and gold ones were springing up. I stayed in the right lane and slowed down because from past drives out this way I knew the Norristown exit was easy to miss and the prison had no sign of its existence in the world for a mile beyond the exit ramp. I guess they didn't want tourists to know that some of the reclaimed desert California is famous for holds evil women. Decagon Women's Correctional Center, right outside Norristown, owned by a private company, is worshipped by the locals for the work it provides: serving visitors, guards, clerical staff, cafeteria workers, health care folks and most of all construction laborers repairing the road and fences and adding wing after wing to house the increasing flood of violent, sinful women committing bloody female crimes. Lucky for the state, crime does pay.

The couple of times I drove to Decagon before, I never tried to get inside on some pretext or other. Back then I just wanted to see where the lady monster—that's what they called her—had been caged for fifteen of her twenty-five-to-life sentence. This time was different. She has been granted parole and, according to penal review notices, Sofia Huxley is going to strut through the bars I pushed her behind.

You'd think with Decagon being all about corporate money that a Jaguar wouldn't stand out. But behind the curbside buses, old Toyotas and secondhand trucks, my car, sleek, rat gray with a vanity license, looked like a gun. But it was not as sinister as the white limousines I've seen parked there—engines snoring, chauffeurs leaning against gleaming fenders. Tell me, who would need a driver leaping to open the door and make a quick getaway? A grand madam impatient to get back to her designer linens in her tasteful high-rise brothel? Or maybe a teenage hookerette eager to get back to the patio of some sumptuous, degenerate private club where she could celebrate her release among friends by ripping up her prison-issue underwear. No Sylvia, Inc., products for her. Our line is sexy enough but not expensive enough. Like all sex trash, the little hookerette would think the higher the price, the better the quality. If she only knew. Still, she might buy some YOU, GIRL sparkle eye shadow or gold-flecked lip gloss.

No limousines today, unless you count the Lincoln town car. Mostly just worn Toyotas and ancient Chevys, silent grown-ups and jittery children. An old man sitting at the bus stop is digging into a box of Cheerios, trying to find the last circle of sweet oat bran. He's wearing ancient wing-tip shoes and crisp new jeans. His baseball cap, his brown vest over a white shirt, scream Salvation Army store but his manner is superior, dainty, even. His legs are crossed and he examines the bit of dry cereal as though it were a choice grape picked especially for him by groundskeepers to the throne.

Four o'clock; it won't be long now. Huxley, Sofia, a.k.a. 0071140, won't be released during visiting hours. At exactly four-thirty only the town car is left, owned probably by a lawyer with an alligator briefcase full of papers, money and cigarettes. The cigarettes for his client, the money for witnesses, the papers to look like he's working.

"Are you okay, Lula Ann?" The prosecutor's voice was soft, encouraging, but I could barely hear her. "There's nothing to be afraid of. She can't hurt you."

No, she can't and, damn, here she is. Number 0071140. Even after fifteen years I could never mistake her simply because of her height, six feet at least. Nothing has shrunk the giant I remember who was taller than the bailiff, the judge, the lawyers and almost as tall as the police. Only her co-monster husband matched her height. Nobody doubted she was the filthy freak that parents shaking with anger called her. "Look at her eyes," they whispered. Everywhere in the courthouse, ladies' room, on benches lining the halls they whispered: "Cold, like the snake she is." "At twenty? How could a twenty-year-old do those things to children?" "Are you kidding? Just look at those eyes. Old as dirt." "My little boy will never get over it." "Devil." "Bitch."

Now those eyes are more like a rabbit's than a snake's but the height is the same. A whole lot else has changed. She is as thin as a rope. Size 1 panties; an A-cup bra, if any. And she could sure use some GlamGlo. Formalize Wrinkle Softener and Juicy Bronze would give color to the whey color of her skin.

When I step out of the Jaguar I don't wonder or care whether she recognizes me. I just walk over to her and say, "Need a lift?"

She throws me a quick, uninterested glance and turns her gaze to the road. "No. I don't."

Her mouth is trembly. It used to be hard, a straight razor sharpened to slice a kid. A little Botox and some Tango-Matte, not glitter, would have softened her lips and maybe influenced the jury in her favor except there was no YOU, GIRL back then.

"Somebody picking you up?" I smile.

"Taxi," she says.

Funny. She is answering a stranger dutifully like she's

used to it. No "What's it to you?" or even "Who the hell are you?" but going on to explain further. "Called a cab. I mean the desk did."

When I come closer and reach out to touch her arm the cab rolls up and fast as a bullet she grabs the door handle, tosses in her little carrier bag and slams the door shut. I bang on the window shouting, "Wait! Wait!" Too late. The driver negotiates the U-turn like a NASCAR pro.

I rush to my car. Following them isn't hard. I even pass the taxi to disguise the fact that I am tailing her. That turns out to be a mistake. Just as I'm about to enter the exit ramp, I see the taxi shoot ahead of me toward Norristown. Gravel pings my wheels as I brake, reverse and follow them. The road to Norristown is lined with neat, uniform houses built in the fifties and added on repeatedly—a closed side porch, a garage expanded for two cars, backyard patio. The road looks like a kindergarten drawing of light-blue, white or yellow houses with pine-green or beet-red doors sitting smugly on wide lawns. All that is missing is a pancake sun with ray sticks all around it. Beyond the houses, next to a mall as pale and sad as "lite" beer, a sign announces the beginning of the town. Next to it another, bigger sign for Eva Dean's Motel and Restaurant. The taxi turns and stops by the entrance. She gets out and pays the driver. I follow and park a ways back near the restaurant. Only one other car is in the parking area—a black SUV. I am sure she is meeting someone, but after a few minutes at the check-in desk, she goes straight to the restaurant and takes a seat by the window. I can see her clearly and watch her study the menu like a remedial or English-as-a-second-language student—lip-reading, running her finger over the items. What a change. This is the teacher who had kindergartners cut apples into rings to shape the letter *O,* doled out pretzels as *B*'s, slit watermelon chunks into *Y*'s. All to spell BOY—who she liked best according to the women whispering in front of the sinks in the ladies' room. Fruit as bait was a big part of the trial's testimony.

Look at her eat. The waitress keeps placing plate after plate in front of her. Makes sense, sort of, this first out-of-prison meal. She's gobbling like a refugee, like somebody who's been floating at sea without food or water for weeks and just about to wonder what harm it would do to his dying boatmate to taste his flesh before it shrank. She never takes her eyes from the food, stabbing, slicing, scooping helter-skelter among the dishes. She drinks no water, butters no bread, as though nothing is allowed to delay her speed-eating. The whole thing is over in ten or twelve minutes. Then she pays, leaves and hurries down the walkway. Now what? Key in hand, tote bag on her shoulder, she stops and turns in to a break between two stucco walls. I get out of the car and walk-run behind her until I hear the retching sounds of vomit. So I hide behind the SUV until she comes out.

3-A is painted on the door she unlocks. I'm ready. I make sure my knock is authoritative, strong but not threatening.

"Yes?" Her voice is shaky, the humble sound of someone trained to automatic obedience.

"Mrs. Huxley. Open the door, please."

There is silence then, "I uh. I'm sorta sick."

"I know," I say. A trace of judgment in my voice, hoping she thinks it's about the sick she left on the pavement. "Open the door."

She opens it and stands there barefoot with a towel in her hand. She wipes her mouth. "Yes?"

"We need to talk."

"Talk?" She blinks rapidly but doesn't ask the real question: "Who are you?"

I push past her, leading with the Louis Vuitton bag. "You're Sofia Huxley, right?"

She nods. A tiny flash of fear is in her eyes. I'm black as midnight and dressed in all white so maybe she thinks it's a uniform and I'm an authority of some sort. I want to calm her so I hold up the shopping bag and say, "Come on. Let's sit down. I have something for you." She doesn't look at the bag or my face; she stares at my shoes with their high lethal heels and dangerously pointed toes.

"What do you want me to do?" she asks.

Such a soft, accommodating voice. Knowing after fifteen years behind bars that nothing is free. Nobody gives away anything at no cost to the receiver. Whatever it is—

cigarettes, magazines, tampons, stamps, Mars bars or a jar of peanut butter—it comes with strings tough as fishing line.

"Nothing. I don't want you to do a thing."

Now her eyes stray from my shoes to my face, opaque eyes without inquiry. So I answer the question a normal person would have posed. "I saw you leave Decagon. No one was there to meet you. I offered you a lift."

"That was you?" She frowns.

"Me. Yes."

"I know you?"

"My name is Bride."

She squints. "That supposed to mean something to me?"

"No," I say and smile. "Look what I brought you." I can't resist and place the bag on the bed. I reach inside and on top of the gift package of YOU, GIRL I lay two envelopes— the slim one with the airline gift certificate then the fat one with five thousand dollars. About two hundred dollars for each year if she had served her full sentence.

Sofia stares at the display as though the items might be infected. "What's all that for?"

I wonder if prison has done something to her brain. "It's okay," I say. "Just a few things to help you."

"Help me what?"

"Get a good start. You know, on your life."

"My life?" Something is wrong. She sounds as if she needs an introduction to the word.

"Yeah." I am still smiling. "Your new life."

"Why? Who sent you?" She looks interested now, not frightened.

"I guess you don't remember me." I shrug. "Why would you? Lula Ann. Lula Ann Bridewell. At the trial? I was one of the children who—"

I search through the blood with my tongue. My teeth are all there, but I can't seem to get up. I can feel my left eyelid shutting down and my right arm is dead. The door opens and all the gifts I brought are thrown at me, one by one, including the Vuitton bag. The door slams shut, then opens again. My black stiletto-heeled shoe lands on my back before rolling off next to my left arm. I reach for it and am relieved to learn that, unlike the right one, this one can move. I try to scream "help," but my mouth belongs to somebody else. I crawl a few feet and try to stand. My legs work, so I gather up the gifts, push them into the bag and, one shoe on, one left behind, limp to my car. I don't feel anything. I don't think anything. Not until I see my face in the side-view mirror. My mouth looks as though it's stuffed with raw liver; the whole side of my face is scraped of skin; my right eye is a mushroom. All I want to do is get away from here—no 911; it takes too long and I don't want some ignorant motel manager staring at me. Police. There have to be some in this town. Igniting, shifting, steering with a left hand, while the other one lies dead next to my thigh, takes concentration. All of it. So it's not until I get farther into

Norristown and see a sign with an arrow pointing to the police station that it hits me—the cops will write a report, interview the accused and take a picture of my wrecked face as evidence. And what if the local newspaper gets the story along with my photograph? Embarrassment would be nothing next to the jokes directed at YOU, GIRL. From YOU, GIRL to BOO, GIRL.

Hammers of pain make it hard to get out my cellphone and dial Brooklyn, the one person I can trust. Completely.

Brooklyn

She's lying. We are sitting in this dump of a clinic after I've driven over two hours to find this hick town, then I have to locate her car parked in the rear of a closed-shut police station. Of course it's closed; it's Sunday, when only churches and Wal-Mart are open. She was hysterical when I found her bloody and crying out of one eye, the other one too swollen to shed water. Poor thing. Somebody ruined one of those eyes, the ones that spooked everybody with their strangeness—large, slanted, slightly hooded and funny-colored, considering how black her skin is. Alien eyes, I call them, but guys think they're gorgeous, of course.

Well, when I find this little emergency clinic facing the mall's parking lot I have to hold her up to help her walk. She hobbles, wearing one shoe. Finally we get a nurse's bug-eyed attention. She is startled at the pair of us: one white girl with blond dreads, one very black one with silky curls. It takes forever to sign stuff and show insurance cards. Then we sit down to wait for the on-call doctor who lives, I don't know, far off in some other crappy town. Bride doesn't say a word while I drive her here, but in the waiting room she starts the lie.

"I'm ruined," she whispers.

I say, "No you're not. Give it time. Remember what Grace looked like after her face tuck?"

"A surgeon did her face," she answers. "A maniac did mine."

I press her. "So tell me. What happened, Bride? Who was he?"

"Who was who?" She touches her nose tenderly while breathing through her mouth.

"The guy who beat you half to death."

She coughs for some time and I hand her a tissue. "Did I say it was a guy? I don't remember saying it was a guy."

"Are you telling me a woman did this?"

"No," she says. "No. It was a guy."

"Was he trying to rape you?"

"I suppose. Somebody scared him off, I guess. He banged me around and took off."

See what I mean? Not even a good lie. I push a bit more. "He didn't take your purse, wallet, anything?"

She mumbles, "Boy Scout, I guess." Her lips are puffy and her tongue can't manage consonants but she tries to smile at her own stupid joke.

"Why didn't whoever scared him off stay and help you?"

"I don't know! I don't know! I don't know!"

She is shouting and fake-sobbing so I back off. Her single open eye isn't up to it and her mouth must hurt too much to keep it up. For five minutes I don't say a word, just flip through the pages of a *Reader's Digest;* then I try to make my voice sound as normal and conversational as I can. I decide not to ask why she called me instead of her lover man.

"What were you doing up here anyway?"

"I came to see a friend." She bends forward as though her stomach hurts.

"In Norristown? Your friend lives here?"

"No. Nearby."

"You find him?"

"Her. No. I never found her."

"Who is she?"

"Somebody from a long time ago. She wasn't there. Probably dead by now."

She knows I know she's lying. Why wouldn't an attacker take her money? Something has rattled her brainpan otherwise why would she tell me such fucked-up lies? I guess she doesn't give a damn what I think. When I stuffed her little white skirt and top into the shopping bag, I found a rubber band around fifty hundred-dollar bills, an airline gift certificate and samples of YOU, GIRL not yet launched. Okay? No species of would-be rapist would want Nude Skin Glo, but free cash? I decide to let it go and wait until she's seen the doctor.

Afterward, when Bride holds up my compact mirror to

her face, I know what she sees will break her heart. A quarter of her face is fine; the rest is cratered. Ugly black stitches, puffy eye, bandages on her forehead, lips so Ubangi she can't pronounce the *r* in *raw*, which is what her skin looks like—all pink and blue-black. Worse than anything is her nose—nostrils wide as an orangutan's under gauze the size of half a bagel. Her beautiful unbruised eye seems to cower, bloodshot, practically dead.

I shouldn't be thinking this. But her position at Sylvia, Inc., might be up for grabs. How can she persuade women to improve their looks with products that can't improve her own? There isn't enough YOU, GIRL foundation in the world to hide eye scars, a broken nose and facial skin scraped down to pink hypodermis. Assuming much of the damage fades, she will still need plastic surgery, which means weeks and weeks of idleness, hiding behind glasses and floppy hats. I might be asked to take over. Temporarily, of course.

"I can't eat. I can't talk. I can't think."

Her voice is whiny and she is trembling.

I put my arm around her and whisper, "Hey, girlfriend, no pity party. Let's get out of this dump. They don't even have private rooms and that nurse had lettuce in her teeth and I doubt she's washed her hands since graduating from that online nursing course she took."

Bride stops shaking, adjusts the sling holding her right

arm and asks me, "You don't think that doctor did a good job?"

"Who knows?" I say. "In this trailer park clinic? I'm driving you to a real hospital—with a toilet and sink in the room."

"Don't they have to release me?" She sounds like a ten-year-old.

"Please. We're leaving. Now. Look what I bought while you were being patched up. Sweats and flip-flops. No decent hospital in these parts but a very respectable Wal-Mart. Come on. Up. Lean on me. Where did Florence Nightingale put your things? We'll get some ice pops or slurries on the way. Or a milk shake. That's probably better medicine-wise—or some tomato juice, chicken broth, maybe."

I'm rambling, fussing with pills and clothes while she clutches that ugly flowered hospital gown. "Oh, Bride," I say, but my voice cracks. "Don't look like that—it's going to be all right."

I have to drive slowly; every bump or sudden lane switch makes her wince or grunt. I try to get her mind off her pain.

"I didn't know you were twenty-three. I thought you were my age, twenty-one. I saw it on your driver's license. You know, when I was looking for your insurance card."

She doesn't answer, so I keep on trying to get a smile out of her. "But your good eye looks twenty."

It doesn't work. What the hell. I might as well be talking to myself. I decide to just get her home and settled. I'll take care of everything at work. Bride will be on sick leave for a long time, and somebody has to take on her responsibilities. And who knows how that might turn out?

Bride

She really was a freak. Sofia Huxley. The quick change from obedient ex-con to raging alligator. From slack-lipped to fangs. From slouch to hammer. I never saw the signal—no eye squint or grip of neck cords, no shoulder flex or raised lip showing teeth. Nothing announced her attack on me. I'll never forget it, and even if I tried to, the scars, let alone the shame, wouldn't let me.

Memory is the worst thing about healing. I lie around all day with nothing urgent to do. Brooklyn has taken care of explanations to the office staff: attempted rape, foiled, blah, blah. She is a true friend and doesn't annoy me like those fake ones who come here just to gaze and pity me. I can't watch television; it's so boring—mostly blood, lipstick, and the haunches of anchorgirls. What passes for news is either gossip or a lecture of lies. How can I take crime shows seriously where the female detectives track killers in Louboutin heels? As for reading, print makes me dizzy, and for some reason I don't like listening to music anymore. Vocals, both the beautiful and the mediocre, depress me, and instrumentals are worse. Plus something bad has been done to my tongue because my taste buds have disappeared. Everything tastes like lemons—except lemons, which taste like salt. Wine is a waste since Vicodin gives me a thicker, more comfortable fog.

The bitch didn't even hear me out. I wasn't the only witness, the only one who turned Sofia Huxley into 0071140. There was lots of other testimony about her molestations. At least four other kids were witnesses. I didn't hear what they said but they were shaking and crying when they left the courtroom. The social worker and psychologist who coached us put their arms around them, whispering, "You'll be fine. You did great." Neither one hugged me but they smiled at me. Apparently Sofia Huxley has no family. Well she has a husband who is in another prison and still unparoled after seven tries. No one was there to meet her. Nobody. So why didn't she just accept help instead of whatever check-out-counter or cleaning-woman job she might be given? Rich parolees don't end up cleaning toilets at Wendy's.

I was only eight years old, still little Lula Ann, when I lifted my arm and pointed my finger at her.

"Is the woman you saw here in this room?" The lawyer lady smells of tobacco.

I nod.

"You have to speak, Lula. Say 'yes' or 'no.'"

"Yes."

"Can you show us where she is seated?"

I am afraid of knocking over the paper cup of water the lady lawyer gave me.

"Relax," says the prosecutor lady. "Take your time."

And I did take my time. My hand was in a fist until my arm was straight. Then I unfolded my forefinger. *Pow!* Like a cap pistol. Mrs. Huxley stared at me then opened her mouth as though about to say something. She looked shocked, unbelieving. But my finger still pointed, pointed so long the lady prosecutor had to touch my hand and say, "Thank you, Lula," to get me to put my arm down. I glanced at Sweetness; she was smiling like I've never seen her smile before—with mouth and eyes. And that wasn't all. Outside the courtroom all the mothers smiled at me, and two actually touched and hugged me. Fathers gave me thumbs-up. Best of all was Sweetness. As we walked down the courthouse steps she held my hand, my hand. She never did that before and it surprised me as much as it pleased me because I always knew she didn't like touching me. I could tell. Distaste was all over her face when I was little and she had to bathe me. Rinse me, actually, after a halfhearted rub with a soapy washcloth. I used to pray she would slap my face or spank me just to feel her touch. I made little mistakes deliberately, but she had ways to punish me without touching the skin she hated—bed without supper, lock me in my room—but her screaming at me was the worst. When fear rules, obedience is the only survival choice. And I was good at it. I behaved and behaved and behaved. Frightened as I was to appear in court, I did what the teacher-psychologists expected of me. Brilliantly, I know, because after the trial Sweetness was kind of motherlike.

I don't know. Maybe I'm just mad more at myself than at Mrs. Huxley. I reverted to the Lula Ann who never fought back. Ever. I just lay there while she beat the shit out of me. I could have died on the floor of that motel room if her face hadn't gone apple-red with fatigue. I didn't make a sound, didn't even raise a hand to protect myself when she slapped my face then punched me in the ribs before smashing my jaw with her fist then butting my head with hers. She was panting when she dragged and threw me out the door. I can still feel her hard fingers clenching the hair at the back of my neck, her foot on my behind and I can still hear the crack of my bones hitting concrete. Elbow, jaw. I feel my arms sliding and grabbing for balance. Then my tongue searching through blood to locate my teeth. When the door slammed then opened again so she could throw out my shoe, like a whipped puppy I just crawled away afraid to even whimper.

Maybe he is right. I am not the woman. When he left I shook it off and pretended it didn't matter.

Foam spurting from an aerosol can made him chuckle, so he lathered with shaving soap and a brush, a handsome thing of boar's hair swelling from an ivory handle. I think it's in the trash along with his toothbrush, strop and straight razor. The things he left are too alive. It's time to throw all of it out. He left everything: toiletries, clothes and a cloth bag containing two books, one in a foreign language, the other a book of poems. I dump it all, then pick through the trash and take out his shaving brush and bone-handled razor. I put them both in the medicine cabinet and when I close the door I stare at my face in the mirror.

"You should always wear white, Bride. Only white and all white all the time." Jeri, calling himself a "total person" designer, insisted. Looking for a makeover for my second interview at Sylvia, Inc., I consulted him.

"Not only because of your name," he told me, "but because of what it does to your licorice skin," he said. "And black is the new black. Know what I mean? Wait. You're more Hershey's syrup than licorice. Makes people think of whipped cream and chocolate soufflé every time they see you."

That made me laugh. "Or Oreos?"

"Never. Something classy. Bonbons. Hand-dipped."

At first it was boring shopping for white-only clothes until I learned how many shades of white there were: ivory, oyster, alabaster, paper white, snow, cream, ecru, Champagne, ghost, bone. Shopping got even more interesting when I began choosing colors for accessories.

Jeri, advising me, said, "Listen, Bride baby. If you must have a drop of color limit it to shoes and purses, but I'd keep both black when white simply won't do. And don't forget: no makeup. Not even lipstick or eyeliner. None."

I asked him about jewelry. Gold? Some diamonds? An emerald brooch?

"No. No." He threw his hands up. "No jewelry at all. Pearl dot earrings, maybe. No. Not even that. Just you, girl. All sable and ice. A panther in snow. And with your body? And those wolverine eyes? Please!"

I took his advice and it worked. Everywhere I went I got double takes but not like the faintly disgusted ones I used to get as a kid. These were adoring looks, stunned but hungry. Plus, unbeknownst to him, Jeri had given me the name for a product line. YOU, GIRL.

My face looks almost new in the mirror. My lips are back to normal; so are my nose and my eye. Only my rib area is still tender and, to my surprise, the scraped skin on my face has healed the quickest. I look almost beautiful again, so why am I still sad? On impulse I open the medicine cabinet and take out his shaving brush. I finger it. The silky hair is both tickly and soothing. I bring the brush to my chin, stroke it the way he used to. I move it to the underside of my jaw, then up to my earlobes. For some reason I feel faint. Soap. I need lather. I tear open a fancy box containing a tube of body foam "for the skin he loves." Then I squeeze it into the soap dish and wet his brush. Slathering the foam on my face I am breathless. I lather my cheeks, under my nose. This is crazy I'm sure but I stare at my face. My eyes look wider and starry. My nose is not only healed, it's perfect, and my lips between the white foam look so downright kissable I touch them with the tip of my little finger. I don't want to stop, but I have to. I clasp his razor. How did he hold it? Some finger arrangement I don't remember. I'll have to practice. Meantime I use the dull edge and carve dark chocolate lanes through swirls of white lather. I splash water and rinse my face. The satisfaction that follows is so so sweet.

This working from home isn't as bad as I thought it would be. I have authority still, although Brooklyn second-guesses me, even overrides a few of my decisions. I don't mind. I'm lucky she has my back. Besides, when I feel depressed the cure is tucked away in a little kit where his shaving equipment is. Lathering warm soapy water, I can hardly wait for the brushing and then the razor, the combination that both excites and soothes me. Lets me imagine without grief times when I was made fun of and hurt.

"She's sort of pretty under all that black." Neighbors and their daughters agreed. Sweetness never attended parent-teacher meetings or volleyball games. I was encouraged to take business courses not the college track, community college instead of four-year state universities. I didn't do any

of that. After I don't know how many refusals, I finally got
a job working stock—never sales where customers would
see me. I wanted the cosmetics counter but didn't dare ask
for it. I got to be a buyer only after rock-dumb white girls
got promotions or screwed up so bad they settled for somebody who actually knew about stock. Even the interview at
Sylvia, Inc., got off to a bad start. They questioned my style,
my clothes and told me to come back later. That's when
I consulted Jeri. Then walking down the hall toward the
interviewer's office, I could see the effect I was having: wide
admiring eyes, grins and whispers: "Whoa!" "Oh, baby."
In no time I rocketed to regional manager. "See?" said
Jeri. "Black sells. It's the hottest commodity in the civilized
world. White girls, even brown girls have to strip naked to
get that kind of attention."

True or not, it made me, remade me. I began to move
differently—not a strut, not that pelvis-out rush of the
runway—but a stride, slow and focused. Men leaped and I
let myself be caught. For a while, anyway, until my sex life
became sort of like Diet Coke—deceptively sweet minus
nutrition. More like a PlayStation game imitating the safe
glee of virtual violence and just as brief. All my boyfriends
were typecast: would-be actors, rappers, professional athletes, players waiting for my crotch or my paycheck like
an allowance; others, already having made it, treating me
like a medal, a shiny quiet testimony to their prowess. Not

one of them giving, helpful—none interested in what I thought, just what I looked like. Joking or baby-talking me through what I believed was serious conversation before they found more ego props elsewhere. I remember one date in particular, a medical student who persuaded me to join him on a visit to his parents' house up north. As soon as he introduced me it was clear I was there to terrorize his family, a means of threat to this nice old white couple.

"Isn't she beautiful?" he kept repeating. "Look at her, Mother? Dad?" His eyes were gleaming with malice.

But they outclassed him with their warmth—however faked—and charm. His disappointment was obvious, his anger thinly repressed. His parents even drove me to the train stop, probably so I wouldn't have to put up with his failed racist joke on them. I was relieved, even knowing what the mother did with my used teacup.

Such was the landscape of men.

Then him. Booker. Booker Starbern.

I don't want to think about him now. Or how empty, how trivial and lifeless everything seems now. I don't want to remember how handsome he is, perfect except for that ugly burn scar on his shoulder. I stroked every inch of his golden skin, sucked his earlobes. I know the quality of the hair in his armpit; I fingered the dimple in his upper lip; I poured red wine in his navel and drank its spill. There is no place on my body his lips did not turn into bolts of lightning. Oh, God. I have to stop reliving our lovemaking. I have to forget how new it felt every single time, both fresh and somehow eternal. I'm tone-deaf but fucking him made me sing and then, and then out of nowhere, "You not the woman . . ." before vanishing like a ghost.

Dismissed.

Erased.

Even Sofia Huxley, of all people, erased me. A convict. A convict! She could have said, "No thanks," or even "Get out!" No. She went postal. Maybe fistfighting is prison talk. Instead of words, broken bones and drawing blood is inmate conversation. I'm not sure which is worse, being dumped like trash or whipped like a slave.

We had lunch in my office the day before he split—lobster salad, Smartwater, peach slices in brandy. Oh, stop. I can't keep thinking about him. And I'm stir-crazy slouching around these rooms. Too much light, too much space, too lonely. I have to put on some clothes and get out of here. Do what Brooklyn keeps nagging me about: forget sunglasses and floppy hats, show myself, live life like it really is life. She should know; she's making Sylvia, Inc., her own.

I choose carefully: bone-white shorts and halter, high-wedged rope-and-straw sandals, beige canvas tote into which I drop the shaving brush in case I need it. *Elle* magazine and sunglasses too. Brooklyn would approve even though I'm just going two blocks to a park used mostly by dog walkers and seniors this time of day. Later on there will be joggers and skaters, but no mothers and children on a Saturday. Their weekends are for playdates, playrooms, playgrounds and play restaurants, all guarded by loving nannies with delicious accents.

I select a bench near an artificial pond where real ducks sail. And though I quickly block a memory of his describing the difference between wild drakes and yardbirds, my muscles remember his cool, massaging fingers. While I turn the pages of *Elle* and scan pictures of the young and eatable, I hear slow steps on gravel. I look up. The steps belong to a gray-haired couple strolling by, silent, holding hands. Their paunches are the exact same size, although his is lower down. Both wear colorless slacks and loose T-shirts imprinted with faded signs, front and back, about peace. The teenage dog walkers snigger and yank leashes for no reason, except perhaps envy of a long life of intimacy. The couple moves carefully, as though in a dream. Steps matching, looking straight ahead like people called to a spaceship where a door will slide open and a tongue of red carpet rolls out. They will ascend, hand in hand, into the arms of a benevolent Presence. They will hear music so beautiful it will bring you to tears.

That does it. The hand-holding couple, their silent music. I can't stop it now—I'm back in the packed stadium. The screaming audience is no match for the wild, sexy music. Crowds dance in the aisles; people stand on their bench seats and clap to the drums. My arms are in the air waving to the music. My hips and head sway on their own. Before I see his face, his arms are around my waist, my back to his chest, his chin in my hair. Then his hands are on my stomach and I am dropping mine to hold on to his while we dance back to front. When the music stops I turn around to look at him. He smiles. I am moist and shivering.

Before I leave the park, I finger the bristles of the shaving brush. They are soft and warm.

Sweetness

Oh, yeah, I feel bad sometimes about how I treated Lula Ann when she was little. But you have to understand: I had to protect her. She didn't know the world. There was no point in being tough or sassy even when you were right. Not in a world where you could be sent to a juvenile lockup for talking back or fighting in school, a world where you'd be the last one hired and the first one fired. She couldn't know any of that or how her black skin would scare white people or make them laugh and trick her. I once saw a girl nowhere near as dark as Lula Ann and who couldn't be more than ten years old tripped by one of a group of white boys and when she fell and tried to scramble up another one put his foot on her behind and knocked her flat again. Those boys held their stomachs and bent over with laughter. Long after she got away, they were still giggling, so proud of themselves. If I hadn't been watching through the bus window I would have helped her, pulled her away from that white trash. See if I hadn't trained Lula Ann properly she wouldn't have known to always cross the street and avoid white boys. But the lessons I taught her paid off because in the end she made

me proud as a peacock. It was in that case with that gang of
pervert teachers—three of them, a man and two women—
that she knocked it out of the park. Young as she was, she
behaved like a grown-up on the witness stand—so calm and
sure of herself. Fixing her wild hair was always a trial, but I
braided it down tight for the court appearance and bought
her a blue and white sailor dress. I was nervous thinking
she would stumble getting up to the stand, or stutter, or forget what the psychologists said and put me to shame. But
no, thank God, she put the noose, so to speak, around at
least one of those sinful teachers' neck. The things they were
accused of would make you puke. How they got little kids to
do nasty things. It was in the newspapers and on television.
For weeks, crowds of people with and without children in
the school yelled outside the courthouse. Some had home-
made signs saying, KILL THE FREAKS and NO MERCY FOR
DEVILS.

I sat through most of the days of the trial, not all, just
the days when Lula Ann was scheduled to appear, because
many witnesses were postponed or never showed. They
got sick or changed their minds. She looked scared but she
stayed quiet, not like the other child witnesses fidgeting and
whining. Some were even crying. After Lula Ann's performance in that court and on the stand I was so proud of her,
we walked the streets hand in hand. It's not often you see
a little black girl take down some evil whites. I wanted her

to know how pleased I was so I had her ears pierced and bought her a pair of earrings—tiny gold hoops. Even the landlord smiled when he saw us. No pictures were in the newspapers because of privacy laws for children, but the word got out. The drugstore owner, who always turned his mouth down when he saw us together, handed Lula Ann a Clark bar after he heard about her courage.

I wasn't a bad mother, you have to know that, but I may have done some hurtful things to my only child because I had to protect her. Had to. All because of skin privileges. At first I couldn't see past all that black to know who she was and just plain love her. But I do. I really do. I think she understands now. I think so.

Last two times I saw her she was, well, striking. Kind of bold and confident. Each time she came I forgot just how black she really was because she was using it to her advantage in beautiful white clothes.

Taught me a lesson I should have known all along. What you do to children matters. And they might never forget. She's got a big-time job in California but she don't call or visit anymore. She sends me money and stuff every now and then, but I ain't seen her in I don't know how long.

Bride

Brooklyn picks the restaurant. Pirate, it's called, a semi-chic, once-hot, now barely-hanging-on place for tourists and the decidedly uncool. The evening is too chilly for the sleeveless white shift I'm wearing, but I want to impress Brooklyn with my progress, my barely visible scars. She is dragging me out of what she says is classic post-rape depression. Her cure is this overdesigned watering hole where male waiters in red suspenders emphasizing their bare chests will do the trick. She is a good friend. No pressure, she says. Just a quiet dinner in a mostly empty restaurant with cute but harmless beef on display. I know why she likes this place; she loves showing off around men. Long ago, before I met her, she twisted her blond hair into dreadlocks and, pretty as she is, the locks add an allure she wouldn't otherwise have. At least the black guys she dates think so.

We talk office gossip through the appetizer but the giggling stops when the mahimahi arrives. It's the usual over-the-top recipe, swimming in coconut milk, smothered with ginger, sesame seeds, garlic and teeny flakes of green onion. Annoyed by the chef's efforts to make a bland fish thrilling,

I scrape everything from the fillet and blurt out, "I want a vacation, to go somewhere. On a cruise ship."

Brooklyn grins. "Oooh. Where? Finally, some good news."

"But no kids," I say.

"That's easy. Fiji, maybe?"

"And no parties. I want to be with settled people with paunches. And play shuffleboard on a deck. Bingo too."

"Bride, you're scaring me." She dabs the napkin to a corner of her mouth and widens her eyes.

I put down my fork. "No, really. Just quiet. Nothing louder than waves lapping or ice melting in crystal glasses."

Brooklyn puts her elbow on the table and covers my hand with hers. "Aw, girl, you're still in shock. I'm not going to let you make any plans until this rape stuff wears off. You won't know what you want until then. Trust me, all right?"

I'm so tired of this. Next she'll be insisting I see a rape therapist or attend victim fests. I'm really sick of it because I need to be able to have an honest conversation with my closest friend. I bite the tip of an asparagus stalk then slowly cross my knife and fork.

"Look, I lied to you." I push my plate away so hard it knocks over what's left of my apple martini. I mop it up with my napkin carefully, trying to steady myself and make what I'm about to say sound normal. "I lied, girlfriend. I lied to you. Nobody tried to rape me and that was a woman beat the shit out of me. Somebody I was trying to help, for Christ's sake. I tried to help her and she would have killed me if she could."

Brooklyn stares open-mouthed then squints. "A woman? What woman? Who?"

"You don't know her."

"You don't either, obviously."

"I did once."

"Bride, don't give me scraps. Let me have the full plate, please." She pulls her locks behind her ears and fixes me with an intense glare.

It took maybe three minutes to tell it. How when I was a little girl in the second grade, a teacher in the kindergarten building next to the main building played dirty with her students.

"I can't hear this," says Brooklyn. She closes her eyes like a nun faced with porn.

"You asked for the full plate," I say.

"Okay, okay."

"Well, she was caught, tried, and sent away."

"Got it. So what's the problem?"

"I testified against her."

"Even better. So?"

"I pointed. I sat in the witness chair and pointed her out. Said I saw her do it."

"And?"

"They put her in prison. Gave her a twenty-five-year sentence."

"Good. End of story, no?"

"Well, no, not really." I am fidgeting, adjusting my neckline as well as my face. "I thought about her on and off, you know?"

"Uh, uh. Tell me."

"Well, she was just twenty."

"So were the Manson girls."

"In a few years she'll be forty and I thought she probably has no friends."

"Poor thing. No kiddies to rape in the joint. What a drag."

"You're not hearing me."

"Damn straight I'm not listening to you." Brooklyn slaps the table. "You nuts? Who is this female alligator, besides being pond scum, I mean. Is she related to you? What?"

"No."

"Well?"

"I just thought she would be sad, lonely after all these years."

"She's breathing. That not good enough for her?"

This is going nowhere. How can I expect her to understand? I signal the waiter. "Again," I say and nod toward my empty glass.

The waiter lifts his eyebrows and looks at Brooklyn. "None for me, cookie. I need cold sobriety."

He gives her a killer smile full of bright and bonded teeth.

"Look, Brooklyn, I don't know why I went. What I do know is I kept thinking about her. All these years in Decagon."

"You write to her? Visit?"

"No. I've seen her only twice. Once at the trial and then when this happened." I point to my face.

"You dumb bitch!" She seems really disgusted with me. "You put her behind bars! Of course she wants to mess you up."

"She wasn't like that before. She was gentle, funny, even, and kind."

"Before? Before what? You said you saw her twice—at the trial and when she clocked you. But what about seeing her diddling kids? You said—"

The waiter leans in with my drink.

"Okay." I'm irritable and it shows. "Three times."

Brooklyn tongues the corner of her mouth. "Say, Bride, did she molest you too? You can tell me."

Jesus. What does she think? That I'm a secret lesbian? In a company practically run by bi's, straights, trannies, gays and anybody who took their looks seriously. What's the point of closets these days?

"Oh, girl, don't be stupid." I shoot her the look Sweetness always put on when I spilled the Kool-Aid or tripped on the rug.

"Okay, okay." She waves her hand. "Waiter, honey, I've changed my mind. Belvedere. Rocks. Double it."

The waiter winks. "You got it," he says, hitting "got" with a slur that must have earned him a promising phone number in South Dakota.

"Look at me, girlfriend. Think about it. What made you feel so sorry for her? I mean, really."

"I don't know." I shake my head. "I guess I wanted to feel good about myself. Not so disposable. Sofia Huxley— that's her name—was all I could think of, someone who would appreciate some ... something friendly without strings."

"Now I get it." She looks relieved and smiles at me.

"Do you? Really?"

"Absolutely. The dude splits, you feel like cow flop, you try to get your mojo back, but it's a bust, right?"

"Right. Sorta. I guess."

"So we fix it."

"How?" If anybody knows what to do, it's Brooklyn. Hitting the floor, she always says, requires a choice—lie there or bounce. "How do we fix it?"

"Well, not with no bingo." She's excited.

"What then?"

"Blingo!" she shouts.

"You called?" asks the waiter.

. . .

Two weeks later, just as she promised, Brooklyn organizes a celebration—a prelaunch party where I am the main attraction, the one who invented YOU, GIRL and helped create all the excitement about the brand. The location is a fancy hotel, I think. No, a smarty-pants museum. A crowd is waiting and so is a limousine. My hair, and dress are perfect: diamondlike jewels spangle the white lace of my gown, which is tight-fitting above the mermaidlike flounce at my ankles. It's transparent in interesting places but veiled in others—nipples and the naked triangle way below my navel.

All that's left is to choose earrings. I've lost my pearl dots, so I choose one-carat diamonds. Modest, nothing flashy, nothing to detract from what Jeri calls my black-coffee-and-whipped-cream palette. A panther in snow.

Christ. Now what? My earrings. They won't go in. The platinum stem keeps slipping away from my earlobe. I examine the earrings—nothing wrong. I peer at my lobes closely and discover the tiny holes are gone. Ridiculous. I've had pierced ears since I was eight years old. Sweetness gave me little circles of fake gold as a present after I testified against the Monster. Since then I've never worn clip-ons. Never. Pearl dots, usually, ignoring my "total person" designer, and sometimes, like now, diamonds. Wait. This is impossible. After all these years, I've got virgin earlobes, untouched by a needle, smooth as a baby's thumb? Maybe it's from the plastic surgery or side effects of the antibiotics? But that was weeks ago. I am trembling. I need the shaving brush. The phone is ringing. I get the brush out and stroke it lightly at my cleavage. It makes me dizzy. The phone keeps ringing. Okay, no jewelry, no earrings. I pick up the phone.

"Miss Bride, your driver is here."

If I pretend sleep maybe he will just get the hell out. Whoever he is I can't face him to chat or fake after-sex cuddle, especially since I don't remember any of it. He kisses my shoulder lightly, then fingers my hair. I murmur as though dreaming. I smile but keep my eyes closed. He moves the bedclothes and goes into the bathroom. I sneak a touch to my earlobes. Smooth. Still smooth. I am complimented constantly at the party—how beautiful, how pretty, so hot, so lovely, everyone says, but no one questions the absence of earrings. I find that strange, because all through the speeches, the award presentation, the dinner, the dancing, my baby thumb earlobes are so much on my mind I can't concentrate. So I deliver an incoherent thank-you speech, laugh too long at filthy jokes, stumble through conversations with coworkers, drink three, four times more than what I can gracefully hold. Do a single line, after which I flirt like a high school brat campaigning for prom queen, which is how I let whoever he is in my bed. I taste my tongue hoping the film is mine alone. God. Thank you. No handcuffs dangle from the bedposts.

He has finished showering and calls my name while putting his tuxedo back on. I don't answer; I don't look; I just pull the pillow over my head. That amuses him and I hear him chuckle. I listen to kitchen noises as he makes coffee. No, not coffee; I would smell it. He is pouring something— orange juice, V8, flat Champagne? That's all that's in the refrigerator. Silence, then footsteps. Please, please just leave. I hear a tick on the nightstand followed by the sound of my front door opening then closing. When I peep from under the pillow I see a folded square of paper next to the clock. Telephone number. FABULOUS. Then his name. I slump with relief. He is not an employee.

I rush to the bathroom and look in the wastebasket. Thank you, Jesus. A used condom. Traces of steam are on the shower glass near the medicine cabinet whose mirror is clear, sparkling, showing me what I saw last night— earlobes as chaste as the day I was born. So this is what insanity is. Not goofy behavior, but watching a sudden change in the world you used to know. I need the shaving brush, the soap. There is not a single hair in my armpit, but I lather it anyway. Now the other one. The lathering up, the shaving, calms me and I am so grateful I begin to think of other places that might need this little delight. My pudenda, perhaps. It's already hairless. Will it be too tricky using the straight razor down there? Tricky. Yes.

Calmed, I go back to bed and slide under the sheet. Minutes later my head explodes with throbbing pain. I get up and find two Vicodins to swallow. Waiting for the pills to work there is nothing to do but let my thoughts trail, track and bite one another.

What is happening to me?

My life is falling down. I'm sleeping with men whose names I don't know and not remembering any of it. What's going on? I'm young; I'm successful and pretty. Really pretty, so there! Sweetness. So why am I so miserable? Because he left me? I have what I've worked for and am good at it. I'm proud of myself, I really am, but it's the Vicodin and the hangover that make me keep remembering some not-so-proud junk in the past. I've gotten over all that and moved on. Even Booker thought so, didn't he? I spilled my guts to him, told him everything: every fear, every hurt, every accomplishment, however small. While talking to him certain things I had buried came up fresh as though I was seeing them for the first time—how Sweetness's bedroom always seemed unlit. I open the window next to her dresser. Her grown-up-woman stuff crowds her vanity: tweezers, cotton balls, that round box of Lucky Lady face powder, the blue bottle of Midnight in Paris cologne, hairpins in a tiny saucer, tissue, eyebrow pencils,

Maybelline mascara, Tabu lipstick. It's deep red and I try some on. No wonder I'm in the cosmetics business. It must have been describing all that stuff on Sweetness's dresser that made me tell him about that other thing. All about it. Me hearing a cat's meow through the open window, how pained it sounded, frightened, even. I looked. Down below in the walled area that led to the building's basement I saw not a cat but a man. He was leaning over the short, fat legs of a child between his hairy white thighs. The boy's little hands were fists, opening and closing. His crying was soft, squeaky and loaded with pain. The man's trousers were down around his ankles. I leaned over the windowsill and stared. The man had the same red hair as Mr. Leigh, the landlord, but I knew it couldn't be him because he was stern but not dirty. He demanded the rent be paid in cash before noon on the first day of the month and charged a late fee if you knocked on his door five minutes late. Sweetness was so scared of him she made sure I delivered the money first thing in the morning. I know now what I didn't know then—that standing up to Mr. Leigh meant having to look for another apartment. And that it would be hard finding a location in another safe, meaning mixed, neighborhood. So when I told Sweetness what I'd seen, she was furious. Not about a little crying boy, but about spreading the story. She wasn't interested in tiny fists or big hairy thighs; she was interested in keeping our apartment. She said, "Don't you say a word about it. Not to anybody, you hear me, Lula?

Forget it. Not a single word." So I was afraid to tell her the rest—that although I didn't make a sound, I just hung over the windowsill and stared, something made the man look up. And it was Mr. Leigh. He was zipping his pants while the boy lay whimpering between his boots. The look on his face scared me but I couldn't move. That's when I heard him shout, "Hey, little nigger cunt! Close that window and get the fuck outta there!"

When I told Booker about it I laughed at first, pretending the whole thing was just silly. Then I felt my eyes burning. Even before the tears welled, he held my head in the crook of his arm and pressed his chin in my hair.

"You never told anybody?" he asked me.

"Never," I said. "Only you."

"Now five people know. The boy, the freak, your mother, you and now me. Five is better than two but it should be five thousand."

He turned my face up to his and kissed me. "Did you ever see that boy again?"

I said I didn't think so, that he was down on the ground and I couldn't see his face. "All I know is that he was a white kid with brown hair." Then thinking of how his little fingers spread then curled, spread wide then curled tight I couldn't help sobbing.

"Come on, baby, you're not responsible for other folks' evil."

"I know, but—"

"No buts. Correct what you can; learn from what you can't."

"I don't always know what to correct."

"Yes you do. Think. No matter how hard we try to ignore it, the mind always knows truth and wants clarity."

That was one of the best talks we ever had. I felt such relief. No. More than that. I felt curried, safe, owned.

Not like now, twisting and turning between the most expensive cotton sheets in the world. Aching, waiting for another Vicodin to start up while fretting in my gorgeous bedroom, unable to stop scary thoughts. Truth. Clarity. What if it was the landlord my forefinger was really pointing at in that courtroom? What that teacher was accused of was sort of like what Mr. Leigh did. Was I pointing at the idea of him? His nastiness or the curse he threw at me? I was six years old and had never heard the words "nigger" or "cunt" before, but the hate and revulsion in them didn't need definition. Just like later in school when other curses—with mysterious definitions but clear meanings— were hissed or shouted at me. Coon. Topsy. Clinkertop. Sambo. Ooga booga. Ape sounds and scratching of the sides, imitating zoo monkeys. One day a girl and three boys heaped a bunch of bananas on my desk and did their monkey imitations. They treated me like a freak, strange, soiling like a spill of ink on white paper. I didn't complain to the teacher for the same reason Sweetness cautioned me about Mr. Leigh—I might get suspended or even expelled.

So I let the name-calling, the bullying travel like poison, like lethal viruses through my veins, with no antibiotic available. Which, actually, was a good thing now I think of it, because I built up immunity so tough that not being a "nigger girl" was all I needed to win. I became a deep dark beauty who doesn't need Botox for kissable lips or tanning spas to hide a deathlike pallor. And I don't need silicon in my butt. I sold my elegant blackness to all those childhood ghosts and now they pay me for it. I have to say, forcing those tormentors—the real ones and others like them—to drool with envy when they see me is more than payback. It's glory.

Today is Monday or is it Tuesday? Anyway, I've been in and out of bed for two days. I've stopped worrying about my earlobes; I can always get them pierced again. Brooklyn telephones and keeps me up to date on office matters. I asked for and got an extension on my leave. She is "acting" regional manager now. Good for her. She deserves it just for getting me out of that Decagon catastrophe, taking care of me for days, seeing to the return of my Jaguar, hiring a cleaning crew, choosing the plastic surgeon. She even fired Rose, my maid, for me when I could no longer stand the sight of her—fat, with cantaloupe breasts and watermelon behind. I couldn't have healed without Brooklyn. Still, her calls are fewer and fewer.

Brooklyn

I thought he was a predator. I don't care how wild a dancing crowd is, you just don't grab somebody from behind
like that unless you know them. But she didn't mind at all.
She let him squeeze her, rub up against her and she didn't
know a thing about him, still doesn't. But I do. I saw him
with a bunch of raggedy losers at the subway entrance.
Panhandling, for Christ's sake. And once I'm pretty sure I
saw him sprawled on the steps of the library, pretending he
was reading a book so the cops wouldn't tell him to move
on. Another time I saw him sitting at a coffee shop table
writing in a notebook, trying to look serious, like he had
something important to do. It was surely him I saw walking aimlessly in neighborhoods far from Bride's apartment.
What was he doing there? Seeing another woman? Bride
never mentioned what he did, what, if any, job he had. Said
she liked the mystery. Liar. She liked the sex. Addicted to it
and believe me I know. When the three of us were together
she was different somehow. Confident, not so needy or constantly, obviously soliciting praise. In his company she shim-
mered, but quietly kind of. I don't know. Yes, he was one

good-looking man. So what? What else did he offer besides a rut between sheets? He didn't have a dime to his name.

I could have warned her. I'm not a bit surprised he left her like a skunk leaves a smell. If she knew what I knew she would have thrown him out. One day just for fun I flirted with him, tried to seduce him. In her own bedroom, mind you. I was bringing something to Bride, mock-ups of packaging. I have her key and just unlocked and opened the door. When I called her name, he answered saying, "She's not here." I went into her bedroom—there he was lying in her bed reading. Naked too, under a sheet that reached to his waist. On impulse, and it really was impulse, I dropped the package, kicked off my shoes and then like in a porn video the rest of my clothes slowly followed. He watched me closely while I stripped but didn't say a word so I knew he wanted me to stay. I never wear underthings so when I unzipped my jeans and kicked them away I simply stood there naked as a newborn. He just stared, but only at my face and so hard I blinked. I fingered my hair then joined him: slipped between the sheets; put my arm around his chest and planted light kisses there. He put his book away.

Between kisses, I whispered, "Don't you want another flower in your garden?"

He said, "Are you sure you know what makes a garden grow?"

"Sure do," I said. "Tenderness."

"And dung," he answered.

I elbowed myself up and stared at him. Bastard. He wasn't smiling but he wasn't pushing me away either. I jumped off the bed and picked up my clothes as quickly as I could. He didn't even watch me get dressed, asshole. He went back to reading his book. If I'd wanted to I could have made him make love to me. I really could have. I probably shouldn't have come on so sudden. Maybe if I had eased up a bit, slowed down. Taken it easy.

Well, anyway, Bride doesn't know a thing about her used-to-be lover. But I do.

Bride

I don't get it. Who the hell is he? His duffel bag, which I am determined to trash like the other one, is stuffed with more books, one in German, two books of poetry, one by somebody named Hass and some paperback books by more writers I've never heard of.

Christ. I thought I knew him. I know he has degrees from some university. He owns T-shirts that say so, but I never thought about that part of his life because what was important in our relationship, other than our lovemaking and his complete understanding of me, was the fun we had. Dancing in the clubs, other couples watching us with envy, boat rides with friends, hanging out on the beach. Finding these books prove how little I know about him, that he was somebody else, somebody thinking things he never talked about. True, our conversations were mostly about me but they were not the joke-filled, sarcastic ones I usually had with other men. To them, anything besides my flirting or their pronouncements would lead to disagreements, arguments, breakups. I could never have described my childhood to them as I did to Booker. Well, there were times when he talked to me at length, but none of it was intimate—it was more like a lecture. Once when we were at the shore stretched out in beach chairs, he started talking to me about the history of water in California. A bit boring, yes, and I was sort of interested. Still, I fell asleep.

I have no idea what occupied him when I was at the office and I never asked. I thought he liked me especially because I never probed, nagged or asked him about his past. I left him his private life. I thought it showed how much I trusted him—that it was him I was attracted to, not what he did. Every girl I know introduces her boyfriend as a lawyer or artist or club owner or broker or whatever. The job, not the guy, is what the girlfriend adores. "Bride, come meet Steve. He's a lawyer at—" "I'm dating this fabulous film producer—" "Joey is CFO at—" "My boyfriend got a part in that TV show—"

I shouldn't have—trusted him, I mean. I spilled my heart to him; he told me nothing about himself. I talked; he listened. Then he split, left without a word. Mocking me, dumping me exactly as Sofia Huxley did. Neither of us had mentioned marriage, but I really thought I had found my guy. "You not the woman" is the last thing I expected to hear.

Days, weeks of mail fill the basket on the table near my door. After searching the refrigerator for something to nibble on, I decide to examine the pile—toss out the pleas for money from every charity in the world, the promises of gifts from banks, stores and failing businesses. There are just two first-class letters. One is from Sweetness. "Hi, Honey," then stuff about her doctors' advice before the usual hint for money. The other is addressed to Booker Starbern from Salvatore Ponti on Seventeenth Street. I tear it open and find a reminder invoice. Sixty-eight dollars overdue. I don't know whether to trash the invoice or go see what Mr. Ponti did for sixty-eight dollars. Before I can make up my mind, the telephone rings.

"Hey, how was it? Last night. Fab, huh? You were a knockout, as usual." Brooklyn is slurping something between words. A calorie-free, energy-filled, diet-supporting, fake-flavored, creamy, dye-colored something. "Wasn't that after-party the bomb?"

"Yeah," I answer.

"You don't sound sure. Did that guy you left with turn out to be Mr. Rogers or Superman? Who is he anyway?"

I go to my bedside table and look again at the note. "Phil something."

"How was he? I went to Rocco's with Billy and we—"

"Brooklyn, I have to get out of here. Away somewhere."

"What? You mean now?"

"Didn't we talk about a cruise somewhere?" My voice is whiny, I know.

"We did, sure, but after YOU, GIRL starts shipping.

The sample gift bags are in and the ad guys have several really cool ideas for . . ."

She rattles on until I stop her. "Look, I'll call you later. I'm a bit hung over."

"No kidding." Brooklyn giggles.

When I hang up I've already decided to check out Mr. Ponti's.

Sofia

I am not allowed to be near children. Home care was my first job after I was paroled. It suited me because the lady I cared for was nice. Grateful, even, for my help. And I liked being away from noise and a lot of people. Decagon is loud, packed with mistreated women and take-no-shit guards. My first week in Brookhaven, before being moved to Decagon, I watched an inmate get smacked across the back of her head with a belt just because she knocked her plate of food on the floor. The guard made her get down on all fours and eat it. She tried but started vomiting, so they took her to the infirmary. The food wasn't all that bad—corn pudding and Spam. I think she was probably sick with flu or something. Decagon is better than Brookhaven, where they loved to strip-search us at every exit and entrance, or just because. But still, at the second place there was always some prisoner-guard drama and when there wasn't, when we worked at our jobs, the noise, quarrels, fights, laughter, shouts went on and on. Even lights out just toned it down from a roar to a bark. At least I thought so. Quiet is mostly what I liked about being a home-care helper. After one month, though,

I had to quit because my patient's grandchildren visited her on weekends. My parole officer found me something similar but without children—a nursing home that didn't call itself a hospice but that is what it mostly was. At first I didn't like being around so many people in another institution, especially ones I had to answer to. But I got used to it since my superiors were not menacing me even though they wore uniforms. Anything that looked or felt like prison gave me a bad attitude.

Somehow I survived those fifteen years. Had it not been for weekend basketball games and Julie, my cellmate and only friend, I wonder if I would have made it. For the first two years we two, sentenced for child abuse, were avoided in the cafeteria. We were cursed and spit on, and the guards tossed our cell every now and then. After a while they mostly forgot about us. We were at the bottom of the heap of murderers, arsonists, drug dealers, bomb-throwing revolutionaries and the mentally ill. Hurting little children was their idea of the lowest of the low—which is a hoot since the drug dealers could care less about who they poison or how old they were and the arsonists didn't separate the children from the families they burned. And bomb throwers are not selective or known for precision. If anybody doubted their hatred of me and Julie all they had to do was notice how the love of children was posted everywhere—pictures of babies and kids were all over the cell walls. Anybody's kid would do.

Julie was serving time for smothering her disabled daughter. The little girl's photograph was posted on the wall above her bed. Molly. Big head, slack mouth, the loveliest blue eyes in the world. Julie whispered to Molly's photo at night or whenever she could. Not asking for forgiveness, but telling her dead daughter stories—fairy tales, mostly, all about princesses. I never told her, but I liked those stories too—helped me sleep. We worked in the sewing shop, making uniforms for a medical company that paid us twelve cents an hour. When my fingers got too stiff to work the machine properly, I was moved to the kitchen where I dropped whatever food I didn't scorch and was sent back to the sewing machines. But Julie wasn't there. She was in the infirmary after trying to hang herself. She didn't know how. A few of the cruelest inmates offered to show her. When she returned to population she was different—quiet, sad and not much company. I guess it was the gang rape by four women, then later the loving enslavement she was in with one of the elderly women—a husband called Lover whom no one trifled with. Nobody, guards or inmates, liked me enough to want more than a casual hookup. I was a fighter and too tall, I guess, almost a giant in that place. Fine, I thought—the less licking the better.

In all those years I received exactly two letters from Jack, my husband. The first was a Dear Honey letter that turned into complaints like "I'm being [blacked-out word] here." Beaten? Fucked? Tortured? What other word would the prison mail censor deny? The second letter began, "What the hell were you thinking, bitch?" No blacked-out word there. I didn't answer. My parents sent me packages at Christmas and on my birthday: nutritious candy bars, tampons, religious pamphlets and socks. But they never wrote, called or visited. I wasn't surprised. They were always hard to please. The family Bible was placed on a stand right next to the piano, where my mother played hymns after supper. They never said so, but I suspect they were glad to be rid of me. In their world of God and Devil no innocent person is sentenced to prison.

I mostly did what I was told. And I read a lot. That was one good thing about Decagon—its library. Since real public libraries don't need or want books anymore, they send them to prisons and old-folks' homes. Anything other than religious tracts and the Bible were banned in my family's home. As a teacher I thought I was well read although in college, as an education major, I was not required to read any literature. Until I was in prison I'd never read *The Odyssey* or Jane Austen. None of it taught me much, but concentrating on escapes, deceits, and who would marry whom was a welcome distraction.

In the taxicab on the first day of my parole I felt like a little kid seeing the world for the first time—houses surrounded by grass so green it hurt my eyes. The flowers seemed to be painted because I didn't remember roses that shade of lavender or sunflowers so blindingly bright. Everything seemed not just remodeled but brand-new. When I rolled down the window to smell the fresh air, the wind caught my hair—whipping it backward and sideways. That's when I knew I was free. Wind. Wind fingering, stroking, kissing my hair.

That same day one of the students who testified against me—all grown up now—knocked on the door. I was in a sleazy motel room desperate to eat and sleep in solitude for once. No petty arguments or sex grunts, loud sobs or snores from nearby cells. I don't think many people appreciate silence or realize that it is as close to music as you can get. Quiet makes some folks fidget or feel too lonely. After fifteen years of noise I was hungry for silence more than food. So I gobbled everything, puked it up and was just about to get some deep solitude when I heard banging on the door.

I didn't know who she was although something about her eyes seemed familiar. In another world her black skin would have been remarkable, but living all those years in Decagon it wasn't. After fifteen years of wearing ugly flat shoes, I was more interested in her fashionable ones— alligator or snakeskin, pointy toes and heels so high they were like the stilts of circus clowns. She spoke as if we were friends but I didn't know what she was talking about or what she wanted until she threw money at me. She was one of the students who testified against me, one of the ones who helped kill me, take my life away. How could she think cash would erase fifteen years of life as death? I blanked. My fists took over as I thought I was battling the Devil. Exactly the one my mother always talked about— seductive but evil. As soon as I threw her out and got rid of her Satan's disguise, I curled up into a ball on the bed and waited for the police. Waited and waited. None came. If they had bashed in the door they would have seen a woman finally broken down after fifteen years of staying strong. For the first time after all those years, I cried. Cried and cried and cried until I fell asleep. When I woke up I reminded myself that freedom is never free. You have to fight for it. Work for it and make sure you are able to handle it.

Now I think of it, that black girl did do me a favor. Not the foolish one she had in mind, not the money she offered, but the gift that neither of us planned: the release of tears unshed for fifteen years. No more bottling up. No more filth. Now I am clean and able.

PART II

✤

⚜

A taxi was preferable because parking a Jaguar in that neighborhood was as dim-witted as it was risky. That Booker frequented this part of the city startled Bride. Why here? she wondered. There were music shops in unthreatening neighborhoods, places where tattooed men and young girls dressed like ghouls weren't huddled on corners or squatting on curbs.

Once the driver stopped at the address she'd given him, and after he told her, "Sorry, lady. I can't wait here for you," Bride stepped quickly toward the door of Salvatore Ponti's Pawn and Repair Palace. Inside it was clear that the word "Palace" was less a mistake than an insanity. Under dusty glass counters row after row of jewelry and watches crouched. A man, good-looking the way elderly men can be, moved down the counter toward her. His jeweler's eyes swept all he could take in of his customer.

"Mr. Ponti?"

"Call me Sally, sweetheart. What can I do you for?"

Bride waved the overdue notice and explained she'd come to settle the bill and pick up whatever had been repaired. Sally examined the notice. "Oh, yeah," he said. "Thumb ring. Mouthpiece. They're in back. Come on."

Together they went into a back room where guitars and horns hung on the walls and all sorts of metal pieces covered the cloth of a table. The man working there looked up from his magnifying glass to examine Bride and then the notice. He went to a cupboard and removed a trumpet wrapped in purple cloth.

"He didn't mention the pinkie ring," said the repairman, "but I gave him one anyway. Picky guy, real picky."

Bride took the horn thinking she didn't even know Booker owned one or played it. Had she been interested she would have known that that was what caused the dark dimple on his upper lip. She handed Sally the amount owed.

"Nice, though, and smart for a country boy," said the repairman.

"Country boy?" Bride frowned. "He's not from the country. He lives here."

"Oh, yeah? Told me he was from some hick town up north," said Sally.

"Whiskey," said the repairman.

"What are you talking about?" asked Bride.

"Funny, right? Who could forget a town called Whiskey? Nobody, that's who."

The men burst into snorts of laughter and started calling

out other memorable names of towns: Intercourse, Pennsylvania; No Name, Colorado; Hell, Michigan; Elephant Butte, New Mexico; Pig, Kentucky; Tightwad, Missouri. Exhausted, finally, by their mutual amusement, they turned their attention back to the customer.

"Look here," said Sally. "He gave us another address. A forward." He flipped through his Rolodex. "Ha. Somebody named Olive. Q. Olive. Whiskey, California."

"No street address?"

"Come on, honey. Who says they have streets in a town called Whiskey?" Sally was having a good time keeping himself amused as well as keeping the pretty black girl in his shop. "Deer tracks maybe," he added.

Bride left the shop quickly, but realized just as quickly that there were no roaming cabs. She was forced to return and ask Sally to phone one for her.

Sofia

I ought to be sad. Daddy called my supervisor to say Mommy died. I asked for an advance to buy a ticket to fly out for the funeral, assuming my parole officer would let me. I remember every inch of the church where the funeral would be held. The wooden Bible holders on the backs of the pews, the greenish light from the window behind Reverend Walker's head. And the smell—perfume, tobacco and something more. Godliness, perhaps. Clean, upright and very good for you like the dining room corner in Mommy's house. The blue-and-white wallpaper I came to know better than my own face. Roses, lilacs, clematis all shades of blue against snowy white. I stood there, sometimes for two hours; a quiet scolding, a punishment for something I don't remember now or even then. I wet my underwear? I played "wrestle" with a neighbor's son? I couldn't wait to get out of Mommy's house and marry the first man who asked. Two years with him was the same—obedience, silence, a bigger blue-and-white corner. Teaching was the only pleasure I had.

I have to admit, though, that Mommy's rules, her strict

discipline helped me survive in Decagon. Until the first day of my release, that is, when I blew. Really blew. I beat up that black girl who testified against me. Beating her, kicking and punching her freed me up more than being paroled. I felt I was ripping blue-and-white wallpaper, returning slaps and running the devil Mommy knew so well out of my life.

I wonder what happened to her. Why she didn't call the police. Her eyes, frozen with fear, delighted me then. The next morning with my face bloated from hours of sobbing, I opened the door. Thin streaks of blood were on the pavement and a pearl earring nearby. Maybe it belonged to her, maybe not. Anyway I kept it. It's still in my wallet as what? A kind of remembrance? When I tend to my patients—put their teeth back in their mouths, rub their behinds, their thighs to limit bed sores, or when I sponge their lacy skin before lotioning it, in my mind I am putting the black girl back together, healing her, thanking her. For the release.

Sorry Mommy.

⚜

The sun and the moon shared the horizon in a distant friendship, each unfazed by the other. Bride didn't notice the light, how carnival it made the sky. The shaving brush and razor were packed in the trumpet case and stowed in the trunk. She thought about both until she became distracted by the music on the Jaguar's radio. Nina Simone was too aggressive, making Bride think of something other than herself. She switched to soft jazz, more suitable for the car's leather interior as well as a soothing background for the anxiety she needed to tamp down. She had never done anything this reckless. The reason for this tracking was not love, she knew; it was more hurt than anger that made her drive into unknown territory to locate the one person she once trusted, who made her feel safe, colonized somehow. Without him the world was more than confusing—shallow, cold, deliberately hostile. Like the atmosphere in her mother's house where she never knew the right thing to do or say or remember what the rules were. Leave the spoon in the cereal bowl or place it next to the bowl; tie her shoelaces with a bow or a double knot; fold her socks down or pull them straight up to the calf? What were the rules and when did they change? When she soiled the bedsheet with her first menstrual blood, Sweetness slapped her and then pushed her into a tub of cold water. Her shock was alleviated by the satisfaction of being touched, handled by a mother who avoided physical contact whenever possible.

How could he? Why would he leave her stripped of all comfort, emotional security? Yes, her quick response to his exit was silly, stupid. Like the taunt of a third grader who had no clue about life.

He was part of the pain—not a savior at all, and now her life was in shambles because of him. The pieces of it that she had stitched together: personal glamour, control in an exciting even creative profession, sexual freedom and most of all a shield that protected her from any overly intense feeling, be it rage, embarrassment or love. Her response to physical attack was no less cowardly than her reaction to a sudden, unexplained breakup. The first produced tears; the second a flip "Yeah, so?" Being beaten up by Sofia was like Sweetness's slap without the pleasure of being touched. Both confirmed her helplessness in the presence of confounding cruelty.

Too weak, too scared to defy Sweetness, or the landlord, or Sofia Huxley, there was nothing in the world left to do but stand up for herself finally and confront the first man she had bared her soul to, unaware that he was mocking her. It would take courage though, something that, being successful in her career, she thought she had plenty of. That and exotic beauty.

According to the men at Sally's he was from a place called Whiskey. Maybe he had gone back there. Maybe not. He could be living with Miss Q. Olive, another woman he didn't want, or he might have moved on. Whatever the case, Bride would track him, force him to explain why she didn't deserve better treatment from him, and second, what did he mean by "not the woman"? Who? This here woman? This one driving a Jaguar in an oyster-white cashmere dress and boots of brushed rabbit fur the color of the moon? The beautiful one, according to everybody with two eyes, who runs a major department in a billion-dollar company? The one who was already imagining newer product lines—eyelashes, for example. In addition to breasts, every woman (his kind or not) wanted longer, thicker eyelashes. A woman could be cobra-thin and starving, but if she had grapefruit boobs and raccoon eyes, she was deliriously happy. Right. She would get right on it after this trip.

The highway became less and less crowded as she drove east and then north. Soon, she imagined, forests would edge the road watching her, as trees always did. In a few hours she would be in north valley country: logging camps, hamlets no older than she was, dirt roads as old as the Tribes. As long as she was on a state highway, she decided to look for a diner, eat and freshen up before driving into territory too sparse for comfort. A collection of signs on a single billboard advertised one brand of gas, four of food, two of lodging. Three miles on, Bride left the highway and turned in to the oasis. The diner she chose was spotless and empty. The smell of beer and tobacco was not recent, nor was the framed Confederate flag that nestled the official American one.

"Yeah?" The counter waitress's eyes were wide and roving. Bride was used to that look, as well as the open mouth that accompanied it. It reminded her of the reception she got on the first days of school. Shock, as though she had three eyes.

"May I have a white omelet, no cheese?"

"White? You mean no eggs?"

"No. No yolks."

Bride ate as much as she could of that redneck version of digestible food, then asked where the ladies' room was. She left a five-dollar bill on the counter in case the waitress thought she was skipping. In the bathroom she confirmed that there was still reason to be alarmed by her hairless pudenda. Then standing at the mirror over the sink, she noticed the neckline of her cashmere dress was askew, slanting down so much her left shoulder was bare. Adjusting it, she saw that the shoulder slide was due neither to poor posture nor to a manufacturing flaw. The top of the dress sagged as if instead of a size 2 she had purchased a 4 and just now noticed the difference. But the dress had fit her perfectly when she started this trip. Perhaps, she thought, there was a defect in the cloth or the design; otherwise she was losing weight—fast. Not a problem. No such thing as too thin in her business. She would simply choose clothes more carefully. A scary memory of altered earlobes shook her but she dared not connect it to other alterations to her body.

While collecting the change and deciding on the tip, Bride asked directions to Whiskey.

"Ain't all that far," said the bug-eyed, smirking waitress. "A hundred miles, maybe one fifty. You'll make it before dark."

Is that what backwoods trash called "not far"? wondered Bride. One hundred and fifty miles? She gassed up, had the tires checked and followed the loop away from the oasis back onto the highway. Contrary to the waitress's certainty, it was very dark by the time she saw the exit marked not by a number but a name—Whiskey Road.

At least it was paved, narrow and curvy but still paved. Perhaps that was the reason she trusted the high-beam headlights and accelerated. She never saw it coming. The automobile overshot a sharp bend in the road and crashed into what must have been the world's first and biggest tree, which was circled by bushes hiding its lower trunk. Bride fought the air bag, moving so fast and in such panic she did not notice her foot caught and twisted in the space between the brake pedal and the buckled door, until trying to free it flattened her with pain. She managed to unbuckle the seat belt but nothing else helped. She lay there awkwardly on the driver's seat, trying to ease her left foot out of the elegant rabbit-furred boot. Her efforts proved both painful and impossible. Stretching and twisting, she managed to get to her cellphone, but its face was blank except for the "no service" message. The likelihood of a passing car was dim in the dark but possible, so she pressed the car's horn, desperate for the honk, to do more than frighten owls. It frightened nothing because it made no sound. There was nothing she could do but lie there the rest of the night, by turns afraid, angry, in pain, weepy. The moon was a toothless grin and even the stars, seen through the tree limb that had fallen like a throttling arm across the windshield, frightened her. The piece of sky she could glimpse was a dark carpet of gleaming knives pointed at her and aching to be released. She felt world-hurt—an awareness of malign forces changing her from a courageous adventurer into a fugitive.

The sun merely hinted at its rise, an apricot slice teasing the sky with a promise of revealing its whole self. Bride, whipped by body cramp and leg pain, felt a tingle of hope along with the dawn. A helmetless motorcyclist, a truck full of loggers, a serial rapist, a boy on a bike, a bear hunter— was there no one to lend a hand? While imagining who or what might rescue her, a small bone-white face appeared at the passenger's side window. A girl, very young, carrying a black kitten, stared at her with the greenest eyes Bride had ever seen.

"Help me. Please. Help me." Bride would have screamed but she didn't have the strength.

The girl watched her for a long, long time, then turned away and disappeared.

"Oh, God," Bride whispered. Was she hallucinating? If not, surely the girl had gone for help. Nobody, not the mentally disabled or the genetically violent, would leave her there. Would they? Suddenly, as they hadn't in the dark, the surrounding trees coming alive in the dawn really scared her, and the silence was terrifying. She decided to turn on the ignition, shift into reverse and blast the Jaguar out of there—foot or no foot. Just as she turned the ignition key to the withering sound of a dead battery a man appeared. Bearded with long blond hair and slit black eyes. Rape? Murder? Bride trembled, watching him squint at her through the window. Then he left. What seemed to Bride like hours were only a few minutes before he returned with a saw and a crowbar. Swallowing and stiff with fear she watched him saw the branch from the hood then, taking a vise from his back pocket, pry and yank the door open. Bride's scream of pain startled the green-eyed girl standing by who watched the scene with her mouth open. Carefully the man eased Bride's foot from under the brake pedal and away from the car's smashed door. His hair hung forward as he lifted her out of the car seat. Silently, asking no questions and offering no verbal comfort, he positioned her in his arms. With the emerald-eyed girl tagging along, he carried Bride half a mile down a sandy path leading to a warehouse-looking structure that might serve a killer as a house. Enclosed in his arms and in unrelenting pain, she said, "Don't hurt me, please don't hurt me," over and over before fainting.

"Why is her skin so black?"

"For the same reason yours is so white."

"Oh. You mean like my kitten?"

"Right. Born that way."

Bride sucked her teeth. What an easy conversation between mother and daughter. She was faking sleep, eavesdropping under a Navajo blanket, her ankle propped on a pillow, throbbing with pain in its furry boot. The rescuing man had brought Bride to this sort-of house, and instead of raping and torturing her, asked his wife to look after her while he took the truck. He wasn't sure, he said, but there was a chance it wasn't too early for the only doctor in the area to be found. He didn't think it was just a sprain, the bearded man said. The ankle might be broken. Without phone service, he had no choice but to get in his truck and drive into the village for the doctor.

"My name is Evelyn," said the wife. "My husband's is Steve. Yours?"

"Bride. Just Bride." For the first time her concocted name didn't sound hip. It sounded Hollywoody, teenagey. That is until Evelyn motioned to the emerald-eyed girl. "Bride, this is Raisin. Actually we named her Rain because that is where we found her, but she prefers to call herself Raisin."

"Thank you, Raisin. You saved my life. Really." Bride, grateful for another vanity name, let a tear sting its way down her cheek. Evelyn gave her one of her husband's plaid, lumberjack shirts after helping her undress.

"Can I fix you some breakfast? Oatmeal?" she asked. "Or some warm bread and butter. You must have been trapped in there all night."

Bride declined, sweetly, she hoped. She just wanted to take a nap.

Evelyn tucked the blanket around her guest, mindful of the propped-up leg, and did not trouble to whisper the black or white kitten conversation as she moved toward the sink. She was a tall woman with unfashionable hips and a long chestnut braid swinging down her back. She reminded Bride of someone she had seen in the movies, not a recent one but something made in the forties or fifties when film stars had distinguishing faces unlike now, when hairstyles alone separated one star from another. But she could not put a name to the memory—actress or film. Little Raisin, on the other hand, resembled no one Bride had ever seen— milk-white skin, ebony hair, neon eyes, undetermined age.

What had Evelyn said? "That is where we found her"? In the rain.

Steve and Evelyn's house seemed to be a converted studio or machine shop: one large space, containing table, chairs, sink, wood-burning cook stove and the scratchy couch Bride lay on. Against a wall stood a loom with small baskets of yarn nearby. Above was a skylight that needed a good power-cleaning. All over the room, light, unaided by electricity, moved like water—a shadow here could be gone in an instant, a shaft hitting a copper pot might take minutes to dissolve. An open door to the rear revealed a room where two beds, one of rope, another of iron, stood. Something meaty, like chicken, roasted in the oven while Evelyn and the girl chopped mushrooms and green peppers at the rough home-made table. Without warning they began to sing some dumb old hippie song.

"This land is your land, this land is my land . . ."

Bride quickly dashed a bright memory of Sweetness humming some blues song while washing panty hose in the sink, little Lula Ann hiding behind the door to hear her. How nice it would have been if mother and daughter could have sung together. Embracing that dream, she did fall into a deep sleep, only to be awakened around noon by booming male voices. Steve, accompanied by a very old, rumpled doctor, clumped into the house.

"This is Walt," said Steve. He stood near the couch, showing something close to a smile.

"Dr. Muskie," said the doctor. "Walter Muskie, MD, PhD, LLD, DDT, OMB."

Steve laughed. "He's joking."

"Hello," said Bride, looking back and forth from her foot to the doctor's face. "I hope it's not too bad."

"We'll see," answered Dr. Muskie.

Bride sucked air through clenched teeth as the doctor sliced through her elegant white boot. Expertly and without empathy he examined her ankle and announced it fractured at the least and unfixable here in Steve's house—she needed to go to the clinic for an X-ray, cast and so on. All he could do, or would do, is clean and bind it so its swell wouldn't worsen.

Bride refused to go. She was suddenly so hungry it made her angry. She wanted to bathe and then eat before being driven to another tacky rural clinic. Meantime she asked Dr. Muskie for painkillers.

"No," said Steve. "No way. First things first. Besides, we don't have all day."

Steve carried her to his truck, squeezed her between himself and the doctor and took off. Two hours later as the two of them drove back from the clinic she had to admit the splint had eased her pain, as had the pills. Whiskey Clinic was across the street from a post office on the first floor of a charming sea-blue clapboard house, which also contained a barbershop. Windows on the second floor advertised used clothes. Quaint, thought Bride, expecting to be helped into an equally quaint examination room. To her surprise the equipment was as cutting edge as her plastic surgeon's.

Dr. Muskie smiled at her astonishment. "Loggers are like soldiers," he said. "They have the worst wounds and need the best and quickest care."

After examining the screen-shot from a sonogram, Dr. Muskie told her she would live but she would probably need a month at the least to heal—maybe six weeks. "Syndesmosis," he said to his uncomprehending patient. "Between the fibula and the tibia. Maybe surgery—probably not, if you do what I say."

He put her ankle in a splint, saying he would give her a cast when the swelling decreased. And she would have to come back to his office for it.

An hour later she was back in the truck sitting next to a silent Steve with her left leg sticking as straight under the dashboard as the splint allowed. After being carried back to the house, Bride found that her earlier hunger had dissipated as the awareness of being unwashed and sour-smelling overwhelmed her.

"I'd like to take a bath, please," she said.

"We don't have a bathroom," said Evelyn. "I can sponge you for now. When your ankle is ready, I'll heat water for the washtub."

Slop jar, outhouse toilet, metal washtub, broke-down scratchy couch for a month? Bride started to cry, and they let her while Rain and Evelyn went on preparing a meal.

Later, after the family finished eating, Bride tried to overcome her embarrassment and accepted a basin of cold water to rinse her face and armpits. Then she roused herself enough to smile and take the plate Evelyn held before her. Quail, as it turned out, not chicken, with thick mushroom gravy. Following the meal, Bride felt more than embarrassed; she was ashamed—crying every minute, petulant, childish and unwilling to help herself or accept aid gracefully from others. Here she was among people living the barest life, putting themselves out for her without hesitation, asking nothing in return. Yet, as was often the case, her gratitude and embarrassment were short-lived. They were treating her like a stray cat or a dog with a broken leg that they felt sorry for. Sullen and picking at her fingernails, she asked Evelyn whether she had a nail file or any nail polish. Evelyn grinned and held up her own hands without speaking. Point taken—Evelyn's hands were less for holding the stem of a wineglass and more for chopping kindling and wringing the necks of chickens. Who are these people, wondered Bride, and where did they come from? They hadn't asked her where she was from or where she was going. They simply tended her, fed her, arranged for her car to be towed for repair. It was too hard, too strange for her to understand the kind of care they offered—free, without judgment or even a passing interest in who she was or where she was going. She wondered on occasion if they were planning something. Something bad.

But the days passed with boredom unbroken. Steve and Evelyn occasionally spent time after supper sitting outside singing songs by the Beatles or Simon and Garfunkel— Steve strumming his guitar, Evelyn joining him in tuneless soprano. Their laughter tinkling between wrong lines and missed notes.

In the following weeks of more visits to the clinic, leg exercises and waiting for the Jaguar to be repaired, Bride learned that her hosts were in their fifties. Steve had graduated from Reed College, Evelyn from Ohio State. With constant bursts of laughter they described how they met. First in India (Bride saw the light of pleasant memories shining in the looks they exchanged), then London, again in Berlin. Finally in Mexico they agreed to stop meeting that way (Steve touched Evelyn's cheek with his knuckle) so they got married in Tijuana and "moved to California to live a real life."

Bride's envy watching them was infantile but she couldn't stop herself. "By 'real' you mean poor?" She smiled to hide the sneer.

"What does 'poor' mean? No television?" Steve raised his eyebrows.

"It means no money," said Bride.

"Same thing," he answered. "No money, no television."

"Means no washing machine, no fridge, no bathroom, no money!"

"Money get you out of that Jaguar? Money save your ass?"

Bride blinked but was smart enough to say nothing. What did she know anyway about good for its own sake, or love without things?

She stayed with them for six difficult weeks, waiting until she could walk and her car was repaired. Apparently the single automobile-repair place had to send away for hinges or a completely new door for the Jaguar. Sleeping in a house of such deep darkness at night felt to Bride like being in a coffin. Outside the sky would be loaded with more stars than she had ever seen before. But in here under a filthy skylight and no electricity she had a problem sleeping.

Finally Dr. Muskie returned to remove her cast and give her a removable foot brace so she could limp about. She glimpsed the disgusting skin that had been hidden underneath the cast and shivered. Even more than having the cast removed, the best thing was Evelyn, true to her word, pouring pail after pail of hot water into a zinc tub. Then she handed Bride a sponge, a towel and a bar of hard-to-lather brown soap. After weeks of bird-washing Bride sank into the water with gratitude, prolonging the soaping until the water had cooled completely. It was when she stood to dry herself that she discovered that her chest was flat. Completely flat, with only the nipples to prove it was not her back. Her shock was so great she plopped back down into the dirty water, holding the towel over her chest like a shield.

I must be sick, dying, she thought. She plastered the wet towel above the place where her breasts had once upon a time announced themselves and risen to the lips of moaning lovers. Fighting panic she called out to Evelyn.

"Please, do you have something I can wear?"

"Sure," said Evelyn, and after a few minutes brought Bride a T-shirt and a pair of her own jeans. She said nothing about Bride's chest or the wet towel. She simply left her to get dressed in private. When Bride called her back saying the jeans were too large to stay on her hips, Evelyn exchanged them for a pair of Rain's, which fit Bride perfectly. When did I get so small? she wondered.

She meant to lie down just for a minute, to quiet the terror, collect her thoughts and figure out what was happening to her shrinking body, but without any drowsiness or warning she fell asleep. There out of that dark void sprang a vivid, fully felt dream. Booker's hand was moving between her thighs, and when her arms flew up and closed over his back he extracted his fingers, and slid between her legs what they called the pride and wealth of nations. She started to whisper or moan but his lips were pressing hers. She wrapped her legs around his rocking hips as though to slow them or help them or keep them there. Bride woke up moist and humming. Yet when she touched the place where her breasts used to be the humming changed to sobs. That's when she understood that the body changes began not simply after he left, but because he left.

Stay still, she thought; her brain was wobbly but she would straighten it, go about as if everything was normal. No one must know and no one must see. Her conversation and activity must be routine, like an after-bath washing of hair. Limping to the kitchen sink she poured water from the standing pitcher into a bowl, soaped then rinsed her hair. As she looked around for a dry towel Evelyn came in.

"Ooh, Bride," she said, smiling. "You got too much hair for a dish towel. Come on, let's sit outside and we can dry it in sunlight and fresh air."

"Okay, sure," said Bride. Acting normal was important, she thought. It might even restore the body changes—or halt them. She followed Evelyn to a rusty iron bench sitting in the yard bathed in bright platinum light. Next to it was a side table where a tin of marijuana and a bottle of unlabeled liquor sat. Toweling Bride's hair, Evelyn chatted away in typical beauty-parlor mode. How happy living here under stars with a perfect man made her, how much she had learned traveling, housekeeping without modern amenities, which she called trash-ready junk since none of it lasted, and how Rain had improved their lives.

When Bride asked her when and where Rain came from, Evelyn sat down and poured some of the liquor into a cup.

"It took a while to get the whole story," she said. Bride listened intently. Anything. Anything to stop thinking first about how her body was changing and second how to make sure no one noticed. When Evelyn handed her the T-shirt as she stepped out of the tub, Evelyn didn't notice or say a word. Bride had spectacular breasts when rescued from the Jaguar; she had them in Whiskey Clinic. Now they were gone, like a botched mastectomy that left nipples intact. Nothing hurt; her organs worked as usual except for a strangely delayed menstrual period. So what kind of illness was she suffering? One that was both visible and invisible. Him, she thought. His curse.

"Want some?" Evelyn pointed to the tin box.

"Yeah, okay." She watched Evelyn's expertise and took the result with gratitude. She coughed with the first toke, but none thereafter.

They were silently smoking for a while until Bride said, "Tell me what you meant by finding her in the rain."

"We did. Steve and I were driving home from some protest, I forget what, and saw this little girl, sopping wet on a brick doorstep. We had an old Volkswagen back then and he slowed down, then put on the brakes. Both of us thought she was lost or her door key was. He parked, got out and went to see what was the matter. First he asked her name."

"What did she say?"

"Nothing. Not a word. Drenched as she was, she turned her head away when Steve squatted down in front of her, but wow! when he touched her on her shoulder she jumped up and ran splashing off in wet tennis shoes. So he just got back in the car so we could continue our drive home. But then rain started really coming down—so hard we had trouble seeing through the windshield. So we called it quits and parked near a diner. Bruno's, it was called. Anyway, rather than wait in the car we went inside, more for shelter than for the coffee we ordered."

"So you lost her?"

"Then, yes." Evelyn, having exhausted the joint, replenished her cup and sipped from it.

"Did she come back?"

"No, but when the rain let up and we left the diner, I spotted her hunched up next to a Dumpster in the alley behind the building."

"Jesus," said Bride, shuddering as though it were she herself in that alley.

"It was Steve who decided not to leave her there. I wasn't so sure it was any of our business but he just went over and grabbed her, threw her over his shoulder. She was screaming, 'Kidnap! Kidnap!' but not too loud. I don't think she wanted attention, especially from pigs, I mean cops. We pushed her into the backseat, got in and locked the doors."

"Did she quiet down?"

"Oh no. She kept hollering 'Let me out,' and kicking the back of our seats. I tried to talk to her in a soft voice so she wouldn't be frightened of us. I said, 'You're soaking wet, honey.' She said, 'It's raining, bitch.' I asked her if her mother knew she was sitting outside in the rain and she said, 'Yeah, so?' I didn't know what to do with that answer. Then she started cursing—nastier words in a little kid's mouth you couldn't imagine."

"Really?"

"Steve and I looked at each other and without talking we decided what to do—get her dry, cleaned and fed, then try to find out where she belonged."

"You said she was about six when you found her?" asked Bride.

"I guess. I don't really know. She never said and I doubt she knows. Her baby teeth were gone when we took her. And so far she has never had a period and her chest is flat as a skateboard."

Bride shot up. Just the mention of a flat chest yanked her back to her problem. Had her ankle not prohibited it, she would have run, rocketed away from the scary suspicion that she was changing back into a little black girl.

One night and a day later Bride had calmed down a little. Since no one had noticed or commented on the changes in her body, how flat the T-shirt hung on her chest, the unpierced earlobes. Only she knew about unshaved but absent armpit and pubic hair. So all of this might be a hallucination, like the vivid dreams she was having when she managed to fall asleep. Or were they? Twice at night she woke to find Rain standing over her or squatting nearby—not threatening, just looking. But when she spoke to the girl, she seemed to disappear.

Helpless, idle. It became clear to Bride why boredom was so fought against. Without distraction or physical activity, the mind shuffled pointless, scattered recollections around and around. Focused worry would have been an improvement over disconnected, rags of thought. Minus the limited coherence of a dream, her mind moved from the condition of her fingernails to the time she walked into a lamppost, from judging a celebrity's gown to the state of her own teeth. She was stuck in a place so primitive it didn't even have a radio while watching a couple going about their daily chores—gardening, cleaning, cooking, weaving, mowing grass, chopping wood, canning. There was no one to talk to, at least not about anything she was interested in. Her determined refusal to think about Booker invariably collapsed. What if she couldn't find him? What if he's not with Mr. or Ms. Olive? Nothing would be right if the hunt she was on failed. And if it succeeded what would she do or say? Except for Sylvia, Inc., and Brooklyn, she felt she had been scorned and rejected by everybody all her life. Booker was the one person she was able to confront—which was the same as confronting herself, standing up for herself. Wasn't she worth something? Anything?

She missed Brooklyn whom she thought of as her only true friend: loyal, funny, generous. Who else would drive miles to find her after that bloody horror at a cheap motel then take such good care of her? It wasn't fair, she thought, to leave her in the dark as to where she was. Of course she couldn't tell her friend the reason for her flight. Brooklyn would have tried to dissuade her, or worse, taunt and laugh at her. Persuade her how ill-advised and reckless the idea was. Nevertheless, the right thing to do was to contact her.

Since she couldn't call, Bride decided to drop her a note. When asked, Evelyn said she didn't have any stationery but she offered Bride a sheet of the tablet paper used to teach Rain to write. Evelyn promised she would get Steve to mail it.

Bride was expert at company memos but not personal letters. What should she say?

I'm okay, so far . . . ?

Sorry to leave without telling . . . ?

I have to do this on my own because . . . ?

When she put down the pencil she examined her fingernails.

Usually the sound of Evelyn's weaving at the loom soothed her, but this day the click, knock, click, knock of the shuttle and pedal was extremely irritating. Whatever road her thoughts traveled, the possibility of shame waited at the end. Suppose Booker wasn't living in a town called Whiskey. And if he was, what then? What if he was with another woman? What did she have to say to him anyhow, besides "I hate you for what you did" or "Please come back to me"? Maybe she could find a way to hurt him, really hurt him. Muddled as her thoughts were, they coalesced around one necessity—an unrelenting need to confront him, regardless of the outcome. Annoyed and irritated by the "what-ifs" and the sound of Evelyn's loom, she decided to hobble outside. She opened the door and called, "Rain, Rain."

The girl was lying in the grass watching a trail of ants going about their civilized business.

"What?" Rain looked up.

"Want to go for a walk?"

"What for?" By the tone of her voice it was clear the ants were far more interesting than Bride's company.

"I don't know," said Bride.

That answer seemed to please. She jumped up smiling and brushing her shorts. "Okay, if you wanna."

The quiet between them was easy at first as each appeared to be deep in her own thoughts. Bride limping, Rain skipping or dawdling along the verge of bushes and grass. Half a mile down the road Rain's husky voice broke the silence.

"They stole me."

"Who? You mean Steve and Evelyn?" Bride stopped and watched Rain scratch the back of her calf. "They said they found you, sitting in the rain."

"Yep."

"So why did you say 'stole'?"

"Because I didn't ask them to take me and they didn't ask if I wanted to go."

"Then why did you?"

"I was wet, freezing too. Evelyn gave me a blanket and a box of raisins to eat."

"Are you sorry they took you?" I guess not, thought Bride—otherwise you would have run away.

"Oh, no. Never. This is the best place. Besides there's no place else to go." Rain yawned and rubbed her nose.

"You mean you don't have a home?"

"I used to but my mother lives there."

"So you ran away."

"No I didn't. She threw me out. Said 'Get the fuck out.' So I did."

"Why? Why would she do that?" Why would anybody do that to a child? Bride wondered. Even Sweetness, who for years couldn't bear to look at or touch her, never threw her out.

"Because I bit him."

"Bit who?"

"Some guy. A regular. One of the ones she let do it to me. Oh, look. Blueberries!" Rain was searching through roadside bushes.

"Wait a minute," Bride said. "Do what to you?"

"He stuck his pee thing in my mouth and I bit it. So she apologized to him, gave back his twenty-dollar bill and made me stand outside." The berries were bitter, not the wild sweet stuff she expected. "She wouldn't let me back in.

I kept pounding on the door. She opened it once to throw me my sweater." Rain spit the last bit of blueberry into the dirt.

As Bride imagined the scene her stomach fluttered. How could anybody do that to a child, any child, and one's own? "If you saw your mother again what would you say to her?"

Rain grinned. "Nothing. I'd chop her head off."

"Oh, Rain. You don't mean that."

"Yes I do. I used to think about it a lot. How it would look—her eyes, her mouth, the blood shooting out of her neck. Made me feel good just thinking about it."

A smooth ridge of rock jutted parallel to the road. Bride took Rain's hand and led her gently to the stone. They both sat down. Neither saw the doe and her fawn standing among the trees on the other side of the road. The doe watching the pair of humans was as still as the tree she stood next to. The fawn nestled her flank.

"Tell me," said Bride. "Tell me."

At the sound of Bride's voice, mother and child fled.

"Come on, Rain." Bride put her hand on Rain's knee. "Tell me."

And she did, her emerald eyes sometimes sparkling wide other times narrowed to dark olive slits as she described the savvy, the perfect memory, the courage needed for street life. You had to find out where the public toilets were, she said; how to avoid children's services, police, how to escape drunks, dope heads. But knowing where sleep was safe was the most important thing. It took time and she had to learn what kinds of people would give you money and what for, and remember the back doors of which food pantries or restaurants had kind and generous servers. The biggest problem was finding food and storing it for later. She deliberately made no friends of any kind—young or old, stable or wandering nuts. Anybody could turn you in or hurt you. Corner hookers were the nicest and the ones who warned her about dangers in their trade—guys who didn't pay, cops who did before arresting them, men who hurt them for fun. Rain said she didn't need reminding because once when some really old guy hurt her so bad she bled, her mother slapped him and screamed, "Get out!" then she douched her with a yellow powder. Men scared her, Rain confessed, and made her feel sick. She had been waiting on some steps at the Salvation Army truck stop when it began to rain. A lady on the truck might give her a coat or shoes this time like other times when she had slipped her food. That's when Evelyn and Steve came along, and when he touched her she thought of the men who came to her mother's house, so she had to run off, miss the food lady and hide.

Rain giggled on occasion as she described her homeless life, relishing her smarts, her escapes, while Bride fought against the danger of tears for anyone other than herself. Listening to this tough little girl who wasted no time on self-pity, she felt a companionship that was surprisingly free of envy. Like the closeness of schoolgirls.

Rain

She's gone, my black lady. That time I saw her stuck in the car her eyes scared me at first. Silky, my cat, has eyes like that. But it wasn't long before I began to like her a lot. She's so pretty. Sometimes I used to just look at her when she was sleeping. Today her car came back with a busted-up door of another color. Before she left she gave me a shaving brush. Steve has a beard and doesn't want it so I use it to brush my cat's fur. I feel sad now she's gone. I don't know who I can talk to. Evelyn is real good to me and so is Steve but they frown or look away if I say stuff about how it was in my mother's house or if I start to tell them how smart I was when I was thrown out. Anyway I don't want to kill them like I used to when I first got here. But then I wanted to kill everybody—until they brought me a kitten. She's a cat now and I tell her everything. My black lady listens to me tell how it was. Steve won't let me talk about it. Neither will Evelyn. They think I can read but I can't, well maybe a little— signs and stuff. Evelyn is trying to teach me. She calls it home-schooling. I call it home-drooling and home-fooling. We're a fake family—okay but fake. Evelyn is a good substi-

tute mother but I'd rather have a sister like my black lady. I
don't have a daddy, I mean I don't know who he is because
he didn't live in my mother's house but Steve is always here
unless he's doing some day work somewhere. My black lady
is nice but tough too. When we started walking back home
after I told her everything about my life before Evelyn and
Steve, a truck with big boys in it passed us. One of them
hollered "Hey, Rain. Who's your mammy?" My black lady
didn't turn around but I stuck out my tongue and thumbed
my nose at him. One of them was Regis, a boy I know
because he comes to our house sometimes with his father to
give us firewood or baskets of corn. The driver, an older boy,
turned the truck around so they could come after us. Regis
pointed a shotgun just like Steve's at us. My black lady saw
him and threw her arm in front of my face. The birdshot
messed up her hand and arm. We fell, both of us, her on
top of me. I saw Regis duck down as the truck gunned its
engine and shot off. What could I do but help her up and
hold on to her bloody arm as we hurried back to our house
as fast as her ankle would let her. Steve picked the tiny pel-
lets out of her hand and arm, saying he was going to warn
Regis's father. Evelyn washed the blood off my black lady's
skin and poured iodine all over her hand. My black lady
made a hurt face but she didn't cry. My heart was beating
fast because nobody had done that before. I mean Steve and
Evelyn took me in and all but nobody put their own self in

danger to save me. Save my life. But that's what my black lady did without even thinking about it.

She's gone now but who knows maybe I'll see her again sometime.

I miss my black lady.

PART III

❧

Blood stained his knuckles and his fingers began to swell. The stranger he'd been beating wasn't moving anymore or groaning, but he knew he'd better walk away quickly before a student or campus guard thought he was the lawless one instead of the man lying on the grass. He'd left the beaten man's jeans open and his penis exposed just the way it was when he first saw him at the edge of the campus playground. Only a few faculty children were near the slide and one was on the swing. None apparently had noticed the man licking his lips and waving his little white gristle toward them. It was the lip licking that got to him— the tongue grazing the upper lip, the swallowing before its return to grazing. Obviously the sight of the children was as pleasurable to the man as touching them because just as obviously, in his warped mind, they were calling to him and he was answering their plump thighs and their tight little behinds, beckoning in panties or shorts as they climbed up to the slide or pumped air on the swing.

Booker's fist was in the man's mouth before thinking about it. A light spray of blood dappled his sweatshirt, and when the man lost consciousness, Booker grabbed his book bag off the ground and walked away—not too fast, but fast enough to cross the road, turn his shirt inside out and make it to class on time. He didn't make it, but there were a few others sneaking into the lecture hall when he arrived. The latecomers took seats in the last rows and plopped backpacks, briefcases or laptops on their desks. Only one of them took a notebook out. Booker preferred pencil on paper too, but his swollen fingers made writing difficult. So he listened a little, daydreamed a little and covered his mouth to hide his yawns.

The professor was going on and on about Adam Smith's wrongheadedness, as he did in almost every lecture, as though the history of economics had only one scholar worth trashing. What about Milton Friedman or that chameleon Karl Marx? Booker's obsession with Mammon was recent. Four years ago, as an undergraduate, he'd nibbled courses in several curricula, psychology, political science, humanities, and he'd taken multiple courses in African-American Studies, where the best professors were brilliant at description but could not answer to his satisfaction any question beginning with "Why." He suspected most of the real answers concerning slavery, lynching, forced labor, sharecropping, racism, Reconstruction, Jim Crow, prison labor, migration, civil rights and black revolution movements were all about money. Money withheld, money stolen, money as power, as war. Where was the lecture on how slavery alone catapulted the whole country from agriculture into the industrial age in two decades? White folks' hatred, their violence, was the gasoline that kept the profit motors running. So as a graduate student he turned to economics—its history, its theories—to learn how money shaped every single oppression in the world and created all the empires, nations, colonies with God and His enemies employed to reap, then veil, the riches. He habitually contrasted the beaten, penniless, half-naked King of the Jews screaming betrayal on a cross with the bejeweled, glamorously dressed pope whispering homilies above the Vatican's vault. *The Cross and the Vault* by Booker Starbern. That would be the title of his book.

Unimpressed by the lecture, he let his thoughts slide toward the man lying exposed near the playground. Bald. Normal-looking. Probably an otherwise nice man—they always were. The "nicest man in the world," the neighbors always said. "He wouldn't hurt a fly." Where did that cliché come from? Why not hurt a fly? Did it mean he was too tender to take the life of a disease-carrying insect but could happily ax the life of a child?

Booker had been raised in a large, tight family with no television in sight. As a freshman in college he lived surrounded by a television/Internet world where both the methods of mass communication and the substance of mass communication seemed to him loaded with entertainment but mostly free of insight or knowledge. The weather channels were the only informative sources but they were off-base and hysterical most of the time. And the video games—mesmerizing in pointlessness. Having grown up in a book-reading family with only radio and newspapers for day-to-day information and vinyl records for entertainment, he had to fake his classmates' enthusiasm for the screen sounds of games blasting from every dorm room, lounge and student-friendly bar. He knew he was way, way out of the loop—a Luddite incapable of sharing the exciting world of tech, and it had embarrassed him as a freshman. He had been shaped by talk in the flesh and text on paper. Every Saturday morning, first thing before breakfast, his parents held conferences with their children requiring them to answer two questions put to each of them: 1. What have you learned that is true (and how do you know)? 2. What problem do you have? Over the years answers to the first question ranged from "Worms can't fly," "Ice burns," "There are only three counties in this state," to "The pawn is mightier than the queen." Topics relevant to the second question might be "A girl slapped me," "My acne is back," "Algebra," "The conjugation of Latin verbs." Questions about personal problems prompted solutions from anyone at the table, and after they were solved or left pending, the children were sent to bathe and dress—the older ones helping the younger. Booker loved those Saturday morning conferences rewarded by the highlight of the weekend—his mother's huge breakfast feasts. Banquets, really. Hot biscuits, short and flaky; grits, snow-white and tongue-burning hot; eggs beaten into pale saffron creaminess; sizzling sausage patties, sliced tomatoes, strawberry jam, freshly squeezed orange juice, cold milk in Mason jars. Some food she stored up for those weekend feasts because during the rest of the week they ate frugally: oatmeal, in-season fruit, rice, dried beans and whatever green leaf was available: kale, spinach, cabbage, collards, mustard or turnip greens. Those weekend breakfast menus were deliberately sumptuous because they followed days of scarcity.

Only during the long months when no one knew where Adam was did the family conferences and sumptuous breakfasts stop. During those months quiet ticked through the house like a time bomb that would often explode into quarrels, silly and pointlessly mean.

"Ma, he's looking at me!"

"Stop looking at her."

"He's looking back!"

"Stop looking back."

"Ma!"

When the police responded to their plea for help in searching for Adam, they immediately searched the Starberns' house—as though the anxious parents might be at fault. They checked to see if the father had a police record. He didn't. "We'll get back to you," they said. Then they dropped it. Another little black boy gone. So?

Booker's father refused to play even one of his beloved ragtime, old-time, jazzy records, some of which Booker could do without but not Satchmo. It was one thing to lose a brother—that broke his heart—but a world without Louis Armstrong's trumpet crushed it.

Then at the beginning of spring, when lawn trees started preening, Adam was found. In a culvert.

Booker went with his father to identify the remains. Filthy, rat-gnawed, with a single open eye socket. The maggots, overfed and bursting with glee, had gone home leaving fastidiously clean bones under the strips of his mud-caked yellow T-shirt. The corpse wore no pants or shoes. Booker's mother could not go there. She refused to have etched in her brain anything other than her image of her firstborn's young, outrageous beauty.

The closed-coffin funeral seemed cheap and lonely to Booker in spite of the preacher's loud eloquence, the crowds of neighbors attending, the dish after dish of carefully cooked food delivered to their kitchen. The very excess made him lonelier. It was as though his older brother, close as a twin, was being buried again, suffocating under song, sermon, tears, crowds and flowers. He wanted to redirect the mourning—make it private, special and, most of all, his alone. Adam was the brother he worshipped, two years older and sweet as cane. A flawless replacement for the brother he'd curled up with in the womb. A brother, he was told, who didn't take a single living breath. Booker was three when they let him know he was a twin to the one who did not survive birth, but somehow he'd always known it—felt the warm void walking by his side, or waiting on the porch steps while he played in the yard. A presence that shared the quilt under which Booker slept. As he grew older the shape of the void faded, transferred itself into a kind of inner companion, one whose reactions and instincts he trusted. When he started first grade and walked to school every day with Adam the replacement was complete. So, following Adam's murder, Booker had no companion. Both were dead.

The last time Booker saw Adam he was skateboarding down the sidewalk in twilight, his yellow T-shirt fluorescent under the Northern Ash trees. It was early September and nothing anywhere had begun to die. Maple leaves behaved as though their green was immortal. Ash trees were still climbing toward a cloudless sky. The sun began turning aggressively alive in the process of setting. Down the sidewalk between hedges and towering trees Adam floated, a spot of gold moving down a shadowy tunnel toward the mouth of a living sun.

Adam was more than brother to Booker, more than the

"A" of parents who'd named their children alphabetically. He was the one who knew what Booker was thinking, feeling, whose humor was both raucous and instructive but never cruel, the smartest one who loved each of his siblings but especially Booker.

Unable to forget that final glow of yellow tunneling down the street, Booker placed a single yellow rose on the coffin lid and another, later, graveside. Family members came long distances to bury the dead and comfort the Star-berns. Among them was Mr. Drew, his mother's father. He was the successful one, the grandfather openly hostile to everybody not as rich as he was, the one even his daughter called not "Daddy" or "Papa" but "Mr. Drew." Yet the old man, who had made his money as an unforgiving slumlord, minded what was left of his manners and did not show the contempt he felt for this struggling family.

After the funeral the house returned tentatively to its routine, with the encouraging sounds of Louis, Ella, Sidney Bechet, Jelly Roll, King Oliver and Bunk Johnson floating from the record player in the background. And the confer- ences and breakfast feasts returned, with Booker and his siblings, Carole, Donovan, Ellie, Favor and Goodman, all trying to think up interesting answers to the routine ques- tions. In time the whole family perked up like *Sesame Street* puppets, hoping that cheer, if worked at hard enough, could sugar the living and quiet the dead. Booker thought their joking strained and their made-up problems both misguided and insulting. During the funeral and for a few days after, a visiting relative, an aunt they called Queen, was the exception to what Booker thought was mindless rote. She had a last name that no one remembered since she was rumored to have had many husbands—one a Mexican, then two white men, four black men, one Asian, but in a sequence no one recalled. Heavy-set with fire-red hair, she surprised the grieving family by traveling all the way from California to attend Adam's funeral. She alone sensed her nephew's anger-mixed sorrow and pulled him aside.

"Don't let him go," she said. "Not until he's ready. Meantime, hang on to him tooth and claw. Adam will let you know when it's time."

She comforted him, strengthened him and validated the unfairness of the censure he was feeling from his family.

Wary of another crisis that might eliminate the soul-stretching music his father played, which Booker counted on to oil and straighten his tangled feelings, he asked his father if he could take trumpet lessons. Sure, said Mr. Starbern, provided his son earned half the teacher's fee. Booker nagged his neighbors for chores and earned enough to skip the Saturday conferences for trumpet lessons that dampened his budding intolerance for his siblings. How could they pretend it was over? How could they forget and just go on? Who and where was the murderer?

His trumpet teacher, already slightly drunk early in the morning, was nevertheless an excellent musician and an even better instructor.

"You got the lungs, the fingers, now you need the lip. When you get all three together you can forget about them and let the music out."

Which, with persistence, he did.

Six years later when Booker was fourteen and a faintly accomplished trumpet player, the nicest man in the world was caught, tried and convicted of SSS, the sexually stimulated slaughter of six boys, each of whose names, including Adam's, was tattooed across the shoulders of the nicest man in the world. Boise. Lenny. Adam. Matthew. Kevin. Roland. Clearly an equal-opportunity killer, his victims seemed to be representative of the *We Are the World* video. The tattoo artist said he thought they were the names of his client's children, not those of other people.

The nicest man in the world was an easygoing, retired auto mechanic who solicited home repairs. He was especially helpful with old refrigerators—the Philcos and GE's built in the fifties to last, and ancient gas stoves and furnaces. "Dirt," he used to say. "Most machinery died because it was never cleaned." Everyone who had hired him recalled that advice. Another feature some remembered was his smile, how welcoming, attractive, even. Otherwise he was fastidious, capable and, well, nice. The single other thing people remembered most about him was that he always traveled with a cute little dog in his van, a terrier he called "Boy." The police withheld what details they could but the families of the murdered boys could not be stopped or silenced. Nightmares about what might have been done to their children did not outweigh the facts. Six years of grief and unanswered questions coalesced around their recollections of time spent in the morgue, heaving, weeping, stone-faced or on their backs in helpless faints.

There was not much left of Adam when he was found, but the details of the more recent abductions were Gothic. Apparently the children were kept bound while molested, tortured and there were amputations. The nicest man in the world must have used his small white terrier as a lure. A central witness, an elderly widow, remembered that she had seen a child in the passenger side of his van laughing and holding a little dog up to his face. Later, after seeing the missing-child posters displayed in store windows, on telephone poles and trees, she thought she recognized a face as that of the laughing boy. She called the police. Of course they knew the van. It advertised in red and blue letters its promise: PROBLEM? SOLVED! WM. V. HUMBOLDT. HOME REPAIR. When Mr. Humboldt's house was searched a dirty mattress sporting dried blood was found in the basement along with an elaborately decorated candy tin that held carefully wrapped pieces of dry flesh, which, on not very close inspection, turned out to be small penises.

Public demands and cries for vengeance disguised as

justice were rampant and harrowing. Signs, rallies in front of the courthouse, editorials—all seemed unassuageable by anything less than the culprit's beheading. Booker joined the chorus but was not impressed by so facile a solution. What he wanted was not the man's death; he wanted his life, and spent time inventing scenarios involving pain and despair without end. Wasn't there a tribe in Africa that lashed the dead body to the back of the one who had murdered it? That would certainly be justice—to carry the rotting corpse around as a physical burden as well as public shame and damnation. The rage, the public clamor upon the conviction of the nicest man in the world, shook him almost as much as Adam's death. The trial itself was not long but the preliminaries seemed eternal to Booker. Throughout the days of newspaper headlines, talk radio and neighborhood gossip he struggled to find some way to freeze and individualize his feelings, to separate them from the sorrow and frenzied anger of other families. Adam's calamity, he thought, was not public fare to be confined to one line in a newspaper's list of the six victims. It was private, belonging only to the two brothers. Two years later, a satisfactory and calming solution came to him. Reenacting the gesture he'd made at Adam's funeral, he had a small rose tattooed on his left shoulder. Was this the same chair the predator sat in, the same needle used on his paste-white skin? He didn't ask. The tattoo artist didn't have the dazzling yellow of Booker's memory, so they settled for an orangish kind of red.

Being accepted into college offered relief as well as distraction and he soon became enchanted with campus life— not the classes, not the professors, but his lively, know-it-all classmates, an enchantment that did not wane for two years. All he did from freshman year through sophomore was react—sneer, laugh, dismiss, find fault, demean—a young man's version of critical thinking. He and his dorm mates ranked girls according to men's magazines and porn videos, ranked one another according to characters in action movies they had seen. The clever ones breezed through classes; the geniuses dropped out. It was as a junior that his mild cynicism morphed into depression. The views of his classmates began to both bore and bother him, not only because they were predictable but also because they blocked serious inquiry. Unlike his effort to perfect "Wild Cat Blues" on his trumpet, no new or creative thinking was required in undergraduate society and none penetrated the blessed fog of young transgression. Student agitation about the war in Iraq that once roiled the campus had quieted. Now sarcasm fluttered its triumphant flag and giggles became its oath; now the docile manipulation of professors became routine. So Booker replayed those questions posed by his parents during those Saturday conferences on Decatur Street: 1. What have you learned that is true (and how do you know)? 2. What problem do you have?

1. So far nothing. 2. Despair.

So, hoping to learn something of value and perhaps find an accommodating place for despair, he applied to graduate school. There he focused on tracking wealth from barter to bombs. To him it was a riveting intellectual journey that policed his anger, caged it and explained everything about racism, poverty and war. The political world was anathema; its activists, both retro and progressive, seemed wrongheaded and dreamy. The revolutionaries, armed or peaceful, had no notion of what should happen after they "won." Who would rule? The "people"? Please. What did that mean? The best outcome would be to introduce a new idea into the population that perhaps a politician would act on. The rest was theater seeking an audience. Wealth alone explained humanity's evil, and he was determined to live without deference to it. He knew exactly the subjects and themes of the articles and books he would write and kept notes on his research. Other than the scholarship in his field he read a little poetry and some journals. No novels—great or lesser. He liked certain poems because they paralleled music, journals because the essays bled politics into culture. It was during his graduate school days that he began to write something other than outlines for future essays. He began trying to shape unpunctuated sentences into musical language that expressed his questions about or results of his thinking. Most of these he trashed; a few he kept.

Assured finally of his master's degree, Booker traveled home alone for the celebratory dinner his mother had arranged. He thought about asking Felicity, his on-again, off-again girlfriend, to accompany him, but decided against it. He didn't want an outsider judging his family. That was his job.

Everything was smooth and almost cheerful at the family gathering until he went upstairs to his old bedroom, the one he once shared with Adam. Looking for what, he was not sure. The room was not simply different; it was antagonistic— a double bed instead of his and Adam's twin set, white transparent curtains instead of shades, a cutesy rug under a tiny desk. Worst of all, the closet that used to be jammed with their playthings—bats, basketballs, board games—now held his sister Carole's girl clothes. But resentment choked him when he discovered that his old skateboard, identical to the one that disappeared along with Adam, was gone. Weak with sadness, Booker went back downstairs. But when he saw his sister, his pallid weakness changed into its blazing twin—fury. He picked a quarrel with Carole; she argued back. Their fight escalated and disturbed the whole family until Mr. Starbern shut it down.

"Stop it, Booker! You not the only one grieving. Folks

mourn in different ways." His father's voice was like the steel of a knife's edge.

"Yeah, sure." Booker's tone was hostile, laced with contempt.

"You acting like you the only one in this family who loved him. Adam wouldn't want that," said his father.

"You don't know what he'd want." Booker successfully fought back tears.

Mr. Starbern rose from the couch. "Well, I do know what I want. I want you civil in this house or out of it."

"Oh, no," Mrs. Starbern whispered. "Don't say that."

Father and son stared at each other, their eyes locking in military aggression. Mr. Starbern won the battle and Booker left the house, closing the door firmly behind him.

It was fitting, perhaps, that after leaving the only home he had ever known he would step out into a downpour. Rain forced him to raise his collar and duck his head like an intruder thankful for the night. Shoulders high, eyes squinting, he moved down Decatur Street in a mood the rainstorm complemented. Before his quarrel with Carole he'd tried to persuade his parents to think of some sort of memorial for Adam—a modest scholarship in his name, for example. His mother warmed to the idea, but his father frowned and was decidedly against it.

"We can't waste money like that and we can't waste time raising it," he said. "Besides, the people who admired and remember Adam don't need to be reminded."

Booker was already feeling a poisonous vein of disapproval not only from Carole, but his younger siblings as well. To Favor and Goodman it seemed Booker wanted a statue of a brother who died when they were babies. What Booker understood as family loyalty, the others saw as manipulation—as trying to control them—outfathering their father. Just because he had two college degrees he thought he could tell everybody what to do. They rolled their eyes at his arrogance.

When he visited his and Adam's old bedroom, the thread of disapproval he'd felt during his proposal of a memorial became a rope, as he saw the savage absence not only of Adam but of himself. So when he shut the door on his family and stepped out into the rain it was an already belated act.

Felicity said, "Okay, sure," when Booker asked if he could bunk at her place for a while. He was grateful for her quick response since he had no address of his own once he cleared out of the graduate dorm. On the bus back to campus reading the back issue of *Daedalus* he'd brought along distracted him from currying his disappointment with his family. But it surfaced powerfully when he got back to the dorm and began to throw the remnants of his college life into boxes—texts, running shoes, shapeless clothes, notebooks, journals—all except his loved trumpet. When he stopped wallowing in the self-pity of being outrageously misunderstood, he called his girlfriend. Felicity was a substitute teacher and their relationship had lasted two years primarily because there were sustained blocks of time when they didn't see each other. Her call-ups, based as they were on the sudden illness of a permanent teacher, were irregular and often to distant districts. So he felt comfortable asking whether he could move in for a bit since both knew it was about convenience and had nothing to do with commitment. It was summer, and since Felicity would probably have no requests for substituting, they could enjoy each other's company without deadlines: go to movies, eat out, run trails—whatever they felt like.

One evening Booker took Felicity to Pier 2, a run-down dinner-and-dancing club that boasted a live combo. Over the shrimp and rice Booker thought, as he often did, that the quartet on the little stage needed brass. Virtually all popular music was saturated with strings: guitars, basses and piano keys aided by percussion. Other than the big-star musicians like the E Street Band, or Wynton Marsalis's orchestra, groups seldom featured, in backup or solo, a sax, clarinet, trombone or trumpet, and he felt the void intensely. So this evening at the break he went backstage to the narrow dressing room full of weed smoke and laughing musicians to ask if he could join their group sometime. Not wanting to cut their earnings with another player, especially one they didn't know, they dismissed him quickly.

"Go to hell, man."

"Who let you back here?"

"Well you could at least hear me," he pleaded. "I play trumpet and you could do with a horn."

The guitarists rolled their eyes, but the drummer said, "Bring it to the Friday set. That's when it won't matter if you screw up."

He didn't mention his future audition to Felicity. She couldn't be less interested in his trumpet playing.

Booker did as the drummer suggested, trying out before them in the dressing room with as close as he could come to a Louis Armstrong solo. The drummer nodded, the piano player smiled and the two guitarists had no objection. From then on during the summer Booker joined the group calling itself The Big Boys on Fridays, when the place was so crowded the drinkers and diners paid no attention to the music.

When in September The Big Boys broke up—the drummer moved away; the piano player got a bigger, better gig—Booker and the guitarists, Michael and Freeman Chase, began to play on streets dappled with homeless veterans with cold fury in their eyes. Their anger was not dampened by the fact that they got more generous offerings by being surrounded by music. It was the sweetest season of Booker's life but it didn't last. By the end of summer the relationship with Felicity had frayed beyond any stitched-up remedy. They had enjoyed being roommate

lovers the whole summer before each began to annoy the
other with habits they had not previously paid close attention to. Felicity complained about his loud trumpet practice
and his refusal to party every single night with her friends.
He hated her cigarette smoke, her choices of take-out food,
music and wine. In addition to insisting on constant visits from members of her family, she was nosy, forever prying into his life. Most of all he found her to be insufferably
opinionated. In fact Felicity found him as unpleasant and
annoying as he found her. She believed she might lose her
sanity if she had to listen one more time to Donald Byrd
or Freddie Hubbard or Blue Mitchell or any of his other
favorite musicians. She began to regard him as a misogynist
loser. Nevertheless they might have stayed together, in spite
of the mutual hostility that was growing like mold between
them, except for one event: Booker's arrest and the night he
spent in a holding cell.

He had passed a couple, parked near an empty lot,
taking turns sucking on a crack pipe. The sight was of no
interest to him until he noticed a child, maybe two years
old, screaming and crying while standing in the backseat of
the crackheads' Toyota. He walked over to the car, yanked
open the door, dragged the man out, smashed his face and
kicked away the pipe that had fallen to the ground. Then
the woman jumped out and ran to help her partner. The
three-person fight was more hilarious than lethal, but it

was long enough and loud enough to get the attention first of shoppers, then the police. All three were arrested and the little screaming girl given to childcare services.

Felicity had to pay the fine. The judge was lenient with Booker because the crackhead parents disgusted him as much as they did Booker. He arraigned the couple and issued a disturbing-the-peace ticket for Booker. The entire incident enraged Felicity who wondered aloud why he meddled in things that didn't concern him.

"Who do you think you are? Batman?"

Booker fingered his right molar to see if it was loose or broken. The female had had more strength than the man, who swung wildly but never got in a hit. It was her knuckles that connected with his jaw.

"There was a little kid in that car. A baby!" he said.

"It wasn't your kid and it wasn't your business," shouted Felicity.

A mite loose, decided Booker, but he would see a dentist anyway.

On the bus home each knew it was over without saying so. Felicity continued nagging for an hour or so after they arrived at her apartment, but up against Booker's leaden silence, she quit and took a shower. He didn't join her, as had been their practice.

Booker's work history was thin—one embarrassing and disaster-ridden semester teaching music in a junior high school, the only public school teaching he could do since he had no certificate, and he was cut from the few music auditions he signed up for. His trumpet talent was adequate but not exceptional.

His luck changed at the precise moment it needed to when Carole tracked him down to forward a letter addressed to him from a law firm. Mr. Drew had died and to everyone's surprise he had included his grandchildren— but not his own children—in his will. Booker was to share the old man's constantly-bragged-about fortune with his siblings. He refused to think about the greed and criminality that produced his grandfather's fortune. He told himself the slumlord money had been cleansed by death. Not bad. Now he could rent his own place, a quiet room in a quiet neighborhood, and continue playing either on the street or in more little rundown clubs. Having access to no studio, the men played on corners. Not for money, which was pitiful enough, but to practice and experiment with one another in public before a nonpaying, therefore uncritical, undemanding audience.

Then came a day that changed him and his music.

Simply dumbstruck by her beauty Booker stared openmouthed at a young blue-black woman standing at the curb laughing. Her clothes were white, her hair like a million black butterflies asleep on her head. She was talking to another woman—chalk white with blond dreadlocks. A limousine negotiated the curb and both waited for the driver to open the door for them. Although it made him sad to see the limo pull away, Booker smiled and smiled as he walked on to the train entrance, where he played with the two guitarists. Neither one was there, not Michael or Chase, and it was only then that he noticed the rain—soft, steady. The sun still blazed so the raindrops falling from a baby-blue sky were like crystal breaking into specks of light on the pavement. He decided to play his trumpet alone in the rain anyway, knowing that no pedestrians would stop to listen; rather, they closed umbrellas as they rushed down the stairs to the trains. Still in thrall to the sheer beauty of the girl he had seen, he put the trumpet to his lips. What emerged was music he had never played before. Low, muted notes held long, too long, as the strains floated through drops of rain.

Booker had no words to describe his feelings. What he did know was that the rain-soaked air smelled like lilac when he played while remembering her. Streets with litter at their curbs appeared interesting, not filthy; bodegas, beauty shops, diners, thrift stores leaning against one another looked homey, downright friendly. Each time he imagined her eyes glittering toward him or her lips open in an inviting, reckless smile, he felt not just a swell of desire but also the disintegration of the haunt and gloom in which for years Adam's death had clouded him. When he stepped through that cloud and became as emotionally content as he had been before Adam skated into the sunset—there she was. A midnight Galatea always and already alive.

A few weeks after that first sighting of her waiting for a limousine, there she was again, standing in line at the stadium where the Black Gauchos were performing—a hot band, new, upcoming, playing a blend of Brazilian and New Orleans jazz, one show only. The line was long, loud and jittery but when the doors opened to the crush he managed first to slip four bodies behind her and then, when the crowd found bench seats, he was able to stand right at her back.

In music-powered air, with body rules broken and sexual benevolence thick as cream, circling her waist with his arms seemed more than a natural gesture; it was an inevitable one. And together they danced and danced. When the music stopped, his Galatea turned to face him and surrender to him the reckless smile he'd always imagined.

"Bride," she said when he asked her name.

God damn, he whispered.

Their lovemaking from the very beginning was serene, artful and long-lasting, so necessary to Booker that he deliberately withheld for nights in a row to make the return to her bed brand-new. Their relationship was flawless. He especially liked her lack of interest in his personal life. Unlike with Felicity there was no probing. Bride was knock-down beautiful, easy, had something to do every day and didn't need his presence every minute. Her self-love was consistent with her cosmetic company milieu and mirrored his obsession with her. So if she rattled on about coworkers, products and markets, he watched her mesmerizing eyes that were so deeply expressive they said much more than mere language could. Speaking-eyes, he thought, accompanied by the music of her voice. Every feature— the ledge of her cheekbones, her invitational mouth, her nose, forehead, chin as well as those eyes—was more exquisite, more aesthetically pleasing because of her obsidian-midnight skin. Whether he was lying under her body, hovering above it or holding her in his arms, her blackness thrilled him. Then he was certain that he not only held the night, he owned it, and if the night he held in his arms was not enough, he could always see starlight in her eyes. Her innocent, oblivious sense of humor delighted him. When she, who wore no makeup and worked in a business all about cosmetics, asked him to help her choose the most winning shade of lip gloss, he laughed out loud. Her insistence on white-only clothes amused him. Unwilling to share her with the public he was seldom in the mood for clubbing. Yet dancing with her in down-lit uncool clubrooms to tapes of Michael Jackson's soprano or James Brown's shouts was irresistible. Pressing close to her in crowded rap bars bewitched them both. He refused her nothing except accompanying her on shopping sprees.

Once in a while she dropped the hip, thrillingly successful corporate woman façade of complete control and confessed some flaw or painful memory of childhood. And he, knowing all about how childhood cuts festered and never scabbed over, comforted her while hiding the rage he felt at the idea of anyone hurting her.

Bride's complicated relationship with her mother and repellent father meant that, like him, she was free of family ties. It was just the two of them, and with the exception of her obnoxious pseudo-friend Brooklyn there were fewer and fewer interruptions from her colleagues. He still played with Chase and Michael on weekends, some afternoons, but there were glorious mornings of sun at the shore, cool evenings holding hands in the park in anticipation of the sexual choreography they would perform in every nook of her apartment. Sober as priests, creative as devils, they invented sex. So they believed.

When Bride was at her office, Booker relished the solitude for trumpet practice, scribbling notes to mail to his favorite aunt, Queen, and since there were no books in Bride's apartment—just fashion and gossip magazines— he visited the library often to read or reread books he had ignored or misunderstood while at university. *The Name of the Rose,* for one, and *Remembering Slavery,* a collection that so moved him he composed some mediocre, sentimental music to commemorate the narratives. He read Twain, enjoying the cruelty of his humor. He read Walter Benjamin, impressed by the beauty of the translation, he read Frederick Douglass's autobiography again, relishing for the first time the eloquence that both hid and displayed his hatred. He read Herman Melville, and let Pip break his heart, reminding him of Adam alone, abandoned, swallowed by waves of casual evil.

Six months into the bliss of edible sex, free-style music, challenging books and the company of an easy undemanding Bride, the fairy-tale castle collapsed into the mud and sand on which its vanity was built. And Booker ran away.

PART IV

Brooklyn

Nothing. A call to our CO asking for more extended leave. Rehab. Emotional rehab—whatever. But nothing about where she's headed or why until today. A note scribbled on a piece of yellow lined tablet paper. Christ. I didn't have to read it to know what it said. "Sorry I ran away. I had to. Except for you everything was falling apart blah, blah, blah . . ."

Beautiful dumb bitch. Nothing about where she's going or how long she'd be gone. One thing I know for sure she's tracking that guy. I can read her mind like a headline crawling across the bottom of a TV screen. It's a gift I've had since I was a little kid. Like when the landlady stole the money lying on our dining room table and said we were behind in the rent. Or when my uncle started thinking of putting his fingers between my legs again, even before he knew himself what he was planning to do. I hid or ran or screamed with a fake stomachache so my mother would wake from her drunken nap to tend to me. Believe it. I've always sensed what people want and how to please them. Or not. Only once did I misread—with Bride's loverman.

I ran away, too, Bride, but I was fourteen and there was nobody but me to take care of me so I invented myself, toughened myself. I thought you did too except when it came to boyfriends. I knew right away that the last one—a conman if ever I saw one—would turn you into the scared little girl you used to be. One fight with a crazy felon and you surrendered, stupid enough to quit the best job in the world.

I started out sweeping a hairdresser's shop then waitressing until I got the drugstore job. Long before Sylvia, Inc., I fought like the devil for each job I ever got and let nothing, nothing stop me.

But for you it's "Wah, wah, I had to run . . ." Where to? In some place where there is no real stationery or even a postcard?

Bride, please.

A city girl is quickly weary of the cardboard boredom of tiny rural towns. Whatever the weather, iron-bright sunshine or piercing rain, the impression of worn boxes hiding shiftless residents seems to sap the most attentive gaze. It's one thing for onetime hippies to live their anticapitalist ideals near the edge of a seldom-traveled country road. Evelyn and Steve had lived exciting lives of risk and purpose in their adventurous pasts. But what about regular plain folks who were born in these places and never left? Bride wasn't feeling superior to the line of tiny, melancholy houses and mobile homes on each side of the road, just puzzled. What would make Booker choose this place? And who the hell is Q. Olive?

She had driven one hundred and seventy miles on and off dirt roads some of which must have been created originally by moccasin-shod feet and wolf packs. Truckers could navigate them but a Jaguar repaired with another model's door had serious trouble. Bride drove carefully, peering ahead for obstacles, alive or not. By the time she saw the sign nailed to the trunk of a pine tree, her exhaustion quieted a growing alarm. Although there were no more physical disappearances, she was disturbed by the fact that she'd had no menstrual period for at least two, maybe three, months. Flat-chested and without underarm or pubic hair, pierced ears and stable weight, she tried and failed to forget what she believed was her crazed transformation back into a scared little black girl.

Whiskey, it turned out, was half a dozen or so houses on both sides of a gravel road that led to a stretch of trailers and mobile homes. Parallel to the road beyond a stretch of sorrowful-looking trees ran a deep but narrow stream. The houses had no addresses but some mobile homes had names painted on sturdy mailboxes. Under eyes suspicious of strange cars and stranger visitors, Bride cruised slowly until she saw QUEEN OLIVE printed on a mailbox in front of a pale-yellow mobile home. She parked, got out and was walking toward the door when she smelled gasoline and fire that seemed to be coming from behind the home. When she crept toward the backyard she saw a heavyset red-headed woman sprinkling gasoline on a metal bedspring, carefully noting where flames needed to be fed.

Bride hurried back to her car and waited. Two children came along, attracted, perhaps, by the fancy automobile, but distracted by the woman at the wheel. Both stared at her for what seemed like minutes in unblinking wonder. Bride ignored the dumbstruck children. She knew well what it was to walk into a room and see the exchange of looks between white strangers. The looks were dismissible because, most often, the gasps her blackness provoked were invariably followed by the envy her beauty produced. Although, with Jeri's help, she had capitalized on her dark skin, stressing it, glamorizing it, she recalled an exchange she once had with Booker. Complaining about her mother, she told him that Sweetness hated her for her black skin.

"It's just a color," Booker had said. "A genetic trait—not a flaw, not a curse, not a blessing nor a sin."

"But," she countered, "other people think racial—"

Booker cut her off. "Scientifically there's no such thing as race, Bride, so racism without race is a choice. Taught, of course, by those who need it, but still a choice. Folks who practice it would be nothing without it."

His words were rational and, at the time, soothing but had little to do with day-to-day experience—like sitting in a car under the stunned gaze of little white children who couldn't be more fascinated if they were at a museum of dinosaurs. Nevertheless, she flat out refused to be derailed from her mission simply because she was outside the comfort zone of paved streets, tight lawns surrounded by racially diverse people who might not help but would not harm her. Determined to discover what she was made of—cotton or steel—there could be no retreat, no turning back.

Half an hour passed; the children were gone and a nickel-plated sun at the top of the sky warmed the car's interior. Taking a deep breath, Bride walked to the yellow door and knocked. When the female arsonist appeared she said, "Hello. Excuse me. I'm looking for Booker Starbern. This is the address I have for him."

"That figures," said the woman. "I get a lot of his mail—magazines, catalogs, stuff he writes himself."

"Is he here?" Bride was dazzled by the woman's earrings, golden discs the size of clamshells.

"Uh-uh." The woman shook her head while boring into Bride's eyes. "He's nearby, though."

"He is? Well how far is nearby?" Relieved that Q. Olive was not a young rival, Bride sighed and asked directions.

"You can walk it, but come on in. Booker ain't going nowhere. He's laid up—broke his arm. Come on in. You look like something a raccoon found and refused to eat."

Bride swallowed. For the past three years she'd only been told how exotic, how gorgeous she was—everywhere, from almost everybody—stunning, dreamy, hot, wow! Now this old woman with woolly red hair and judging eyes had deleted an entire vocabulary of compliments in one stroke. Once again she was the ugly, too-black little girl in her mother's house.

Queen curled her finger. "Get in here, girl. You need feeding."

"Look, Miss Olive—"

"Just Queen, honey. And it's Ol-li-vay. Step on in here. I don't get much company and I know hungry when I see it."

Well, that's true, thought Bride. Her anxiety during

the long trip had masked her stomach-yelling hunger. She obeyed Queen and was pleasantly surprised at the room's orderliness, comfort and charm. She had wondered for a second if she was being seduced into a witch's den. Obviously Queen sewed, knitted, crocheted and made lace. Curtains, slipcovers, cushions, embroidered napkins were elegantly handmade. A quilt on the headboard of an empty bed, whose springs were apparently cooling outside, was pieced in soft colors and, like everything else, cleverly mismatched. Small antiques such as picture frames and side tables were oddly placed. One whole wall was covered with photographs of children. A pot simmered on the two-burner stove. Queen, unaccustomed to being rebuffed, placed two porcelain bowls on linen mats along with matching napkins and silver soup spoons with filigreed handles.

Bride sat down at a narrow table on a chair with a decorative seat cushion and watched Queen ladle thick soup into their bowls. Pieces of chicken floated among peas, potatoes, corn kernels, tomato, celery, green peppers, spinach and a scattering of pasta shells. Bride couldn't identify the strong seasonings—curry? Cardamom? Garlic? Cayenne? Black pepper and red? But the result was manna. Queen added a basket of warm flat bread, joined her guest and blessed the food. Neither spoke for long minutes of eating. Finally, Bride looked up from her bowl, wiped her lips, sighed and asked her hostess, "Why were you burning your bedsprings? I saw you back there."

"Bedbugs," answered Queen. "Every year I burn them out before the eggs get started."

"Oh. I never heard of that." Then, feeling more comfortable with the woman, asked, "What kind of stuff did Booker send you? You said he sent some writings."

"Uh-huh. He did. Every now and then."

"What were they about?"

"Beats me. I'll show you some, if you like. Say, why you looking for Booker? He owe you money? You sure can't be his woman. You sound like you don't know him too good."

"I don't, but I thought I did." She didn't say so, but it suddenly occurred to her that good sex was not knowledge. It was barely information.

Bride touched the napkin to her lips again. "We were living together, then he dumped me. Just like that." Bride snapped her fingers. "He left me without a word."

Queen chuckled. "Oh he's a leaver, all right. Left his own family. All except me."

"He did? Why?" Bride didn't like being classified with Booker's family, but the news surprised her.

"His older brother was murdered when they was kids and he didn't approve of his folks' response."

"Awww," Bride murmured. "That's sad." She made the acceptable sound of sympathy but was shocked to learn she knew nothing about it.

"More than sad. Almost ruined the family."

"What did they do that made him leave?"

"They moved on. Started to live life like it was life. He wanted them to establish a memorial, a foundation or something in his brother's name. They weren't interested. At all. I have to take some responsibility for the breakup. I told him to keep his brother close, mourn him as long as he needed to. I didn't count on what he took away from what I said. Anyhow, Adam's death became his own life. I think it's his only life." Queen glanced at Bride's empty bowl. "More?"

"No thanks, but it was delicious. I don't remember eating anything that good."

Queen smiled. "It's my United Nations recipe from the food of all my husbands' hometowns. Seven, from Delhi to Dakar, from Texas to Australia, and a few in between." She was laughing, her shoulders rocking. "So many men and all of them the same where it counts."

"Where does it count?"

"Ownership."

All those husbands and still all alone, thought Bride. "Don't you have any kids?" Obviously she did; their photographs were everywhere.

"Lots. Two live with their fathers and their new wives; two in the military—one a marine, one in the air force; another one, my last, a daughter, is in medical school. She's my dream child. The next to last is filthy rich somewhere in New York City. Most of them send me money so they

don't have to come see me. But I see them." She waved to
the photographs gazing out from exquisite frames. "And
I know how and what they think. Booker always stayed
in touch with me, though. Here, I'll show you how and
what he thinks." Queen moved to a cabinet where sewing
materials were neatly hanging or stacked. From its floor
she lifted an old-fashioned breadbox. After sorting through
its contents, she removed a thin sheaf of papers clipped
together and handed it to her guest.

What lovely handwriting, thought Bride, suddenly real-
izing that she'd never seen anything Booker wrote—not
even his name. There were seven sheets. One for each
month they were together—plus one more. She read the
first page slowly, her forefinger tracing the lines, for there
was little or no punctuation.

Hey girl what's inside your curly head besides dark
rooms with dark men dancing too close to comfort
the mouth hungry for more of what it is sure is there
somewhere out there just waiting for a tongue and some
breath to stroke teeth that bite the night and swallow
whole the world denied you so get rid of those smokey
dreams and lie on the beach in my arms while i cover
you with white sands from shores you have never seen
lapped by waters so crystal and blue they make you
shed tears of bliss and let you know that you do belong

finally to the planet you were born on and can now join
the out-there world in the deep peace of a cello.

Bride read the words twice, understanding little if anything. It was the second page that made her uncomfortable.

Her imagination is impeccable the way it cuts and
scrapes the bone never touching the marrow where
that dirty feeling is thrumming like a fiddle for fear its
strings will break and screech the loss of its tune since
for her permanent ignorance is so much better than the
quick of life.

Queen, having finished washing the dishes, offered her guest a drink of whiskey. Bride declined.

Reading the third page, she thought she remembered a conversation she'd had with Booker that could have provoked what he wrote, the one in which she described the landlord and details of her childhood.

You accepted like a beast of burden the whip of a
stranger's curse and the mindless menace it holds along
with the scar it leaves as a definition you spend your life
refuting although that hateful word is only a slim line
drawn on a shore and quickly dissolved in a seaworld
any moment when an equally mindless wave fondles it

*like the accidental touch of a finger on a clarinet stop
that the musician converts into silence in order to let the
true note ring out loud.*

Bride read three more pages in quick succession.

*Trying to understand racist malignancy only feeds it,
makes it balloon-fat and lofty floating high overhead
fearful of sinking to earth where a blade of grass could
puncture it letting its watery feces soil the enthralled
audience the way mold ruins piano keys both black and
white, sharp and flat to produce a dirge of its decay.*

*I refuse to be ashamed of my shame, you know, the one
assigned to me which matches the low priority and the
degraded morality of those who insist upon this most
facile of human feelings of inferiority and flaw simply to
disguise their own cowardice by pretending it is identical
to a banjo's purity.*

*Thank you. You showed me rage and frailty and hostile
recklessness and worry worry worry dappled with such
uncompromising shards of light and love it seemed a
kindness in order to be able to leave you and not fold
into a grief so deep it would break not the heart but the
mind that knows the oboe's shriek and the way it tears
into rags of silence to expose your beauty too dazzling*

to contain and which turns its melody into the grace of
livable space.

Puzzled, Bride raised her eyes from the pages and looked at Queen, who said, "Interesting, is it?"

"Very," answered Bride. "But strange too. I wonder who he was talking to."

"Himself," said Queen. "I bet they're all about him. Don't you think so?"

"No," murmured Bride. "These are about me, our time together." Then she read the last page.

You should take heartbreak of whatever kind seriously
with the courage to let it blaze and burn like the
pulsing star it is unable or unwilling to be soothed into
pathetic self-blame because its explosive brilliance rings
justifiably loud like the din of a tympani.

Bride put the papers down and covered her eyes.

"Go see him," said Queen, her voice low. "He's down the road, the last house beside the stream. Come on, get up, wash your face and go."

"I'm not sure I should, now." Bride shook her head. She had counted on her looks for so long—how well beauty worked. She had not known its shallowness or her own cowardice—the vital lesson Sweetness taught and nailed to her spine to curve it.

"What's the matter with you?" Queen sounded annoyed. "You come all this way and just turn around and leave?" Then she started singing, imitating the voice of a baby:

Don't know why
There's no sun up in the sky . . .
Can't go on.
Everything I had is gone,
Stormy weather . . .

"Damn!" Bride slapped the table. "You're absolutely right! Totally right! This is about me, not him. Me!"

"You? Get out!" Booker rose from his narrow bed and pointed at Bride, who was standing in the door of his trailer.

"Fuck you! I'm not leaving here until you—"

"I said get out! Now!" Booker's eyes were both dead and alive with hatred. His uncast arm pointed toward the door. Bride ran nine quick steps forward and slapped Booker's face as hard as she could. He hit her back with just enough force to knock her down. Scrambling up, she grabbed a Michelob bottle from a counter and broke it over his head. Booker fell back on his bed, motionless. Tightening her fist on the neck of the broken bottle, Bride stared at the blood seeping into his left ear. A few seconds later he regained consciousness, leaned on his elbow and, with squinty, unfocused eyes, turned to look at her.

"You walked out on me," she screamed. "Without a word! Nothing! Now I want that word. Whatever it is I want to hear it. Now!"

Booker, wiping blood from the left side of his face with his right hand, snarled, "I don't have to tell you shit."

"Oh, yes you do." She raised the broken bottle.

"You get out of my house before something bad happens."

"Shut up and answer me!"

"Jesus, woman."

"Why? I have to know, Booker."

"First tell me why you bought presents for a child molester—in prison for it, for Christ's sake. Tell me why you sucked up to a monster."

"I lied! I lied! I lied! She was innocent. I helped convict her but she didn't do any of that. I wanted to make amends but she beat the crap out of me and I deserved it."

The room temperature had not risen, but Bride was sweating, her forehead, upper lip, even her armpits were soaking.

"You lied? What the hell for?"

"So my mother would hold my hand!"

"What?"

"And look at me with proud eyes, for once."

"So, did she?"

"Yes. She even liked me."

"So you mean to tell me—"

"Shut up and talk! Why did you walk out on me?"

"Oh, God." Booker wiped more blood from the side of his face. "Look. Well, see. My brother, he was murdered by a freak, a predator like the one I thought you were forgiving and—"

"I don't care! I didn't do it! It wasn't me who killed your brother."

"All right! All right! I get that, but—"

"But nothing! I was trying to make up to someone I ruined. You just ran around blaming everybody. You bastard. Here, wipe your bloody hand." Bride threw a dish towel toward him and put down what was left of the bottle. After wiping her palms on her jeans and brushing hair from her damp forehead, she looked steadily at Booker. "You don't have to love me but you damn well have to respect me." She sat down in a chair by the table and crossed her legs.

In a long silence cut only by the sound of their breathing, they stared not at each other but away—at the floor, their hands, through the window. Minutes passed.

At last Booker felt he had something definitive and vital to say, to explain, but when he opened his mouth his tongue froze—the words were not there. No matter. Bride was asleep in the chair, her chin pointing toward her chest, her long legs splayed.

Queen didn't knock; she simply opened the door to Booker's trailer and stepped in. When she saw Bride sprawled asleep in a chair and the bruise over Booker's eye she said, "Good Lord. What happened?"

"Dustup," said Booker.

"Is she okay?"

"Yeah. Knocked herself out and fell asleep."

"Some 'dustup.' She came all this way to beat you up? For what? Love or misery?"

"Both, probably."

"Well, let's get her out of that chair and on the bed," said Queen.

"Right." Booker stood up. With Queen's help and his one working arm they got her on his narrow, unmade bed. Bride moaned, but did not wake.

Queen sat down at the table. "What you gonna do about her?"

"I don't know," answered Booker. "It was perfect for a while, the two of us."

"What caused the split?"

"Lies. Silence. Just not saying what was true or why."

"About?"

"About us as kids, things that happened, why we did things, thought things, took actions that were really about what went on when we were just children."

"Adam for you?"

"Adam for me."

"And for her?"

"A big lie she told when she was a kid that helped put an innocent woman in prison. A long sentence for child rape the woman never did. I walked out after we quarreled about Bride's strange affection for the woman. At least it seemed strange at the time. I didn't want to be anywhere near her after that."

"What'd she lie for?"

"To get some love—from her mama."

"Lord! What a mess. And you thought about Adam—again. Always Adam."

"Yep."

Queen crossed her wrists and leaned on the table. "How long is he going to run you?"

"I can't help it, Queen."

"No? She told her truth. What's yours?"

Booker didn't answer. The two of them sat in silence with Bride's light snoring the only sound until Queen said, "You need a noble reason to fail, don't you? Or some really deep reason to feel superior."

"Aw, no, Queen. I'm not like that! Not at all."

"Well what? You lash Adam to your shoulders so he can work day and night to fill your brain. Don't you think he's tired? He must be worn out having to die and get no rest because he has to run somebody else's life."

"Adam's not managing me."

"No. You managing him. Did you ever feel free of him? Ever?"

"Well." Booker flashed back to standing in the rain, how his music changed right after he saw Bride stepping into a limousine, how the gloom he had been living in dissipated. He thought about his arms around her waist while they danced and her smile when she turned around. "Well," he repeated, "for a while it was good, really good being with her." He couldn't hide the pleasure in his eyes.

"I guess good isn't good enough for you, so you called Adam back and made his murder turn your brain into a cadaver and your heart's blood formaldehyde."

Booker and Queen stared at each other for a long time until she stood up and, not taking the trouble to hide her disappointment, said, "Fool," and left him slouched in his chair.

Taking her time Queen walked slowly back to her house. Amusement and sadness competed for her attention. She was amused because she hadn't seen lovers fight in decades—not since she lived in the projects in Cleveland where young couples acted out their violent emotions as theatrical performances, aware of a visible or invisible audience. She had experienced it all with multiple husbands, all of whom were now blended into no one. Except her first,

John Loveday, whom she'd divorced—or had she? Hard to remember since she hadn't divorced the next one either. Queen smiled at the selective memory old age blessed her with. But sadness cut through the smile. The anger, the violence on display between Bride and Booker, were unmistakable and typical of the young. Yet, after they hauled the sleeping girl to the bed and laid her down, Queen saw Booker smooth the havoc of Bride's hair away from her forehead. Glancing quickly at his face she was struck by the tenderness in his eyes.

They will blow it, she thought. Each will cling to a sad little story of hurt and sorrow—some long-ago trouble and pain life dumped on their pure and innocent selves. And each one will rewrite that story forever, knowing the plot, guessing the theme, inventing its meaning and dismissing its origin. What waste. She knew from personal experience how hard loving was, how selfish and how easily sundered. Withholding sex or relying on it, ignoring children or devouring them, rerouting true feelings or locking them out. Youth being the excuse for that fortune-cookie love—until it wasn't, until it became pure adult stupidity.

I was pretty once, she thought, real pretty, and I believed it was enough. Well, actually it was until it wasn't, until I had to be a real person, meaning a thinking one. Smart enough to know heavyweight was a condition not a disease; smart enough now to read the minds of selfish people right away. But the smarts came too late for her children.

Each of her "husbands" snatched a child or two from her, claimed them or absconded with them. Some spirited them away to their home countries; another had his mistress capture two; all but one of her husbands—the sweet Johnny Loveday—had good reasons to pretend love: American citizenship, U.S. passport, financial help, nursing care or a temporary home. She had no opportunity to raise a single child beyond the age of twelve. It took some time to figure out the motives for faking love—hers and theirs. Survival, she supposed, literal and emotional. Queen had been through it all, and now she lived alone in the wilderness, knitting and tatting away, grateful that, at last, Sweet Jesus had given her a forgetfulness blanket along with a little pillow of wisdom to comfort her in old age.

Restless and deeply displeased with the turn of events, especially Queen's open disgust with him, Booker went outside and sat on his doorstep. Soon it would be twilight and this haphazard village minus streetlights would disappear in darkness. Music from a few radios would be as distant as the lights flickering from TV sets: old Zeniths and Pioneers. He watched a couple of local trucks rumble by and a few motorcyclists that followed soon after. The truckers wore caps; the motorcyclists wore scarves tied around their foreheads. Booker liked the mild anarchy of the place, its indifference to its residents modified by the presence of his aunt, the single person he trusted. He'd found some on-and-off work with loggers, which was enough until he fell out of a rig and wrecked his shoulder. At every turn, cutting into his aimless thoughts was the picture of the spell-binding black woman lying in his bed, exhausted after screaming and trying her best to kill him or at minimum beat him up. He really didn't know what made her drive all this way except vengeance or outrage—or was it love?

Queen's right, he thought. Except for Adam I don't know anything about love. Adam had no faults, was innocent, pure, easy to love. Had he lived, grown up to have flaws, human failings like deception, foolishness and ignorance, would he be so easy to adore or be even worthy of adoration? What kind of love is it that requires an angel and only an angel for its commitment?

Following that line of thought, Booker continued to chastise himself.

Bride probably knows more about love than I do. At least she's willing to figure it out, do something, risk something and take its measure. I risk nothing. I sit on a throne and identify signs of imperfection in others. I've been charmed by my own intelligence and the moral positions I've taken, along with the insolence that accompanies them. But where is the brilliant research, the enlightening books, the masterpieces I used to dream of producing? Nowhere. Instead I write notes about the shortcomings of others. Easy. So easy.

What about my own? I liked how she looked, fucked, and made no demands. The first major disagreement we had, and I was gone. My only judge being Adam who, as Queen said, is probably weary of being my burden and my cross.

He tiptoed back into his trailer and, listening to Bride's light snoring, retrieved a notebook to once again put on paper words he could not speak.

I don't miss you anymore adam rather i miss the emotion that your dying produced a feeling so strong it defined me while it erased you leaving only your absence for me to live in like the silence of the japanese gong that is more thrilling than whatever sound may follow.

I apologize for enslaving you in order to chain myself to the illusion of control and the cheap seduction of power. No slaveowner could have done it better.

Booker put away his notebook. Dusk enveloped him and he let the warm air calm him while he looked forward to the dawn.

Bride woke in sunshine from a dreamless sleep—deeper than drunkenness, deeper than any she had known. Now having slept so many hours she felt more than rested and free of tension; she felt strong. She didn't get up right away;

instead she remained in Booker's bed, eyes closed, enjoying a fresh vitality and blazing clarity. Having confessed Lula Ann's sins she felt newly born. No longer forced to relive, no, outlive the disdain of her mother and the abandonment of her father. Pulling herself away from reverie she sat up and saw Booker drinking coffee at the pull-down table. He looked pensive rather than hostile. So she joined him, picked a strip of bacon from his plate and ate it. Then she bit into his toast.

"Want more?" Booker asked.

"No. No thanks."

"Coffee? Juice?"

"Well, coffee, maybe."

"Sure."

Bride rubbed her eyelids trying to replay the moments before she fell asleep. The swelling over Booker's left temple helped. "You got me over to your bed with one working arm?"

"I had help," said Booker.

"Who from?"

"Queen."

"God. She must think I'm crazy."

"Doubt it." Booker placed a cup of coffee in front of her. "She's an original. Doesn't recognize crazy."

Bride blew away the coffee's steam. "She showed me the things you mailed her. Pages of your writing. Why did you send them to her?"

"I don't know. Maybe I liked them too much to trash but not enough to carry around. I suppose I wanted them to be in a safe place. Queen keeps everything."

"When I read them I knew they were all about me—right?"

"Oh, yeah." Booker rolled his eyes and heaved a theatrical sigh. "Everything is about you except the whole world and the universe it floats in."

"Would you stop making fun of me? You know what I mean. You wrote them when we were together, right?"

"They're just thoughts, Bride. Thoughts about what I was feeling or feared or, most often, what I truly believed—at the time."

"You still believe heartbreak should burn like a star?"

"I do. But stars can explode, disappear. Besides, what we see when we look at them may no longer be there. Some could have died thousands of years ago and we're just now getting their light. Old information looking like news. Speaking of information, how did you find out where I was?"

"A letter came for you. An overdue bill, I mean, from a music repair shop. The Pawn Palace. So I went there."

"Why?"

"To pay them, idiot. They told me where you might be. This dump of a place, and they had a forwarding address to a Q. Olive."

"You paid my bill then drove all this way to slap my face?"

"Maybe. I didn't plan it, but I have to say it did feel good. Anyway I brought you your horn. Is there more coffee?"

"You got it? My trumpet?"

"Of course. It's fixed too."

"Where is it? At Queen's?"

"In the trunk of my car."

Booker's smile traveled from his lips to his eyes. The joy in his face was infantile. "I love you! Love you!" he shouted and ran out the door down the road toward the Jaguar.

It began slowly, gently, as it often does: shy, unsure of how to proceed, fingering its way, slithering tentatively at first because who knows how it might turn out, then gaining confidence in the ecstasy of air, of sunlight, for there was neither in the weeds where it had curled.

It had been lurking in the yard where Queen Olive had burned bedsprings to destroy the annual nest of bedbugs. Now it traveled quickly, flashing now and then a thin red lick of flame, then dying down for seconds before springing up again stronger, thicker, now that the way and the goal were clear: a tasty length of pine rotting at the trailer's pair of back steps. Then the door, more pine, sweet, soft. Finally there was the joy of sucking delicious embroidered fabric of lace, of silk, of velvet.

By the time Bride and Booker got there, a small cluster of people were standing in front of Queen's house—the jobless, several children and the elderly. Smoke was sneaking from the sills and the door saddle when they broke in. First Booker, then Bride right behind him. They dropped to the floor where smoke was thinnest and crawled to the couch where Queen lay still, seduced into unconsciousness by the smiles of smoke without heat. With his one good arm and Bride's two, their eyes watering and throats coughing, they managed to pull the unconscious woman to the floor and drag her out to the tiny front lawn.

"Further! Come on, further!" shouted one of the men standing there. "The whole place could blow!"

Booker was too intent on forcing air into Queen's mouth to hear him. At last in the distance the sirens of fire truck and ambulance excited the children almost as much as the cartoon beauty of a roaring fire. Suddenly, a spark hiding in Queen's hair burst into flame, devouring the mass of red hair in a blink—just enough time for Bride to pull off her T-shirt and use it to smother the hair fire. When, with stinging, singed palms, she tore away the now sooty, smoking shirt, she grimaced at the sight of a few tufts of hair hard to distinguish from the fast-blistering scalp. All the while, Booker was whispering, "Yeah, yeah. Come on, love, come on, come on, lady." Queen was breathing— at least coughing and spitting, major signs of life. As the ambulance parked, the crowd became bigger and some of the onlookers seemed transfixed—but not at the moaning patient being trundled into the ambulance. They were focused, wide-eyed, on Bride's lovely, plump breasts. However pleased the onlookers were, it was zero compared to Bride's delight. So much so she delayed accepting the blanket the medical technician held toward her—until she saw the look on Booker's face. But it was hard to suppress her glee, even though she was slightly ashamed at dividing her attention between the sad sight of Queen's slide into the back of the ambulance and the magical return of her flawless breasts.

Bride and Booker ran to the Jaguar and followed the ambulance.

Once Queen was admitted, Bride spent the days with her, Booker the nights, three of which passed before Queen opened her eyes. Head bandaged, its contents drugged, she recognized neither of her rescuers. All they were able to do was watch the tubes attached to the patient, one clear as glass turning like a rainforest vine, others thin as telephone wire, all secondary to the white clematis bloom covering the soft gurgle from her lips.

Lines of primary colors bled across the screen above the hospital bed. Transparent bags of what looked like flat Champagne dripped into a vine feeding Queen's flaccid arm. Unable to rise to a bedpan, she had to be scoured, oiled and rewrapped—all of which Bride, not trusting the indifferent hands of the nurse, did herself as tenderly as possible. And she bathed her one section at a time, making sure the lady's body was covered in certain areas before and after cleansing. She left Queen's feet untouched because in the evening when Booker relieved her he insisted, like a daily communicant at Easter, on the duty of assuming that act of devotion. He maintained the pedicure, soaped then rinsed Queen's feet, finally massaging them slowly, rhythmically, with a lotion that smelled like heather. He did the same for Queen's hands, all the time cursing himself for the animosity he had felt during their last conversation.

Neither one spoke during those ablutions and, except for Bride's occasional humming, the quiet served as the balm they both needed. They worked together like a true couple, thinking not of themselves, but of helping somebody else. Sitting among other people in a hospital waiting room with nothing to do but worry was an ordeal. But so was staring helplessly at the patient noting every stir, breath or shift of the prone body. After three days of waiting broken by what acts of comfort they could provide, Queen spoke, her voice a rough, unintelligible croak through the oxygen mask. Then late one evening the oxygen mask was removed and Queen whispered, "Am I going to be all right?"

Booker smiled.

"No question. No question at all." He leaned in and kissed her nose.

Queen licked her dry lips, closed her eyes again and began to snore.

When Bride returned to relieve him and he told her what had happened, they celebrated by eating breakfast together in the hospital cafeteria. Bride ordered cereal, Booker orange juice.

"What about your job?" Booker raised his eyebrows.

"What about it?"

"Just asking, Bride. Breakfast conversation, you know?"

"I don't know about my job and don't care. I'll get another one."

"Oh, yeah?"

"Yeah. And you? Logging forever?"

"Maybe. Maybe not. Loggers move on after they destroy a forest."

"Well, don't worry about me."

"But I do."

"Since when?"

"Since you broke a beer bottle over my head."

"Sorry."

"No kidding. Me too."

They chuckled.

Away from Queen's hospital bed, relieved about her progress and in a fairly relaxed mood, they amused themselves with banter like an old couple.

Suddenly, as though he'd forgotten something, Booker snapped his fingers. Then he reached into his shirt pocket and took out Queen's gold earrings. They had been removed to bandage Queen's head. All this time they had been in a little plastic bag tucked in the drawer of her bedside table.

"Take these," he said. "She prized them and would want you to wear them while she recovers."

Bride touched her earlobes, felt the return of tiny holes and teared up while grinning.

"Let me," said Booker. Carefully he inserted the wires into Bride's lobes, saying, "Good thing she was wearing them when the place caught fire because nothing at all is left. No letters, address book, nothing. All burned. So I called my mother and asked her to get in touch with Queen's kids."

"Can she contact them?" asked Bride swerving her head gently back and forth the better to relish the gold discs. Everything was coming back. Almost everything. Almost.

"Some," Booker replied. "A daughter in Texas, medical student. She'll be easy to find."

Bride stirred her oatmeal, tasted a spoonful, found it cold. "She told me she doesn't see any of them, but they send her money."

"They all hate her for some reason or another. I know she abandoned some of them to marry other men. Lots of other men. And she didn't or couldn't take the kids with her. Their fathers made sure of that."

"I think she loves them though," said Bride. "Their photographs were all over the place."

"Yeah, well the motherfucker who murdered my brother had all his victims' photos in his fucking den."

"Not the same, Booker."

"No?" He looked out the window.

"No. Queen loves her children."

"They don't think so."

"Oh, stop it," said Bride. "No more stupid arguments about who loves who." She pushed the cereal bowl to the center of the table and took a sip of his orange juice. "Come on, hateful. Let's go back and see how she's doing."

Standing on either side of Queen's bed, they were extremely happy to hear her speaking loudly and clearly.

"Hannah? Hannah?" Queen was staring at Bride and breathing hard. "Come here, baby. Hannah?"

"Who's Hannah?" asked Bride.

"Her daughter. The medical student."

"She thinks I'm her daughter? God. Drugs, medicine, I guess. That stuff confuses her."

"Or focuses her," said Booker. He lowered his voice. "There was a thing with Hannah. Rumor in the family was that Queen ignored or dismissed the girl's complaint about her father—the Asian one, I believe, or the Texan. I don't know. Anyway she said he fondled her and Queen refused to believe it. The ice between them never melted."

"It's still on her mind."

"Deeper than her mind." Booker sat in a chair near the foot of Queen's bed listening to her persistent call—a whisper now—for Hannah. "Now I think of it, it explains why she told me to hang on to Adam, to keep him close."

"But Hannah isn't dead."

"In a way she is, at least to her mother. You saw that photo display she had on her wall. Takes up all the space. It's like a roll call. Most of the pictures are of Hannah though—as a baby, a teenager, a high school graduate, winning some prize. More like a memorial than a gallery."

Bride moved behind Booker's chair and began to massage his shoulders. "I thought those photos were of all her children," she said.

"Yeah, some are. But Hannah reigns." He rested his head on Bride's stomach and let the tension he didn't know was in him drift away.

Following a few days of cheer-inspiring recovery, Queen was still confused but talking and eating. Her speech was hard to follow since it seemed to consist of geography—the places she had lived in—and anecdotes addressed to Hannah.

Bride and Booker were pleased with the doctor's assessment: "She's doing much better. Much." They relaxed and began to plan what to do when Queen was released. Get a place where all three were together? A big mobile home? At least until Queen could take care of herself, without delving too closely, they assumed the three of them would live together.

Slowly, slowly their bright plans for the immediate future darkened. The carnival-colored lines on the screen began to wiggle and fall, their sliding punctuated by the music of emergency bells. Booker and Bride took shallow breaths as Queen's blood count dropped and her temperature rose. A vicious hospital-borne virus, as sneaky and evil as the flame that had destroyed her home, was attacking the patient. She thrashed a bit then held her arms raised high, her fingers clawing, reaching over and over for the rungs of a ladder that only she could see. Then all of it stopped.

Twelve hours later Queen was dead. One eye was still open, so Bride doubted the fact. It was Booker who closed it, after which he closed his own.

During the three days waiting until Queen's ashes were ready, they argued over the choice of an urn. Bride wanted something elegant in brass; Booker preferred something environmentally friendly that could be buried and in time enrich the soil. When they discovered there was no grave-yard within thirty-five miles, or a suitable place in the trailer park for her burial, they settled for a cardboard box to hold ashes that would be strewn into the stream. Booker insisted on performing the rites alone while Bride waited in the car. She watched him carefully, anxiously, as he walked away toward the river, holding the carton of ashes in his right elbow and his trumpet dangling from the fingers of his left. These last days, thought Bride, while they were fig-uring out what to do, were congenial because their focus was on a third person they both loved. What would happen now, she wondered, when or if there was just the two of them again? She didn't want to be without him, ever, but if she had to she was certain it would be okay. The future? She would handle it.

Although heartfelt, Booker's ceremony to honor his beloved Queen was awkward: the ashes were lumpy and difficult to toss and his musical tribute, his effort at "Kind of Blue," was off-key and uninspired. He cut it short and, with a sadness he had not felt since Adam's death, threw his trumpet into the gray water as though the trumpet had failed him rather than he had failed it. He watched the horn float for a while then sat down on the grass, resting his forehead in his palm. His thoughts were stark, skeletal. It never occurred to him that Queen would die or even could die. Much of the time, while he tended her feet and listened to her breath he was thinking about his own unease. How disrupted his life had become, what with caring for an aunt he adored and who was now dead due to her own carelessness—who the hell burns bedsprings these days? How acute his predicament had become by the sudden return of a woman he once enjoyed, who had changed from one dimension into three—demanding, perceptive, daring. And what made him think he was a talented trumpet player who could do justice to a burial or that music could be his language of memory, of celebration or the displacement of loss? How long had childhood trauma hurtled him away from the rip and wave of life? His eyes burned but were incapable of weeping.

Queen's remains, touched by a rare welcome breeze, drifted farther and farther down-current. The sky, too sullen to keep its promise of sunlight, sent hot moisture instead. Feeling unbearable loneliness as well as profound regret, Booker stood up and joined Bride in the Jaguar.

Inside the car the quiet was thick, brutal, probably because there were no tears and nothing important to say. Except for one thing and one thing only.

Bride took a deep breath before breaking into the deathly silence. Now or never, she thought.

"I'm pregnant," she said in a clear, calm voice. She looked straight ahead at the well-traveled road of dirt and gravel.

"What did you say?" Booker's voice cracked.

"You heard me. I'm pregnant and it's yours."

Booker gazed at her a long time before looking away toward the river where a smattering of Queen's ashes still floated but the trumpet had disappeared. One by fire, one by water, two of what he had so intensely loved gone, he thought. He couldn't lose a third. With just a hint of a smile he turned around to look again at Bride.

"No," he said. "It's ours."

Then he offered her the hand she had craved all her life, the hand that did not need a lie to deserve it, the hand of trust and caring for—a combination that some call natural love. Bride stroked Booker's palm then threaded her fingers through his. They kissed, lightly, before leaning back on the headrests to let their spines sink into the seats' soft hide of cattle. Staring through the windshield, each of them began to imagine what the future would certainly be.

No lonesome wandering child with a fishing pole passed by and glanced at the adults in the dusty gray car. But if one had, he or she might have noticed the pronounced smiles of the couple, how dreamy their eyes were, but would not care a bit what caused that shine of happiness.

A child. New life. Immune to evil or illness, protected from kidnap, beatings, rape, racism, insult, hurt, self-loathing, abandonment. Error-free. All goodness. Minus wrath.

So they believe.

Sweetness

I prefer this place—Winston House—to those big, expensive nursing homes outside the city. Mine is small, homey, cheaper, with twenty-four-hour nurses and a doctor who comes twice a week. I'm only sixty-three—too young for pasture—but I came down with some creeping bone disease, so good care is vital. The boredom is worse than the weakness or the pain, but the nurses are lovely. One just kissed me on the cheek before congratulating me when I told her I was going to be a grandmother. Her smile and her compliments were fit for someone about to be crowned.

I had showed her the note on blue paper that I got from Lula Ann—well, she signed it "Bride," but I never pay that any attention. Her words sounded giddy. "Guess what, S. I am so so happy to pass along this news. I am going to have a baby. I'm too too thrilled and hope you are too." I reckon the thrill is about the baby, not its father, because she doesn't mention him at all. I wonder if he is as black as she is. If so, she needn't worry like I did. Things have changed a mite from when I was young. Blue blacks are all over TV, in fashion magazines, commercials, even starring in movies.

There is no return address on the envelope. So I guess I'm still the bad parent being punished forever till the day I die for doing the well-intended and, in fact, necessary way I brought her up. I know she hates me. As soon as she could she left me all alone in that awful apartment. She got as far away from me as she could: dolled herself up and got some big-time job in California. The last time I saw her she looked so good, I forgot about her color. Still, our relationship is down to her sending me money. I have to say I'm grateful for the cash because I don't have to beg for extras like some of the other patients. If I want my own fresh deck of cards for solitaire I can get it and not need to play with the dirty, worn one in the lounge. And I can buy my special face cream. But I'm not fooled. I know the money she sends is a way to stay away and quiet down the little bit of conscience she's got left.

If I sound irritable, ungrateful, part of it is because underneath is regret. All the little things I didn't do or did wrong. I remember when she had her first period and how I reacted. Or the times I shouted when she stumbled or dropped something. How I screamed at her to keep her from tattling on the landlord—the dog. True. I was really upset, even repelled by her black skin when she was born and at first I thought of . . . No. I have to push those memories away—fast. No point. I know I did the best for her under the circumstances. When my husband ran out on us, Lula Ann was a burden. A heavy one but I bore it well.

Yes, I was tough on her. You bet I was. After she got all that attention following the trial of those teachers, she became hard to handle. By the time she turned twelve going on thirteen I had to be even tougher. She was talking back, refusing to eat what I cooked, primping her hair. When I braided it, she'd go to school and unbraid it. I couldn't let her go bad. I slammed the lid and warned her of the names she'd be called. Still, some of my schooling must have rubbed off. See how she turned out? A rich career girl. Can you beat it?

Now she's pregnant. Good move, Lula Ann. If you think mothering is all cooing, booties and diapers you're in for a big shock. Big. You and your nameless boyfriend, husband, pickup—whoever—imagine OOOH! A baby! Kitchee kitchee koo!

Listen to me. You are about to find out what it takes, how the world is, how it works and how it changes when you are a parent.

Good luck and God help the child.

HARRY & MEGHAN

AN INVITATION TO THE ROYAL WEDDING

THIS IS A CARLTON BOOK

Published in 2018 by Carlton Books Limited
20 Mortimer Street
London W1T 3JW

10 9 8 7 6 5 4 3 2 1

Text © Carlton Books 2018
Design © Carlton Books 2018

A CIP catalogue record for this book is available from the British
Library.

ISBN 978 1 78739 133 8

Printed in Spain

HARRY & MEGHAN

AN INVITATION TO THE ROYAL WEDDING

CARLTON
BOOKS

CONTENTS

FOREWORD

On 11 December 1936, King Edward VIII told the British people in a radio address that he could no longer continue as monarch "without the help and support of the woman I love". Edward was determined to marry Wallis Simpson, an American divorcee, and was forced to abdicate.

Eighty-one years later, on Christmas Day, another American divorcee, an actress of mixed race, walked to St Mary Magdalene Church on the Sandringham estate in Norfolk. It was a short walk, but for the Royal Family it represented a giant step. Meghan Markle was arm in arm with Prince Harry and alongside the Duke and Duchess of Cambridge. She was greeted by the Queen.

Meghan Markle is not, of course, the first divorcee to marry into the House of Windsor. The Duchess of Cornwall, then Mrs Camilla Parker Bowles, married the Prince of Wales in 2005. But no other fiancée of a Royal has been invited by the Queen to join her at Sandringham for Christmas. Not the Duchess of Cornwall, not Diana, Princess of Wales, not the Duchess of Cambridge. It was a deeply significant gesture by the Queen: a sign of how warmly Meghan has been welcomed into a family that calls itself "the Firm". Perhaps more importantly it was evidence of how far that family has come in the process of change and modernization.

Most of those who report on the Royal Family for a living have developed a particular affection for Prince Harry. He has provided some good copy, of course, but his lack of stuffiness and increasing approachability have made him a popular figure. He has also earned much respect. He was on the front line in Afghanistan and went on to champion the cause of those injured, both physically and mentally, in the service of their country.

Through all of this, during many of the interviews he gave to promote the causes he supports, Harry fielded the "settling down" question from reporters fishing for an insight into his private life. He deflected it with little more than mild irritation, but when his relationship with Meghan became public he reacted with fury to the tone of some of the coverage. A statement on his behalf referred to fictional stories and comment pieces with racial undertones. On social media there had been "outright sexism and racism".

If there remained any doubt about the intensity of this relationship it was dispelled when Harry and Meghan gave a television interview to mark their engagement. Harry described how he fell in love "incredibly quickly", adding that "all the stars were aligned, everything was just perfect".

Not all the Royal Family's love stories have had happy endings. Some have faltered and then collapsed under the relentless glare of public attention. Joining "the Firm" brings extraordinary exposure and often ruthless scrutiny. No one knows that better than the sons of Diana, Princess of Wales. But all the signs are that Prince Harry has found true love and that Meghan Markle will not merely adjust to the Royal Family, she may very well transform it.

TIM EWART, FORMER ITV NEWS ROYAL EDITOR

INTRODUCTION

OPPOSITE:

Prince Harry and Meghan Markle are radiant as they announce their engagement in the Sunken Garden at Kensington Palace on 27 November 2017. Their relationship had been made public a year earlier.

NEXT PAGE:

Prince Philip, Meghan and Prince Harry arrive at the Royal Family's traditional Christmas Day church service at St Mary Magdalene Church in Sandringham.

The wedding between Henry Charles Albert David Windsor and Rachel Meghan Markle is simply unprecedented in almost every conceivable way. When Harry's own parents married, it was deemed that the bride must come from a suitable background and have had no other significant suitors in her background. Princess Diana made the grade because she was too young to have had any other serious boyfriends, and because her forebears, the Spencers, were one of Britain's most prominent aristocratic families and her father had been an equerry to the King.

Meghan Markle could not be more different. A biracial actress who has already been married once and who comes from the United States, she will be 36 on the day she marries Harry – the same age Diana was when she died. But their union has not only failed to raise any eyebrows, regal or otherwise, it has been warmly welcomed, both by the Royal Family and the rest of the country. It is an indication as to quite how much the monarchy has changed since 1981, the year Harry's parents got married, although then, as now, it is the Queen who is still in charge.

The Windsors have, in fact, been adept at constantly reinventing themselves throughout their history and have now done so again in the second decade of the twenty-first century – twice. The wedding of Harry's older brother, William, was already a step away from tradition in that his bride, Catherine Middleton, was, herself, a middle-class girl, not a member of the aristocracy or any foreign royal family. The two lived together before getting married – an unprecedented occurrence. But the circumstances surrounding Harry's marriage are more unusual still.

In 1936, the monarchy was shaken to its very foundations when another American divorcee, Wallis Simpson, caused Edward VIII, Harry's great-great uncle, to abdicate the throne. The crown went to his younger brother, George VI, father of the present Queen, but it was that abdication that rocked the nation to such an extent that Elizabeth II will not, despite her great age, countenance standing down today. To the Windsors, duty is everything and Edward did not do his duty. It would not have been surprising if there had been a judder of terror when Meghan arrived on the scene.

But there wasn't. Of course, circumstances have changed: the world, as well as the House of Windsor, has moved on. Nor is Harry in the same position as Edward VIII: by the time of the wedding, he will be sixth in line to the throne, not the incumbent. It is very unlikely that Harry will ever become Henry IX.

But he is, and will remain, a senior Royal and, as such, his choice of bride will always attract a huge amount of attention. And that Meghan is so markedly different from other Royal brides shows quite how much attitudes have changed. For the great irony, of course, is that, while the abdication crisis was caused by a divorcee, divorce has featured in the Royal Family in almost every generation since. The Queen's sister, Princess Margaret, was forced to give up the great love of her life, Peter Townsend, on the grounds that he was divorced, only to later split from her own husband, the Earl of Snowdon. Three of the Queen's children are divorced, including Harry's father, Prince Charles. Lessons have clearly been learned, as the Queen put it in another context, and now, rather than forcing the Royal princes into quasi-arranged unions, they have been allowed to marry for love.

And so, as with his older brother, William, Harry could not only choose his own bride regardless of background, but protocol has been relaxed to the extent that Meghan was able to spend Christmas with him at the Queen's Norfolk home in Sandringham (again unprecedented before the actual wedding – even Kate had to wait to become the Duchess of Cambridge before that honour was extended to her) and relax into life at Nottingham Cottage (Nott Cott), their home in the grounds of Kensington Palace. And Meghan is clearly the right choice for him. This book will look at the background of both of them, of what shaped them, and of why they are so compatible. They are the ultimate modern Royal couple – and this is why.

CHAPTER 1

PRINCE HARRY

"WHEN DID I KNOW SHE WAS THE ONE?

VERY FIRST TIME WE MET."

PRINCE HARRY, NOVEMBER 2017

His birth, when it came, marked yet another high in the Royal Family's fortunes in the early 1980s. Prince Henry Charles Albert David was born on 15 September 1984 in the Lindo Wing of St Mary's Hospital in Paddington, London. Known as Harry right from the start, he was the second son of Prince Charles and Princess Diana, and (at that stage) third in line to the British throne. To the public, it was a huge cause of celebration and appeared to be a sign of the happiness between Charles and Diana; in private, alas, it was a different story. But no one knew it back then.

Little Harry was baptized into the Church of England by the Archbishop of Canterbury, Robert Runcie, and sent to Mynors' nursery school and pre-preparatory Wetherby School in London. This was followed by Ludgrove School and Eton, both of which were also attended by his elder brother, William. Away from school the brothers divided their time between Kensington Palace and Highgrove, their parents' homes in London and Gloucestershire. Harry was introduced to public life early – his first official trip happened in 1986 when he was taken to Italy.

Behind the scenes, however, matters were far more complicated than the public realized at the time. Harry's mother, Diana, far from being the pliable spouse that she had initially seemed destined to be, was turning into the most famous and most photographed woman in the world. There was a big age gap between her and Charles – when they married, she was 20 and he was 32 – and it further emerged that they had little in common. Moreover, Diana was determined to bring her sons up in a way that was brand new to the Royal Family, taking them to homeless shelters, exposing them to the less fortunate in life. Both boys grew up understanding that theirs was a privileged life; in

later years it also became clear that Harry had inherited his mother's empathy when dealing with people less fortunate than himself. He also inherited her rebelliousness: Harry was a mischievous little boy, far more so than his staid older brother, and was known to lead his Royal protection officers a merry dance. There were trips to the Caribbean, to Florida's Disney World, to Alton Towers. They were probably the first Royal princes to be taken to McDonalds, just down the road from Kensington Palace.

But his childhood had its own fair share of travails, which would culminate in tragedy. As his parents' marriage fell apart, both pursued other relationships: Diana with James Hewitt and Charles with his first great love, Camilla Parker Bowles, whom he would later go on to marry. Stories began to leak out into the press about the terrible state of the Wales's marriage and, in 1992, the publication of *Diana: Her True Story* blew the idea of the Royal marriage as a real-life fairy tale out of the water. The couple separated, and Prince Charles moved out to St James's Palace. While Kensington Palace remained Harry's London home,

ABOVE:

Harry was always the naughty one. Here he is sticking his tongue out on the royal balcony following the Trooping the Colour parade. Lady Gabriella Windsor and Lady Rose Windsor are also present.

OPPOSITE:

Harry's first day at Wetherby School, which William also attended.

ABOVE:

In the aftermath of
Princess Diana's
shocking death, Prince
Charles takes his two
young sons to inspect
the massive floral
tribute left outside
Kensington Palace.

he still spent time with his father in the country, keeping pets and learning countryside pursuits. From 1993, he and William had a *de facto* nanny in the jolly shape of Tiggy Legge-Bourke, who was, herself, the source of controversy when she said of her charges, "I give them what they need at this stage: fresh air, a rifle and a horse. She [Diana] gives them a tennis racket and a bucket of popcorn at the movies." She further irritated Diana by referring to the two of them as "my babies".

In 1996, Harry's parents divorced and, the following year, the great tragedy of his young life occurred. He was just 12 years old when his mother was killed in a car crash in Paris with her lover Dodi al Fayed. The hearts of the nation went out to the bereaved little boy as they saw him walking alongside his brother, father, grandfather and Uncle Charles Spencer behind the funeral cortège as it moved from Kensington Palace to Westminster Abbey. In later years, he was to talk of the huge gap in his life after losing his mother at such a young age, of the anger it built up and the sadness he was unable to cope with. It created the need in his life for a mother figure and it is, perhaps, not surprising that his eventual fiancée was a couple of years older than him and with a very maternal, cherishing air. In the wake of Diana's death, Harry and William continued in the care of Tiggy Legge-Bourke, who again managed to cause controversy when she allowed the princes to abseil down a 50-metre dam without safety lines or helmets. That might have been it for Tiggy, but the boys adored her so much that she retained her position after all.

There were signs of rebellion, even then. Harry was just 17 when he was photographed smoking cannabis and drinking (underage), provoking his father to take him to a drugs clinic to see what could happen if a problem really got out of hand. There was further trouble when he unwisely wore a Nazi German Afrika Korps uniform complete with a swastika armband to a fancy-dress party, for which he later apologized. However, despite the lack of judgement on his part, there was widespread sympathy among the public. This was a young man who had lost his mother and, even before Harry spoke about the impact of what had happened to him, as he only did many years later, there was an understanding that, if Harry was sometimes a little too OTT, it was because, despite Tiggy's efforts, the guiding hand of a mother was not there.

In June 2003, Harry left Eton with two A-levels, which qualified him to join the army, and, after a gap year in Australia in

LEFT:

A pensive-looking Prince Harry in his room at Eton. A photo of his mother sits on the desk behind him.

OPPOSITE:

Prince Harry distinguished himself as a soldier when serving in Afghanistan. Here he is holding an SLR rifle while on patrol in the deserted town of Garmisir.

ABOVE:

A prince on parade. The Queen smiles at her grandson as she inspects soldiers at the Sovereign's Parade at Sandhurst.

in which he worked on a cattle ranch, he entered Sandhurst in May 2005. Officer Cadet Wales, as he was known, joined the Alamein Company and, after completing his officer training within a year, was commissioned as a cornet in the Blues and Royals. The army was the making of him. In his spare time, Harry was developing the reputation of being something of a party prince, photographed falling out of nightclubs and fighting with photographers – a direct result, it is clear in hindsight, of losing his mother so young – but no one doubted his bravery and commitment to the armed forces. There was early debate about whether he should be allowed to serve in Iraq – Harry, himself, was very keen to see action, saying, "If they said, 'No, you can't go front line,' then I wouldn't drag my sorry ass through Sandhurst and I wouldn't be where I am now." Ultimately, however, it was deemed that he and the soldiers around him would be too much at risk as a high-profile target but, in October 2008, like his father and brother before him, it was announced he would learn to fly military helicopters. After learning to fly the Apache attack

helicopter, he was presented with his wings by his father in 2010.

Harry proved to be a very adept Apache pilot and, after further training in California and Arizona in 2012, he went to serve on a four-month combat tour of Afghanistan. He was threatened by the Taliban, but served for 20 weeks, having successfully qualified as an Apache aircraft commander. Back in London, he became a staff officer and, at the same time, conceived the idea for the Invictus Games, a Paralympic-style event for injured servicemen and -women, which is how he was to meet one Meghan Markle. The inaugural games were held on 10–14 September 2014 and are probably Harry's most impressive contribution to public life to date.

After a secondment to the Australian Defence Force, Harry left the Armed Forces in June 2015. But, apart from his ongoing involvement with the Invictus Games, he had taken on numerous other roles. He had been appointed Counsellor of State when he was just 21 and, as such, was heavily involved in the Commonwealth. Nor were the Invictus Games his only work for the underprivileged. Harry had early conceived of a great love for Africa, and the plight of the people in the former British colony of Lesotho had touched

ABOVE:

Prince Harry set up a charity, Sentebale, to help vulnerable children in Lesotho. Here he is playing with a three-year-old blind girl named Karabo while visiting Phelisanong Children's Home in Pitseng in December 2014.

him deeply. As early as 2004, he launched Sentebale: The Princes' Fund for Lesotho, to help children with HIV/Aids, and, in 2007, organized the Concert for Diana at Wembley Stadium to help fund it. There have been numerous other charitable involvements as well, including WellChild and polo matches in aid of various causes.

In 2009, Harry and William set up their own Royal household in St James's Palace, separate from their father's, guided by the former British ambassador to Washington, Sir David Manning, and that year also launched The Foundation of Prince William and Prince Harry to further their charitable work. Harry's immense popularity was growing both at home and abroad: in March 2012, as part of the Queen's Diamond Jubilee Celebrations, Harry visited Belize, the Bahamas and Jamaica, where his presence went down so well that he was even credited with stopping the prime minister, Portia Simpson-Miller, from cutting the ties between Jamaica and the monarchy. Numerous international visits were to follow, with Harry as one of the most senior members of the Royal Family representing the Windsors all over the world.

In 2012, there was also a return to controversy, when pictures of Harry and an unknown young woman – both naked in a Wynn Las Vegas hotel room playing strip billiards – emerged. Initially, UK newspapers were reluctant to publish the photos, although the *Sun*

ABOVE:

On the same visit, he went to Mokhotlong, where he showed children a photo he had taken on a Fuji X100s camera.

ultimately did so, while St James's Palace maintained that Harry's privacy had been invaded. It made no difference whatsoever to his standing, with the public polls later that year showing Harry to be the third most popular member of the Royal Family after the Queen and Prince William.

He was also one of the most eligible men in the world and was to have two serious relationships before meeting Meghan. The first of these was Chelsy Davy, daughter of the (controversial) Zimbabwean businessman Charles Davy. The two were together for about seven years, between 2004 and 2011, with a gap in the middle. In an interview that took place to coincide with his twenty-first birthday, Harry commented that he "would love to tell everyone how amazing she is but once I start talking about that, I have left myself open... There is truth and there is lies and unfortunately I cannot get the truth across."

Chelsy accompanied him to the wedding of William and Catherine Middleton but, ironically, that was said to have brought it home to her that they could not marry because she could not cope with the pressures of such a public life. "She has watched what Kate has gone through and how much she has had to sacrifice, and says it's not for her," a friend of hers said. "Chelsy thought the wedding was wonderful and she had a ball, but there's no way marriage is on the cards for her. She wants her freedom and to start a career. That's her focus

BELOW:

Prince Harry charmed Jamaica when he visited to mark Queen Elizabeth's Diamond Jubilee. Posing with Usain Bolt, Harry later pretended to try to steal the race.

BELOW RIGHT:

Laden with garlands on a visit to Gauda Secondary School, which had been damaged by an earthquake in Okhari, Nepal.

at the moment, she and Harry are going to see how things go." In the end, of course, they split up, and Harry embarked on a two-year relationship with the actress Cressida Bonas, after being introduced to her by his cousin, Princess Eugenie. Cressida, too, found it difficult to cope with being in the public eye and in April 2014 it was announced that there had been an amicable split. Harry was alone again.

Despite his eligible-man status, it was to be a while before Harry finally found the woman he was destined for, not least because any woman knew that, by dating him, she would be the subject of a good deal of attention, which put them off. "If or when I do find a girlfriend, I will do my utmost to ensure that me and her can get to the point where we're actually comfortable with each other before the massive invasion that is inevitably going to happen into her privacy," he told the *Sunday Times*. "The other concern is that even if I talk to a girl, that person is then suddenly my wife, and people go knocking on her door." In other words, Harry needed to find someone who could handle the spotlight. And he did.

ABOVE:

Prince Harry chats to USA Invictus Team Member Elizabeth Marks during the Invictus Games Orlando 2016 before trying on her jersey. One of Harry's proudest achievements was establishing the Invictus Games to help injured and disabled people.

CHAPTER 2

MEGHAN MARKLE

"REFLECTING ON WHERE I CAME FROM HELPS ME TO
APPRECIATE AND BALANCE WHAT I HAVE NOW."

MEGHAN MARKLE, DECEMBER 2016

PREVIOUS PAGE:

*A glamorous Meghan
Markle looks stunning
at Elle's 6th Annual
Women in Television
dinner in Los Angeles
in January 2016.*

ABOVE:

*A fresh-faced
Meghan attends Kari
Feinstein's Pre-Emmy
Style Lounge in Los
Angeles in 2005.*

When Thomas W. Markle and Doria Ragland first set eyes on one another at some point towards the end of the 1970s, they could not have dreamed that one day their daughter was going to marry a prince of the House of Windsor. Indeed, even the life she had before she met Harry would have seemed a lot to grasp: actress in a hit TV show and with a reputation as a humanitarian. Hers was to be an active life.

In fact, the couple's union raised eyebrows even then in some eyes, because Doria is African-American and can trace her forebears back to slaves (an even more remarkable precedent in a Royal bride than Kate Middleton's coal-mining ancestors), while Thomas came from Dutch-Irish stock. Thomas had been married before, giving Meghan an older half-brother and half-sister, and by the time his daughter came along on 4 August 1981, he was working as a lighting director in Los Angeles. Meghan was aware from the start that her status as a biracial woman caused comment:

"My dad is Caucasian and my mom is African-American," she said in later years. "I'm half black and half white ... I have come to embrace [this and] say who I am, to share where I'm from, to voice my pride in being a strong, confident, mixed-race woman."

Shortly after her relationship with Harry came to light – and, with it, a renewed focus on her racial identity – Meghan tackled the subject head on in *Elle*. "It was the late Seventies when my parents met, my dad was a lighting director for a soap opera and my mom was a temp at the studio," she wrote. "I like to think he was drawn to her sweet eyes and her Afro, plus their shared love of antiques. Whatever it was, they married and had me. They moved into a house in The Valley in LA, to a neighborhood that was leafy and affordable. What it was not, however, was diverse. And there was my mom, caramel in complexion with her light-skinned baby in tow, being asked where my mother was since they assumed she was the nanny."

It did, at least, tackle the elephant in the room because this was new and uncharted territory, although for Meghan it was an issue she'd had to deal with throughout her entire life. And it wasn't always easy. While growing up at school, she was asked to tick a box identifying her racial background (she couldn't) and, when her father found out why she was so upset about it, he advised her

BELOW:

High-school yearbook photographs of young Meghan. She had a love of performing from a young age.

29

to draw her own box in the future (which she most certainly did as an adult in life). Her parents did what they could, buying two sets of dolls – one black and one white – and combining them to create a mixed-race family, but the sensitivity to the subject remained.

The couple divorced when Meghan was just six, but she remained close to her father, visiting him on the set of *Married… with Children*, where he was the lighting director. She was thus given a taste for acting from an early age. She was educated at the Immaculate Heart Catholic High School, which wrongly gave some people the impression that she was a Catholic (both parents were Protestants) and, early on, she picked up some of the interests that were to stay with her into later life. Doria was a yoga teacher and she and Meghan would practise yoga together, as they still do. They also travelled from early on, and Meghan's philanthropic streak came out when she was as young as 13 and helped out in a soup kitchen.

"I started working at a soup kitchen in skid row of Los Angeles when I was 13 years old, and the first day I felt really scared," she told *The Game Changers*, a book by Samantha Brett and Steph Adams. "I was young, and it was rough and raw down there, and though I was with a great volunteer group, I just felt overwhelmed. I remember one of my mentors (Mrs. Maria Pollia) told me that 'life is about putting others' needs about your own fears.' That has always stayed with me." It was to stand her in good stead. She was an early campaigner as well, managing to get a company to change a national television commercial at the age of just 11 because she believed it was sexist. One of her first jobs was earning $4 an hour at Humphrey Yogart, a frozen yoghurt store in LA: "Meghan was still at school – maybe a little older than 13 as the rules are strict in California," her boss Paula Sheftel later recalled. "She earned minimum wage and was very popular with customers. She had to prove she had an outgoing personality and would work well with staff."

After leaving school, Meghan attended Northwestern University in Evanston, Illinois, where she studied theatre and international studies and, partly because of the latter, spent some time as an intern at the US embassy in Buenos Aires, before deciding to opt for an acting career. But it was tough, not least because of the ethnic issue: "I wasn't black enough for the black roles and I wasn't white enough for the white ones, leaving me somewhere in the middle

OPPOSITE:

A thoughtful looking Meghan attends the Some Kind-a Gorgeous Style and Beauty Lounge at the Chateau Marmont in California, 2010.

as the ethnic chameleon who couldn't book a job," she later said. To help make ends meet, Meghan became a freelance calligrapher: "It was because I went to an all-girls Catholic school for, like, six years during the time when kids actually had handwriting class," she later told *Esquire*. "I've always had a propensity for getting the cursive down pretty well. What it evolved into was my pseudo-waitressing job when I was auditioning. I didn't wait tables. I did calligraphy for the invitations for, like, Robin Thicke and Paula Patton's wedding."

But work gradually began to come in. Her first television appearance was on the daytime soap *General Hospital*, then small roles on the likes of *Century City*, *The War at Home* and *CSI:NY* came in. Meghan also became a "briefcase girl" on the US game show *Deal or No Deal*, something that came back to haunt her when her relationship with Harry came out and cheesy pictures of Meghan emerged, brandishing her suitcase. She often sounded a little embarrassed talking about that: "I would put that in the category of things I was doing while I was auditioning to try to make ends meet," she told *Esquire*. "I went from working in the US Embassy in Argentina to ending up on *Deal*. It's run the gamut. Definitely working on *Deal or No Deal* was a learning experience, and it helped me to understand what I would rather be doing. So if that's a way for me to gloss over that subject, then I will happily shift gears into something else."

More brief appearances in television shows and films, including *Get Him to the Greek*, *Remember Me*, *Cuts* and *Love, Inc.*, ensued, until July 2011 when she had her major breakthrough in the role of Rachel Zane in *Suits*. It was to make her name. Rachel was a paralegal at the legal firm Pearson Hardman, and becomes the love interest of Mike Ross (Patrick J. Adams), which again sent the media into a frenzy when the news about her Royal boyfriend emerged. There were plenty of shots when a scantily clad Meghan was pictured in a clench with her on-screen love interest, which often appeared when anything about Harry and Meghan came out. *Suits* was filmed in Toronto, although it was set in New York, and so Meghan upped sticks to the Canadian city, which is where she was to make her home for the best part of seven years.

The character of Rachel was, in part, based on Meghan: for example, the two of them are both foodies, interested in the cooking and eating of food, and restaurants. This was one of the many reasons that Meghan, like a number of other Hollywood actresses (most famously Gwyneth Paltrow) set up her lifestyle website, which she called The Tig: the name derived from her favourite Italian wine, Tignanello. It was, said Meghan, a "hub for the discerning palate – those with a hunger for food, travel, fashion & beauty". This gave an insight into Meghan's life as curiosity in her grew: she shared details of favourite vacation reads (Michael Ondaatje's *The English Patient*), sustainable travel, famous acquaintances (Michael Bublé), playlists, favourite food and much, much more. The blog ran for three years until Meghan shut it down – another clear hint that she was soon to be entering into a lifestyle that it would be unwise to share online.

It was early on in the success of *Suits* that Meghan entered into her first brief marriage, to Trevor Engelson. Trevor (who bears a passing resemblance to Harry) was a film producer, born on 23 October 1976 in New York. His best-known film, in which Meghan appeared, is the Robert Pattinson vehicle *Remember Me*. The couple first met in 2004 and, after six years of dating, got engaged in 2010. They eventually tied the knot at the Jamaica Inn in Ocho Rios, Jamaica, in the course of a four-day affair with 102 guests. The wedding would be nothing like her second wedding; in some ways it resembled nothing more than a casual beach party. However, the marriage only lasted two years. Trevor had remained

in LA while Meghan moved to Toronto and the long-distance aspect of their marriage was said to be a problem, to say nothing of Meghan's growing success. The divorce cited "irreconcilable differences"; the marriage was done.

Meghan was not lacking in admirers and her next boyfriend was Cory Vitiello, a well-known Canadian chef who ran one of the best-known restaurants in Toronto, The Harbord Room. They were an item between 2014 and 2016, and rumours persist that they were still an item when Harry and Meghan first met, although no one involved was keen to comment. At any rate, Cory soon found himself a single man once more.

It was during her involvement with *Suits* that Meghan found she had a global profile that she could put to good use – much as Harry's mother, Diana, had done a couple of decades earlier. She became a counsellor for the international charity One Young World, and spoke at the 2014 annual summit on the subjects of

ABOVE:

Meghan made her name in the television show Suits, *set in a New York law firm. She is pictured with co-stars, from left to right, Gina Torres, Rick Hoffman, Gabriel Macht and Patrick J. Adams, who plays her love interest in the show.*

gender equality and slavery in the modern day. That same year, she also went to Afghanistan and Spain as part of the USO Chairman of the Joint Chiefs of Staff Holiday Tour. Two years after that, she became a global ambassador for World Vision Canada, in which role she visited Rwanda for the Clean Water Campaign, as well as taking a trip to India to raise awareness on the subject of issues about women. On top of that, she has carried out work with the United Nations Entity for Gender Equality and the Empowerment of Women. All of this must have had a tremendous impact on Harry, who is both extensively involved in his own charitable work and grew up with a mother who did exactly the same. It was also a good omen for her future with the Royal Family, in which charitable work and duty play a huge part.

So that is Meghan Markle, a thoroughly modern Royal bride with a background that has never been seen in the Royal Family before. Perhaps most crucial of all, however, given the pressures she is having to face, is her personality. Warm, relaxed and easy going, albeit with a serious side, Meghan has the ability to put those around her at ease. As an actress of many years' standing, she also has the ability to cope with the spotlight in a way that Harry's earlier girlfriends found difficult. And now, of course, just as she had established herself as a successful actress and charity worker, was going to come the meeting that would change her life.

OPPOSITE:

A super-stylish Meghan on her way to The Today Show *taping at New York's Rockfeller Center in July 2016. She and Harry were already dating by then.*

BELOW:

As Rachel Zane in Suits.

CHAPTER 3

A BLIND DATE

"I'VE LONGED FOR KIDS SINCE I WAS VERY, VERY YOUNG.
AND SO . . . I'M WAITING TO FIND THE RIGHT PERSON,
SOMEONE WHO'S WILLING TO TAKE ON THE JOB."

PRINCE HARRY, NOVEMBER 2017

Misha Nonoo is a New York-based fashion designer who was born in Bahrain to an Iraqi father and English mother. She grew up in Chelsea and attended the ACS International School in Surrey and the Ecole Supérieure du Commerce Extérieure in Paris. More to the point, she is also one of Meghan Markle's closest friends and, indeed, designed the "Husband" shirt Meghan was wearing when the couple made their first joint appearance at the Invictus Games in September 2017. "We were seated next to one another at a lunch and we got along like a house on fire," Misha told the London *Evening Standard* of the time she and Meghan first met. "She has the most remarkable and generous spirit. I aspire to be as philanthropic as she is, and to have as much of an impact as her."

The friendship might never have been commented on were it not for one fact – Misha seems to have played a crucial role in bringing Harry and Meghan together. Misha is now divorced, but she, too, was married, to the Old Etonian Alexander Gilkes, who was co-founder of auctioneers Paddle 8 (where Harry's cousin, Princess Eugenie, briefly worked) and also, crucially, a close friend of Harry's. Misha met her husband-to-be when she was just 17 and a summer intern at Quintessentially, the concierge company. They married in 2012 and divorced five years later, which gave her yet more in common with Meghan – they were both young divorcees. They had more in common, too: interest in spiritual issues, charity work and a love of animals.

Misha and Meghan's friendship just grew, with Instagram pictures showing the two of them on holiday in Ibiza and Formentera, rather sweetly captioned with the words, "When only children find sisters". (Meghan's half-siblings are much older than her.) It has never been confirmed that it was Misha who set Harry and Meghan up on a blind date together, and she, herself, will not talk about it but, given that she is Meghan's closest friend and was married to Harry's equivalent, it seems possible. However, there has also been intensive speculation that the real matchmaker was Meghan Markle's friend Violet von Westenholz, daughter of former Olympic skier Baron Piers von Westenholz, a close friend of the Prince of Wales.

It was on a blind date that Harry and Meghan finally met, with neither knowing a great deal about the other from the outset, which they revealed after the engagement was announced, without naming their Cupid ("We should protect her privacy and not reveal

too much of that," Meghan said.) There had been a great deal of speculation that the couple had met via the Invictus Games, but it emerged that it was good, old-fashioned matchmaking that brought the two together. And neither knew exactly what to expect.

For a start, Meghan was totally new to all things Royal, and took it remarkably in her stride when told that her blind date was actually a prince, although the way it was put to her seemed more to be a case of meeting someone she might like. However, romance was clearly on the cards. "It was definitely a set-up. It was a blind date for sure. We talk about it now. Because I'm from the States, you don't grow up with the same understanding of the Royal Family," Meghan said in the couple's joint television interview after the engagement was announced. But she had been taken aback to realize quite how much interest this new relationship would provoke. She might have been used to television stardom, but the aura surrounding the Royal Family was in another league

ABOVE:

Harry and Meghan whisper to one another as they watch a wheelchair tennis match during the Invictus Games 2017.

OPPOSITE:

Meghan attends the opening ceremony of the Invictus Games. She and Harry were seated separately but by the end of the week were inseparable.

all together. "And so, while I now understand very clearly there is a global interest there, I didn't know much about him and so the only thing that I had asked her when she said she wanted to set us up was, I have one question: 'Well, is he nice?' Because if he wasn't kind, it just didn't seem like it would make sense."

Nor did Prince Harry know much about Meghan in return, contrary to speculation that he'd seen her on television previously and had voiced a desire to meet her. "I'd never even heard of her until this friend said 'Meghan Markle' – I was, like, 'Right, OK, give me a bit of background.' I'd never watched any of *Suits*," he admitted. "I was beautifully surprised when I walked into that room and saw her sitting there. I was, like, wow, I really have done well, I've got to up my game, sit down and make sure I have good chat."

He did. The date clearly went extremely well and, if anyone was star struck, it was Harry, not Meghan, who is a woman who can take pretty much anything in her stride. One Royal observer noted that she was "funny, feisty, confident and she wasn't swayed or knocked by the fact he was Prince Harry. She thought he was terribly cute." Harry was very impressed to hear about Meghan's charity work in Rwanda, and started bombarding her with texts until he could get her to agree to meet again. "And then it was, like, right, diaries," Harry continued. "We need to get the diaries out and find out how we're going to make this work, because I was off to Africa for a month, she was working. And we just said, 'Right, where's the gap?' And the gap happened to be in the perfect place."

Given the identity of the people involved, and the fact that the two lived on opposite sides of the Atlantic, they were clearly going to have to decide early on whether this had the potential to be serious

LEFT:

She's made her mark. In late 2016 a piece of street art appeared in north London. Artist Pegasus depicted Meghan wearing a dress based on the US flag, flanked by soldiers of the Queen's Guard.

and whether they wanted to give it a go. They did. "We met once and then twice, two dates back to back in London, last July," Harry said in their joint interview. "Then it was about three, maybe four weeks later that I managed to persuade her to come and join me in Botswana, and we camped out with each other under the stars for five days. Then we were really by ourselves, which was crucial to me to make sure we had a chance to get to know each other." This was a crucial test: Harry had a long-standing love of Africa (as did his brother, William, who proposed to Kate in Kenya) and, if the two of them could bond there, there was clearly a good prognosis

ABOVE:

Meghan attends the eighth day of the Wimbledon Championships in July 2016.

for the future. It was also a place where there was utter privacy, no concerns about diners in nearby restaurants taking pictures of them, just a stark and beautiful landscape where they could get to know one another well.

And both were in the market for something more serious. Both were in their thirties, with Meghan two years older than Harry, and there was none of the coyness there might have been if they had been much younger at the time. In some ways, it was fortunate for everyone concerned that the relationship was so obviously serious so quickly, simply because, given the effort the two of them were going to have to make, they both had to know there was an actual point in doing so. "The fact that I fell in love with Meghan so incredible quickly was confirmation to me that all the stars have aligned and everything was just perfect," Harry said in their joint interview. "This beautiful woman just tripped and fell into my life. We're a fantastic team, we know we are and, over time, we hope to have as much impact as possible."

From that early meeting and the time in Botswana, the couple managed to meet every two weeks, keeping it as low key as possible. "Just to take the time to be able to go on long country walks and just talk," said Meghan, who said that the courtship had not felt like a whirlwind. "I think we were able to really have so much time just to connect, and we never went longer than two weeks without seeing each other, even though we were obviously doing a long-distance relationship. So we made it work."

In the world of the smartphone, they had to stay as private as possible, too – there were "cozy nights in in front of the television, cooking dinner in our little cottage," said Prince Harry. "It's made us a hell of a lot closer in a short space of time. For us, it's an opportunity for really getting to know each other without people looking or trying to take photos on their phones."

William and Kate lived nearby, so it was easy to

BELOW:

The couple are seen swapping a quick embrace following polo at Cowarth Park in May 2017.

ABOVE:

The couple will start their married life in Nottingham Cottage, circled above, a bijoux residence in the middle of Kensington Palace, which is where the Duke and Duchess of Cambridge also lived after their wedding.

make off-the-radar introductions without the wider world noticing: "William was longing to meet her and so was Catherine, so, you know, being our neighbours, we managed to get that in quite a few times now," said Harry. "Catherine has been absolutely amazing, as has William as well, you know, fantastic support." Of course, his brother and sister-in-law were as aware as Harry on the difficulties of Royal dating, for the wider public would have been desperate for more information as soon as they knew something was going on.

In retrospect, there were signs that something really was going on. Meghan was seen in the Royal Box at Wimbledon that summer, although no one made the connection at the time. Indeed, no one was really sure who Meghan was: although *Suits* was shown in the UK – first on Dave and later via Netflix – she still was an unknown quantity for most of the British public, which suited Harry just fine. Both his previous serious girlfriends had been scared off by media attention and, although Meghan might have been able to cope with it in her own right, Harry did not want to expose her to it just yet.

There was also the minor matter of introducing her to his grandmother, the Queen. While this might not have been an important element in most relationships, in this particular one it was crucial, not least because Harry was going to have to ask his grandmother's permission to marry. Meghan proved herself to be just as unfazed about this as she was about everything else.

"It's incredible to be able to meet her through his lens: not just with his honour and respect for her as the monarch, but the love that he has for her as his grandmother," Meghan said. "All of those layers have been so important for me so that, when I met her, I had such a deep understanding and, of course, incredible respect for being able to have that time with her. She's an incredible woman."

And it didn't hurt that Meghan, like the Royals, was an animal lover, with a particular affection for dogs. "And the corgis took to you straight away," Harry added. "I've spent the last thirty-three years being barked at; this one walks in, absolutely nothing. Just wagging tails and I was just, like, 'argh'. The family together have been absolutely a solid support. My grandparents, as well, have been wonderful throughout this whole process, and they've known for quite some time. So how they haven't told anybody is, again, a miracle in itself. But now the whole family have come together and have been a huge amount of support."

That first date had clearly been a momentous one and the whole Royal romance did manage to stay under the radar for months, until Harry, who had spoken publicly of his pain at not being able to protect his own mother from the interests of the world outside, finally lashed out in an extraordinary and unprecedented statement, of which more anon. But for anyone in the know, the hints just grew bigger and bigger, and nor was the entire courtship just cozy evenings in at Nottingham Cottage (Nott Cott), Harry's Kensington Palace home. So what really went on between that first blind date and the announcement of the engagement? How did Prince Harry really conduct the courtship with the woman who would one day become his wife?

CHAPTER 4

SECRET COURTSHIP

"WE'VE JUST FOCUSED ON WHO WE ARE AS A COUPLE.
AND SO WHEN YOU TAKE ALL THOSE EXTRA LAYERS AWAY
AND ALL OF THAT NOISE, I THINK IT MAKES IT REALLY EASY
TO JUST ENJOY BEING TOGETHER."

MEGHAN MARKLE, NOVEMBER 2017

Harry and Meghan met in the spring of 2016; as they later confessed, much of their courtship went on away from public glare, at least to begin with. "We were very quietly dating for about six months before it became news, and I was working during that whole time, and the only thing that changed was people's perception," Meghan told *Vanity Fair*. "Nothing about me changed. I'm still the same person that I am, and I've never defined myself by my relationship."

At around that time, a series of images began to appear on Meghan's Instagram account that, in retrospect, are highly revealing. First, there was a picture of Meghan with a bunch of people and the caption, "Swooning over these. #London #peonies #spoiledrotten". There followed a love heart with "Kiss me" stamped on it, captioned, "Lovehearts in #London". This was followed by a couple of matches in a heart shape, a card bearing the motto "The foolish wait" (as if), more peonies and, finally, a game changer, of which more below.

But any couple happy and in love wants to share the news with the rest of the world, and so, gradually – perhaps even subconsciously on their part – hints began to emerge that something was afoot. In the UK, the *Sunday Express* announced that the pair were an item and that Harry was happier than he had been in years. Coincidentally, or not, perhaps, Meghan posted a picture on her Instagram account of two bananas snuggling up together with the words, "Sleep tight". And from that moment, global curiosity levels shot sky high – and there they stayed.

At first, no one knew quite what to make of it. Not only was this a first in every conceivable way possible, but was it serious? Or was it a fling? Some members of William and Harry's circle had been a little sniffy about Kate Middleton – how would they react to Meghan? Politely and warmly, if they had any sense, because there quickly came another indication that this was something serious – it was reported in *People* magazine that Meghan had already met Prince Charles. "Harry is pretty serious about her and she is pretty serious about him," said a source. "It's great. They have a lot in common and I'm sure they will get on very well."

That was enough to spark a feeding frenzy. Suddenly, everyone – but everyone – wanted to know more about Meghan and, when it

PREVIOUS PAGE:

During their visit to Nottingham, Harry and Meghan found time to attend Nottingham Academy. Bystanders were impressed by Meghan's natural style and the way she related to well-wishers.

OPPOSITE:

Prince Harry is pictured attending a StreetGames "Fit and Fed" holiday activity session in Central Park, East Ham, in July 2017. On the other side of the Atlantic, Meghan was spotted wearing a very similar bracelet.

emerged that she was a biracial divorced actress, interest soared to an all-time high. In yet another totally unprecedented move, Harry issued a strongly worded statement asking everyone to back off and give the couple a little space.

"Since he was young, Prince Harry has been very aware of the warmth that has been extended to him by members of the public," it read. "He feels lucky to have so many people supporting him and knows what a fortunate and privileged life he leads. He is also aware that there is significant curiosity about his private life. He has never been comfortable with this, but he has tried to develop a thick skin about the level of media interest that comes with it. He has rarely taken formal action on the very regular publication of fictional stories that are written about him and he has worked hard to develop a professional relationship with the media focused on his work and the issues he cares about.

"But the past week has seen a line crossed. His girlfriend, Meghan Markle, has been subject to a wave of abuse and harassment. Some of it has been hidden from the public – the nightly legal battles to keep defamatory stories out of papers; her mother having to struggle past photographers in order to get to her front door; the attempts of reporters and photographers to gain illegal entry to her home and the calls to police that followed; the substantial bribes offered by papers to her ex-boyfriend; the bombardment of nearly every friend, co-worker and loved one in her life. It is not right, that a few months into a relationship with him that Ms Markle should be subjected to such a storm. He knows commentators will say this is 'the price she has to pay' and that 'this is all part of the game'. He strongly disagrees. This is not a game – it is her life and his."

Amid speculation that William might have thought this unwise, another Royal statement was issued to the *Daily Telegraph*: "The Duke of Cambridge absolutely understands the situation concerning privacy and supports the need for Prince Harry to support those closest to him." It was clear: they were all singing from the same hymn sheet.

It worked – to an extent – but at the same time, it had the possibly unanticipated effect of actually confirming the relationship. Until then, no one had been sure how seriously to take the rumours – now it was not only clear that it was all true, but that the relationship was serious, as well. And that subconscious desire to proclaim their relationship to the world was also still clear – they were spotted wearing matching bracelets on either side of the Atlantic.

Interest in Meghan remained as strong as ever, although the edge was taken off the aggressiveness with which some people were attempting to find out more about her, and, in some ways, the publication of that statement seemed to take the pressure off the two of them. Neither seemed quite so worried about keeping it a secret: in December, Harry went on an official trip to Barbados, but rather than coming straight back to London as had originally been planned, he made an unofficial stopover in Toronto. Around that time, Meghan was spotted wearing a necklace with the initials "M" and "H".

The couple were sticking to their resolve of not being apart for more than two weeks: in mid-December, the two of them were seen in London's West End, wearing beanie hats to protect against the cold, walking hand in hand through the throng. They took in a performance of *The Curious Incident of the Dog in the Night-Time* and, elsewhere, were seen buying a Christmas tree. Meghan may not have graduated to Christmas-at-Sandringham status yet, but they were clearly happy in their domestic life together, although that year they were to spend Christmas apart.

As 2017 began, Meghan was becoming quite a regular, albeit unofficial, visitor to the UK's capital. Early in the year, the couple were spotted again, having dinner at London's trendy Soho House, and then in March, another indication that the relationship was really serious came through. One of Harry's best friends, Tom "Skippy" Inskip (who had been present at the Las Vegas weekend) was getting married to software developer Lara Hughes-Young in Montego Bay, Jamaica (about 60 miles away from where Meghan first got married), and Harry was one of the ushers.

He took Meghan to the wedding with him – another clear indication that she was a permanent fixture in his life – and the duo stayed at the chic Round Hill Resort, which, at £5,000 a night, showed Harry certainly knew how to treat the woman in his life. Indeed, JFK and Jackie Kennedy had gone there for their honeymoon. Harry's aunt, Sarah, Duchess of York, and her daughter, Eugenie, were also in attendance, allowing Meghan to get used to moving in Windsor circles while still in an unofficial and relaxed ambience. The whole occasion was, in fact, an

enormous success, even when Harry sent a waitress and a tray of drinks flying when he tried to do Michael Jackson's moonwalk. That prompted much hilarity, but it was noticeable to everyone how close the couple were by now. Totally at ease in each other's company, it was now becoming inconceivable that there wouldn't be an engagement announcement soon.

A princess (or duchess) cannot be seen to promote anything, however, and so it was in April that year that Meghan quietly and without fanfare closed down her blog, The Tig. There was intense speculation that she had been advised to do this by the Palace, although that was not confirmed. Shortly afterwards, Meghan was seen cheering Harry on at the polo, and then it was another high-profile wedding – that of Pippa Middleton, Harry's sister-in-law, to financier James Matthews in the Berkshire village of Bucklebury, where the Middleton's lived. Everyone had to play it carefully here. There were already concerns that Pippa would be eclipsed by the appearance of her sister Kate, and Meghan's presence raised the risk even more. In the event, Meghan kept a very low profile; she didn't attend the actual ceremony and, instead, turned up at the evening reception, after Harry had driven off to collect her.

"[Harry] knew this was all about Pippa's big day and he and Meghan jointly decided they didn't want to upstage her," a source told the *Sun*. "Harry went all the way back to London to get Meghan and bring her to the party. He was determined not to upstage Pippa but also really wanted them to enjoy the wedding together. He didn't want Meghan having to arrive alone, without him alongside her, at the reception." And given that this was their second wedding together in a matter of months, it was once again clear that the two were both in sync and serious about one another. Meghan was to reveal as much very soon.

But before she did so, Harry whisked her off on holiday to Africa to celebrate her 36th birthday. It was back to Botswana (this time at £650 a night) to the Meno a Kwena camp, where they stayed in a luxurious tent overlooking the Boleti River. Botswana, which Harry has described as his "second home", is where they had first bonded just over a year previously; now they were staying in the height of luxury. Their tent – one of just nine at the resort – was furnished with a king-sized bed, open-air shower and traditional wooden carved furniture; it overlooked a

OPPOSITE:

Brothers in arms. Princes William and Harry attend the wedding of the Duchess of Cambridge's sister Pippa Middleton to James Matthews at St Mark's Church, Englefield Green in May 2017. Meghan attended the evening reception.

stretch of the river where elephants and zebras came out to drink.

Back home again, an interview with Meghan was published in *Vanity Fair* that gave the clearest indication to date that the couple were to wed. It made global headlines because of a small quote from Meghan, which was actually in the context of a much longer interview that was really about her life, not her relationship with Harry. But perhaps no one should have been surprised by the intense interest she aroused.

"We're a couple," she said. "We're in love. I'm sure there will be a time when we will have to come forward and present ourselves and have stories to tell, but I hope what people will understand is that this is our time. This is for us. It's part of what makes it so special, that it's just ours. But we're happy. Personally, I love a great love story."

Of course, Meghan would never have spoken so openly were she not at liberty to do so and, given her words, it was clear that a major announcement was in the air. But there were still a few more months to go before Harry and Meghan were to make it official, still a little while even before they were to make their first official appearance together, although it was pretty clear to everyone that this was a very modern Royal romance, more so even than that of William and Catherine. It was to be a case of

ABOVE:

Meghan mingles with the crowd at the Audi Polo Challenge at Coworth, Berkshire, in May 2017.

OPPOSITE:

In January 2017, it was announced that Harry would be Patron of Rhino Conservation Botswana (RCB). This picture was taken the previous September, when he joined an RCB operation to fit tracking devices to rhinos.

Californian sunshine beaming into the heart of the Windsors. The nation was on tenterhooks. With an unstable political situation both within the UK and also out in the wider world, the nation was in need of a good Royal love story. And in the story of Harry and Meghan, so unusual and yet so in keeping with the new modern Britain, that is exactly what they were going to get.

CHAPTER 5

TWENTY-FIRST CENTURY ROMANCE

"THE FACT THAT I FELL IN LOVE WITH MEGHAN SO INCREDIBLY QUICKLY IS CONFIRMATION TO ME THAT ALL THE STARS ARE ALIGNED."

PRINCE HARRY, NOVEMBER 2017

E ver since Harry's acknowledgement of their relationship via his plea to the press to leave Meghan alone, interest in the duo had mounted but, to date, they had only been seen in an unofficial context together, never at a formal engagement. That was about to change, and it was appropriate that it did so at the Invictus Games, the project that was closest to Harry's heart and his greatest contribution to public life to date. And so it was, in September 2017, in Toronto, Meghan's home since she had started filming *Suits*, that they were finally seen in public.

They took it in stages. Both were there during the opening ceremony of the Games, but they were seated apart: Harry was with American First Lady Melania Trump and the Canadian Prime Minister Justin Trudeau (and looking as if he'd rather be with his girlfriend), while Meghan was seated in the next section along, next to Markus Anderson, a mutual friend of the couple. (After the official opening, however, Harry went to join them). Then, over the course of the week, things changed.

A couple of days on from the opening ceremony, they turned up hand in hand to a wheelchair tennis match and, by the closing

ceremony, they were "snuggling, kissing, with their arms around each other", according to *US Weekly*. The duo appeared in the Air Canada Centre with Meghan's mother, Doria Ragland, and their friends, Jessica Mulroney, daughter-in-law of a former Canadian prime minister, Brian Mulroney, and Markus Anderson. Harry was seen kissing Meghan in public for the first time; there was no attempt at all at concealing their feelings for one another. Back in the UK, a poll by *Hello!* magazine had a massive two-thirds of those taking part saying the couple should wed.

Harry was content to comment just on the games, not his relationship: "We have a social responsibility to continue this for as long as it's needed. The world needs Invictus, these guys need Invictus, I need Invictus, we all need our fix," he said, but friends were commenting that he had never looked happier, more settled and confident.

Now that the romance was well and truly out in the open, so, too, was comment surrounding its implications. Many were pointing out that this truly would be a very modern Royal Family. Harry and his brother, William, had already broken the taboos surrounding the discussion about mental health by talking about how they both had suffered in the wake of the death of their mother (Meghan's influence could be detected in the background there, too), and now Harry was going one step further by choosing a bride who reflected modern Britain.

Admittedly, she was American, but the fact that she did not come from a traditional aristocratic/European-princess background meant that she was far more in keeping with the multi-racial society that Britain had become. When Meghan first appeared on the scene, eyebrows were raised when some commentators used

OPPOSITE:

At the opening ceremony of the Invictus Games Toronto in September 2017, Harry sat with dignitaries including American First Lady Melania Trump, Sophie Grégoire Trudeau and Canadian Prime Minister Justin Trudeau.

ABOVE RIGHT:

Prince Harry shakes hands with Justin Trudeau at the Royal York Hotel in Toronto.

the word "exotic" to describe her, but now other commentators with different ethnic backgrounds were coming forward to say that, at last, there would be a member of the Royal Family they could relate to. Britain was no longer all white and now neither were the Royals. In other quarters, it was noticeable that it simply wasn't an issue at all and, although the Queen did not make her views on this particular topic public, she was known to have a huge affection for the Commonwealth, the hugely diverse grouping of 52 nations that were mainly former territories of the British Empire and included many different racial groupings. It can, at least, be assumed that she would have been delighted to see her family changing in a way that reflected the country over which she reigned.

Elsewhere, it plainly wasn't a point of concern. It helped that Meghan, herself, had so often spoken out about her racial heritage: she had not ignored or ducked the issue and had spoken about how her mother had been subjected to some very unpleasant language in the past, but the very fact that she had addressed the topic meant there was nothing more to say. And given the Windsors' own recent history in divorce, neither could that be raised as an issue.

Of course, there was one other set of people taking an active interest in Meghan's life – her own family. Meghan's family, on her father's side, had been a source of fascination from the moment she arrived on the scene: her father, Thomas, half-brother, Thomas, Jr, and half-sister, Samantha, had all played a minor role in the proceedings and now their names came up again. Thomas, Jr had caused waves the previous January when he was arrested after holding a gun to his girlfriend's head and had then compounded matters by publicly stating that Meghan was a "hot commodity" and that Harry "better get on with it". Samantha, it then emerged, was writing a book called *The Diary of Princess Pushy's Sister*: initially, this was billed as a tell-all, although Samantha had backtracked somewhat and declared that the title was ironic and that the book would be very affectionate.

Now Thomas, Jr's son, somewhat confusingly also called Thomas, decided to speak out, revealing that there was a feud between Thomas, Meghan's father, and Thomas, Jr and that the two hadn't spoken for years. "My dad and aunt are crazy. I feel terrible for Meghan," he said in an interview with the *Sunday Mirror*.

OPPOSITE: *During his time in office, Barack Obama got to know Prince Harry. They appear to enjoy each other's company as they watch the wheelchair basketball at the Invictus Games in 2017.*

"Me and my brother, Tyler, have nothing to do with our dad. His behaviour since Meghan began dating Prince Harry has been completely appalling. I want people to know I have nothing to do with it and just apologize to her. It's just a shame her own family are making up stories about her... She is a lovely, warm and caring person and she seems super happy with Prince Harry. I believe it was fate they fell for each other and I wish them both the best.

The rest of the family did continue to make their presence felt, however. Samantha Markle turned up on *Good Morning Britain* to deny that her book was going to be a tell-all: "There's so much the public doesn't know," she said. "I think the British people and the world will be surprised. It's a beautiful, warm, witty story. She is lively, very animated and charming. I go through and sort of recant some of the beautiful nuances of our lives." As for

Meghan being a member of the Royal Family, "She's lovely. She's very strong, she's very worldly, very educated, very graceful. She will absolutely be a compliment to her role." For this, it must be said, she got something of a pasting on social media, with people pointing out she hadn't actually seen her half-sister in years; nor could she say with any certainty that she would be likely to get a wedding invitation. It looked pretty unlikely, in truth.

But the reaction to all this proved that the public was firmly in favour of Meghan: again and again, it came up that she was a biracial divorced actress who had frequently been seen in steamy clinches with her co-star – and no one cared. There was no opposition from within the Royal Family, from senior politicians, from taste makers and, above all, from the public. This was partly down to the fact that Harry was looking so happy these days – more than he had done in years. And to a country that had never forgotten seeing a little 12-year-old boy bereaved of his mother and walking steadily behind her coffin on the day of the funeral, the wish to see Harry happy was palpable. If Meghan was the person who could make him so, that alone would have given her the backing of the people. Her own warm, outgoing personality was already showing through as well, which endeared her to the country all the more.

There had already been a great deal of interest in Meghan's origins, especially on her mother's side, but thanks to a Channel 4 documentary, *When Harry Met Meghan: A Royal Romance*, more details emerged. It turned out that Meghan could have British roots after all: a historian, Andy Ulicny, had managed to trace her great-great-grandmother, Martha Sykes, back to England. Martha left the UK for the States with her parents when she was just one year old: "Most likely, the Sykes family came from Yorkshire, a coal-mining region, and the name Sykes was popular up that way," he said. The family ended up in the mining region of Pennsylvania, although Martha's father, Thomas, died just eight years later, leaving her mother, Mary, with five children to cope with. Martha was later to marry into the Markle family.

This news caused some amusement: Meghan actually came from doughty Yorkshire stock? She was a Yorkshire lass at heart? "Eeh bah gum," said the commentators, somewhat inevitably, but rather more to the point, the documentary also revealed

OPPOSITE:

Meghan and her mother, Doria Ragland, attend the Closing Ceremony of the Invictus Games Toronto in September 2017.

NEXT PAGE:

All his life, Harry has been exposed to grand state ceremonial occasions, and is pictured here in the Trooping the Colour ceremony in 1992. With him in the carriage are his mother, Princess Diana ,and his great-grandmother, Queen Elizabeth The Queen Mother.

ABOVE:

Princess Diana places her hands protectively on her younger son's shoulders during the 50th Anniversary of the Battle of Britain Parade on the balcony at Buckingham Palace in September 1990. Sarah, Duchess of York is beside them.

that, of the five bereaved children, the girls were sent into domestic service, while the boys became coal miners, making the difference in Meghan and Harry's forebears all the more acute. "What has happened is the merging of two families," said Ulicny. "Harry's family has wealth and power and Meghan's had to fight."

That was true enough but the documentary was salutary in that it, too, raised no eyebrows: no one implied that Meghan was not good enough for her prince. But then again – they may even have been related. The investigation into all things Meghan now turned up the fact that they possibly had a distant ancestor via the Queen Mother, Harry's great-grandmother. He was traced back to 1480 and called Ralph Bowes, a High Sheriff of County Durham; his granddaughter, Bridget Bowes, married John Hussey of Dorking, Surrey, and his grandson, Christopher Hussey, moved to America in 1632. Meghan stemmed from that line. Elsewhere, the Bowes married into the Lyon family, which eventually produced Elizabeth Bowes-Lyon, the future Queen Mum.

No one really cared. Nor were they overly worried when actress Abby Wathen, who described herself as a "friend" and

had co-starred with Meghan in the film *Random Encounters*, described the period in which the two actresses got divorced at the same time, as part of ITV documentary *Harry and Meghan: Truly, Madly, Deeply*. "Meghan, she's not one of these people that dwells," she said. "I was destroyed and Meghan was really, 'It was great to feel empowered.' I feel she took her power back. It wasn't the marriage she needed to be in and she moved on."

If so, that could only bode well for the future because, behind the scenes, a great deal was going on to prepare Meghan for the life that lay ahead. As with the other more recent Royal brides, a lot was being done to help their entry into "The Firm", as Prince Philip always called it; after the crises with Princess Diana and Sarah Ferguson, chances were not being taken any more. No one cared about Meghan's race or divorced status, but they cared a great deal about whether she would be able to deal with being a member of the House of Windsor. And that was going to mean changing her life completely – and giving up the day job.

CHAPTER 6

COMING TO ENGLAND

"I THINK I CAN VERY SAFELY SAY, AS NAIVE AS IT SOUNDS NOW,

HAVING GONE THROUGH THIS LEARNING CURVE IN THE PAST

YEAR AND A HALF, I DID NOT HAVE ANY UNDERSTANDING OF

JUST WHAT IT WOULD BE LIKE."

MEGHAN MARKLE, NOVEMBER 2016

The news, when it came, was significant. Meghan Markle was to stand down from the television series *Suits*, the show that had made her name. She had spent seven seasons playing Rachel Zane, the paralegal-turned-attorney, but the end had come – and not just for that, but for her acting career as a whole. It was a momentous decision and a sign of how much her life was to change; it was also reminiscent of Grace Kelly, who also gave up her acting career to marry a prince. Meghan may have been a breath of fresh air in almost every conceivable way in the Royal Family, but the fact is that being a Windsor and being an actress could not mix. That is, it couldn't mix as far up the food chain as Harry, though there was a Windsor actress, Sophie Winkleman, who was married to Lord Frederick Windsor. However, he was the son of Prince and Princess Michael of Kent, and, therefore, not so close to the throne.

The formal announcement that Meghan was quitting her job came after the engagement itself, of which far more anon. USA

Network and Universal Cable Productions said in a statement, "From all of us at USA Network and Universal Cable Productions, we want to send our most heartfelt congratulations to Meghan Markle and Prince Harry on their engagement. Meghan has been a member of our family for seven years and it has been a joy to work with her. We want to thank her for her undeniable passion and dedication to *Suits*, and we wish her the very best."

In actual fact, the development was far more momentous than that statement initially suggested – Meghan had spent her entire adult life as an actress, carving out a career. That was something else that made her such a modern bride: she had a vocation. And Meghan was similarly upbeat when talking about it in the couple's joint television interview: "I don't see it as giving anything up. I just see it as a change," she said. "It's a new chapter, right? And also, keep in mind, I've been working on my show for seven years. We were very, very fortunate to have that sort of longevity on a

ABOVE:

Meghan took part in the DirectTV 8th Annual Celebrity Beach Bowl in New York in 2014.

series… I've ticked this box, and I feel very proud of the work I've done there, and now it's time to work with you [Harry] as a team."

But the signs that she was going to leave had been there for months and it had put the makers of the show in quite a tricky position – what to do with her character as it became increasingly obvious that she was going to have to step down. They couldn't be put in the position of having been in the know before anyone else; nor could they be too intrusive, given the identity of the people involved. A high-wire act was required. *Suits* creator Aaron Korsh told the BBC's *Today* programme that he only found out that

ABOVE: *In December 2014, Meghan visited Vicenza, Italy, where US soldiers of the 173rd Airborne Brigade showed her how to wear a parachute.*

Meghan was leaving the show after her engagement was announced, but the fact is that preparations for her departure had been going on for the best part of a year. In a show like that – a ratings winner, with a lot of money and careers hanging on the line – a major character like Rachel cannot just vanish without a back-up plan being in place. That takes time and Korsh clearly knew that something was on the cards. They had been gently paving the way for Rachel/Meghan's departure for some time.

"When the announcement came out was when I officially knew the script planning [for her exit] was correct, but we just got the sense... that they were in love and it was going to work out for them," Korsh said.

"I had a decision to make because I didn't want to intrude and ask her, 'What's going on?' So we decided to take a gamble that these two people were in love and that it was going to work out. As the season progressed, I thought: I would rather have good things happen in Meghan's life, which would likely mean her leaving the show, so let's plan on that."

None of this was, of course, a shock. Before the engagement had been announced, *Insider* ran a speculative piece that made it clear what was going on: "If Meghan decides not to come back for season eight, the show will still keep going if everyone else signs on," an unnamed source said. Adding, to *E! News*, "She isn't the main cast member on the show, and quite frankly, everyone already thinks she's not coming back. Even before Harry, she was starting to think about transitioning out of acting. She wants to focus on other worldly endeavors she is passionate about, like her philanthropy." That was, of course, a part of her old life that Meghan would not have to give up, although, in the future, it would be more Windsor-related as she and Harry started work as

ABOVE:

A radiant Meghan at the Elton John AIDS Foundation's 13th Annual An Enduring Vision benefit at Cipriani's Wall Street, in New York in 2014.

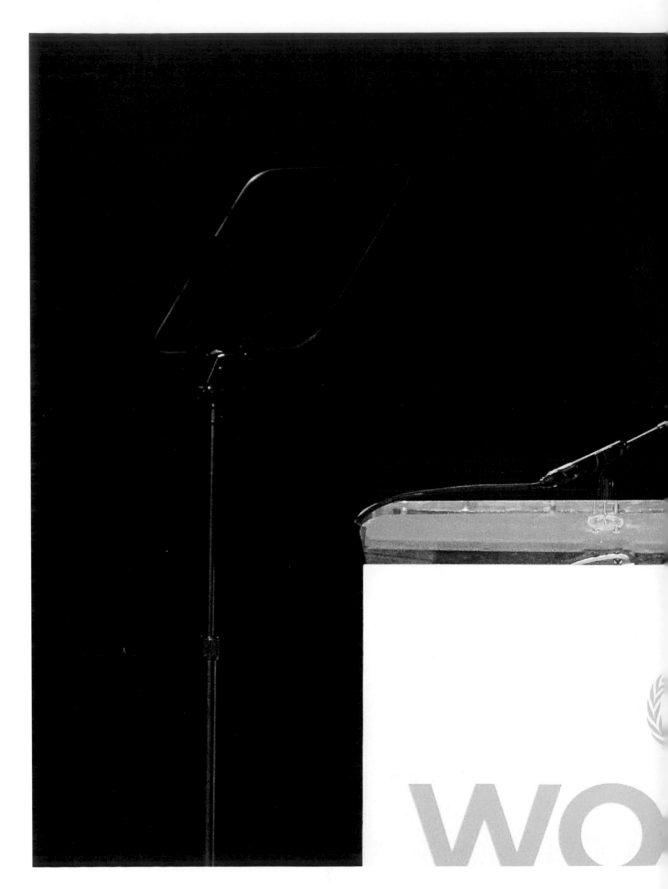

PREVIOUS PAGE:

*Meghan has long
been a committed
campaigner. She is
pictured here at a UN
Women Event in New
York, a cause she
strongly supported,
but has now given
up to concentrate
on charity work
with Harry.*

a team. It was later confirmed, though, that she would be giving up her charity work for the United Nations.

Aaron Korsh had also previously dropped some large hints as to what was happening. He might not have been officially told of Meghan's plans until the big announcement, but he certainly realized that something was in the offing. Asked in advance of the announcement by tvline.com about Meghan's future – and, indeed, that of her co-star Patrick J. Adams, who played Mike Ross, her love interest on the show – he said, "They all have things going on in their lives, we'll see what happens. This is true on all long-running shows, and people have things happening in their lives."

And, as if that were not enough, Meghan's stand-in, Nicky Bursic, also took to Instagram, again pre-announcement, revealing that something was quite definitely afoot. "It's been an absolute pleasure and honour being your 'STAND-IN' for the last 2 seasons," she posted. "Though I've been on @suits_usa for 6 years, the latter 2 has been my most memorable. Wishing you all the happiness in the world Bella."

To adorn this she added a love heart emoji and one of a champagne glass toast alongside the hashtags #youdeserveitall #loveher.

Of course, this new phase in Meghan's life was affecting her co-stars as well – above all, Patrick. When the show started, he had been one of the two central characters but, by this time, he and Meghan were so heavily associated with one another on screen that, in some ways, he had no choice but to leave. Another love interest could have been found, but it would have unbalanced the show. Fortunately, however, he appeared to want this, too: "Patrick was always leaving the show," a source told *US Weekly*. "He made his mind up a while ago. Patrick wants to pursue other things and he's realized his time at *Suits* has come to an end." The face of the show was clearly going to change completely because of Meghan's new direction. That might well have happened anyway, as it does on many long-running series, but Meghan's new life had certainly hastened the change.

OPPOSITE:

With Suits *co-star Patrick J. Adams. In the wake of the engagement it was announced they would both be leaving the show.*

In actual fact, when Meghan and Patrick left, it could not have been a happier way of leaving the show or a more direct reference to what was happening in Meghan's personal life: their on-screen characters, Rachel and Mike, got married. And this development became public in September 2017, two months before the engagement announcement. Aaron Korsh was asked if the characters would wed: "I'm going to go ahead and say, 'Yes. How's that?'" he responded. The wedding was shot at Toronto's King Edward Hotel, with Meghan wearing the Anne Barge gown she was supposed to have married Mike in several seasons earlier in the show. Of course, it attracted a huge amount of attention and comment – how could it not?

In the run-up to the announcement, there were other indications that life was changing rapidly for Meghan, too. Removal vans were spotted outside her rented home in Toronto – is it possible that she was relocating to London? The answer, of course, was yes. "Meghan has officially moved out of her Toronto apartment," a source told *US Weekly*. "Meghan's furniture from her Toronto home will be going into storage and her personal belongings are being sent to the UK. There are no plans for them to live separately. Meghan will move right in [to Harry's home.]" Indeed, she was

spotted throughout November in London, shopping and carrying her yoga mat, clearly at home in the city that would, from then on, be her base. The fact that she did this before the official announcement was proof of how carefully everything was being mapped out in advance and how much was being done to make her feel at home. Nothing was being left to chance.

Then there was the matter of the dogs. It was always a positive sign when a new member of the Royal Family showed an affinity for hounds, and Meghan did: she had rescued Bogart, a Labrador-shepherd cross, from a Los Angeles dog shelter, she said to *Best Health* magazine, and she wanted to provide him with a little buddy, and thus adopted Guy, a beagle, who had been lost in the woods of Kentucky. Moving them to the UK was not a totally straightforward process: they would need to be microchipped, given vaccinations and blood tests, and then spend some time in quarantine once in the UK. At first, it was thought that Meghan was going to move both dogs over, but it emerged that Bogart was considered too old to travel and that Meghan was going to have to leave him behind. It was a wrench; Meghan had previously described her dogs as "my boys" and "my loves", and giving up one of them was clearly going to be hard.

Kensington Palace refused to comment on the details, but Meghan later confirmed that he had been rehoused with a friend. "I have two dogs that I've had for quite a long time, both my rescue pups," she told Mishal Husain in the couple's joint interview. "And one is now staying with very close friends and my other little guy is, yes, he's in the UK. He's been here for a while. I think he's doing just fine."

Not entirely, however. Shortly afterwards, it was reported that Meghan had been left "distraught" when Guy broke two of his legs in an accident; he was tended to by Professor Noel Fitzpatrick, a "world-class orthopaedic-neuro veterinary surgeon" who had appeared on television and was famous for his bionic-surgery techniques. Guy was said to be at a facility in Surrey. Harry accompanied his fiancée there to make sure everything would be all right. The news made headlines – as everything did about Meghan these days – with people taking to Twitter to wish Guy a speedy recovery and news coming out that the dog was on the way to feeling better. So, settled down together, just what was the couple's London life like now?

OPPOSITE: *During their visit to Cardiff, Harry and Meghan dropped into Star Hub, where they watched a game of Jenga. Harry seemed particularly engrossed.*

CHAPTER 7

LIVING AT NOTT COTT

"I KNOW THAT AT THE END OF THE DAY, SHE CHOOSES ME.
I CHOOSE HER. WHATEVER WE HAVE TO TACKLE WILL BE
US TOGETHER AS A TEAM."

PRINCE HARRY, NOVEMBER 2017

Nottingham Cottage is modest by Royal standards. Situated in the grounds of Kensington Palace, where William and Harry grew up, and the home of their mother Diana both before and after her divorce, Nottingham Cottage is a 1,300 square-foot, 2-bedroom establishment, which had been Harry's home since 2013, when William and Kate had moved out of the cottage and set up in the 20-room Apartment 1A in the next courtyard, within the palace itself. William was said to have had to duck in order to avoid knocking his head on the ceiling, and nor did it have every luxury, such as air conditioning – the couple had had to use fans.

And Meghan was certainly stepping into history. Originally a two-story Jacobean mansion built in 1605 and designed by Sir George Coppin, Kensington Palace, situated at the east end of Kensington High Street (and thus in one of the plushest residential areas in the world), had been a Royal residence since 1689 (nearly a century before the United States declared independence). William III bought Nottingham House, as it then was, for £20,000 and moved in with his wife, Mary II. Sir Christopher Wren was called in to remodel the building and, in the eighteenth century, George I created new Royal premises, including Apartments 8 and 9, which is where Diana lived.

Many kings and queens had it as their main palace after that, including Queen Anne, Queen Victoria and George II, although he was the last monarch to use it as his main base. However, Kensington Palace is much less stuffy than Buckingham Palace, partly because it is not used for state occasions in the way Buckingham Palace is. It has played home to the likes of Princess Margaret, who entertained there, and, as mentioned, of course, Diana herself. It has a rooftop garden and long passageways, making it ideal for children, and there were other Royals in situ, including the Kents and the Gloucesters. In 2012, the whole place underwent a £12-million refurbishment: "We have set out to awake the sleeping beauty of Kensington Palace," said Charles Mackay, chair of the Historic Royal Palaces board.

Much of the interior was left untouched for historic reasons, but some areas now have a more minimalist feel than once they did, with art installations such as light sculptures now included in the building. The grounds include the beautiful Sunken Garden – modelled on the style of an eighteenth-century garden, although it

was not completed until 1908 – which is composed of symmetrical plantings of a variety of flowers, including tulips, based around a large pond. It is a very far cry from where Meghan grew up in Los Angeles, or, indeed, her home in Toronto, which was perfectly pleasant, but did not carry with it centuries of Royal history.

"Nott Cott" is a cosy little place – the smallest residence on the estate – but the reception rooms were designed by Sir Christopher Wren, and the property also boasted a small garden, in which Harry had set up a hammock when he first moved in. Previous occupants had included Diana's sister, Lady Jane Fellowes, and her husband, Sir Robert Fellowes, who had been the Queen's private secretary, as well as Brigadier Sir Miles Hunt-Davis, Prince Philip's private secretary, who had lived there with his wife, Gay. Marion Crawford, the Queen's governess, had written a memoire about her charges (and had been expelled from Royal ranks for doing so); she

PREVIOUS PAGE:

Meghan and Harry in
the Sunken Garden
of Kensington
Palace following the
announcement of
their engagement

ABOVE:

When they were
young: the two small
princes play the piano
under the watchful
gaze of their mother,
Princess Diana.

described it by saying it "looks as if it had got to London quite by mistake from some distant country place". In other words, it was charming. It was to be the place where the new Royal couple would start their married life, although, if and when their family started to grow, they would be expected to move to larger premises within the palace itself, such as Wren House or Apartment 1.

Apartment 1 is currently home to Prince Richard, the Duke of Gloucester, who is 24th in line to the throne and lives there with his wife, Birgitte; they offered to move out when William and Kate were deciding where to live, and might do so again. Wren House, overlooking a beautiful walled garden, is home to the Duke and Duchess of Kent, while Prince Michael of Kent and his wife, Marie Christine, were settled in Apartment 10, a grand, five-bedroom, five-reception-room establishment.

By the time Meghan joined her prince in November 2017, she already knew Nott Cott well. It had been her base whenever she came to London and, indeed, she had spent some time there the previous December in the run-up to Christmas, when the two were seen buying a Christmas tree to adorn their little nest. They were able to lead a cozy, intimate life away from the public gaze, cooking together in the kitchen (both were keen cooks and Meghan was not, as had been widely described, strictly vegan) and sheltering from the media; Kensington Palace was quite big enough to protect them from prying eyes. It was also widely expected that, like all senior members of the Royal Family, Harry would be given a country home, possibly as a wedding present, by the Queen.

The couple's social circle was an interesting one. Right at the heart of London, both geographically and socially, Harry and Meghan had a wide mix of acquaintances.

They were not just at the heart of Royal and aristocratic circles, but an international crowd as well, starting with their matchmaker, Misha Nonoo.

The circle also included Meghan's close friend Markus Anderson (who had originally been thought to be the one who introduced the couple). Originally from Ontario, Markus moved to London at the age of 19, where he worked for the private club (which now has global outposts) Soho House. He moved back to Canada to open a branch of the club in Toronto, where he became a consultant for Soho House Group. On the opening night of the Toronto club, one of the guests was Cory Vitiello, the well-known chef who had been Meghan's boyfriend before she met Harry. The Canadian branch was, as someone put it, "the pre-eminent meeting place for upwardly mobile hobnobbers", with Anderson having "a bloodhound's nose for tastemakers".

Meghan's Canadian clique – who could be expected not just to attend the wedding, but to visit the couple once they had established themselves – also included Sophie Trudeau, a former television reporter who was now married to Canadian Prime Minister Justin Trudeau and, as such, was Canada's First Lady. Like Meghan, she

BELOW:

Meghan and her friend Markus Anderson attend a fashion event in October 2014 in Toronto, Canada.

was a yoga aficionado and social activist and, again like Meghan, she had also been thrust into the international limelight through her marriage, and was able to offer some advice on how to handle it. There was an enormous amount of publicity centred on her charismatic husband, in addition to which the couple had three young children, who had to be protected from the spotlight. Sophie had had to learn how to lead both public and private lives.

Another confidante was the seven-times Wimbledon winner Serena Williams, whom Meghan met in 2014 and with whom she formed an immediate bond. "She quickly became a confidante I would text when I was travelling, the friend I would rally around for her tennis matches, and the down-to-earth chick I was able to grab lunch with a couple of weeks ago in Toronto," Meghan once said. "We are both the same age, have a penchant for hot sauces and adore fashion, but what connects us more than those things is perhaps our belief in exceeding expectations – our endless ambition." Serena was yet another person who had had to learn to deal with the limelight, and Meghan's interest in tennis chimed in with her Middleton in-laws – she and Pippa Middleton, Kate's sister, had both seen Serena play at Wimbledon in 2016. "We hit it off immediately, taking pictures, laughing and chatting not about tennis or acting

ABOVE:

One of Meghan's close friends is the tennis pro Serena Williams. They are pictured here with Hannah Davis at the DirecTV Celebrity Beach Bowl in New York in February 2014.

OPPOSITE:

Meghan and Jessica Mulroney go for similar shades of blue at an Instagram Dinner in May 2016 in Toronto.

but about good old-fashioned girly stuff. So began our friendship," Meghan wrote of Serena in her blog.

Then there was Priyanka Chopra, an ex-Miss World and Bollywood star who, as well as being the first Indian actress to play the lead in a big-name US TV drama (*Quantico*), was a UNICEF ambassador who had recently been highlighting the plight of Syrian refugees. Jessica Mulroney, daughter-in-law of the former Canadian prime minister Brian Mulroney, has already been mentioned, but she was, indeed, another of the gang, as was the New York socialite Olivia Palermo, who had taken part in Meghan's so-called "Girl Squad" of people who posted memories of their mothers on her blog.

The identities of many of these friends was easy to establish: Meghan had been open about sharing details of her life on The Tig before closing it down, as, indeed, were her friends in using other social media. Jessica – who was known as Meghan's Girl Friday as well as "Toronto's answer to Gwyneth Paltrow" – had posted numerous pictures of the Royal bride-to-be on her Instagram account, and a few of them had also contributed to Meghan's *Vanity Fair* profile. Priyanka had been quoted as saying, "It would have been nice to write about her, not just her boyfriend. I mean, she's an actor, she's an activist, she's a philanthropist. It's just a little sexist... There needs to be a certain sense of equality where a woman is not just a plus-one, you know. It's nice to be your own identity, too."

So it wasn't exactly the usual crowd of aristos that surrounded the Royal Family and, when these various identities came to light, there was some feverish speculation about which of them might morph into a Royal bridesmaid. It was certainly an eclectic number to choose from.

Harry, of course, had his own inner circle, who were also expected to feature in the crowd at Nott Cott, foremost among them being Harry's fellow old Etonian, Tom Inskip and his wife, Lara Hughes-

ABOVE LEFT:

Harry and Tom Inskip attend the wedding of James Meade and Lady Laura Marsham in September 2013.

OPPOSITE:

Princes William and Harry and their friend Guy Pelly at the start of the Enduro 2008 Motorcycle Rally in South Africa.

Young, to whose wedding Harry had already taken Meghan.

Harry's circle also included Arthur Landon, one of the richest young men in Britain, who had inherited £500 million from his father, Brigadier Tim Landon, the "White Sultan" said to have made a fortune after orchestrating a coup in Oman. His girlfriend, the American Alessandra Balazs, is the daughter of the international hotelier Andre Balazs. Another old Etonian chum was Jake Warren, son of the Queen's racing manager and a godson of Princess Diana.

Then, of course, there was Guy Pelly, a friend of both William and Harry; a bar owner and one of the group's most outgoing members, married to another American, Lizzy Wilson, heiress to the Holiday Inn empire. Meghan would, at least, have some fellow Americans within the group. Stockbroker Adam Bidwell, who had once dated the singer Katherine Jenkins, was also a chum. And finally, of course, there were Harry's two significant ex-girlfriends, Chelsy Davy and Cressida Bonas, both of whom he had remained on good terms with and still bumped into occasionally at society events.

All in all, it was quite a backdrop to live in, to be at the heart of such an eclectic crowd. As William's younger brother, Harry had always been the more free-spirited of the two, and that showed through in the set-up, with the Harry and Meghan circle seemingly a little more informal than the ceremony that was always bound to surround William, the future king. It was even conceivable that, in the early days, at least, the couple would do their entertaining on an informal basis in Nott Cott – after all, both were very good cooks. Meghan had done her fair share of entertaining in her early years, as well as during her time in Toronto – it was just the circumstances that were marking a change.

And Meghan was certainly learning the ropes as quickly as she could because, for all the grandeur of the couple's immediate surroundings, they were nothing compared to what Meghan would experience next. For Meghan to marry into the Royal Family, there were two people whose opinions were crucial: the Queen and Prince Charles, both of whom carried the centuries of Royal tradition on their shoulders and both of whom had been watching anxiously for years as Harry sought to find the woman who would be his life partner.

So just how did Meghan get on with the head of one of the world's longest and most important reigning monarchies? And what did the Queen think of her?

OPPOSITE:

Harry is in morning dress as he joins his grandmother the Queen and Jake Warren for day three of Royal Ascot in June 2014.

CHAPTER 8

MEETING
HER MAJESTY

"AND THE CORGIS TOOK TO YOU STRAIGHT AWAY. IN THE LAST

33 YEARS, I'VE BEEN BARKED AT. THIS ONE WALKS IN,

ABSOLUTELY NOTHING. JUST WAGGING TAILS."

PRINCE HARRY, NOVEMBER 2017

Meeting the in-laws can be nerve-wracking under any circumstances, but when the in-laws are the Windsors, anyone could be forgiven for feeling a little unsure of themselves. Meghan was not that sort of woman, however: in her thirties by the time she met Harry, at ease in the spotlight and with a fairly generous dollop of self-esteem, she was not going to be easily intimidated. Even so, it was all a lot to take on board.

Harry and Meghan knew that their relationship was serious from very early on; because of their age, it also moved a lot faster than that of William and Kate, who were together for seven years before they finally got engaged. That also meant that Meghan was introduced to the rest of the family much sooner than she might otherwise have been, although Harry did keep his cards close to his chest at first. First up, of course, were William and Kate themselves, who were their near neighbours at Kensington Palace, and thus could meet in private without worrying about prying eyes. William and Harry had always been very close as brothers and Harry had been enormously supportive during William's wooing of Kate; now the tables were turned.

"I'd been seeing her for a period of time and I literally didn't tell anybody at all," Harry disclosed during the couple's joint television interview. But when he did, "William was longing to meet her and so was Catherine so, being our neighbours, we managed to get that in... quite a few times now." And Kate and Meghan got on well. "Catherine's been absolutely amazing," said Harry.

"She's been wonderful," Meghan added. And, of course, no one knew better than Kate what it was like to go as an outsider into the very heart of the Royal Family; she, more than anyone, could guide Meghan in the ways of her new world. There was some speculation that there might be rivalry between them – both were stunning brunettes with a very stylish dress sense, added to which there was the fact that Meghan bore a striking resemblance to Pippa Middleton – but the fact was that it was Kate who was destined to be Queen, not Meghan. She could afford to be generous and show her the ropes.

Next up was Prince Charles. A generation previously, he might have been concerned that his son was becoming increasingly serious about a divorcee but, given his own extremely chequered romantic history and the fact that he, too, was married to someone who had been married before, it meant he could hardly complain.

And he didn't. Again, a series of meetings was held behind closed doors, "teas and meetings", Harry later explained. "The family together have been a solid support." The meetings were held at Charles and Camilla's sumptuous residence at Clarence House, a couple of miles away from Kensington Palace, on The Mall and attached to St James's Palace. Before Charles moved in, it had been the home of the Queen Mother; Harry and William had also made it their base until they moved to Kensington Palace.

Neither Harry nor Meghan provided detailed information about when the meetings took place, but it did seem that there were a number of them, with intense speculation that the couple had also visited Charles at his Scottish residence, Birkhall, a grand hunting lodge on the Balmoral estate. He visited there every summer and, given the importance that Scotland held for the whole of the Royal clan, it was another taste for Meghan of what she could expect her

PREVIOUS PAGE:

Meghan mania was in evidence during the couple's first joint engagement in Nottingham. Meghan stunned in a regal blue coat.

ABOVE:

Harry with the Duke and Duchess of Cambridge spearheading a campaign on mental health called Heads Together in April 2016.

ABOVE:

The Prince of Wales was one of the first of the Royals to marry a divorcee, Camilla Parker Bowles. The wedding took place in Windsor, where Harry and Meghan are to wed, Here, the couple are surrounded by their children: William and Harry and Laura and Tom Parker Bowles.

future life to be like. It was also another way of getting to know everyone behind closed doors: she was, according to Charles, "a very nice girl and very pleasant". And Camilla got on with her too. "America's loss is our gain," she said after the engagement was announced, but then Camilla also knew how difficult it could be to join the Royal Family. She was now well established as a senior Royal, but that certainly hadn't always been the case. She had faced a huge amount of opposition at some stages in her relationship with Charles and, to this day, opinion is divided over whether she should be crowned Queen. She was another one who could provide Meghan with the guidance she would need.

And so to the Queen herself. No matter how self-assured anyone is, meeting Elizabeth II is a cause for nerves and, even though Meghan had been meeting senior members of the Royal Family, it was not until she met the monarch herself and gained her approval that the relationship could move to the next step. In their joint interview, of which there is more in the next chapter, Meghan enthused about meeting an "incredible woman", although, again,

OPPOSITE:

The Queen in relaxed mode at Sandringham with her corgis. In their joint television interview, Harry said that the corgis had taken to Meghan immediately.

it was not entirely clear when that initial meeting took place.

But, as with so many of the other personnel involved, it happened over afternoon tea and, according to some reports, at least, took place at Buckingham Palace in September. Meghan was said to have been driven into the grounds in a Ford Galaxy with blacked-out windows – a necessity because, if anyone had spotted her there and realized she was meeting Harry's grandmother, news of the almost certain engagement would have spread instantly. The meeting is thought to have taken place in the Queen's private lounge on the first floor of the palace at around 5pm; Prince Philip, by now retired from Royal duties due to his age, was not there. Sandwiches, scones and cake were served, along with a blend of Darjeeling and Assam tea.

The culmination of all this came in December, after the engagement had been announced, when Harry and Meghan attended a Christmas lunch at Buckingham Palace, which was filled with members of the Royal Family who Meghan had not yet met. This was an annual event held for the extended Windsor clan: hosted by the Queen, it was for those who would not be attending the celebrations on Christmas Day at Sandringham. All the senior Royals were in attendance, along with family members that Meghan had not previously met, such as Prince and Princess Michael of Kent and their son, Lord Frederick Windsor, he who was also married to an actress. By this time, the tables had been turned to the extent that many were said to be excited about meeting Harry's new love, rather than the other way around, and Meghan lived up to billing: after an initial spate of slight nerves, she began to dazzle, reeling the guests under her spell.

"Everyone wanted to meet Meghan and welcome her to the family and she didn't disappoint," an insider told the *Daily Mail*. "Harry was clearly very happy and very proud of her and everyone thought she was delightful. It was your typical Christmas lunch in spite of who was there – turkey, crackers… the lot." Meghan joined in enthusiastically: she was seen pulling a cracker with Prince Charles, putting on a paper hat and reading out a joke.

ABOVE:

Meghan sported a hat by Philip Treacy for the Royal Family's traditional Christmas Day church service in 2017.

Afterwards, Harry drove the two of them back to Kensington Palace. Meghan was, by now, relaxed enough to beam and flash her ring. This also provided proof positive that the "Meghan Markle effect" was real in that, like her sister-in-law-to-be, anything she wore could be guaranteed to sell out: on that day, she was wearing the Self-Portrait Nightshade Midi Dress by Jules B. One glimpse of Meghan wearing it meant it sold out in every size.

If that had been a dress rehearsal for a Royal outing, now came the real thing. Royal fiancées usually had to wait to get the actual ring on their finger before they were invited to Christmas lunch at Sandringham, but in December 2017, with a huge break in tradition, Meghan was there as well. She and Harry actually stayed at nearby Anmer Hall, which was William and Kate's country home, and which took the pressure off slightly, but a first time at Sandringham is a lot for anyone.

Meghan was exposed to the full experience, too: wearing a chic brown coat and hat, she and the Royals made the walk from

ABOVE:

Meghan showed no sign of nerves as she and Harry attended St Mary Magdalene Church in Sandringham on Christmas Day.

Sandringham House to St Mary Magdalene Church, an annual ritual that Harry would have been familiar with since he was a young child. For Meghan, however, it was all new, and she and Harry walked alongside William and Kate, an image that personified the future of the monarchy, with Kate the middle-class girl who had married into the Windsors and Meghan the biracial American divorcee about to do the same. It was certainly a far cry from what Meghan had grown up with, celebrating Christmas in the Californian sunshine. At chilly Sandringham, there were all the formal customs the Royals followed, from giving gifts on Christmas Eve to games of charades (although Meghan, as an actress, could be expected to be adept at that pursuit, at least.) If she had ever had any doubts about how much her life was about to change, those doubts were certainly to be erased now.

A few days later, Harry summed it up in an interview with Sarah Montague, when he guest-edited Radio 4's *Today* programme: "The family loved having her there," he said. "There's always that family part of Christmas [where] there's always that work element there as well, and, I think, together, we had an amazing time.

BELOW:

Harry and Meghan greet well-wishers outside the church after attending the Christmas Day ceremony. It gave Meghan the chance to experience how her life would take shape from now on.

We had great fun staying with my brother and sister-in-law and running round with the kids. Christmas was fantastic." And were there any British traditions to be explained? "Oh, plenty. I think we've got one of the biggest families that I know of, and every family is complex as well," said Harry with some understatement. "No, look, she's done an absolutely amazing job. She's getting in there and it's the family, I suppose, that she's never had."

That last comment was to cause some controversy within Meghan's own family but, back on the day itself, everyone was concentrating on what they had to do. The Queen, Prince Philip, Charles and Camilla were also there, of course, but all eyes were on Meghan. If she felt the pressure, she managed to hide it from the crowds. Hundreds of well-wishers were out in force and she worked the crowd like a pro, hanging on to Harry's arm as she chatted to people who had turned out to wish them all well. "She said lots of things," confided one person in the crowd, Mrs Judith Wallis, who was sitting in a wheelchair; she was in her seventies, and had come from Chesterfield to see the Royal Family. "She was very, very lovely." It was a sentiment that was extensively voiced elsewhere.

ABOVE:

The Queen and the Duke of Edinburgh lead the rest of the Royal Family after the church service, including Charles and Camilla, William and Kate and Harry and Meghan.

Meghan had another hurdle to cross: curtsying to the Queen. William and Harry stood in a line with Kate and Meghan outside the church to greet their grandmother as she arrived: when she did so, both women bobbed down into a curtsy, while both men bobbed their heads. Seemingly trivial, it was another nerve-wracking ordeal for someone new to Royal circles; nor was this exactly a standard custom in the United States. But Meghan pulled it off without looking too nervous. After that, she joined the rest of the Royals for the traditional Christmas lunch before the family convened around the television later in the afternoon to watch the Queen's Speech, which she delivers every year on Christmas Day.

And what a speech it was. To round it all off, the Queen, again, gave her tacit seal of approval to her grandson's romantic relationship: the engagement photo of Harry and Meghan was clearly visible on her desk; within the speech itself, the Queen emphasized that she was looking forward to welcoming new members of the family in 2018. That was not a reference to Meghan alone, as William and Kate were expecting their third child in April that year, but it was a clear indication that Meghan had passed a succession of tests with flying colours. She was ready to join The Firm.

CHAPTER 9

A ROYAL
ENGAGEMENT

"PERSONALLY, I LOVE A GREAT LOVE STORY."

MEGHAN MARKLE, SEPTEMBER 2017

November 2017, and a cozy night in for the happy couple at Nott Cott. Harry had been a dab hand at cooking since his Eton days and Meghan was a self-acknowledged foodie who had frequently posted recipes on her blog, so what could have been more natural than the two of them to be roasting a chicken together? Or "trying to roast a chicken", as Harry later said.

Harry's mind might, indeed, not have been on the task in hand, for a much bigger preoccupation was looming. There was no doubt as to how serious his relationship with Meghan had become, and Harry had often spoken longingly of settling down, as his brother had done, into palpable domestic happiness with his wife and children. William had proposed in the wilds of Africa; would Harry do likewise? No: warm and happy in front of the kitchen stove, the moment to do it was now.

But Harry was a traditional sort of chap, and so he proposed in the traditional way. "It was so sweet and natural and very romantic. He got down on one knee," Meghan said later in the television interview the pair gave when the announcement of their engagement was made on 27 November. "As a matter of fact, I could barely let you finish proposing. I said, 'Can I say yes now?'"

Harry took over the story: "There was hugs, and I had the ring in my finger. I was, like, 'Can I give you the ring?' She goes, 'Oh, yes! The ring!'" And slowly the couple opened up about the relationship: Harry revealed that they had only been on a couple of dates together when he persuaded her to go away – and it was that that had sealed the deal. "I managed to persuade her to come and join me in Botswana," he said. "And we camped out with each other under the stars... she came and joined me for five days out there, which was absolutely fantastic." It was a proper chance for the two of them to get to know one another, he said, and decide that they were prepared to embark on a long-distance relationship. The gamble had clearly paid off.

The actual announcement was made from Clarence House, home to Prince Charles. "His Royal Highness The Prince of Wales is delighted to announce the engagement of Prince Harry to Ms Meghan Markle," it read.

"The wedding will take place in Spring 2018. Further details about the wedding will be announced in due course. His Royal Highness and Ms Markle became engaged in London earlier in the month. Prince Harry has informed Her Majesty The Queen and other close members of his family. Prince Harry has also sought and received the blessing of Ms Markle's parents. The couple will live in Nottingham Cottage at Kensington Palace."

In the immediate aftermath of the announcement – and in time-honoured tradition – the pair appeared to answer a few questions and show off the ring. Somewhat poignantly, their first appearance as an engaged couple took place in the sunken garden in Kensington Palace, which is the site of the memorial garden created to commemorate the twentieth anniversary of Princess Diana's death. But whatever melancholy thoughts might have been in Harry's mind on its creation were clearly long gone; he and Meghan were beaming with happiness, Harry in a blue suit and tie, Meghan in a chic white overcoat and very high heels. When did

Harry know Meghan was The One? he was asked. "The very first time we met," Harry replied. Meghan said she was "so very happy, thank you". Harry added that he was "thrilled, over the moon". And, of course, Meghan was only too happy to show off her ring.

The engagement ring that William had given to Catherine was the one their mother had worn and now Harry was determined to refer to his mother in the ring he gave to Meghan, too. "The ring is obviously yellow gold because that's (what's) her favourite and the main stone itself I sourced from Botswana and the little diamonds either side are from my mother's jewellery collection to make sure that she's with us on this crazy journey together," he said. "I think she would be over the moon, jumping up and down, you know, so excited for me, but then, as I said, would have probably been best friends with Meghan. It is days like today when I really miss having her around and miss being able to share the happy news."

Unsurprisingly, there was immediate and global worldwide interest in the announcement, with Meghan's long-term co-star on *Suits*, Patrick J. Adams, tweeting somewhat mischievously, "She said she was just going out to get some milk…" This was followed up by a rather more serious message, however: "Playing Meghan's television partner for the better part of a decade uniquely qualifies me to say this: Your Royal Highness, you are a lucky man and I know your long life together will be joyful, productive and hilarious. Meghan, so happy for you, friend. Much love."

RIGHT:

The Town Crier, Tony Appleton, outside Kensington Palace, announcing the engagement of HRH Prince Harry and Ms Meghan Markle on 27 November 2017.

The Obamas also sent their congratulations, while – rather more pertinently – the rest of the Royal Family and Meghan's parents expressed their delight. Prince Charles was on a visit to the model town of Poundsbury that he had created in Dorset; he was "thrilled" and "very happy indeed", he said. It

was "very good" and he was "thrilled for them both. They'll be very happy indeed." The Duke and Duchess of Cambridge said, "We are very excited for Harry and Meghan. It has been wonderful getting to know Meghan and to see how happy she and Harry are together." And Meghan's own parents released a joint statement: "We are incredibly happy for Meghan and Harry. Our daughter has always been a kind and loving person. To see her union with Harry, who shares the same qualities, is a source of great joy for us as parents."

It was not long before further details about the wedding began to emerge. It was to be held in May 2018 at St George's Chapel, Windsor Castle, which is where Harry's uncle Prince Edward had married Sophie Rhys-Jones, and where his father and the Duchess of Cornwall had attended a service of prayer after their ceremony at the Windsor Guildhall. It was, in a way, a tactful choice: the other two alternatives – St Paul's Cathedral, which is where Harry's parents had married, and where his mother's funeral had taken place, and Westminster Abbey, which is where William and Catherine wed – were just too grand, not least as Meghan was, after all, a divorcee. Almost every rule in the Royal

BELOW:

A media frenzy: the front pages of British newspapers following the announcement of the engagement.

wedding book was being rewritten for Meghan and Harry, but one of those venues might have been thought to have been a step too far.

At any rate, Harry and Meghan, a Royal couple unlike any other, were clearly determined to do it their way. For a start, not many Royal grooms would have been engaged in cooking a chicken when the proposal took place; meanwhile, Meghan's New Age tastes were well known and there was speculation that the duo might have something slightly different planned. The couple were "leading the planning process for all aspects of the wedding", said their spokesman, Jason Knauf, adding that they were working on ideas that would allow the public to "feel part of the celebrations. This wedding, like all weddings, will be a moment of fun and joy that will reflect the characters of the bride and groom," he continued. Windsor was a "special place" for the couple, he said, and added that it was "an incredibly happy day" and that they were "overwhelmed by support from the UK and around the world".

ABOVE:

The couple share a smile on an official visit to Nottingham in December 2017.

But, of course, this remained a highly unusual situation for a member of the Royal Family to be in and there had clearly been a huge amount of work behind the scenes to resolve what had to be done. Because Meghan had attended a Catholic school, it was erroneously thought that she was, herself, a Catholic. She was, in fact, a Protestant, but her grandmother-in-law-to-be was the Head of the Church of England, so it was announced that Meghan would be baptized into the Church as well and would also be confirmed before the wedding. Her future grandmother-in-law was also the Head of State (her father-in-law-to-be and brother-in-law-to-be would also one day inhabit that position), so it was also announced that Meghan would take British citizenship. An American marrying a Prince of the Royal blood was deemed quite acceptable these days, but she couldn't stay American, it seemed. Or would she adopt dual nationality? It was not yet clear.

Further details of their life together and, in particular, Meghan's new life began to emerge. It was then that it was widely reported that Meghan had two dogs (the interest she had in common with most of the Royal Family): one of them, Guy, would be joining her in the UK but the other, Bogart, would not. Meghan would be giving up some of her charity preoccupations, such as the work she did on gender with the United Nations, and, instead, would concentrate on the Royal Family's own work, becoming the fourth patron of the Royal Foundation of the Duke and Duchess of Cambridge and Prince Harry.

It was not long before Meghan got her first taste of what life as a Royal was to be. Just four days after the engagement was announced, she and Harry went on their first joint walkabout, to Nottingham, a place that Harry said has become "very special" to him (it was his eighth visit in five years). In their engagement interview, Meghan had said she was keen to get her "boots on the ground"; this was her first chance to do so and she carried it off magnificently.

Beaming and waving to the crowds, Meghan might not have come from the more typical background for a Royal princess but that certainly didn't seem to concern the many well-wishers who thronged their route. Radio Nottingham had prepared an enormous engagement card to be signed by the locals: "You've got to believe in the fairytale. That's part of the excitement," said one of them, Kathryn Moran, a 25-year-old barrister. Meanwhile, the fact that Meghan was an American divorcee made her "more relatable",

Abbie Goodband, an administrator at Boots the Chemist, said.

Irene Hardman, 81, had met Harry twice before. "I've got him a little goody bag," she said. "I've bought two fridge magnets with Nottingham on. I bought lots of information leaflets on surrounding places, such as Newstead Abbey and the castle.

I've bought him Haribo and some Nottingham fudge, and a Christmas card with Nottingham on, and also a card with 'Congratulations' on." She had met a good many of the other Royals over the years, including Diana, and, on Meghan, she was adamant: "She's just beautiful. I honestly think she's going to be the right one for him. If I get the chance, I will make sure I say, 'Look after Harry for us.'"

If this was to test the waters of the public's reaction to Meghan, it went staggeringly well. The weather was freezing but thousands turned out, waving both British and American flags. Many were carrying cards to be handed over, while Harry and Meghan looked like a couple of old pros as Harry took on one side of the street and Meghan the other. Harry, of course, had done this countless times before but, for Meghan, it was all new. That said, appearing in front of crowds and dealing with excited well-wishers, of course, went with the territory of being an actress, so she was not as overwhelmed as others in her position might have been.

The crowds could be heard chanting, "Harry, Harry" and "Meghan, Meghan"; Meghan gracefully accepted cards and flowers, saying, "Thank you so much," and, "I really appreciate that." She could have been born for the role. She was also seen giving Harry a reassuring pat on the back, just as she had been the encourager and the nurturer during their engagement interviews. The body language between them said it all.

CHAPTER 10
SPRING WEDDING

"THEY ARE DELIGHTED THAT THE BEAUTIFUL
GROUNDS OF WINDSOR CASTLE WILL BE WHERE THEY
BEGIN THEIR LIVES AS A MARRIED COUPLE."

KENSINGTON PALACE SPOKESMAN JASON KNAUF, NOVEMBER 2017

Saturday, 19 May 2018 was to be quite a day: the day that Harry and Meghan would wed – as well as being the day of the FA Cup Final, which Prince William would normally attend as FA President. In this case, however, he clearly had other duties to handle: news of his brother's marriage to Meghan Markle at St George's Chapel in Windsor Castle had already attracted worldwide attention. Unusually for a Royal wedding, it was to take place on a Saturday (the Queen had wed on a Thursday, Prince Charles on a Wednesday and Prince William on a Friday), and excitement surrounding the event was immense. Meghan, who was adjusting well to all the attention, was, by now, experiencing what it really meant to be a member of the Royal Family, making headlines just by whatever she wore.

On the day the date of the wedding was announced, Harry returned to Sandhurst to take the salute of the passing out of the latest cadets, as he had done every year since graduating 11 years earlier, representing the Queen. As he presented the Sword of Honour to the latest standout officer cadet, and the International Sword and Queen's Medal, and represented the Queen at the Sovereign's Parade, it was a reminder that this was not a showbiz wedding – it was a Royal one.

The House of Windsor represented a monarchy that had stood for 1,000 years and, while Harry, himself, was edging further

PREVIOUS PAGE:

The Order of the Garter Ceremony outside WIndsor Castle.

ABOVE:

As the wedding date is announced, Harry is pictured attending the Sovereign's Parade at Sandhurst, where he represented the Queen. He had himself been inspected by his grandmother 11 years earlier.

and further away from the throne with every new addition to the Cambridge household, he was still one of the most senior members of one of the world's oldest ruling elites. Harry looked every inch the prince and soldier as he attended the commissioning service in the Royal Memorial Chapel: "You are now part of something much bigger than yourself... No matter how challenging the road ahead becomes, the time you have spent in this great place has prepared you to face any test," he told the recruits.

But if the announcement of the wedding date had been timed to coincide with the visit, underlining Harry's status as a senior Royal, it did nothing to scale back the intensity of the interest in the big day, starting with the venue. It might not have been one of the central-London locations, but it was as grand as a prince and his bride could wish for. Initially established in the fourteenth century by Edward III, and extensively embellished in the late fifteenth century, it is both a Royal Peculiar (which means it is exempt from the jurisdiction of the diocese in which it lies and is subject to the jurisdiction of the Head of the Church of England; namely, the Queen) and a Chapel of the Order of the Garter.

It seats 800 and has been the site of many Royal weddings, especially those of the children of Queen Victoria. More recently, as mentioned in the previous chapter, it saw the service of prayer for Harry's father, and the nuptials of his Uncle Edward, and also his cousin, Peter Phillips, in 2008. It is also the resting site of various Royals, including the Queen's father, George VI, the Queen Mother and Princess Margaret. There are also symbols of pageantry everywhere, most obviously in the form of the Queen's (or King's) beasts: 76 heraldic statues on the roof of the chapel. They represent 14 of the heraldic animals: the lion of England, the red

RIGHT:

Harry appeared at ease during his time at the Sovereign's Parade.

dragon of Wales, the panther of Jane Seymour, the falcon of York, the black bull of Clarence, the yale of Beaufort, the white lion of Mortimer, the greyhound of Richmond, the white hart of Richard II, the collared silver antelope of Bohun, the black dragon of Ulster, the white swan of Hereford, the unicorn of Edward III and the golden hind of Kent. In other words, the pair were marrying right at the very heart of monarchy.

Royal weddings, of course, had always been showstoppers and always had the effect of uniting the country. The Queen (then Princess Elizabeth) and Prince Philip married on 20 November 1947 in Westminster Abbey. It was a hugely grand affair, as befitted the heiress to the throne, with eight bridesmaid's, including Princess Margaret, presided over by the Archbishops of Canterbury and York, with huge numbers of Royals from all over Europe in attendance, three exceptions being Prince Philip's sisters, because of their German connections (this was just two years after the war). Princess Elizabeth was dazzling in her Norman Hartnell dress (she'd had to collect coupons to get the material), and Prince Philip was strikingly handsome in his naval uniform. It set the standard for Royal weddings and, indeed, Royal marriages, with the couple celebrating their 70th wedding anniversary around the time that Harry and Meghan got engaged.

The Queen's sister and other children all had their own big days, of course, but none could really compete with that of the

OPPOSITE:

The wedding of Princess Elizabeth to Philip Mountbatten at Westminster Abbey was broadcast to 200 million radio listeners.

ABOVE:

Prince Charles and Princess Diana kiss on the Balcony of Buckingham Palace to the delight of the crowds on their wedding day.

Queen's son, Harry's father, Prince Charles. Taking place on 29 July 1981 at St Paul's Cathedral, it seemed to the watching nation – and the world – as if it really were the stuff that fairy tales were made of. Speculation had surrounded the prince for years about his choice of future bride: at the time, it occurred to no one that a 12-year age gap and totally different interests and characters were actually a disaster in waiting. Instead, the beautiful Lady Diana Spencer, already visibly morphing from shy country-girl aristo to international beauty, was walked up the aisle by her father, Earl Spencer, dressed in a cream silk puffball of a dress made by Elizabeth and David Emanuel. There were seven bridal attendants looking after them, and the ceremony was taken by the Archbishop of Canterbury, Robert Runcie. Most of the crowned heads of Europe were present, as well as Nancy Reagan, then the First Lady of the United States. Afterwards, there was a reception at Buckingham Palace, complete with 27 wedding cakes. The family came out on to the Palace's balcony where, much to the delight of the vast crowd of spectators, Charles and Diana kissed.

This latest wedding would not quite be on that scale, but the considerations were the same. Who would be there? Harry and Meghan's intimate circle of friends, as detailed in previous chapters, would almost certainly be on the guest list, as would all of the Windsors, but a Royal wedding involves a great deal more than a few personal friends. It is fraught with difficulty and the opportunity for causing offence, which, when it involves powerful people, can run the real risk of resulting in diplomatic crises. The most obvious example of this with regard to Harry and Meghan's wedding involved two American presidents. Before her relationship with Harry became public, Meghan had made her distaste for President Trump very clear, while, at the same time, the younger members of the Windsor clan were becoming very friendly with the Obamas.

When Barack Obama had been president, he was introduced to William, Harry and William's son, Prince George, who was then still a toddler. President Obama had clearly been very taken with young George. Ties were strengthened when the former president attended the Invictus Games in Toronto when Harry and Meghan were there, and further proof of how well the prince and the president were got on came in December 2017 when Harry was a guest editor on Radio 4's *Today* programme.

He managed to pull in two A-list guests: one was his own father and the other was President Obama. The banter between Harry and Obama showed a clear rapport. Already, speculation had arisen as to whether the Obamas would be on the guest list for the wedding, which would risk offending the US incumbent President Donald Trump (especially if he wasn't on the list), thus alienating Britain's greatest international ally. Harry was asked outright about this: "We haven't even put the invites or the guest list together yet," he said. "Who knows whether he's [Obama's] going to be invited or not? I wouldn't want to ruin that surprise."

It was a diplomatic answer, but the situation was so sensitive that it was thought that the Prime Minister, no less, might get drawn in. "Harry has made it clear he wants the Obamas at the wedding; so it's causing a lot of nervousness," a senior government source told iNews. "Trump could react very badly. Conversations are ongoing… and ministers will eventually have to decide. If the PM lays down the law, Harry will just have to suck it up." And as the presence of Nancy Reagan at Charles and Diana's wedding implied, it was not unreasonable of the current president to expect an invitation, too.

OPPOSITE:

The wedding of Prince Charles and Lady Diana Spencer was watched by an estimated global television audience of 750 million.

Ultimately, however, it was Buckingham Palace that was compiling the guest list, not Downing Street, although the two would be in constant consultation. Very senior Royal weddings are state occasions, which means that other heads of state are invited; this one was not. Buckingham Palace was also paying for it, not the taxpayer, so there was more leeway than there would have been at William and Kate's wedding. However, it could safely be assumed that other European royal families (many, of course, related to the Windsors) would be there, along with heads of the Queen's beloved Commonwealth. Although the Royal Family rose above party politics, issues of statesmanship were always there.

Then there was Meghan's family. Harry had, somewhat unwisely, upset some of them by saying that, in marrying into the Windsors, "It's the family that, I suppose, she's never had," prompting a sharp rebuke from her half-sister, Samantha, and reports that her father was very upset. But Samantha had not been slow in the past to share her sometimes controversial views of Meghan, and the sisters were not close; nor had Samantha seemed very hopeful of getting an invitation. It was not clear if Meghan's half-brother, Thomas, and his family would be there either – there had been the very embarrassing episode in which he'd been arrested for pulling a gun on his girlfriend. Meghan's parents would be there, of course, and her father had already expressed a wish to walk her up the aisle.

Who would design the dress? There was always intense secrecy surrounding this: both Diana (the Emanuels) and Kate Middleton (Alexander McQueen) managed to keep their secret up until the wedding day, and it looked certain that Meghan would attempt to do the same. She had previously said that her dream gown would be "classic and simple". She further added, "I personally prefer dresses that are whimsical or subtly romantic."

Certainly, she could have her pick of designers, and the odds were that it would be a British one, although there was some speculation that she might enlist the services of her friend and matchmaker Misha Nonoo. She had also already been pictured in a classic wedding design when Rachel got married in *Suits*; she was wearing an Anne Barge number for that. Could she do so again? Meghan had also previously said that she would always be a fan of the Lebanese fashion designer Elie Saab, but, perhaps, the strongest contender was the British fashion house Ralph & Russo. Meghan had worn one of their numbers for the engagement pictures.

Who would preside over the wedding? It was not immediately clear but the chances were that it would be the Archbishop of Canterbury, Justin Welby. He had already given the couple his blessing: "I am very, very sure after conversations that this is no tick-box exercise, 'we ought to get married in a church'," he told Radio 4's *Today* programme. "There is a profound sense of commitment and seriousness both about faith and their life together, which is quite inspirational," he went on. Would he preside himself? "That is up to them," the Archbishop replied. The jury was still out.

The details of Meghan's bouquet were also being kept secret, but it was almost certain to contain a sprig of myrtle. That was a tradition that dated back to 1840, when Queen Victoria married Prince Albert, and it had been used in the bouquets of Royal brides ever since. Symbolizing matrimony, love and hope, Kate Middleton had had a sprig in her bouquet, and also lily of the valley, to pay tribute to Princess Diana, which Meghan might also want to do. Meghan was also known to love peonies, putting many pictures of them on her Instagram feed. Indeed, she had posted a bouquet of peonies once that appeared to have been sent to her by Prince Harry. A hint, perhaps, as to what the nation could expect for the big day…

ABOVE:

Prince William and Catherine Middleton walk down the aisle at the close of their wedding ceremony at Westminster Abbey on 29 April 2011.

CHAPTER 11

THOROUGHLY MODERN ROYALS

"IT WAS JUST A CHOICE, RIGHT? I THINK THAT VERY EARLY ON,

WE REALIZED WE WERE GOING TO COMMIT TO EACH OTHER."

MEGHAN MARKLE, NOVEMBER 2017

Prince Harry is very unlikely ever to become King but, in his choice of bride and his own lifestyle and concerns, he and Meghan represent the future of the Royal Family. One of the reasons that the monarchy has survived so long is its adaptability: Harry's ancestors changed their image time and again to reflect the society in which they lived. It was only in Queen Victoria's time that the concept of the "Royal Family" as such began to emerge, while it was just over 100 years ago, in 1917, that the family changed its name from Saxe-Coburg-Gotha to Windsor. It followed a proclamation by George V, who realized that the name was too German, not least as Britain was still fighting World War II.

So the advent of Meghan Markle could not have been more positive for the future of the monarchy. The face of Britain had changed enormously over the Queen's hugely long reign and it was important that the Royal Family reflect that. The process had begun with Princess Diana and, after her untimely death at the age of just 36 – the same age Meghan would be when she married

PREVIOUS PAGE:

Harry and Meghan
visit charity
Reprezent in London
in January 2018.

OPPOSITE:

Meeting the team
at the Reprezent
training programme,
established in 2008
to fight knife crime.

ABOVE:

Meghan meets well-
wishers as she and
Harry leave after the
visit to Reprezent.
"Meghan mania"
was going strong.

Harry – it was quite clearly carrying forward with her two sons. In the year leading up to the engagement announcement, William, Kate and Harry had been campaigning for better understanding of mental-health issues – a far cry from the "stiff upper lip" approach the Windsors had adopted in the past. Some of this was, undoubtedly, influenced by Meghan: a California girl in both background and outlet, she was no stranger to concepts such as therapy, something that would never have featured in Windsor-speak before.

The fact that she is a biracial divorced actress has been touched on previously, but it, too, shows how open the monarchy is to change. In 1936, an American divorcee caused the downfall of a king amid the Abdication Crisis: in 2018 no one batted an eyelid. Instead, there was widespread rejoicing that Harry had finally met someone who was going to be the Duchess of Right: the loss of his mother at such a young age and the failure of his two significant relationships before Meghan had produced in Harry a desire to settle down. One of the most popular of the Royals, there was also a palpable need among the public to see him do so. The vast majority of the public was delighted at his choice: times were changing, and the Royals were changing, too.

The sibling to the monarch is always in a slightly tricky position: the Queen's sister, Princess Margaret, is often portrayed as a grand and difficult woman who never really seemed to find a role in life. But Margaret had been denied the chance to marry the great love of her life, Group Captain Peter Townsend, and there had always been a sense that that event cast a shadow that never left her. Harry, on the other hand, was being allowed to marry exactly who he wanted, and he made it clear from the outset that they were going to work as a team. Meghan's commitment to their future was equally great: she was going to be a member of the Royal Family, but she was sacrificing a great deal in order to do so. She was leaving her country, her career, her nationality, even her lifestyle – for, no matter how great the opportunities and luxuries that lay before her, she was also sacrificing her freedom. The life of a modern princess is not a fairy tale. It involves a lot of hard work.

But then, unlike any Royal bride before her – even Kate Middleton – Meghan had been a career girl. She knew the value

BELOW:

Cheering crowds carrying the Welsh flag greet Harry and Meghan as they visit Cardiff Castle in January 2018.

OPPOSITE:

Unusually for the Royals, Harry and Meghan signed autographs for the waiting crowds.

of hard work. She was not an ingénue coming into a situation she didn't fully understand; she was a mature woman who had made her name in the cut-throat world of television. She was also clearly able to provide the steadying influence that Harry needed, and was clearly prepared to take on the responsibilities of being a Royal bride.

After the wedding, there will, of course, have to be changes. Nott Cott is perfect for a newly married couple, but it is not big enough for a growing family and, if the couple have children, they will almost certainly have to move to one of the grander abodes at Kensington Palace. But to a certain extent, they will be able to live their lives in their own way, in a manner that William and Kate cannot. Being the "spare" to William's "heir" might have some drawbacks, but it does mean that Harry will have more flexibility than his brother ever did or will have. Harry has made it plain he wishes to be a campaigning Royal, just like his mother before him, and he has also, so far, skilfully negotiated the pitfalls that his father sometimes slips into: namely, avoiding anything that is too political. The Windsors cannot allow themselves to have any perceived political bias. The Queen has spent a lifetime managing to stay above the realm of politics and both her grandsons by Charles seem set to do the same.

So it looks as if Harry and Meghan will continue rewriting the rule book, even as they settle into married life. And the wedding comes at an auspicious moment. As life in Britain looks fractious and difficult due to the changing political situation in Europe and across the Atlantic, the Royal Family are doing what they have so often done before: uniting the country behind them. This country does royalty and pageantry as no other, and Harry and Meghan are just the latest thoroughly modern chapter in a story that has continued for a thousand years. Invitations to the wedding will be sought after, and interest in their married life will continue to burn as strongly as ever, especially if and when they start building a family. But the signs are that theirs is a stable relationship, with each complementing the other. Together, as in all the best relationships, they are stronger than the sum of their parts.

OPPOSITE:

Meghan looks touched as she receives flowers from well-wishers in Brixton, London.

OVERLEAF:

Wrapped up against the biting cold, the beaming couple greeted the crowds that lined the streets of Cardiff.

INDEX

CREDITS

Alamy: DOD: 76; /Ivan Nikolov/WENN.com: 78-79; /Amanda Rose: 115

Getty Images: Jean-Paul Aussenard/WireImage for Kari Feinstein PR: 28; /Steve Back: 112-113; /Ben Birchall - WPA Pool: 60, 140-141; /Hugo Burnand/Pool: 100; /Adrian Dennis/WPA Pool: 4, 102, 106, 138; /Adrian Dennis/AFP: 10-11, 103, 104; /Paul Edwards – Pool: 24 (right); /Billy Farrell/Patrick McMullan via Getty Images: 32; /Christopher Furlong: 117; /Sylvain Gaboury/Patrick McMullan via Getty Images: 34; /Charley Gallay/Getty Images For Benefit Cosmetics: 31; /Gallo Images: 125; /Tim Graham: 14, 15, 16, 17, 19, 21, 87, 127, 129; /Anwar Hussein/WireImage: 18, 93, 101; /Samir Hussein/WireImage: 8, 38, 43, 65, 66, 108, 110, 111, 132, 136; /Chris Jackson/WPA Pool: 23, 24 left, 137; /Chris Jackson-Pool/Getty Images for Invictus: 25, 42, 63; /Chris Jackson/Getty Images for Ascot Racecourse: 95; /Chris Jackson/Getty Images for Sentebale: 22; /Keystone-France/Gamma-Rapho: 88; /Daniel Leal-Olivas/AFP: 84; /David Levenson: 71; /Dominic Lipinski - WPA Pool: 72, 131, 135; /Heathcliff O'Malley/WPA Pool: 12; /Kevin Mazur/Getty Images for DirecTV: 90; /Max Mumby/Indigo: 53, 92, 96, 119, 122, ; /National Geographic: 10; /Julian Parker/UK Press: 68-69, 70; /George Pimentel/WireImage: 89, 91; /Popperfoto: 125, 126; /Geoff Pugh - WPA Pool: 82; /Rhino Conservation Botswana/Kensington Palace: 59; /Vaughn Ridley/for the Invictus Games Foundation: 7; /Nicky J Sims: 99; /Andy Stenning - WPA Pool: 50; /John Stillwell - WPA Pool: 107; /John Stillwell POOL/Tim Graham Picture Library; 74; /Ray Tamarra/GC Images: 36; /Justin Tallis - WPA Pool: 56; /Karwai Tang/WireImage: 46, 62, 123; /Jack Taylor: 134; /Andrew Toth: 40

REX/Shutterstock: 48; /Facundo Arrizabalaga/EPA: 44-45; /Tom Buchanan/SilverHub: 58; /Dutch Oven/Kobal: 80; /Neil Hall/EPA-EFE: 114; /Rupert Hartley: 47; /Steve Meddle: 116; /Frank Ockenfels/Dutch Oven/Kobal: 35; /Erik Pendzich: 75; /John Salangsang/BFA: 26; /Charles Sykes/Invision/AP: 77; /USA Network/Netflix/Kobal: 37

Seth Poppel/Yearbook Library: 29

COUNTRIES OF THE WORLD

UNITED KINGDOM

ROB BOWDEN

Evans

TITLES IN THE COUNTRIES OF THE WORLD SERIES:
BRAZIL • FRANCE • JAPAN • KENYA • UNITED KINGDOM • USA

Published by Evans Brothers Limited
2A Portman Mansions
Chiltern Street
London W1U 6NR

Produced for Evans Brothers Limited by
Monkey Puzzle Media Limited
Gissing's Farm, Fressingfield
Suffolk IP21 5SH

First published 2002
© copyright Evans Brothers 2002
© copyright in the text Rob Bowden 2002

The right of Rob Bowden to be identified as the author of this Work has been asserted by him in accordance with the Copyright, Designs and Patents Act 1988.

British Library Cataloguing in Publication Data
United Kingdom. - (Countries of the world)
1.Great Britain - Juvenile literature
I.Title
941

ISBN 0 237 52268 3

Editor: Katie Orchard
Designer: Jane Hawkins
Map artwork by Peter Bull
Charts and graphs produced by Encompass Graphics Ltd

Endpapers (front): The stunning landscape of the Scottish Highlands.
Title page: St Paul's Cathedral – a key feature of the London skyline.
Imprint and Contents page: The mysterious structures of Stonehenge date back 5,000 years.
Endpapers (back): The Queen's Guards march down Pall Mall towards Buckingham Palace.

All photograhs taken by Rob Bowden (images@easi-er.co.uk) except for the following, which were kindly supplied by: *Chapel Studios* front endpapers (Graham Horner), title page (Patrick Cockell), 11 (top/Zul Mukhida), 11 (bottom/David Thomas), 12 (Graham Horner), 14 (top/Graham Horner), 14–15 (bottom/Zul Mukhida), 16 (bottom/Zul Mukhida), 20 (top and bottom/Graham Horner), 21 (top/Zul Mukhida), 23 (Graham Horner), 25 (top/Graham Horner), 28 (Zul Mukhida), 35 (bottom/Graham Horner), 37 (Zul Mukhida), 42 (Graham Horner), 44 (top/Graham Horner), 45 (Rafe Harwood), 46 (top/Tim Garrod), 48 (Graham Horner), 57 (top and bottom/Zul Mukhida); *Corbis* 60 (Grant Smith); *Corbis Digital Stock* imprint and contents pages, back endpapers; *FLPA* 38 (Chris Demetriou), 51 (J Watkins).

CONTENTS

The Union Jack flag, combining the flags of England, Scotland and Wales.

INTRODUCING THE UK

Liverpool's famous waterfront across the River Mersey. Liverpool was one of the many cities that benefited from trade during the colonial period.

A UNITED KINGDOM?

The UK is a political union between the island of Great Britain (made up of England, Scotland and Wales) and Northern Ireland. However, the union as it stands today was only formed in 1921, when the Anglo-Irish Treaty agreed to the partition, or division, of Ireland. The oldest part of the union is between England and Wales (1536). Scotland joined later to form Great Britain in 1707. A union between Great Britain and Ireland in 1801 led to the formation of the United Kingdom of Great Britain and Ireland, which survived until the 1921 Anglo-Irish Agreement. This agreement eventually led to the present union and name.

The UK's complicated past continues to present fresh challenges today. Scotland and Wales are arguing for greater independence, and there has been a long-standing struggle for power in Northern Ireland between those loyal to Ireland and those loyal to Great Britain.

There is often confusion about the use of the name 'UK': many people use the terms 'Great Britain' or even 'England' instead. This is perhaps understandable given that the capital, London, is in England and the national language is English.

RULE BRITANNIA

In its prime the UK controlled over a quarter of the earth's surface and ruled over almost half of the world's population. These were the days of the British Empire, which began with the colonisation of North America and the Caribbean in the early 1600s and peaked in the late 1800s before starting to decline after the First World War (1914–18). During this period the UK became the world's greatest trading and military nation, amassing great wealth from its colonies and territories around the world. This wealth helped fund the Industrial Revolution that began in Britain around 1760, nearly 40 years before the USA began to industrialise and 70 years before the rest of western Europe.

By the time of the First World War, however, the British Empire was starting to lose its world superiority. The USA and Germany had taken over as the primary industrial powers and political control was being challenged by colonies throughout the empire. The enormous loss of human life (1.2 million

Castles are a reminder of the power struggles before the creation of the union. This one, built in 1285, is at Harlech in Wales.

people) and the massive economic costs of fighting two wars in close succession left the UK crippled. After the end of the Second World War (1939–1945), the UK was unable and unwilling to maintain its empire. In 1947 India gained its independence and this set off a series of movements that saw most colonies secure independence in the following 30 years. Some of the last colonies to gain independence were Zimbabwe in 1980 and Hong Kong, which became part of China in 1997.

This monument in Ironbridge is dedicated to the thousands who died during the two world wars.

KEY DATA

Official Name:	United Kingdom of Great Britain and Northern Ireland (UK)
Area:	244,100km^2
Population:	58.8 million (mid-2000 estimate)
Official Language:	English
Main Cities:	London (capital), Birmingham, Manchester, Edinburgh, Cardiff, Belfast
GDP per capita:	US$ 22,093 (1999)*
Currency:	Pound Sterling (£)
Exchange Rate:	US$1 = £0.69 (1 November 2001)

* Calculated on Purchasing Power Parity basis

Rebuilding the UK

After the loss of so many lives during the two world wars, the UK had to rebuild both its economy and its population. Rebuilding the economy was a slow process, but with financial assistance from the newly established international community (including organisations such as the United Nations and the World Bank) the UK economy was soon growing again. By 1957 Prime Minister Harold Macmillan famously stated that Britain 'had never had it so good'. Rebuilding the population, however, would take longer. The government created the Welfare State, setting up institutions such as the National Health Service (NHS) and providing free education to encourage and support families. This led to a baby boom in the population, but there were still not enough people of working age to help rebuild the economy in the short term. The UK turned to its colonies and encouraged people to come to the UK to live and work. Many thousands took up the invitation, with most arriving from India, Pakistan and the Caribbean, and settling in London and the big industrial cities of central England such as Birmingham, Sheffield and Manchester. The arrival of these people not only aided economic recovery, but also made the UK into the multi-cultural society that it is today.

Manchester is one of many multi-ethnic cities in the UK.

By the 1960s the UK was again showing its strength with a booming economy and a thriving cultural scene that become known as 'the swinging sixties'. This period produced some of the UK's best-known symbols such as the Mini motor car, the music of *The Beatles* and *The Rolling Stones*, and the World Cup winning football champions of 1966.

The UK and Europe

In 1973 the UK joined the European Economic Community (now the European Union – EU) and so began a debate that is as current today as it was then – the relationship between the UK and Europe. Europe is vital to the UK economy, accounting for well over 50 per cent of all trade, but as other European countries introduce policies to further strengthen such ties, the UK has so far been reluctant to join them. The main argument surrounds the replacement of the UK currency with a common European currency (the Euro – €). Many British people believe this would mean a further loss of independence and power for the UK economy. Others believe the UK must join the European Monetary Union (EMU) if it is to stay competitive with its European partners and that failure to do so could be disastrous for the UK economy.

TWENTY-FIRST CENTURY UK

The position of the UK at the beginning of the twenty-first century was very different from what it had been only a century before. No longer a world superpower, the UK is having to form new relationships with Europe and beyond in order to keep its position as a major world economy. At home it is also having to examine itself and the relationships between the different parts of the union. In 1997 the people of Scotland and Wales voted to have greater control over their own affairs in a process known as devolution. Northern Ireland, too, has a national assembly, but tension between the rival parties there constantly threaten its work.

With such diversity in the UK today, many people are now questioning what it means to be British. The early part of the twenty-first century is likely to see more changes to the nature of the UK.

ABOVE: Protestant Orangemen in Northern Ireland still celebrate the victory of William III over the Catholic forces of James II in 1690.
BELOW: Edinburgh is the seat of the newly devolved Scottish parliament.

LANDSCAPE AND CLIMATE

Dramatic hills tower over Scotland's stunning Loch Lomond.

The landscape of the UK is very varied, from the peaks of the Scottish Highlands to the low-lying areas of flat land in Norfolk that are no higher than sea level. Images of rolling hills are often associated with the UK, which has earned a reputation as a 'green and pleasant land', benefiting from fertile soil and a temperate climate. As an island nation, the UK's varied coastline is also an important aspect of the landscape.

THE HIGHLANDS

Scotland is the highest part of the UK, consisting of the North-west Highlands and Southern Uplands (bordering England) and the Grampian Mountains. There is a low-lying area in between where the main population centres (Edinburgh, Glasgow and Dundee) are found. The Highlands are carved up by numerous rivers and lochs (lakes). Loch Ness is world famous and has long been rumoured to be the home of a mysterious prehistoric creature. The western coastline is indented with steep-sided sea lochs and surrounded by most of Scotland's 790 islands, which include the Hebrides, Orkneys and Shetlands. People living on some of the 130 inhabited islands are amongst the most remote populations in the UK. Fierce seas and stormy weather often isolate these communities from the mainland for weeks at a time. Western Scotland's Grampians (including the Cairngorms) are the UK's highest range and include the UK's highest point, Ben Nevis, at 1,343m.

The Grampians are the only part of the UK high enough to support arctic vegetation. Wales is also dominated by highland and mountains, with the Cambrian Mountains running the length of the country. Better known, however, are the Brecon Beacons in the south-east and Snowdonia in the north-west. Snowdonia includes Mount Snowdon, Wales' highest peak at 1,085m. This is a popular tourist attraction, receiving over 500,000 visitors each year. Popular activities include walking or taking the train to the summit, complete with its own café!

THE LOWLANDS

The UK's lowlands are located mainly in England, particularly in the east of the country. In parts of Lincolnshire and East Anglia (Norfolk, Suffolk and Cambridgeshire) the land barely rises above sea level. Much of this area was once fertile wetlands known as 'the Fens'. In the eighteenth century the Fens were drained to create farmland that is today

ABOVE: A haunting mist rolls over Cader Idris, part of the spectacular mountain scenery of Snowdonia National Park in Wales.
RIGHT: Gently rolling hillsides dominate much of the UK and are extensively farmed, with sheep farming being the most widespread.

the main arable farming area of the UK with fields of grains or vegetables stretching as far as the eye can see. In the south-west, the Somerset Levels form another area of lowland which was drained for farming, but also for harvesting peat used as a fuel and, more recently, to enrich garden soils. During heavy rainfall this area often floods, returning the landscape to what it may have looked like several hundred years ago.

There is very little of the UK's landscape that has not been altered in some form by human activities. Originally much of the country would have been covered in woodland but most of this has now disappeared with only a few areas surviving such as the New Forest, near Southampton, and Sherwood Forest (made famous in the tales of Robin Hood), near Nottingham.

ROLLING HILLS

Between the extremes of the highlands and lowlands, the rest of the UK consists of gently rolling countryside. This land is generally well watered and fertile. Most of the UK population lives in this area and many of the main population centres are located near the country's major rivers such as London on the Thames, Nottingham on the Trent and Newcastle on the Tyne. Farming in this region is a mixture of arable and livestock with some regional specialisms. For example, dairy production is significant in the south-west – Devon cream is world famous.

LANDSCAPE OF THE UK

Rock climbers at Brimham Rocks, near Harrowgate in Yorkshire, make the most of the dramatic landscape.

Landscapes are important for tourism, too, and many of the most popular attractions are located in the UK's countryside areas. The Lake District in Cumbria is perhaps the best known, but other popular landscapes include the Pennines, the Peak District, the Yorkshire Moors, the Cotswolds, Dartmoor, Exmoor and the South Downs, all of which attract millions of visitors every year.

COASTAL LANDSCAPES

The UK is surrounded by water and has a coastline stretching a total of 12,429km – equivalent to travelling almost a third of the way around the world. This coastline varies dramatically from the pebbly beaches and chalk cliffs of Sussex to the expansive sands of north Norfolk, and the sheer cliffs and lochs of Scotland's west coast. One of the most popular coastal regions is south-west England, where the mixture of rugged granite cliffs, white sand beaches and picturesque fishing villages attract tourists in their millions. Some of the UK's best-loved towns are also on the coast, such as Brighton with its famous pier and Blackpool with its pleasure beach. These have become highly developed tourist centres for both foreign and UK visitors. One of the UK's more unusual coastal features is the world famous Giant's Causeway in County Antrim, Northern Ireland. This 5km-long stretch of basalt columns was formed by molten lava erupting from beneath the sea and cooling very quickly. The columns, which are hexagonal in shape, are between 37–50cm wide and vary in height up to 6m tall. From the air the Giant's Causeway looks like a giant honeycomb.

UNPREDICTABLE WEATHER

British people are famous for their discussions about the weather. When it rains they long for sunshine and yet after just a few weeks of dry, sunny weather they start to complain that their gardens are drying out and that it is too hot. In reality the UK's climate is usually somewhere in between these extremes and is classified as maritime temperate. This means it is generally mild and damp – rarely too hot and dry or too cold and wet.

British people are quick to enjoy the summer sunshine whilst it lasts!

The UK's weather is difficult to predict and can change very rapidly in a single day. Some general patterns can be identified, however. Temperatures tend to be warmer in the south than in the north. Average temperatures in the south of England range from 4°C in January to 18°C in July, whilst in the north of Scotland the averages range from 3°C to 15°C during the same months. Rainfall is higher in the west of the UK and on higher ground. The Scottish Highlands receive over 3,000mm per year, and in parts of the Pennines and the Lake District rainfall of up to 4,500mm has been recorded. Eastern and low-lying areas of the UK are generally drier, averaging around 1,000–1,500mm, but falling as low as 600mm in London and parts of neighbouring Kent and Essex.

The white chalk cliffs dominate the view at the Seven Sisters Country Park in Sussex.

TEMPERATURE AND RAINFALL

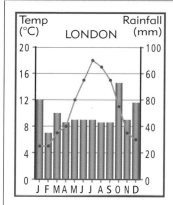

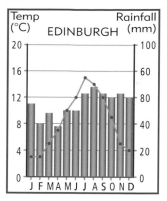

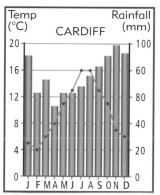

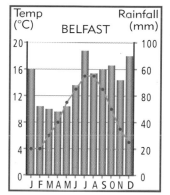

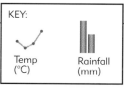

KEY:

Temp (°C)

Rainfall (mm)

CASE STUDY
STORMS AHOY!

In October 2000 and again in March 2001 parts of the UK experienced exceptional rainfall leading to serious flooding with damage to property and massive disruption to travel and daily life. In Lewes, in south-east England, 800 homes and businesses and over 700 cars were damaged or written-off by the floods. Rainfall in the area was more than three times its normal level during October 2000, yet by June 2001 rainfall was four times less than normal, causing localised drought in the same area. Such extremes are expected to become more common in future as a result of climate change and records suggest that this is already happening – 2001 saw the wettest March in the UK since 1766.

NATURAL RESOURCES

This old slate train in north Wales now provides scenic tourist rides.

RESOURCES FOR INDUSTRIALISATION

Although the UK does not have abundant supplies of natural resources, it has significant reserves of key resources that were vital to the start of the Industrial Revolution in the eighteenth century. Coal, iron ore and water were three highly significant resources that came together in the development of the first steam engine by James Watt in 1769. The invention of the steam engine changed the world for ever, providing industry with power and allowing the development of machinery for mass production. In the UK this led to rapid industrialisation, particularly in areas such as Nottingham where supplies of coal and water were plentiful.

Traditional industrial skills utilised local resources such as iron. This blacksmith is using his hammer to bend iron heated in a furnace.

Canals were built to transport coal, raw materials and finished products to and from the factories and mills. The canals were followed by the development of the railway network in the 1800s. The railways dramatically reduced journey times, allowing businesses and industry to flourish. The journey between London and Birmingham, for example, was reduced from almost 24 hours in 1821 (by stagecoach) to around four hours by train in 1845. The railways were also significant for the development of British colonies. Networks were built in India and eastern and southern Africa, easing the movement and export of raw materials to the UK where they were turned into manufactured goods.

FOSSIL FUELS

The UK's dependence on fossil fuels has changed little since the Industrial Revolution. In 1997 fossil fuels accounted for 87.8 per cent of the UK's energy needs. Coal, which met over 90 per cent of the UK's energy requirements in 1950, has since reduced in significance. By 1997 it accounted for only 18 per cent of UK energy. This decline was due to the exhaustion of the most accessible reserves and the increased costs of deep-mining, which made British coal more expensive than imported coal from countries such as the USA and Australia. In addition, the pollution from burning coal for heating and power was considered a primary cause of London's Great Smogs in 1952 and 1968, which led to the deaths of around 4,700 people. As a result of this the government introduced Clean Air Acts in 1956 and 1968 to reduce the use of coal in built-up areas. Since then most homes and businesses now use natural gas, a much cleaner fuel extracted from under the North Sea and Irish Sea.

GAS – PROS AND CONS

The UK now has around 90 gas fields supplying natural gas for domestic and industrial use and increasingly for electricity generation in gas-fired power stations. Natural gas does not emit sulphur dioxide (SO_2), which is one of the main gases responsible for producing acid rain and smog. Largely as a result of conversion to natural gas, emissions of SO_2 from UK cities have been cut by 60 per cent since 1960. However, natural gas is non-renewable – once used it cannot be replaced. Current UK reserves will probably be exhausted long before 2050. Natural gas also emits carbon dioxide (CO_2) when burnt – the main greenhouse gas responsible for global warming.

ENERGY RESOURCES

REDUCTION OF UK COAL PRODUCTION, 1970–2000

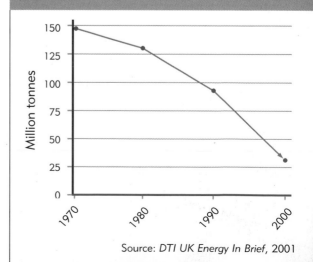

Source: DTI UK Energy In Brief, 2001

CASE STUDY
UK OIL INDUSTRY

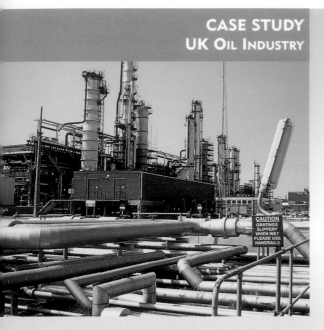

Ellesmere Port on the Mersey estuary is one of the UK's main oil refineries.

Oil was discovered in the UK under the North Sea in the early 1970s and first came into production in 1975. Its location, however,

presented problems for extraction due to treacherous seas and the fact that the oil fields were a long distance from land. Platforms (oil rigs) were constructed to provide a stable surface for drilling into the seabed to extract the crude oil. The oil was then sent via special pipelines laid along the seabed to Sullom Voe, Europe's biggest oil refinery, on the Shetland Isles. Having overcome extraction difficulties the oil industry has grown rapidly and by 1996 the UK was the ninth-biggest producer in the world, accounting for 3.9 per cent of the world total. Despite fears that North Sea oil (and gas) would run out shortly after the year 2000, recently discovered reserves are now being exploited. These reserves are expected to last until at least 2030. Extraction, however, is becoming more expensive as new supplies are discovered in increasingly remote locations. The UK will have to look to alternative sources of energy in the coming years if it is to continue to meet its own needs in the future.

REGIONAL RESOURCES

The UK has some regional natural resources and these have led to the development of localised and specialist industries in certain areas. For example, Cornwall in south-west England was historically a major producer of tin, whilst north Wales was the major source of slate used to make tiles for roofing. Many of these local industries have declined as resources became scarce or as new and cheaper alternatives became available. Slate tiles for example, were gradually replaced by manufactured clay tiles starting in the early 1900s. Today most of the slate mines have closed, although a few are now being turned into tourist attractions. One of the most famous regional industries in the UK was the pottery industry in Stoke-on-Trent, an area still known as 'the Potteries'.

The area around Stoke-on-Trent had the ideal combination of local clays and wood, and later coal fuel, needed to produce pottery. Specialist materials such as China clay from Cornwall were brought in using the region's canal network, which developed to meet the needs of the Potteries. Hundreds of small potteries sprang up in the area, identified by their bottle-shaped kilns, which dotted the landscape. The Clean Air Acts saw the end of the polluting bottle kilns, and many potteries closed as modern and highly mechanised technology was introduced. However, some of the most famous factories including Wedgwood and Royal Doulton continue to produce pottery, and their popularity with collectors around the world means they are also major tourist attractions.

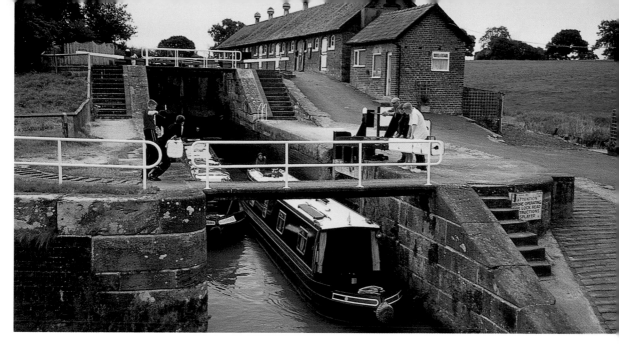

WATER RESOURCES

Historically, the UK's inland waterways played an important role in the Industrial Revolution. Today they are still significant, attracting more than 10 million visitors every year to enjoy boating, and walking or cycling along the old towpaths. Water is an important resource in other ways. Many large industries such as steel and paper manufacturing require large quantities of water during their production processes, and modern intensive farming uses irrigation to improve the growth and yield of

Canal holidays are increasingly popular with tourists such as these on the Trent and Mersey Canal, south of Manchester.

crops – especially vegetables. Water is also an important source of energy. Water wheels provided one of the earliest forms of energy and can still be seen in a few carefully preserved locations. Today the power of water is used to generate electricity in the form of hydroelectric power (HEP), as it passes through dams built across narrow river valleys. Scotland is the main producer of HEP in the UK, but the biggest single scheme is in north Wales at Dinorwig, near Llanberis.

The Wedgwood visitor centre near Stoke-on-Trent tells the story of the Potteries' development.

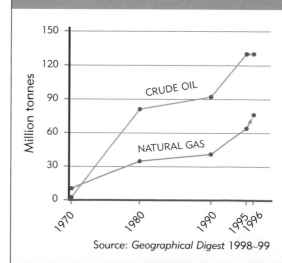

GROWTH IN UK OIL AND GAS PRODUCTION, 1970–1996

Source: *Geographical Digest* 1998–99

Silage making takes place in early summer. It is an important part of the dairy farmers' calendar.

OF LAND AND SEA

In addition to the resources extracted from the earth, the land and waters of the UK are important resources in themselves, supporting industries such as agriculture, forestry, fishing and tourism. In total UK agriculture meets around 60 per cent of food needs, despite employing only around 1 per cent of the labour force. Fertile soils enable intensive agricultural production of cereals such as wheat and barley, as well as fruit and vegetable crops such as carrots, potatoes, apples and berries. Other crops that are grown include flax, which is used to make linen, and rapeseed, which is pressed to obtain rapeseed oil. UK rapeseed cultivation has grown dramatically in recent years, increasing from just 274,000 tonnes in 1980 to over 1,200,000 tonnes by 1995, making the UK the world's seventh biggest producer.

CASE STUDY
UK FISHERIES

Fishermen sort through the daily catch at Whitby, Yorkshire.

The fisheries surrounding the UK are an important natural resource. However, in recent years many of the species caught have been in decline due to over-fishing by modern commercial fishing fleets. Cod is under particular pressure, with North Sea stocks down to around 10 per cent of their 1970 level. Cod stocks are likely to decline further still, with up to 85 per cent of the young fish being killed before they have matured and bred. In 1999 quotas (limits) on cod fishing were reduced by 90 per cent. Fishing fleets failed to catch even this amount, suggesting that stocks are much lower than predicted. The decline in fish stocks is affecting coastal communities around the UK, threatening family businesses that, in some cases, stretch back hundreds of years. In Scotland, hard-hit fishermen are facing an added threat to their livelihoods from the local seal population, which has grown from around 30,000 in 1978 to an estimated 120,000 in mid-2001. Fishermen estimate that grey seals consume 200,000 tonnes of fish from Scottish waters each year – more than the fishermen are allowed to catch. Fishermen are now arguing for a cull of seals to help protect fish stocks, but conservationists oppose the plan and say it will damage the tourist industry, which generates around £36 million per year from seal-watching tours.

Farmers haggle over the price of cattle at a market in Sussex.

Livestock rearing is important in the UK with sheep and cattle (for meat and milk) being the most significant, but pigs and poultry (mainly chickens) are also important. In recent years, however, the livestock industry has been troubled by falling prices and diseases such as BSE (mad cow disease) in cattle, and an outbreak of foot and mouth in 2001 (see pages 32–33).

Forestry in the UK is controlled by the Forestry Commission. The Forestry Commission was established in 1919 to manage British forests at a time when only 4 per cent of the UK was forest land. The conservation of remaining forests and replanting of trees for commercial use increased the forest cover in the UK to around 10 per cent by the mid-1990s.

RIGHT: Commercial forestry is carefully managed in the UK and forest cover is slowly increasing.

FOREST MANAGEMENT

Early forest plantations were almost entirely coniferous softwoods planted in uniform rows to make them easy to manage and harvest when mature (after about 50 years). Today plantations are less uniform and include a variety of deciduous trees and traditional species such as Scots pine. This change has been in recognition of the role that forests play in conserving environments and wildlife, and of their value to visitors. Many forests now contain walks or cycle paths for visitors to use.

A CROWDED ISLAND

The UK is less than half the size of France, yet it has almost the same population. This makes the UK a very crowded island, with a population density in 1999 of 241 people per km², compared to 107 per km² in France and just 29 people per km² in the USA. However, people in the UK are not evenly distributed. The West Midlands of England, for example (the heart of the Industrial Revolution), has almost 3,000 people per km², compared to just 8 people per km² in the rugged Highland region of Scotland.

In urban areas population densities are much higher than in their rural surroundings. Oxfordshire and Norfolk are both rural counties with population densities below the national average and yet their principal towns of Oxford and Norwich have over 3,000 people per km². Among the most densely populated parts of the UK are the historic industrial cities such as Birmingham, Glasgow and Manchester. London is the most densely populated, with over 13,000 people per km² in districts such as Kensington and Chelsea.

POPULATION DENSITIES

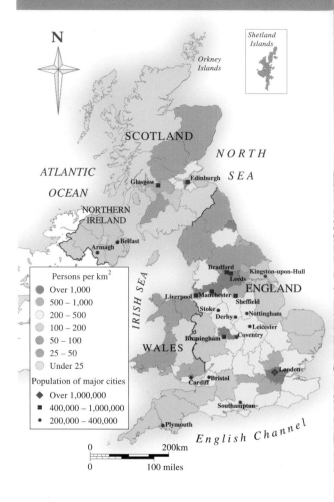

URBAN POPULATION
(% OF TOTAL, 1950–2015)

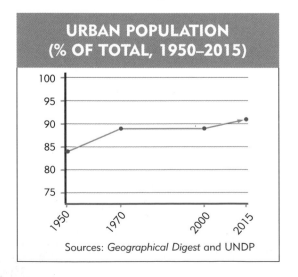

Sources: *Geographical Digest* and UNDP

POPULATION, 1950–2050

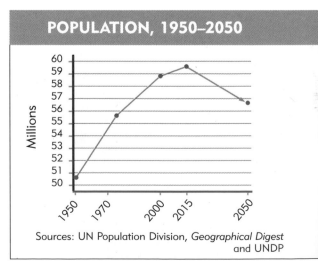

Sources: UN Population Division, *Geographical Digest* and UNDP

AN AGEING POPULATION

People in the UK are living longer than ever before because of dramatic improvements in healthcare and life expectancy during the last century. At the same time, young people are marrying later and having fewer children than before. This means that the total UK population is actually expected to decline by about 4 per cent between 2000 and 2050. However, the proportion of people over the age of 65 is expected to increase by 56 per cent over the same period, from about 16 per cent of the UK population in 2000 to around 19 per cent in 2015 and 25 per cent by 2050. This ageing of the UK population is starting to have significant impacts on the UK economy that are likely to become more severe in the coming decades. Healthcare systems are being stretched as they attempt to cope with more elderly patients needing care and employers in some areas are finding it increasingly difficult to find staff as fewer young people are entering the labour force. In the retail industry some firms are now employing people over the age of 65 on a part-time basis in order to fill this gap. Another dramatic impact on the UK economy is the increased demand for leisure and tourist activities from

People in the UK are living longer and enjoying greater leisure time in their retirement.

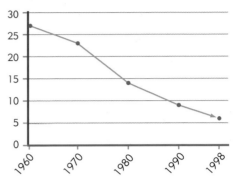

SOCIAL INDICATORS

UNDER-FIVE MORTALITY RATE (PER 1,000 LIVE BIRTHS)

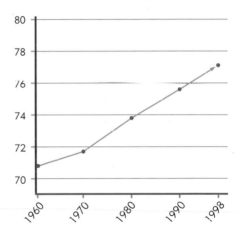

Sources: UNICEF, UNDP and World Bank

LIFE EXPECTANCY AT BIRTH

Source: WHO (World Health Organisation)

older generations, which, with better health, increased mobility and higher incomes, are better able to enjoy their later life. The government calls this spending 'the grey pound' and also recognises the importance of keeping older generations content because of the growing power of 'the grey vote'.

If population growth continues to decline, the consequences for the UK would be dramatic. For example, if the working population were to be maintained at 1995 levels then the UK would require over 6 million additional migrant workers by 2050.

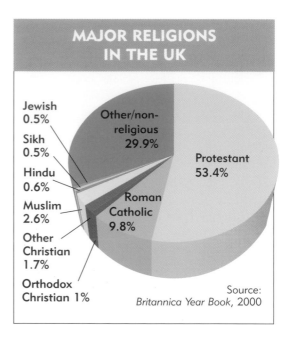

MAJOR RELIGIONS IN THE UK

Jewish 0.5%

Sikh 0.5%

Hindu 0.6%

Muslim 2.6%

Other Christian 1.7%

Orthodox Christian 1%

Other/non-religious 29.9%

Roman Catholic 9.8%

Protestant 53.4%

Source: *Britannica Year Book*, 2000

The UK today has many people of Asian origin. Birmingham is one city where they make up a large proportion of the population.

MIGRATION INTO THE UK

In the aftermath of the Second World War, the UK was desperately short of labour to help rebuild its tattered economy. Although the British themselves set about replenishing the population in a flurry of births that became known as 'the baby boom', there was still the immediate problem of labour shortages. This was met by government policies encouraging migrants to come to the UK from the former colonial territories of India and Pakistan, the Caribbean and British-controlled Africa. Hundreds of thousands of people arrived during the 1950s and 1960s, boosting the UK economy and settling, for the main part, in the UK's industrial cities.

By the early 1990s it was estimated that the UK had received about 4 million migrant residents accounting for around 7 per cent of the total population. As more migrants arrived in the UK they tended to settle close to those who arrived ahead of them, forming strong local communities that, in some cases, are almost entirely comprised of ethnic minority groups. Leicester, Bradford and Birmingham all have significant populations of Asian origin, whereas London has a particularly large number of people who were originally from the Caribbean and Africa. There has also been migration within the UK, with most movement being from Scotland, Wales and Northern Ireland into England.

A CULTURAL MELTING-POT

With the historical influence of the UK's colonial empire and the contemporary population mix since the 1950s, the UK has been described as a cultural melting-pot, where different beliefs, influences, tastes and ideas come together. This multi-cultural UK is strongest in the large cities, and centres such as Birmingham and Leicester are expected to be dominated by ethnic minority groups in the near future.

In some areas there have been conflicts caused by such ethnic differences. In the summer of 2001 several multi-ethnic communities in the north of England experienced violent street riots between white and Asian youths. Although such incidents are isolated and unusual they have raised concerns about the inequalities experienced by the UK's ethnic minorities. Ethnic minorities often experience higher levels of unemployment than their white neighbours and find work in lower-paid jobs. This in turn leads to lower standards of living, which may then further increase feelings of inequality.

The government is now looking at different ways to improve relations between such communities, with schools and young people playing a central role. Citizenship has been introduced into the national curriculum to encourage young people to accept and understand differences based not only on ethnic origin, but also as a result of religious beliefs or sexual orientation. It is hoped that such programmes will help everyone in the UK to understand the issues and enjoy the full benefits of a multi-cultural society.

RIGHT: Street carnivals, such as this one in Leeds, are a colourful element of the UK's multi-cultural society.
BELOW: Campaigners work to promote greater understanding between ethnic groups and reduce some of the tensions experienced in some communities.

SHARING CULTURES

The UK's multi-cultural society has influenced all areas of modern life: the most popular UK food is curry; African and Caribbean rhythms have had a strong impact on the UK music scene; Indian prints and fabrics have become popular in modern clothing design. This diversity has enriched life for most UK residents.

POPULAR CULTURE

Despite the wide variations within British culture there are certain elements that cut across such divides and have become known as 'popular culture'. Certain TV programmes, for example, appeal to a range of people from

Pavement cafés and restaurants are a sign of the UK's increasingly European culture.

very diverse backgrounds. Tastes in food, music and clothing are now shared by a broad cross-section of the British people. One aspect in particular has managed to cross social divides better than many others – sport. British people are among the world's most enthusiastic sports fans and follow their national and regional teams avidly. Football, rugby, cricket, athletics and tennis are among the most popular sports. Some of the UK's most successful sports people include Olympic winning athletes Lynford Christie and Denise Lewis, and the footballers John Barnes, Ian Wright and Sol Campbell. Many of these sports stars recognise their ability to cross social and cultural barriers and have become

Chinese people have developed their own communities. This is a Chinese supermarket in China Town, Manchester.

involved in youth sports schemes that encourage people from all backgrounds to get involved.

Pop stars, too, are a big part of modern popular culture and again they manage to bridge social and cultural barriers. Many of the most popular recent acts include individuals from a broad range of ethnic backgrounds. In addition to its own multi-cultural influences, the UK's popular culture is also increasingly influenced by people and cultures from other countries. This is because modern communications and travel are allowing British people to experience previously remote people and places. The USA has perhaps had the biggest influence, particularly in the world of entertainment. Hollywood films and American sitcoms such as *Friends* are especially popular. However, influences from around the world can be seen, such as the recent trend for elements of Japanese culture – water gardens, bonsai trees and *feng shui*.

Bollywood films (the Indian equivalent of Hollywood) can be seen at Star City cinema, on the outskirts of Birmingham.

CASE STUDY
COOL BRITANNIA

With so many different cultures influencing the UK many people are now questioning exactly what it means to be British in the twenty-first century. Certain elements have remained very strong, however, such as the position of the Royal family and the use of the Union Jack flag as a symbol of the UK. In fact there was outrage when British Airways removed the Union Jack from its aircraft tails and a modern version of the flag was quickly reinstated. Other aspects of British culture are perhaps less obvious, but in the 1990s a new sense of Britishness began to emerge in a wave of new fashion, design, music and

entertainment that became known as 'Cool Britannia'. This new image of the UK has embraced the diversity of the country, making it popular overseas as well as in the UK. Films such as *Four Weddings and a Funeral*, *East is East* and *Bridget Jones's Diary*, which deal with different aspects of British culture, have rejuvenated the British film industry. UK bands such as *Oasis* dominated the world music scene with many calling them 'The Beatles of the 1990s'. *Oasis* was just one of many UK bands that marked a revival in the British pop-music scene. Top models such as Naomi Campbell and Kate Moss, and designers such as Alexander McQueen have added to the image of Cool Britannia, which for many people in the UK has given them an identity they can be proud of.

THE UK ECONOMY

Keeping up with the latest technology is essential to the economy. These people are checking circuit boards for computerised equipment.

A MODERN GLOBAL ECONOMY

Once the world's greatest economy, the UK was ranked only the fifth largest in 1998 and in terms of wealth per person the UK did not even make the top twenty. However, the UK remains one of the most important economies in the world and London is still the world's most important financial centre. The UK economy has undergone drastic transformations since the 1950s and continues to do so as it modernises to compete in the global markets of the twenty-first century.

Modern businesses can locate almost anywhere in the world, conducting trade at the click of a button, and transferring money and information around the world in seconds. In such a fast-moving world the UK has to remain at the cutting edge of technology and enterprise if it is to maintain its position as a major world economy. The UK also faces the challenge of having to find alternatives to some of the traditional industries that have declined since the Second World War.

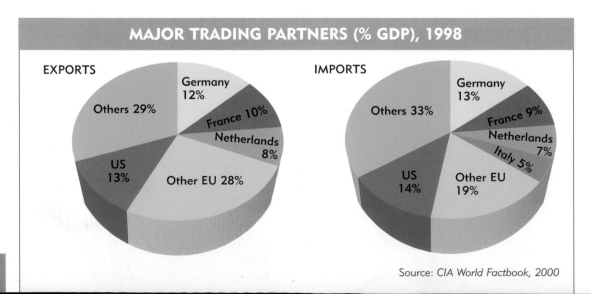

MAJOR TRADING PARTNERS (% GDP), 1998

EXPORTS
- Germany 12%
- France 10%
- Netherlands 8%
- Other EU 28%
- US 13%
- Others 29%

IMPORTS
- Germany 13%
- France 9%
- Netherlands 7%
- Italy 5%
- Other EU 19%
- US 14%
- Others 33%

Source: *CIA World Factbook, 2000*

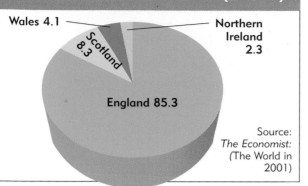

CONTRIBUTION TO THE NATIONAL ECONOMY (% GDP)

Wales 4.1

Scotland 8.3

Northern Ireland 2.3

England 85.3

Source: *The Economist:* (The World in 2001)

INDUSTRIES IN DECLINE

The heavy industries that formed the backbone of the UK economy since the Industrial Revolution have experienced rapid decline during the latter half of the twentieth century. Steel, shipbuilding, textiles and numerous other industries all but vanished from many parts of the UK, leaving land and buildings empty and derelict, and millions of skilled workers unemployed. In 1947, when the coal mines were nationalised (brought under government control), there were nearly 1,000 deep mines employing over 700,000 miners. By the time the government sold the industry to private companies (privatisation) in 1994 there were just 22 deep mines and 32 open-cast mines left, and employment had fallen to just 10,000 miners and support staff. Similar declines were commonplace across many traditional industries and where they still survive, such as the Potteries in Stoke-on-Trent, production has been mechanised and the workforce cut to its bare minimum.

Although the UK's industrial decline has affected the whole economy, its biggest impact has been on those communities that developed around specific industries such as textiles in Manchester, steel in Sheffield or shipbuilding in Glasgow. The impact on these communities was made worse because many businesses were dependent on the main industry and its workers. This is known as a knock-on or multiplier effect. Just as many businesses were established to support the arrival of the industries and their workers (a positive multiplier) they have equally been forced to decline as unemployment increased and people had less money to spend in the local economy (a negative multiplier). The result of this has, in some places, been the collapse of entire communities, and parts of old industrial cities are now experiencing the highest poverty rates in the UK. In many instances the decline of industry and local communities has led to a depopulation of the area as people have moved away to look for work elsewhere. In Wales for example, the town of Blaenau Ffestiniog suffered a 95 per cent decrease in population following the decline and eventual closure of its slate quarry.

Slate spoil heaps dominate the old slate-mining community of Blaenau Ffestiniog, Wales.

Telecommunications, such as mobile phones, have played a major part in the growth of the UK's growing service economy in recent years.

A SERVICE ECONOMY

Today the UK economy is overwhelmingly dominated by the service sector, which accounted for 73 per cent of Gross Domestic Product (GDP – the value of goods and services produced in the UK) in 1998. The service sector includes any businesses or industries that offer services to people or other businesses. Banking and insurance are two of the biggest and oldest industries in this sector, but it also includes services such as leisure, tourism and the travel industry. These newer services have grown rapidly in recent years as a result of people having more leisure time, and new technologies making travel cheaper and easier.

ECONOMIC STRUCTURE (% GDP)

Agriculture
1.7%

Industry
25.3%

Services 73%

Source: CIA World Factbook, 2000

THE CONSTRUCTION INDUSTRY

The construction industry reflects very strongly the overall state of the economy. When the economy is doing well both the government and private sector invest in new buildings or projects to extend or renovate existing property. However, if the economy starts to slow down then spending is often cut and the construction industry experiences a rapid decline as a result. Because of this, the construction industry makes use of a large number of casual employees who are employed as labourers according to the demand for workers at the time.

City redevelopment helps boost employment in the construction industry.

Other new technologies such as personal computers and mobile communications have also led to an increase in this sector, with growth in additional services such as training, support and the Internet. The speed of growth in these information technology (IT) services has been particularly rapid. Reports suggest that the demand for IT professionals in Europe outstripped supply by 600,000 in 2001 and that this figure could rise to 2 million by 2003. The UK government is encouraging businesses to take a leading role in meeting such gaps by training people and developing what has become known as e-commerce (business that takes advantage of the Internet).

INDUSTRY AND MANUFACTURING

Industry accounts for most of the UK's remaining GDP, with construction, manufacturing and energy production being among the most important components. Within manufacturing the greatest contribution to the GDP was made by food products, printing and publishing, machinery,

metal products and motor vehicle production. The UK is also a major producer of chemicals and is rapidly becoming a major centre for hi-tech electronics such as computer and telecommunications equipment. A large proportion of these new manufacturing industries are located in the south of England, while many of the old industries and areas of decline are in the north of the UK.

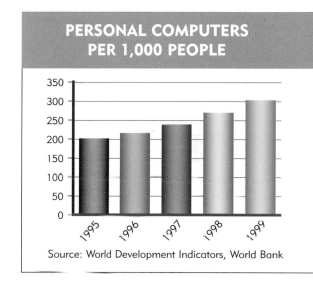

PERSONAL COMPUTERS PER 1,000 PEOPLE

Source: World Development Indicators, World Bank

CASE STUDY
THE UK MOTOR INDUSTRY

The Mini, a classic British car, is now made by the German company BMW.

Increased competition in the motor industry has forced UK manufacturers into a period of restructuring over the last 20 years. Many smaller manufacturers have been taken over by bigger companies, such as Jaguar and Land Rover, now owned by Ford. The Mini is now made by BMW. In 2001 Rover was the only significant UK manufacturer remaining. The closure of plants and loss of jobs as a result of restructuring has been made up for by new investment from Japanese manufacturers deciding to locate their European plants in the UK. Nissan, Honda and Toyota have all built modern hi-tech plants in the UK to take advantage of the skilled labour force and government grants available. As a result of this investment from overseas, UK vehicle production has grown almost every year since 1986 and continues to employ an estimated 400,000 workers.

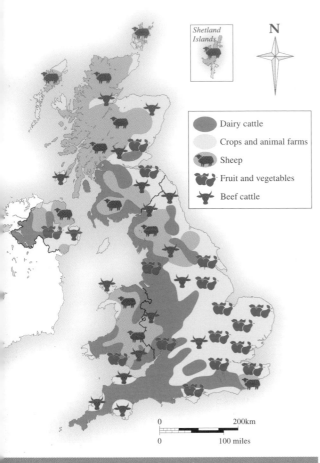

Dairy cattle

Crops and animal farms

Sheep

Fruit and vegetables

Beef cattle

Shetland Islands

N

0   200km

0   100 miles

AGRICULTURAL AREAS

Grazing cows are a typical UK countryside scene, but foot and mouth could have changed all that.

UK AGRICULTURE

Agriculture accounted for just 1.7 per cent of UK GDP in 1998 and employed only around 1 per cent of the labour force. In 2000, however, agriculture contributed to less than 1 per cent of the GDP for the first time in its history and the industry lost 20,000 workers – almost 6 per cent of the total agricultural workforce. Average farm incomes fell to a 25-year low of just £7,800, compared to their high of £25,000 in 1995. This crisis in British agriculture was partly caused by low agricultural prices and an increasingly global food industry in which the UK's traditionally small farms cannot compete. But it was also the result of two major livestock diseases – BSE (mad cow disease) and foot and mouth – which devastated not only the farms that were infected, but also confidence in UK farm produce. As the agricultural economy rebuilds itself, many feel it must use less intensive production methods and meet local food needs as part of a sustainable farming industry. This is starting to happen, with a 720 per cent increase in the area organically farmed during the period 1995–99, and an increase in local farmers' markets and 'veggie-box' schemes, where farmers deliver produce direct to people's homes. Many people feel that the role of farmers as countryside managers should also be better emphasised.

The government is encouraging farmers to use their land in alternative ways such as for forestry or leisure facilities including golf courses, camping sites and rural attractions. Farmers are also being encouraged to manage the environment through policies such as 'set-aside', where land is left fallow, and meadows and natural animal and plant life are allowed to flourish. 'Buffer zones' are another such policy, where strips of land close to rivers and streams are left uncultivated to reduce pollution from chemicals and to provide a habitat for aquatic life. Rural campaign groups such as the UK Countryside Agency believe that farmers could use their land for even more diverse purposes in the future, such as for wind farms to generate renewable energy.

Straw bales are a familiar rural scene during harvest time (July–August).

CASE STUDY
FOOT AND MOUTH

Large parts of the UK were placed under strict disease control during the foot and mouth outbreak in 2001.

In February 2001 a case of foot and mouth disease was identified in England for the first time in 34 years. In the last outbreak (1967–1968) 440,000 animals were slaughtered, hundreds of jobs were lost and the economic cost was over £1.5 billion. By comparison, in 2001 a total of 3.6 million animals had been slaughtered by the end of July with an average of three new cases still being reported each day. The highly contagious nature of foot and mouth meant that the impact of the disease was felt throughout the UK. Footpaths and rural tourist attractions were closed and much of the British countryside became a no-go area. The outbreak worsened just as the tourist industry was preparing for its traditional Easter start, ending all hopes of a swift end to the crisis. By June 2001 it was estimated that foot and mouth disease had cost the UK economy between £10–20 billion. At least half these losses were in the leisure and tourism industries. Even traditional tourist centres such as Stratford-upon-Avon, the birth town of Shakespeare, have been affected despite not having a single case of foot and mouth disease. This town normally receives around 3.8 million visitors a year (second only to London) generating £135 million for the local economy and employing 17 per cent of the local labour force. In 2001, however, visitor numbers were estimated to be down by 30 per cent due to foot and mouth, causing hundreds of job losses and threatening many of the smaller business such as bed and breakfast cottages and restaurants.

TOURISM

The UK tourist industry accounted for 3–4 per cent of GDP in 1999, earning a total of £63.9 billion and employing around 1,860,000 people (7 per cent of all employment) in the UK. The majority of UK tourism is made up of domestic tourists and day-trippers, but the number of overseas visitors increased by 47 per cent between 1991 and 1999 and is expected to increase further still. The main tourist attractions in the UK include historic cities and houses, museums, industrial

Stratford-upon-Avon is a popular tourist destination because of its links with the famous playwright, William Shakespeare.

heritage centres, national parks, and countryside and theme parks. The residences of the Royal family are also a major attraction to overseas visitors, many of whom are keen to see anything with a royal connection. Alton Towers theme park in Staffordshire is the most popular fee-charging attraction, with 2.65 million visitors in 1999, closely followed by

CASE STUDY
OVERSEAS VISITORS

OVERSEAS TOURISTS TO UK IN 2000

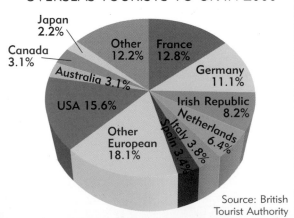

Japan 2.2%
Canada 3.1%
Other 12.2%
France 12.8%
Germany 11.1%
Australia 3.1%
USA 15.6%
Irish Republic 8.2%
Netherlands 6.4%
Italy 3.8%
Spain 3.4%
Other European 18.1%

Source: British Tourist Authority

In 2000 25.2 million tourists visited the UK, making it the sixth most popular destination in the world, accounting for 4 per cent of the world's total number of tourists. Most visitors came from the USA and northern Europe, in addition to significant numbers from Australia, Canada and Japan. They stayed an average of 8.3 days and spent a total of £12.5 billion. Overseas tourism grew rapidly during the 1990s but in 2001 it suffered a set-back as foot and mouth disease meant large parts of the countryside became difficult to move about in. In addition, a slow-down in the global economy led to a reduction in overseas bookings from countries such as the USA, which accounted for almost 16 per cent of visitors in 2000.

Madame Tussaud's waxworks museum and the Tower of London. Many tourist attractions are free, however, such as national parks or historic towns. This type of tourism is on the increase as places throughout the UK try to cash in on the growing number of visitors. Stratford-upon-Avon has long used its Shakespeare connection to encourage tourism, whilst Ironbridge, to the north-west of Birmingham, markets itself as the birthplace of the Industrial Revolution. Even small villages can benefit from their historical past: the Derbyshire village of Eyam advertises itself as the site of a plague outbreak in 1665 that claimed over 70 per cent of the village's population. There is also a very modern type of tourism that uses the UK's revived reputation as 'Cool Britannia'. This appeals to a large number of fashion-conscious and mainly young tourists who have made cities such as Brighton and Manchester popular as much for their 'cool' culture and image as anything else. This can be seen in the number of designer shops, street cafés and night-clubs that have sprung up in these cities.

DOMESTIC TOURISM

In 1999 there were around 146 million domestic tourists in the UK, making up 85 per cent of the total. They spent an amazing £16.25 billion, most of which paid for stays of only one or two nights. City breaks account for nearly 65 per cent of all visits. A further £32 billion was spent during the estimated 1.3 billion day-trips taken in the UK in 1999. These trips do not officially count as tourist visits because they do not involve a stay away for a night, but they are important because they account for over half of all

Dovedale, with its stepping stones, is one of the most popular parts of the Peak District.

earnings from tourism. National parks (see page 55) such as the Lake District or the Brecon Beacons in South Wales are popular destinations for day-trippers. The Peak District is one of the most popular attractions because of its location within easy reach of major cities such as Manchester, Sheffield and Nottingham. With an estimated 30 million day visitors each year the Peak District is beaten only by Mount Fuji in Japan as the most visited national park in the world.

Donkey rides on Blackpool beach are a popular treat for young visitors to the area.

THE 'OUT-OF-TOWN' ECONOMY

While the UK economy used to rely heavily on the physical location of resources, today it depends more on issues such as transport links and ease of customer access. This has given rise to an 'out-of-town' economy, where an increasing number of businesses, industries and services are choosing to locate away from town centres on large open areas of land, often close to major road networks. Business, science, industrial, retail and leisure parks are now a common sight around much of the UK, and in some places they can all be found within a single location. Many of the businesses that locate at these parks are large companies with many outlets or factories around the country or even internationally. Small and local businesses are unable to compete and, as their customers begin to use out-of-town facilities, many have been forced to close down. Even large companies have closed their town centre locations in favour of out-of-town sites, leaving shops, offices and factories abandoned and boarded up in many town centres.

The growing trend of large companies to move away from the town centres has taken its toll on some local economies. Since the late 1990s some town centres have undergone extensive renovations in an attempt to revitalise the local economy. Transport and parking facilities have been improved, purpose-built shopping malls developed and offices modernised or rebuilt to take advantage of the latest technology. Even within these redevelopments, however, it is often large companies that benefit while local independent businesses are increasingly vulnerable.

RISING EMPLOYMENT LEVELS

Despite changes and unemployment black-spots, the overall trend in the UK has been one of increasing employment. In 2001 unemployment fell to below 5 per cent. The number of people claiming unemployment benefit fell below 1 million for the first time since 1975, having peaked at over 3 million in 1986. This turn-around in employment levels is considered by many to be a sign that the UK has overcome the economic declines of the past and is now emerging as a modern economy better able to compete in the new global marketplace.

EMPLOYMENT

Changes in the economy are reflected in UK employment figures. Employment in heavy industry and manufacturing has declined significantly, while the proportion of people working in the service sector has increased to 77 per cent. Agriculture employs only around 1 per cent of the working population – even the UK's energy sector has more employees.

Out-of-town retail parks such as this one, at junction 9 of the M6 motorway, take advantage of new infrastructure.

Shopping malls, with many different shops under the same roof are replacing traditional high street shops.

The location of employment has also changed, with the south of England having the highest employment levels, while many old industrial areas and inner cities have high unemployment. In parts of Wales nearly half of the people of working age are unemployed, while in Liverpool 65 per cent of 16–24 year olds are unemployed. The workforce is also changing. The proportion of women in employment has grown by almost 10 per cent since 1965, although 44 per cent of these jobs are part-time compared to just 9 per cent for men. More people are also choosing to work for themselves. The UK had an estimated 3.2 million people in self-employment in 2001 accounting for over 11 per cent of all employment. Technology such as faxes, e-mail and the Internet also led to an estimated 2 million people working from home by mid-

A job centre in Blaenau, Wales. This area had the highest unemployment levels in the UK in 2001.

2001. This trend is likely to continue as even large businesses are beginning to allow employees to use such technology to work from home while staying in contact with the office and their colleagues. These new work patterns also benefit the environment as they involve less travel and a more efficient use of space.

FEMALE LABOUR FORCE (% OF TOTAL)

Source: ILO (International Labour Organisation)

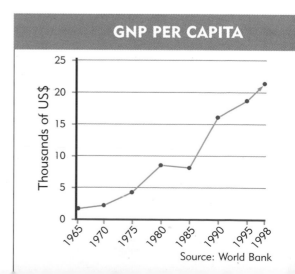

GNP PER CAPITA

Source: World Bank

TRANSPORT AND INFRASTRUCTURE

Traffic jams on the M25 motorway are a common sight, especially in the evening rush hour.

It is perhaps not surprising that in a country with a strong motoring history the car is something of a star in the UK, but the extent to which the car dominates transport is a cause for concern. Cars (and other motor vehicles) are among the biggest contributors to the UK's greenhouse gas emissions and road accidents are the leading cause of death in young people under 15 years old. Despite such problems, British people are using cars more than ever before and the number of cars on the road is increasing.

In 1997 there were an estimated 24.2 million vehicles on the UK's roads, 90 per cent of which were private cars. This represented a 65 per cent increase in the number of vehicles since 1980. As patterns of living and working continue to change, car use is expected to increase by as much as 50 per cent by 2025. With so many vehicles the UK's road network has expanded dramatically over the years and now covers a total distance of 371,603km – only 12,000km short of the distance between the Earth and the Moon. However, traffic congestion remains a major problem in many parts of the UK and is estimated to cost the economy around £15 billion each year in lost time and production. Congestion has been made worse by people using cars for even the shortest of trips.

CAR DEPENDENCY

Nearly half of all car journeys in the UK are less than 3km – a distance that could easily be covered by using public transport, cycling or walking. The car is such a part of British life that there are over 42 cars for every 100 people. This is less than in France or Germany, but the growth in UK car ownership has been especially high at 54 per cent between 1980 and 1996, compared to 35 per cent in Germany and just 23 per cent in France.

Train use is increasing again, but delays and technical problems are still common on many routes.

UK RAILWAYS

The railway network is the most popular alternative to the car for long-distance travel, and connects most major towns and cities in the UK. Developed initially for trade and industry, the railway became a popular mode of public transport from the 1830s and was significant in the early development of tourism in the UK. Trains such as the 'Southern Belle', which ran between London and Brighton until 1933 increased the popularity of tourism by train. The route is still one of the most popular today. Just as the railways replaced the canal network as the main form of transporting cargo, roads have since replaced the railways for all but the bulkiest of goods and many railway lines have closed as a result. Some are maintained as tourist attractions, with restored steam engines providing experiences of a time gone by. Others have been converted into cycle tracks, such as in the Manifold Valley in Derbyshire.

The UK's main railway network was privatised in 1994 and was operated by a number of companies in different parts of the country. There were numerous problems as these operators and the owner of the tracks and signals (Railtrack) attempted to modernise the network to encourage greater use of trains. The biggest problems were caused by mechanical faults and delays to services, but a series of major accidents also raised concern about the safety of the railways. In October 2001 Railtrack collapsed and the railway network returned to government control.

MAIN TRANSPORT NETWORKS

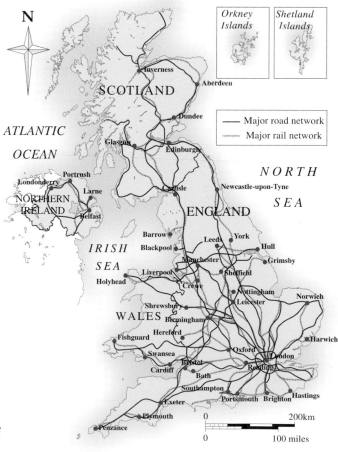

INTEGRATED TRANSPORT SYSTEMS

The key challenge for modern transport policy is to encourage what the government calls 'integrated transport systems'. These are transport systems that reduce problems of congestion and pollution associated with greater road use, but at the same time allow people and goods to move around more efficiently and flexibly. The key to such systems is getting different modes of transport to work together. This already occurs to some extent in terms of moving freight. Packing freight into standardised containers (containerisation) means that the same container can be moved more easily from trains to lorries and ships. Transport 'hubs' provide meeting places for the different forms of transport to transfer the containers. These transport hubs are located in key centres such as ports and industrial cities.

Providing such a system for passenger transport is less straightforward. People are widely distributed and their travel needs are extremely varied, but regular services providing connections between different

Manchester's Metrolink is part of one of the most successful integrated transport systems in the UK so far.

forms of transport have been successful in many cities. In Belfast for example, the Europa Bus Centre and Great Victoria Street Railway Station provide an efficient connection between the bus and rail systems. One of the most successful integrated transport systems is the Greater Manchester Metrolink, which provides regular city centre trams that connect with local and regional bus services. The Metrolink carries 14 million passengers a year and was extended in 2000 to help further reduce the number of cars coming into the city. Similar systems exist or are being constructed in Birmingham, Sheffield, Nottingham and several other cities.

RURAL TRANSPORT

Providing integrated transport for people living in rural areas is more problematic. Low population densities in these areas mean that providing rural services is less profitable for transport companies. As a result, many rural bus services have been reduced to only a few times a week whilst others have been lost altogether. Dial-a-bus schemes (where people can telephone in advance to order a bus service) have been introduced in some areas in an attempt to bring services and demand together, but in rural areas most people tend to use their car for transport. One solution would be to make cars less environmentally harmful. Cleaner fuels such as liquid petroleum gas (LPG) are already on the market, as are specially designed cars that combine petrol and electric engines. The main hope for the future, however, is in hydrogen-powered cars using special fuel cells that release only water vapour but provide the same power as current petrol engines. Buses using this system are already in use in Canada and it is hoped that the first cars using hydrogen fuel cells will be available in the UK in 2005.

Buses are the main form of transport for the 30 per cent of British people who do not have a car.

CASE STUDY
NATIONAL CYCLE NETWORK

The National Cycle Network is intended to contribute to a new era of sustainable travel.

Cycle use in the UK declined by 36 per cent between 1986 and 1998, despite the fact that there are more bicycles in the UK than cars. Many people are concerned about riding bicycles along increasingly polluted and congested roads. The National Cycle Network hopes to reverse this trend by establishing a nationwide network of cycle paths and cycle-friendly roads to make cycling safer. The first 9,600km of the network were opened in the summer of 2000 and a further 6,400km are planned for completion by 2005. The network is intended to benefit commuters, shoppers, children going to school and tourists who want to enjoy an alternative and healthy way of visiting different parts of the UK. Sign-posted routes, and links with railway stations and major population centres will put about 30 million people within easy reach of the network when it is complete.

Regular exercise is a good way of keeping fit and healthy.

UNHEALTHY TRENDS

Although people in the UK are living longer than ever before, they are not necessarily healthier. In fact the health of the nation shows some worrying trends, such as growing rates of obesity and falling levels of exercise. Such trends are linked to changing lifestyles. Watching television, for example, is the UK's favourite leisure activity, especially among younger generations. The average amount of time spent watching television doubled between 1965 and 1995 to 26 hours a week.

People are consuming more high fat and high sugar foods such as burgers, pizzas, crisps and sweets than in previous decades. These foods are high in calories and have contributed to an estimated 51 per cent of adults in the UK being overweight. The proportion of people who are severely overweight (obese) has doubled since 1990. Such problems are not limited to adults. Obesity amongst young people and even toddlers in the UK has increased dramatically in recent years. Recent reports suggest that nearly 25 per cent of children under four years old are overweight and almost 10 per cent are obese. This recently named 'Teletubby generation' could have a serious impact on future UK healthcare spending.

DANGERS OF A POOR DIET

The 'Teletubby generation' could place a serious strain on the health service in the future, adding to the estimated £2.6 billion a year that obesity currently costs the UK economy and health system. There are already signs that diabetes is associated with obesity. Poor diet is increasing amongst teenagers, and other diet-related illnesses such as heart disease and strokes are among the UK's biggest causes of death.

A HEALTH CRISIS

When the National Health Service (NHS) was set up in 1948 it was considered the envy of the world, providing free medical care to everyone in the UK. In the 1990s, however, the NHS has come under increasing criticism as rural and small-town hospitals have closed, and patients have had to wait longer to be treated. The growing elderly population and the decline in the health of the population as a whole is putting the NHS under extreme pressure. In mid-2001 there were over 1 million people waiting for treatment. The ageing population is a particular strain, as shown by the increase in demand for replacement joints such as hips and knees to improve life for elderly people whose natural joints have worn out. Some patients are forced to wait for over a year just to get on to a waiting list for an operation, a fact that annoys many elderly patients in particular, having paid into the NHS (through taxes) for their whole working lives.

The government is investing more money in hospitals and in the training of new health staff, but an increasing number of people are turning to private medical care instead. Such services are not an option for the poorest and most vulnerable in society, however, and many people have little choice but to wait for treatment on the NHS.

The government is investing in healthcare to rebuild confidence in the NHS.

Some experts suggest that not eating a balanced diet that includes fresh fruit and vegetables and other important foods can contribute to poor general health.

The time that people wait for care varies dramatically across the UK. In Cardiff, Wales, 45 per cent of people have to wait over six months for an operation, compared to just 0.5 per cent of those living in Dorset, southern England. The most unhealthy regions of the UK are those areas where poverty is also greatest. This means that those areas with the greatest need for health services are the least able to afford them. Glasgow is one of the worst-affected cities. People living in the poorest areas of Glasgow are three-and-a-half times more likely to die before the age of 65 than those living in Cambridgeshire or Surrey, which are wealthy counties.

POVERTY AND PLENTY

People living in poverty in the UK normally have lower education standards and poorer housing conditions than people living in wealthier communities. Poverty is also closely linked to unemployment and so tends to be highest in former industrial and manufacturing centres where employment has been declining. The division between richer and poorer areas in the UK is sometimes known as the north-south divide, the north being generally poorer than the south. In the north-west of England for example, the average weekly income per person in 1998 was £145, compared with £207 in south-eastern England. Wales and Scotland were in between these levels at £151 and £158 per week respectively, whilst Northern Ireland had the lowest weekly income at just £126 per person. Such figures are only indicators, however, and do not reveal the differing levels of wealth within these regions. Elderly people are among the poorest members of communities throughout the UK. Nearly a fifth of single pensioners were living in poverty in 1999. The poorest group are single parents, with around 40 per cent living in extreme poverty in 1999.

BELOW: In major cities local authorities often house people in tower blocks, but these sometimes lead to greater exclusion from the wider community.

TEENAGE PREGNANCY

The UK has seen a growth in the number of teenage pregnancies and currently has the highest rate in Europe. Every year about 90,000 teenagers in England become pregnant (resulting in 56,000 births), including nearly 8,000 girls under 16 and 2,200 girls aged 14 or younger. This is a worrying trend because many of these girls may not complete their education and learn the skills needed to find employment.

Teenage pregnancy is one of the causes behind the growth in single parents in the UK.

EDUCATION, EDUCATION, EDUCATION

Better education is considered by many to be the main way to reduce poverty and improve the state of society in the UK. Unemployed people, for example, are twice as likely to have low literacy skills as those in paid employment, suggesting that better education would help them find employment and therefore reduce their poverty. Schooling is compulsory in the UK until the age of 16, but the quality of education received varies dramatically. In some areas school absenteeism is a major problem. The worst-performing schools tend to be located in the poorest areas, meaning that children in these areas are less likely to attain enough qualifications for a well-paid job. The challenge is to break this poverty cycle and provide young people in disadvantaged areas with opportunities to improve their education and skills. The UK government has made this its major task for the future. Prime Minister Tony Blair's famous slogan of 'education, education, education' was used repeatedly in the build-up to his party's election victory in June 2001. Schools are being equipped with computers to teach new skills for the twenty-first century and schools in disadvantaged areas are being given specialist teachers to help motivate individual pupils and improve their performance.

One of the government's main aims is to improve the quality of education in the UK.

INCOME INEQUALITY

The gap between the poorest and the richest people in the UK has widened since the 1980s. This led to higher income inequality in the UK in the late 1990s than at any time since the fifteenth century. In 1979 the richest 10 per cent (decile) of the population enjoyed 20 per cent of the UK's total income whilst the poorest decile shared just 4.1 per cent. By 1996 the share in total income had risen to 28 per cent for the richest decile, but fallen to just 2 per cent for the poorest. This growing inequality is even more striking if real incomes are considered. Weekly incomes for the poorest decile fell by 12 per cent between 1979 and 1996 whilst those of the wealthiest decile increased by 68 per cent, providing evidence that 'the rich get richer whilst the poor get poorer'.

Grafitti covers a wall in Brighton, East Sussex.

THE BIG ISSUE

In 1991 a magazine called *The Big Issue* was launched as a self-help programme for homeless people to earn money. *The Big Issue* now sells over 250,000 copies and is read by a million people each week. Apart from the financial rewards, the Big Issue Foundation assists people in rebuilding their lives with the help of training or counselling to allow them to play an active role in society again.

The Big Issue has proven a great success in helping the most vulnerable homeless people.

SOCIAL EXCLUSION

Poor health, low education standards, poverty, family break-ups and unemployment are often found in the same location. They can combine to cause so many social problems that communities and individuals become excluded from wider society because of their circumstances. Many people living in deprived inner cities such as Glasgow and Liverpool face 'social exclusion'. Young people find it particularly difficult to cope with such situations. In the worst cases, exclusion can lead to problems of drug and alcohol abuse or leave people homeless and living rough on the streets.

In 1997 an estimated 131,410 households were classified as homeless in the UK, mainly due to family break-downs or failure to keep up rent payments. Most of these people are taken into the care of local authorities, but this is not always the case, and some end up living rough and may be seen begging for money on the streets of major cities.

CRIME AND PREVENTION

Social exclusion, poverty and unemployment have often been blamed for an increase in crime in the UK in recent decades. Theft, burglaries and car crime have all increased since the 1970s, as have attacks on people related to robberies. Some of the worst-affected areas are also those facing the greatest levels of poverty and unemployment.

An increase in police officers and the introduction of closed circuit television (CCTV) cameras is starting to reduce crime and in 2001 the overall crime rate was 2.5 per cent lower than in 2000. Car theft and burglaries fell furthest by 7.2 and 7.8 per cent respectively, but robbery increased by 12.9 per cent, especially that of mobile phones, which accounted for almost 40 per cent of robberies in some urban areas. Despite some improvements, there were still a total of 5.2 million crimes reported in the UK between 2000 and 2001, of which only 24 per cent were solved by the police.

CASE STUDY
BIG BROTHER

A television series called *Big Brother* was one of the most popular shows in 2000 and 2001. The series was based on a house in which the occupants' daily life was followed by numerous video cameras around the clock and then broadcast on the Internet and nightly TV shows. The idea of cameras following people constantly is becoming a reality in the UK. The UK has the largest network of CCTV cameras in the world. The cameras are concentrated in cities (150,000 in London alone), but most urban areas and small towns now have some form of CCTV. The cameras are installed to make the streets safer and reduce levels of theft and vandalism. Each day, an average city-dweller is filmed at least eight (and up to 300) times.

CCTV cameras in Stoke-on-Trent, West Midlands, capture the movements of shoppers on a busy Saturday afternoon.

This has led some people to see CCTV systems as an intrusion on privacy. The latest systems are even capable of matching people's faces against police records, using sophisticated computers to identify known criminals. The introduction of such a system in the London borough of Newham saw crime fall by 34 per cent in six months, proving to many that CCTV is extremely valuable. With more cameras being installed every year, the idea of a 'Big Brother' watching people's every move may soon become very real.

THE ENVIRONMENT

Beautiful environments such as the Yorkshire Dales are protected so that everyone can enjoy them.

GROWING CONCERN

Concern for the environment in the UK is reaching new heights. More and more people are becoming members of environmental groups such as Greenpeace or Friends of the Earth. This concern is also evident on the streets, where there are more environmentally friendly products for sale, higher rates of recycling and increasing demand for organic food.

Such attitudes are mainly due to people being better informed about the condition of the environment, but also because people have greater leisure time to enjoy and care for their surroundings. Some people, however, have suggested that concern for the environment is a luxury for the better-off in society and that poorer communities and individuals (who often suffer the worst environments) do not have time to share in such luxuries.

The UK government is taking environmental issues more seriously than ever before and implementing various new policies that force or encourage people to help protect the environment. A new vehicle tax system, for example, charges higher taxes to those with bigger, more polluting vehicles, whilst drivers who convert to using cleaner technologies such as liquid petroleum gas (LPG) instead of petrol are supported by government grants. Both of these policies are part of the government's commitment to reduce emissions of carbon dioxide (CO_2) – one of the main greenhouse gases responsible for global warming.

Electric buses, such as this one covering a city centre route in Birkenhead, near Liverpool, are one way to reduce dependence on carbon.

REDUCING GREENHOUSE GASES

Much of the UK economy relies on technologies that produce large quantities of CO_2. Almost 70 per cent of the UK's energy comes from fossil fuels, which emit vast quantities of CO_2 when they are burnt. The UK's dependence on motor vehicles also adds to this burden. In 2001 motor vehicle emissions were the fastest-growing contributor to greenhouse gases. With car use predicted to increase by 17 per cent by 2010 the trend is set to continue. Similar patterns can also be seen in most industrial nations of the world and as the economies of developing nations grow, they, too, are emitting an increasing amount of CO_2. This resulted in all of the world's leaders coming together in Kyoto in Japan in 1997 to agree action that would reduce pressure on the global environment in the coming years. The UK agreed to reduce its greenhouse gas emissions to 12.5 per cent below their 1990 levels by 2010, focusing on renewable energy as the best way of achieving this target.

RENEWABLE ENERGY

In 2000 renewable energy accounted for just 2.8 per cent of the UK's electricity generation, but this was twice as much as in 1993 and the renewable energy sector grew by 8 per cent in 2000 alone. Renewable energy is set to grow very rapidly in the next decade or so, with the government setting targets for it to meet 5 per cent of all needs by 2003 and 10 per cent by 2010. At present the vast majority of renewable energy (82.3 per cent) comes from biofuels such as landfill gas, refuse combustion and industrial wood burning. Hydroelectricity (HEP) provides 14 per cent whilst wind power, the only other major source, provided just 2.7 per cent of renewable energy in 2000.

CO₂ EMISSIONS BY SOURCE, 1970–2000

(bar chart, vertical axis: Millions of tonnes, 0–70; horizontal axis years 1970, 1980, 1990, 2000)

KEY:
Power Generation
Industry
Domestic
Transport
Other

Source: *DTI UK Energy In Brief*, 2001

Solar panels are used to power some parking meters, such as this one in Nottingham.

In 2001 the UK had around 60 wind farms. These wind farms generated about 400 megawatts (MW) of power in total, enough for 300,000 homes. Studies have shown that the UK has the world's highest potential wind power resource – Scotland alone has more than the whole of Europe. Despite this seemingly obvious source of renewable and emission-free energy, wind power has yet to really take off in the UK. One of the problems is that while people may agree with the idea of wind power, they object to turbines being located near their homes – an attitude that has become known as the 'Not In My Back Yard' (NIMBY) syndrome. Complaints about noise are the most common, but turbines are also blamed for spoiling scenic views, affecting radio and television signals, and posing a threat to birds. Some communities have learnt to live with wind turbines, however, such as the people of Swaffham in Norfolk. Their 98m-high wind turbine has become a local landmark. The turbine attracts thousands of tourists who come to learn about wind power and other sustainable technologies.

One solution to complaints about wind turbines is to locate them offshore – a technique already used in Denmark. In 2001 the UK had just two offshore turbines, and a

Tourists pay to climb the Ecotricity wind turbine in Swaffham, Norfolk, the only one in the UK with a viewing platform.

further 18 were scheduled for construction. When finished, these turbines will provide a total of 1,600 MW of power. With more offshore farms expected, wind energy could become a major source of energy for the UK in the coming years.

WASTE AND RECYCLING

In 1999–2000 81 per cent of the UK's municipal waste was disposed of in landfill sites and a further 8 per cent was incinerated. This means that only 11 per cent of the UK's municipal waste was recycled or composted, compared with over 25 per cent in Denmark and the USA, and more than 40 per cent in Switzerland. Such low levels of recycling may have a major impact on the UK's environment.

Landfill sites can contain hazardous materials that take hundreds or even thousands of years to break down. As these materials break down, they release chemicals that mix with water passing through the landfill to form leachate. Leachate can pass into local water supplies, contaminating the environment and making its way into drinking-water supplies. Landfills also generate methane gas as waste decomposes, or breaks down.

WIND ENERGY SITES IN THE UK

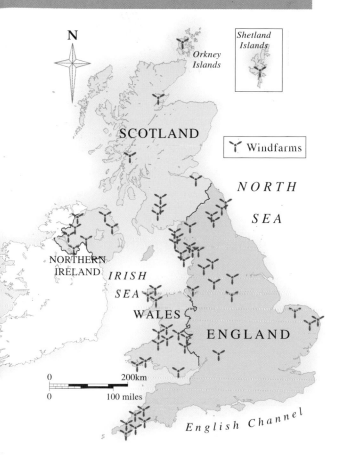

N

Shetland Islands

Orkney Islands

SCOTLAND

Y Windfarms

NORTH SEA

NORTHERN IRELAND *IRISH SEA*

WALES

ENGLAND

0   200km
0   100 miles

English Channel

Methane is a major greenhouse gas and is also highly explosive if not carefully managed. Modern landfills are lined to prevent leachate escaping and have special vents to release methane, but the real solution is to landfill less waste, especially since the UK is running out of landfill space. In recent years incineration has become a more favoured option to landfill because burning waste reduces its bulk by about 90 per cent. However, concern about the safety of emissions from incinerators has led to a backlash from environmentalists and concerned residents. The concern surrounds wastes containing toxic organic micro pollutants (TOMPs) which, unless burnt at over 1,200°C, release toxins into the environment. Some of these toxins have been linked to cancer and birth defects in humans, and deformities and premature deaths in wildlife (especially birds). The latest incinerators are highly efficient and their designers claim to have eradicated these emissions. However, fears concerning the health effects of incinerators mean they will probably meet continued resistance from UK residents.

Most of the UK's municipal waste is disposed of in landfill sites like this one at Rainham, Essex.

The Centre for Alternative Technology in Machynlleth, Wales was one of the first to start educating people about better environmental management.

THE THREE RS

The debate over whether to landfill or incinerate waste in the UK has detracted from the real issue concerning waste, the so-called 'three Rs' – Reduce, Re-use and Recycle. There is a need for the UK to reduce the amount of waste it produces in the first place, to re-use materials and objects wherever possible, and then, if they have no further use, to recycle them instead of disposing of them. Items such as envelopes, glass jars and paper can easily be re-used around the household. Some companies offer specialist re-use facilities such as 'Ink Again', which re-uses old ink cartridges from printers, refilling them to provide cheaper replacements than original parts. Recycling is already practised by most households in the UK, although it is often limited to glass bottles and newspaper, which are collected from the kerbside or taken to special recycling collection points. Other waste products such as cardboard, plastics, metals and old clothing can be recycled into new products or used as the raw material for other objects. Plastic soda bottles marked with the letters PET, for example, are the raw material used to make fleece jackets, whilst a single plastic vending machine cup can be made into a pencil by a UK company called Remarkable Pencils. Composting is another form of recycling that could be greatly improved in the UK. About 40 per cent of the average household's waste is biodegradable, meaning it can be broken down by natural organisms. If composted instead of being thrown away, biodegradable waste provides a valuable fertiliser for the garden and reduces the UK's waste burden.

Perhaps the most difficult of the three Rs to achieve is reducing the level of waste produced in the first instance. The UK is a consumer nation where people want the latest fashions, newest designs and most up-to-date technology, even if they have existing goods that are still useable. In some cases, however, replacing goods can be beneficial for the environment. A modern washing machine, for example, uses about a third of the electricity and half as much water as a machine made in the 1970s.

This energy-efficient office building in Wales is built from recyclable materials and uses renewable solar power to generate electricity.

CASE STUDY
GLASS RECYCLING

Glass is a particularly good material for recycling as it can be used to make up to 90 per cent of new glass, saving both energy and resources. Compared to manufacturing glass with raw materials, recycling glass reduces air pollution by 20 per cent, mining wastes by 80 per cent and water consumption by 50 per cent. Over 6 billion glass containers are used in the UK each year, but only 22 per cent of them are currently recycled, compared to the European average of 50 per cent. With over 22,000 bottle banks around the UK there is little excuse for people not to recycle glass.

There are, however, some problems concerning glass recycling. Around 60 per cent of the glass recycled in the UK is coloured, whereas 70 per cent of manufactured glass is clear, so there is a mismatch between supply and demand. One solution already in use in the USA is to colour bottles using a thin film that disappears when the glass is melted down, instead of colouring the glass itself. This 'ColorCoat' technology also removes the need to sort glass into different colours at bottle banks.

The UK has very poor rates of recycling compared with its European neighbours.

Park-and-ride schemes have been introduced by numerous authorities in the UK to reduce urban traffic pollution.

A SUSTAINABLE FUTURE?

Sustainable development is defined as meeting the needs of the present population without harming the ability of future generations to meet their needs. The UK government is committed to meeting these objectives and it attempts to ensure that its policies work towards such goals. The government introduced a landfill tax to deter people from dumping waste and to encourage them to think about alternative ways to manage it. Education and awareness about sustainable development are also important. The government has set up a national advertising campaign and website called 'Doing Your Bit' as well as introducing sustainable development into the school curriculum. Local authorities are also working towards a more sustainable future by introducing policies as part of Local Agenda 21, a guideline for working towards internationally agreed goals to achieve sustainable development. Park-and-ride schemes, bus and cycle lanes, recycling collections, sustainable housing programmes, and the protection and regeneration of environments are all examples of policies introduced to meet Local Agenda 21.

PROTECTED AREAS

Whilst local authorities can protect and regenerate local environments, the UK has certain environments that are considered of national or even international importance. These areas are protected as national parks or as specially designated Areas of Outstanding Natural Beauty (AONB) or Sites of Special Scientific Interest (SSSI). In Scotland protected areas are referred to as National Scenic Areas.

In 1951 the Peak District was the first national park to be established in the UK: it covers an area of 1,438km^2 between the cities of Manchester and Sheffield. Since then a further ten national parks have been established, and two more national parks in England and three in Scotland were proposed in 2001.

SSSIs can be relatively small areas, such as ponds or meadows that are habitats for endangered species or have special geographical interest. SSSIs can be located within national parks as they have special regulations regarding their protection. AONB are areas considered worthy of protection for their natural scenery, but they do not normally have the same level of protection

as national parks. The South Downs in Sussex is listed as an AONB but will soon become one of the UK's new national parks.

Whilst protected areas are intended to be enjoyed by tourists, the enormous increase in tourism is placing increasing strain on these sites. Certain locations, such as Dovedale in the Peak District are especially popular and are known as 'honeypot attractions', because of the way visitors flock to them as bees would around a honeypot. Honeypot attractions sometimes suffer from excessive visitor numbers, which in turn can lead to road congestion, localised air pollution, footpath erosion and disruption to local communities. There is a delicate balance between encouraging visitors and protecting the environments they come to enjoy. With tourism and car use both increasing, the challenge is likely to become even greater in the future.

Heath and moorlands are among the UK's threatened environments that are protected by national parks.

UK NATIONAL PARKS

THE PEAK DISTRICT	1,438km^2
LAKE DISTRICT	2,292km^2
SNOWDONIA (ERYRI)	2,142km^2
DARTMOOR	954km^2
PEMBROKESHIRE COAST	620km^2
NORTH YORK MOORS	1,432km^2
YORKSHIRE DALES	1,769km^2
EXMOOR	693km^2
NORTHUMBERLAND	1,049km^2
BRECON BEACONS	1,351km^2
THE BROADS	303km^2

Source: The Association of National Park Authorities

This statue shows Birmingham's transition from its industrial past into the modern era. The leading figure represents Maurice Wilkins, a Birmingham-trained scientist who won the Nobel Prize for his work on DNA.

CONTINUED REFORMS

The UK will undergo continued reforms in the early part of the twenty-first century as it completes the modernisation of its economy. Industry will continue to decline except for the specialised manufacture of hi-tech products and components. In contrast, the service sector will continue to expand, particularly in the leisure industry. Agriculture in the UK will become even less significant following the succession of food scares and diseases that have plagued the sector in recent years. The exception to this pattern will be organic farming, which is expected to expand to meet the annual doubling in demand for organic produce, 70 per cent of which is currently imported rather than produced locally. Continued reforms will also be seen in transport and energy, both of which will have to adopt more sustainable approaches if the UK is to meet its various environmental commitments.

In terms of social policy, the main challenges facing the UK are to revive the NHS, and to ensure that everyone in the UK has equal opportunities for high-quality education and the chance to learn the skills necessary for finding employment. This will require special effort in the more deprived areas of the UK that have suffered more than most as industries have closed, scaled down or relocated. The UK will become more ethnically diverse in the future, especially if immigration is encouraged to supply the shortfall of labour expected as a result of an ageing population. Such patterns are already evident, with nurses being recruited from the Philippines in 2000–2001 to fill staff shortages in the NHS. Whilst such diversity should be beneficial to the UK, recent experiences suggest that ethnic differences can be exaggerated into local conflicts, often hiding wider problems such as unemployment, poverty or crime. In the summer of 2001 ethnic conflicts became violent and resulted in damage to both people and property in several UK cities.

INTO EUROPE?

The biggest change to affect the UK in the coming years will be its decision on whether or not to adopt the Euro and extend its links with Europe to monetary union. Opinion is divided at present as to the benefits of the UK joining the so-called 'Euro-zone'. Those who support the Euro claim it would simplify and encourage trade, benefiting UK companies. Critics believe that the UK would become too reliant on Europe, and lose its international reputation and independence. For the British public, the biggest concern seems to be the loss of the British pound as a currency. In fact feelings are so strong that in the 2001 General Election several political parties stood for election purely on the basis of saving the

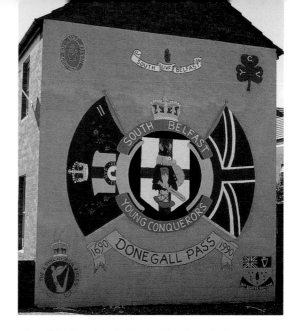

A political wall painting in Northern Ireland. The fragile negotiations between opposing groups in Northern Ireland will hopefully bring lasting peace.

pound. The final decision will be down to the UK people themselves, as the government has promised a referendum allowing them to vote whether or not to join the Euro-zone. The outcome will play a major role in determining the future of the UK. However, since it is less than 100 years since the British ruled over nearly half the world's population and barely 50 years since the end of the last war, the UK is used to change.

The London Eye provides a spectacular platform from which to view the changing landscape of London as it leads the UK into the twenty-first century.

GLOSSARY

Arable farming A farming system that focuses on growing plant crops, normally grains such as wheat, maize and barley, among others.

Basalt A black or dark grey rock formed as a result of cooled molten magma from volcanic activity. Basalt can cool and solidify into hexagonal columns such as those in the Giant's Causeway.

Biodegradable A substance that can be broken down and recycled by naturally occurring organisms.

Biofuels A term used to describe fuels made up of biological material such as timber or methane gas, which is generated as biological matter decomposes.

Colonisation The process whereby one country takes political control of another.

Devolution A process in which part of a country is given greater control of its own affairs and the central government becomes less involved (devolved).

Euro (€) The new common currency used in EMU countries and replacing their old currencies as of January 2002. The UK has so far resisted joining the EMU and so keeps the pound (sterling).

European Monetary Union (EMU) A group of European nations who have agreed to share a common European currency (the Euro – €) and dispose of their own currencies. The EMU should improve trade between member countries.

Global economy Trade and businesses are increasingly operating at a global level thanks to modern communications. Such transactions are said to take place in the global economy.

Grey vote As populations age, elderly people (who often have grey hair) become a larger proportion of the total population and so have a bigger influence on governments by the way they vote.

Gross Domestic Product (GDP) The monetary value of goods and services produced by a country in a single year.

Gross National Product (GNP) The monetary value of the goods and services produced by a country plus any earnings from overseas in a single year.

Hydroelectric power (HEP) Electricity generated by water as it passes through turbines. These normally involve large dams across river valleys that form artificial lakes behind them.

Integrated transport systems Systems in which different forms of transport, such as buses, trains, trams and cars, are co-ordinated to improve people's mobility and reduce pollution pressure on the environment.

Landfill sites Holes or hollows in the ground used for burying waste from human activities. Once full they are covered over and the land is often used for building or leisure activities.

Leachate A liquid formed when water enters a landfill site and carries diluted chemicals and metals with it as it passes through the rubbish. Leachate can pollute local water resources.

Megawatt (MW) A measure of electrical power most often used to describe the power output of electricity sources such as power stations or wind farms (1 MW is equal to 1 million Watts).

Multiplier effect The process whereby one event leads to another. Sometimes known as a 'domino effect' or 'knock-on effect'. This process can be positive or negative and is often used in economics.

National Assembly A group of elected individuals who have a responsibility for governing their people (the nation).

Nationalisation The process of making an organisation or industry the property of the nation as opposed to the property of individuals.

'Out-of-town' economy The pattern whereby large sections of the economy such as businesses, industry, retail stores and leisure facilities move to locations outside main towns, often on specially constructed sites.

Privatisation The process whereby a national property is sold to individuals to become privately owned and managed.

Referendum Allowing members of the public to vote on a major issue. The UK is likely to have a referendum about joining the EMU.

Renewable energy Energy from sources that are continually available, such the wind or the sun. Non-renewable sources include coal, oil and gas – once used, they cannot be used again.

Set-aside An agricultural practice where land is left fallow because it is not needed to produce food or is left to protect the environment. Farmers are normally paid by the government for leaving this land fallow.

Social exclusion When an individual or group of people is isolated from the broader society in which they live.

Sustainable development Development that meets the needs of today without compromising the ability of future generations to meet their needs.

'Teletubby generation' The term used to describe the increasingly overweight child population in the UK.

Toxic Organic Micro Pollutants (TOMPs) A group of pollutants produced by the incomplete burning of fuels or waste. TOMPs are highly toxic, even in small quantities, and some are carcinogenic (believed to cause cancer).

Transport hubs Key points (hubs) where different modes of transport meet. Roads may meet with a railway terminal or port for example, allowing the easy transfer of goods.

Veggie-box schemes Schemes whereby local farm produce is delivered direct from the farms to nearby communities, reducing the need for transportation over long distances.

Welfare State A system of public services and benefits provided by the government and set up in 1948. They include free healthcare under the National Health Service (NHS).

Wind farm A series of wind turbines generating electricity for the national electricity network.

FURTHER INFORMATION

BOOKS TO READ:

Country Fact Files: the United Kingdom by David Flint (Hodder Wayland, 1998). Illustrated reference for KS3.

Exploring Geography Book 1: The UK and the Local Environment by Simon Ross and Peter Eyre (Longman, 1991). Textbook for KS3 looking at the UK and the local environment.

Exploring Geography Book 2: The UK Within Europe by Ann Beckwith and Anne Sutcliffe (Longman, 1991). Textbook for KS3 looking at the UK's relationship with Europe.

Geographical Case Studies: The United Kingdom by Chris Burnett, Keith Flinders and Barnaby Lenon (Hodder & Stoughton Educational, 1995). A case study based text on the UK for KS3–4.

The Rough Guide To Britain by Ron Andrews and others (Rough Guides, 2000). An informative travel guide to Britain though it excludes Northern Ireland.

WEBSITES:

GENERAL INFORMATION
http://msn.expedia.com/wg/Europe/United_Kingdom/P2796.asp/
A good general knowledge and enquiry site to find out more about the UK.

PEOPLE
http://www.royal.gov.uk/
The official website of the British Monarchy.

ENVIRONMENT
http://www.anpa.gov.uk/
Website for The Association of National Park Authorities (ANPA) with information and links to all the UK's national parks.

http://www.doingyourbit.org.uk/
UK government website (from the Department of Environment, Food and Rural Affairs) promoting greater environmental awareness.

http://www.cat.org.uk/
The Centre for Alternative Technology in Machynlleth, Wales, provides information about sustainable development and how to get involved.

PLACES
http://www.aboutbritain.com/
Useful entry website allowing you to search for more about the UK's regions, towns and attractions.

TOURISM
http://www.enjoybritain.com/
A website offering links for everything to do with travel and tourism in the UK.

http://www.visitbritain.com/
The official visitors site for the British Tourist Authority – a useful virtual tour in 'Images of Britain'.

INDEX

Numbers shown in **bold** also refer to pages with maps, graphic illustrations or photographs.

The famous Lloyds building, designed by Richard Rogers, is a dramatic feature of the London skyline.

Sheep graze on rolling green farmland.

R(

Th
Ac
Th
re

Witness to History

Victorian Britain

Sean Connolly

Heinemann
LIBRARY

www.heinemann.co.uk/library

Visit our website to find out more information about **Heinemann Library** books.

To order:

 Phone 44 (0) 1865 888066

 Send a fax to 44 (0) 1865 314091

 Visit the Heinemann Bookshop at www.heinemann.co.uk/library to browse our catalogue and order online.

First published in Great Britain by Heinemann Library,
Halley Court, Jordan Hill, Oxford
OX2 8EJ, part of Harcourt Education.

Heinemann is a registered trademark of
Harcourt Education Ltd.

Produced for Heinemann by Discovery Books Ltd
Editorial: Sarah Eason and Gill Humphrey
Design: Ian Winton
Picture Research: Rachel Tisdale
Production: Edward Moore

Originated by Ambassador Litho Ltd
Printed and bound in Hong Kong, China
by South China Printing

ISBN 0 431 17045 2
07 06 05 04 03
10 9 8 7 6 5 4 3 2 1

British Library Cataloguing in Publication Data
Connolly, Sean
  Victorian Britain. – (Witness to History)
  941'.081

A full catalogue record for this book is available from the
British Library.

Acknowledgements
The publishers would like to thank the following for
permission to reproduce photographs:
Bettmann/Hulton p.16; The Fleming–Wyfold Art
Foundation/Bridgeman Art Library p.33; Hermitage, St
Petersburg/Bridgeman Art Library p.45; Corbis p.21; Mary
Evans Picture Library pp.4, 5, 6, 7, 10, 14, 17, 18, 19, 20,
24, 25, 26, 32, 36, 40, 41, 42, 43, 44, 45, 48, 50; Hulton
Archive pp.34, 46; Hulton Getty p.35; Mansell/Timepix/Rex
Features pp.28, 38; Peter Newark's Historical Pictures pp.8,
12, 22, 30; Robert Opie Collection p.27.

Cover photograph is an 1898 illustration showing a
'crossing-sweeper' boy being paid by a wealthy Victorian
lady for sweeping her pathway on the road. This picture is
reproduced with permission of Mary Evans Picture Library.

The publishers would like to thank Bob Rees, historian and
assistant head teacher, for his assistance in the preparation
of this book.

Disclaimer
All Internet addresses (URLs) given in this book were
valid at the time of going to press. However, due to the
dynamic nature of the Internet, some addresses may have
changed, or sites may have changed or ceased to exist
since publication. While the author and publisher regret
any inconvenience this may cause readers, no
responsibility for any such changes can be accepted by
either the author or the publisher.

Every effort has been made to contact copyright holders
of any material reproduced in this book. Any omissions
will be rectified in subsequent printings if notice is given
to the publishers.

Words appearing in bold, **like this**, are explained in the Glossary.

Contents

Introduction

The Victorian era (1837–1901) was a time of rapid change, economic growth and, for some, great prosperity. At the start of Queen Victoria's reign Britain was mainly an agricultural nation, but by the time of her death more than three-quarters of the population lived in towns or cities. New inventions and faster machines developed as a result of the **Industrial Revolution** fuelled the growth of industrial cities. A few people benefited, becoming very rich, as new factories were built and **manufacturing** and trade flourished. For the vast majority of working people, however, earning a few pennies each day and keeping out of the **workhouse** were their main concerns.

The British Empire

From the seventeenth century onwards Britain had begun to gain control of many other parts of the world. Most of these lands became British **colonies**, where local officials made some decisions, but overall power was still based in London. By the time Victoria became queen, Great Britain controlled Australia, New Zealand and Canada, as well as some parts of Africa, the Caribbean and Asia. During Victoria's reign, this process of colonization continued. British influence, driven by business, military power and a desire to spread the Christian gospel, took root in the colonies. British officials governed many of these areas like smaller versions of Britain itself, with British-style law courts, schools and rail networks. One of the most memorable events of the century came in 1877, when Victoria was crowned Empress of India. The British-controlled lands spread around the world were no longer simply a collection of colonies – they had become the British Empire.

This is one of the most famous photographs of Queen Victoria. It was taken in 1887, ten years after she was crowned Empress of India.

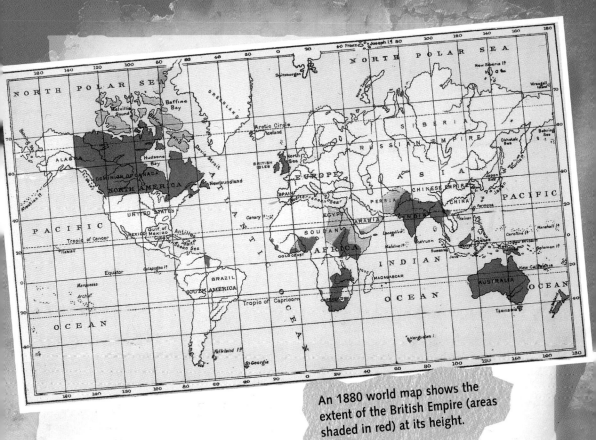

An 1880 world map shows the extent of the British Empire (areas shaded in red) at its height.

Ideas of progress

Many Victorians were concerned with the idea of progress and during this era Great Britain became the most powerful nation on earth. Some Victorians believed that progress would also be good for the rest of the world. For them, having an empire was not only a way of getting cheap goods from around the world, it was a chance to spread British ideas and achievements to other countries.

However, not all Victorians approved of change. People working in towns and in the countryside saw machines taking over traditional jobs. Many looked back fondly to a time when landscapes were not ruined by the sight of factory chimneys billowing black smoke. Others saw their houses and common land cleared away to make way for larger, more efficient farms. Unfortunately it was often the poor who made the biggest sacrifices in the name of progress.

How do we know?

By studying history, we can learn about the events of the past. If we need to find out about, for example, the origin of the Olympic Games in Greece or the French Revolution, we can find many books and articles about these subjects. They can tell us when and how these events took place, as well as who were the leading characters. They often go on to explain not only why things have happened, by giving the background to the events, but also how the events themselves changed the course of history. A historical work that is written after the period it describes is called a **secondary source**.

Getting to the source

This book uses **primary sources** to tell the story of life in Victorian Britain. Secondary sources can give us the broad picture of events and changes in this historical period, but primary sources capture the 'feel'

of the times, highlighting the fast-moving changes that amazed some people and horrified others. These sources, which include diary entries, newspaper reports, **memoirs** and advertisements, put real people back into the historical picture with personal accounts that describe what it was really like to be alive during the reign of Queen Victoria.

For most people letter writing was the only way of communicating before the introduction of the telephone. Nineteenth-century letters give us first-hand accounts of how Victorian people lived and felt.

Photography was developed during the Victorian era, providing us with accurate pictures of lfe at that time, such as this image of Coventry factory workers in 1897.

A varied picture

The Victorian era was a time of new ideas. As happens with many new ideas, people often resisted them at first. You can sense in his writing Charles Darwin's concern about the public response to his great work *On the Origin of Species* (see page 17). Other documents served to alert the public to dangers or to make political points. Annie Besant's description of the working conditions in the match factories (see page 37) and James Greenwood's account of the **temperance** meeting (see page 31) are good examples. However, those who lived away from such problems often found it easy to ignore the cruelty and injustices that flourished throughout Victorian society.

Many of the other accounts are simply descriptions of developments in a fast-changing world. Together these accounts paint a vivid picture of life in this fascinating period of British history.

Forging new links

At the time of Queen Victoria's coronation in 1837, Great Britain was changing fast. Scientists, engineers and company owners were taking advantage of the new technology created by the **Industrial Revolution**. New techniques in mining, farming and **manufacturing** enabled people to produce more goods. These goods were then sold in Great Britain and also shipped and sold to people in other countries around the world.

The Industrial Revolution was dependent on the development of a good transport system. People could no longer rely on horse-drawn vehicles to carry loads, often on rutted, muddy roads. Factory owners needed a regular supply of coal to operate their steam-powered machines and, like farmers, then had to send their goods to towns and cities where people would buy them. Looking for new ways to carry heavy loads, engineers in the eighteenth century had begun developing a network of canals to transport goods in large, flat-bottomed boats. New paving methods, pioneered by engineers such as John McAdam, made road travel quicker and safer. In the 1820s Britain saw the introduction of a new form of transport – the railway. The new steam trains moved goods much faster than canal boats, and by the late 1820s had even begun attracting passengers. During the Victorian era over 32,000 kilometres (20,000 miles) of track would be laid. Journeys that once lasted days now took only hours.

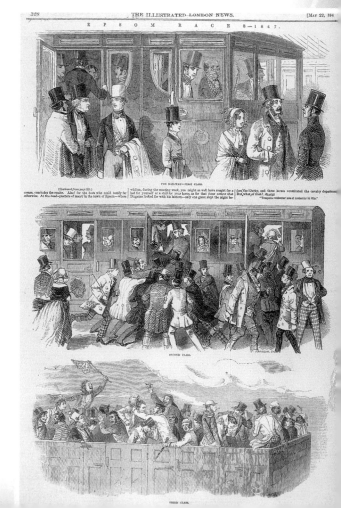

The Aylesbury News

15 June 1839

Monday last was indeed a gay and busy day. At an early hour inhabitants of this town were aroused by the lively strains of the Aylesbury town band, and great numbers of people were present to witness the departure of the seven o'clock (first) train. At ten o'clock the crowd of respectable inhabitants and fashionably dressed people around the station-house was very great, and the pressure to obtain the best seats was severe. None were admitted without a shareholder's ticket, and as soon as the train was full the band struck up and off went the steamer, dragging after it [in the carriages] between 200 and 300 people, and to the amazement of as many thousands outside, who were regretting their ill-luck in not having obtained a ticket. The train returned from Cheddington almost immediately, and from that time till night, the crowd, besieged the station house clamouring for admission.

This humorous illustration from 1847 shows the different conditions for rail passengers in first class (top), second class and third class (bottom).

The Penny Post

British people had been able to post letters before the 1800s, but the service was costly and unreliable. Worse still, the person receiving the letter – and not the sender – had to pay for the delivery. Letter carriers sometimes had to make five or six calls at a house before someone would receive, and pay for, the letter. Then in the mid-1830s a teacher named Rowland Hill made a new suggestion. He said that mail could be delivered more efficiently, and more cheaply, if the sender paid with a stamp. He suggested a flat rate of one penny for each ounce (30g.) a letter weighed. This was far less than the sixpence people had been paying. Hill made his proposal to the government in 1837 and Parliament eventually approved his suggestion in 1839.

The Uniform Penny Post came into force on 10 January 1840. On the first day of the Penny Post 112,000 letters were posted, more than three times the number for that day in the previous year. In 1840, after the introduction of the Penny Post, 168 million letters were posted in Great Britain. Ten years later this figure had risen to 347 million letters.

The Penny Post arrived at a time when many British people could not read or write. Once the educational developments of later decades took effect, the numbers of letters posted skyrocketed.

True or false?

This account describes an incident that may have inspired Rowland Hill to propose the idea of the Penny Post. We can only think of this source as a story, as we do not know if it is true or false. This account does show how the cost of receiving a letter was too much for poor people to pay, and how a more efficient and fairer way of paying for delivery would help people.

By chance he [Hill] witnessed a touching scene, a postman brought a letter from London addressed to a young village girl. She examined the letter, but because the postage on it was so great she refused to accept it. Rowland Hill intervened but the girl was clearly embarrassed by his action. Patiently he questioned her and she finally confessed that the letter was from her fiance working in London, but as she was too poor to afford letters from him they had devised a neat strategem. By various ingenious signs and marks drawn on the covering of the letter the young man was able to let her know that he was keeping well and that he still loved her.

Rowland was profoundly disturbed by this story and he pondered on the problem.

London's first post office letterbox was installed in 1855. Signs gave a clear idea of how far it was from the central post office and when letters would be collected from it.

Public health

For most people, living conditions in London and other major industrial cities were very bad in the first decades of Victoria's reign. Poor **hygiene**, open drains (underground sewers were not built until the 1860s), overcrowded housing, dangerous working conditions and dirty drinking water were a major part of the problem. Added to this were London's famous 'pea-soupers' – days of dense, blinding smog caused by burning coal.

All of these unhealthy factors led to outbreaks of serious illnesses, which spread quickly through the crowded city streets. Most of the victims of these diseases were poor, working people. Thousands died in the **cholera epidemics** of 1831, 1848, 1853 and 1866. **Tuberculosis** also claimed lives because the medical advances needed to cure it had not yet been made.

Edwin Chadwick (author of a public health report in 1842 – *The Sanitary Condition of the Labouring Population*) – argued that it was very difficult for poor people to improve their own living and working conditions. The first Public Health **Act** of 1848, tried to improve sanitation and building standards, but it wasn't until the 1875 Public Health Act became law, and councils were forced to provide lighting, clean water, drainage, sewage disposal and medical inspectors, that dramatic improvements in public health were made.

The French artist Gustave Doré depicted the dismal and unhealthy living conditions of working people in Whitechapel (East London) in 1872.

Hector Gavin describes
One of the leading campaigners for improved living conditions
was the journalist Hector Gavin. This description of life in East
London comes from an investigation, known as 'Sanitary
Ramblings', which he published in 1848.

A gentleman, named Knight, rashly, and in
ignorance of the locality, purchased the lease of
No. 1, which forms the eastern end of Bethnal-
Green-road. Immediately after taking up his
residence there he became ill, and, shortly after, died
of **typhus**, in an aggravated form. On inspection of
the neighbouring premises, I discovered Paradise
Dairy immediately behind his house. In this dairy
sixteen cows and twenty swine are usually kept. The
animal remains and decomposing vegetable refuse
were piled up a considerable height above a hollow
adapted to receive them. This conservation [keeping]
of the refuse takes place in order that a sufficiently
large quantity may accumulate. Moreover, the
soakage from the neighbouring privies [toilets] found
its way into this receptacle for manure and filth. The
surface of the yard was dirty and covered with
refuse. Even in the street, the offensiveness of this
nuisance was obviously apparent to every passer-by.
The occupiers of this dairy nevertheless claimed the
place to be perfectly clean and wholesome.

The long arm of the law

Many of the same conditions that contributed to the poor state of public health also led to a serious crime problem in Victorian Britain. Once again the worst affected areas were London and the major cities. Poverty played a large part in leading some people into a life of crime. Violent attacks and robberies, murder and burglary were common problems in these cities. And with no streetlights in the first decades of Victoria's reign, many law-abiding people were afraid to go out at night. Newspaper reports only added to the public's fears over crime by recounting gruesome tales of murders, including those committed by the notorious Jack the Ripper in London during the late 1880s.

Britain's first police force, had been established in London in 1829. Policemen were called 'Bobbies' after their founder, Sir Robert Peel. These policemen, and similar forces in other cities, set out to make the streets safer. For those criminals who were caught and convicted, the punishments were as fierce as the crimes. Until 1846, many of them were **transported** to Australia or other British **colonies**. For others, the sentence was more clear-cut – death by hanging.

Mounted officers in London and other British cities were part of a growing police force trained to bring criminals to justice. This picture is dated 1867.

I was a witness of the execution at Horsemonger Lane this morning. I went there with the intention of observing the crowd gathered to behold it, and I had excellent opportunities of doing so, at intervals all through the night, and continuously from day-break until after the spectacle was over …The horrors of the **gibbet** and of the crime which brought the wretched murderers to it faded in my mind before the atrocious bearing, looks, and language of the assembled spectators. When I came upon the scene at midnight, the shrillness of the cries and howls that were raised from time to time … made my blood run cold …When the day dawned, thieves, low prostitutes, ruffians, and vagabonds of every kind, flocked on to the ground, with every variety of offensive and foul behaviour …When the two miserable creatures who attracted all this ghastly sight about them were turned quivering into the air, there was no more emotion, no more pity, no more thought that two immortal souls had gone to judgement, no more restraint in any of the previous obscenities, than if the name of Christ had never been heard in this world, and there were no belief among men but that they perished like the beasts.

Science and invention

Scientists, engineers and inventors were seen as important people in Vicorian times. The engineer Isambard Kingdom Brunel built railway lines, bridges and tunnels, steamships and huge new railway stations. British scientists like Michael Faraday conducted numerous tests before coming up with new theories. Faraday's work on electricity took place over 40 years, but his discoveries led to the development of the electric motor, the dynamo and the transformer. A major advance in medicine, made by Joseph Lister, was the use of **antiseptics** in the operating theatre.

Later in the era some of these discoveries were put to practical use. Electricity was used, first to send messages by telegraph and then, at the end of the nineteenth century, to provide lighting in streets and in homes. Engineers and inventors also developed the modern flush toilet, the safety pin, the rubber tyre, the bicycle and the steam **turbine**.

One of the most important scientific advances of the nineteenth century was the theory of **evolution**, developed by the English **naturalist** Charles Darwin. In his book *On the Origin of Species by Means of Natural Selection* (1859), Darwin concluded that all living creatures change over time, with the strongest or most adaptable being most likely to survive and reproduce. His theory caused an outcry by suggesting that human beings evolved from apes. This was shocking to many Christian Victorians who believed in the biblical story, which said that humans had been created by God.

Isambard Kingdom Brunel, the great Victorian engineer, stands in front of his steamship *Great Eastern*, which was launched in 1858.

Charles Darwin writes

At the end of his book *On the Origin of Species*, Darwin, no doubt aware of the controversy it was likely to cause among some Victorian Christians, was careful to include God in his view of the world.

It is interesting to contemplate a tangled bank, clothed with many plants of different kinds, with birds singing on the bushes, with various insects flitting about, and with worms crawling through the damp earth, and to reflect that these elaborately constructed forms, so different from each other, and dependent upon each other in so complex a manner, have all been produced by laws acting around us ... there is grandeur in this view of life, with its several powers, having been originally breathed by the Creator into a few forms or into one; and that, whilst this planet has gone cycling on according to the fixed law of gravity, from so simple a beginning endless forms most beautiful and most wonderful have been, and are being evolved.

Many Victorians mocked Darwin's theory that humans evolved from apes. This magazine illustration from the *London Sketch Book* of 1874 has Darwin trying to show an ape how similar they are.

The Great Exhibition

Inspired by a sense of pride in Britain's achievements – but with an eye on making a profit – a group of Victorians, led by Queen Victoria's husband, Prince Albert, decided to stage a Great Exhibition in London. Albert acted as president of the **Royal Commission**, which planned and later developed the exhibition.

The Great Exhibition was meant to demonstrate British achievement in industrial design while at the same time advertising British products for overseas customers. The exhibition was held in an iron-and-glass structure, known as the Crystal Palace, in London's Hyde Park. The building was enormous, covering an area of 7.5 hectares. Open for five and a half months in the summer of 1851, it attracted more than 6 million visitors, who came to see some 14,000 exhibits from around the world, nearly half of which were British. The displays ranged from examples of decorative arts to scientific instruments, tools and kitchen appliances. A large area was given over to machinery, some of it powered by the Exhibition's own steam engines.

The Exhibition was a great success, and made a huge profit. This money went towards the founding of the Victoria and Albert Museum, the Natural History Museum and the Science Museum in South Kensington, London. The Crystal Palace was taken down and re-erected in South London, but was destroyed by fire in 1936.

Victoria's husband, Prince Albert, played an important role in the planning of the Great Exhibition. He believed that such a collection of works of art and industry would encourage competition. Albert died in 1861 and was mourned by Queen Victoria for the rest of her life.

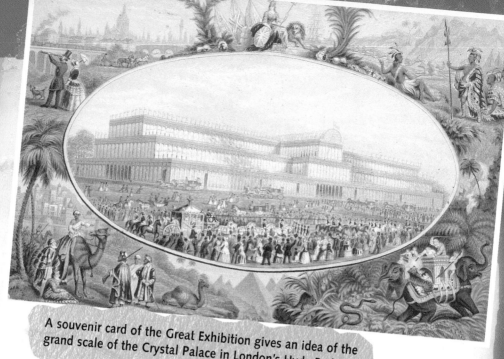

A souvenir card of the Great Exhibition gives an idea of the grand scale of the Crystal Palace in London's Hyde Park.

Responses to the Great Exhibition

The *Art Journal*, in its catalogue of the Exhibition (top), gives a dramatic description of the inside of the Crystal Palace. The quote from the *(Roman) Sun* describes the effect of the Great Exhibition on the surrounding district (bottom).

On entering the building for the first time, the eye is completely dazzled by the rich variety of hues [colours] that burst upon it on every side … in the centre of the building rises the gigantic fountain … whilst at the northern end the eye is relieved by the verdure [lushness] of the tropical plants and the lofty and overshadowing branches of the forest … the first objects which attract the eye are the sculptures…

The *Art Journal 1851*

The roads leading to Hyde Park were rendered almost impassable … It is scarcely necessary to mention that signs of a general holiday were everywhere shown, by the closing of shops and the hanging out of flags, of all nations, from the windows.

The *(Roman) Sun* 1 May 1851

Child labour

Behind Britain's prosperity in the nineteenth century lay a shameful record of harsh working conditions, especially for children. The many new factories that had developed since the beginning of the **Industrial Revolution** relied on the labour of children, some as young as six years old. These children worked long hours, often in horrible conditions, in factories and mines in every city and town. Child labour was one of the most serious problems that Victorian Britain faced. Social reformers called for improvements to working conditions, but they were opposed by both employers, who relied on child labour, and parents, who needed the extra income their children brought to the family.

The activities of social reformers and the evidence of parliamentary reports led to a series of **acts** of parliament which aimed to control and monitor working conditions, especially for children. The Factory Act of 1844 limited the working day for children aged between eight and thirteen to six and a half hours. The 1847 Act limited the working day for under-eighteens to ten hours. The 'Climbing Boys' Act of 1875 made it illegal to use children to climb and clean chimneys. Although these laws were often difficult to enforce, by the time Victoria died in 1901 conditions for children had greatly improved.

A woman lowers two children down a mineshaft in 1842. Children as young as five worked at least eleven hours a day in mines during Victoria's first years as queen.

These children, working in a brickyard, carry heavy lumps of wet clay from the clay heap to the brickmaker's table and back – a distance of some nineteen kilometres (twelve miles).

Factory worker describes the dangers of factory machines

An unidentified girl from Sheffield was interviewed in 1865 about her work in a knife-making factory. She describes the dangers all around the young workers as they laboured through a 14-hour working day.

I have been very careful about machines ever since a girl of nine or ten years old. We girls in some works [factories] of this kind were playing at hiding, and one about fourteen years old hid beside a drum in a wheel then not working, and it was started and crushed her to pieces. they had to pick her bones up in a basket, and that's how they buried her ... girls are soft, giddy things.

A divided society

Society at the start of the nineteenth century was fairly fixed. A wealthy but small upper class earned and maintained its wealth through investments and rents from land. The middle class was made up of merchants, factory owners, professional people, such as lawyers and bankers, and small landowners. These people attributed much of their success to hard work. The largest group of people, the lower or working class, owned no land and worked mainly as farm labourers or in factories. With no paid holidays, no sick leave, no vote and unpleasant and dangerous working conditions, these people faced a difficult life, and no amount of hard work could improve their situation.

Most people – all British women and those men who did not own property – did not have the right to vote in elections. Those with power and money, who could vote, were most likely to benefit from Great Britain's increasing prosperity. The Chartist Movement, organized in 1838, tried to change this. They believed that if all men had the vote then working men would have the power to change the system. However, protests and a petition did nothing to persuade Parliament to take up their cause. Some **trade unions** tried to improve conditions, through education and self-help. Other Victorians, like Samuel Smiles, picked up on this 'self-help' message and used it as a cure for all ills. Like many wealthier Victorians, he had little understanding of the problems faced by workers who were paid a pittance for their labour or who could not find any work at all.

The 'gospel of work' and 'self-help' meant little to those Victorians whose daily life was a struggle in terrible working conditions, in which no amount of hard work would improve their lives.

Samuel Smiles writes

Samuel Smiles was a Scottish-born journalist who moved to England in his twenties. He became convinced that social improvement would come only to those who worked for it themselves. He collected his views in a popular book entitled *Self-Help* (1859). This extract comes from *Self-Help*. The language in this extract is quite difficult to understand. Smiles is saying that it is a man's duty to work hard – for his own sake and for the benefit of his country.

The career of industry which the nation has pursued, has also proved its best education. As steady application to work is the healthiest training for every individual, so is it the best discipline of a state [country]. Honourable industry travels the same road with duty; and **Providence** has closely linked both with happiness ... It is true that no bread eaten by man is so sweet as that earned by his own labour, whether physical or mental. By labour the earth has been subdued, and man redeemed [saved] from barbarism; nor has a single step in civilization been made without it. Labour is not only a necessity and a duty, but a blessing: only the idler feels it to be a curse. The duty of work is written on the ... muscles of the limbs, the mechanism of the hand, the nerves and lobes of the brain – the sum of whose healthy action is satisfaction and enjoyment.

The great house

The very rich formed only a small fraction of the population as a whole, and most upper-class families knew, or had heard of, each other. It was hard to break into their social circle, and there were many ways that they could tell that someone was not 'one of us'. Great formal dances, known as balls, figured largely in upper-class life. They provided entertainment and a chance to meet future husbands and wives. Whether confined to their great house in the country or spending part of their time in a London town house, the **gentry** continued with their rounds of balls, '**coming out**' and hunting.

The great house operated like a small community in itself, often employing up to a hundred servants and staff to run the house and its land and gardens. Most servants worked very long hours doing boring and dirty jobs with little in the way of reward and hardly any time off. There were rigid distinctions between the different sorts of servants, and this was reflected in their wages and some of the privileges they enjoyed.

Members of the wealthy upper class enjoying themselves during refreshment time at a **public school** cricket match. Many wealthy people had no idea how lower–class, working people lived.

Extract from survey of servants' wages

This list of servants' wages (converted into pounds and new pence) was taken from a survey of 2000 houses, conducted in England and Wales in 1891. In 1850 there were 1 million women in **domestic service**; by 1900 this number had doubled. For a comparison with modern money, a pound in 1891 would now be worth about £140.

Class of work	Age	Average annual salary
Between maid	19	£11.90
Scullery (pantry) maid	19	£13.00
Kitchen maid	20	£15.00
Nurse-housemaid	21–25	£16.00
General domestic	21–25	£14.60
Housemaid	21–25	£16.20
Nurse	25–30	£20.10
Parlour maid	25–30	£20.60
Laundry maid	25–30	£23.60
Cook	25–30	£20.20
Lady's maid	30–35	£24.70
Cook-housekeeper	40	£35.60
Housekeeper	40	£52.50

Household servants attended to almost every aspect of life as part of their job. This 1887 illustration shows a maidservant helping her mistress into her place at the dinner table.

The rising middle class

Victorian Britain saw a great surge in the number of people who could describe themselves as middle class. This middle class was made up of people who earned their living from a wide – and growing – number of jobs and professions. The middle class gained more political influence when the Reform **Act** of 1832 was passed, which gave about 250,000 men the right to vote. It also became richer, with many middle-class men making fortunes in new companies and in business generally. George Hudson, who started life as a **draper**, invested money in the railways. By 1844 he controlled more than 1600 kilometres (1000 miles) of railway line and had become one of Britain's first millionaires.

The newly rich middle classes wanted to copy the lifestyles of the landed classes. Some bought estates and built magnificent houses. They wanted servants and liked to give entertainments. To satisfy middle-class aspirations there were a number of publications giving advice on how to run houses and estates, on manners and how to bring up children.

Mrs Beeton's advice on what to wear

Isabella Beeton was an educated Victorian lady who became a popular cookery writer. Her *Book of Household Management* was published in 1861 and included 3000 recipes as well as articles on food preparation and other areas of household management. The book soon became a bible for middle-class women, who would turn to their 'Mrs Beeton's' for advice on social, business and medical matters as well as for reliable recipes. Isabella Beeton died at just 28 years of age after the birth of her fourth child. This is an extract from her *Book of Household Management*.

A lady's dress should be always suited to her circumstances, and varied for different occasions. The morning dress should be neat and simple, and suitable for the domestic duties that usually occupy the early part of the day. This dress should be changed before calling hours; but it is not in good taste to wear much jewellery except with evening dress. A lady should always aim at being well and attractively dressed whilst never allowing questions of costume to establish inordinate claims on either time or purse. In purchasing her own garments, after taking account of the important detail of the length of her purse, she should aim at adapting the style of the day in such a manner as best suits the requirements of her face, figure and complexion, and never allow slavish adherence to temporary fads of fashion to overrule her own sense of what is becoming and befitting. She should also bear in mind that her different costumes have to furnish her with apparel for home wear, outdoor exercise and social functions, and try to allot due relative importance to the claims of each.

"The BEST Cookery Books in the WORLD"

MRS BEETON'S COOKERY BOOKS

1s   2s6d   3s6d   7s6d

NEW-ENLARGED & GREATLY IMPROVED Editions

Price 7s. 6d.

Mrs BEETON'S BOOK of HOUSEHOLD MANAGEMENT

RE-COMPOSED AND REVISED THROUGHOUT (Containing nearly half as much matter again as the Old Edition), in all 1700 PAGES, THOUSANDS OF RECIPES AND INSTRUCTIONS, 13 COLOURED PLATES, 68 FULL-PAGE AND 700 OTHER ENGRAVINGS. With Quantities, Time, Costs, and Seasons, Directions for Carving and Trussing, Management of Children, Duties of Servants, the Doctor, Legal Memoranda, and Bills of Fare and Menus for all Seasons.

Mrs BEETON'S DICTIONARY OF EVERY DAY COOKERY

AND HOUSEKEEPING BOOK. Re-Written and Revised Throughout, and greatly Enlarged and Improved, comprising 570 PAGES, 2000 RECIPES AND INSTRUCTIONS, 600 ENGRAVINGS AND COLOURED PLATES, With Tables of Expenditure, Household Accounts, New Menus, &c.

Price 3s. 6d.

WARD, LOCK, BOWDEN, & Co., London, New York, and Melbourne.

A colourful advertisement for some of Mrs Beeton's books. Cooks today still refer to them for advice.

Trade unions

Although Victorian Britain became the wealthiest country in the world, only a small number of people, usually businessmen or factory owners, benefited from this prosperity. The majority of those who did the actual work – the working population – had to be grateful they had a job at all. Working conditions were often dreadful and could be dangerous, but workers had little say over how much money they could earn.

At the beginning of the century it was illegal to form a **trade union** to improve workers' pay and conditions. When laws banning trade unions were **repealed** in 1824, workers began to organize and **strike** to achieve the improvements they wanted. Large trade unions, such as the Amalgamated Society of Engineers (1851), were formed to represent groups of workers involved in similar trades.

Violent disturbances in Sheffield in 1866 turned Parliament against the trade unions. The Trades Union Congress, representing a number of different unions, was formed in 1868 and pressed for the right of workers to strike peacefully. The Employers and Workmen **Act** (1875) guaranteed this right in law. From then on, workers could – and would – use the power of the strike to achieve better pay.

THE GRAPHIC

AN ILLUSTRATED WEEKLY NEWSPAPER

SATURDAY, SEPTEMBER 7, 1889

MR. JOHN BURNS ADDRESSING THE MEN ON STRIKE AT THE GATES OF THE EAST AND WEST INDIA DOCKS

THE GREAT STRIKE OF DOCK LABOURERS AT THE EAST END

Ben Tillett describes how strikers raised money to support their families while not working

The London Dock Strike of 1889 showed that unions could bring a major industry to a standstill. The strike worked, and after five weeks the employers lost so much money that they gave in to the union's demands. In this passage, union leader Ben Tillett describes how the dockers raised money to support their families during the dispute.

In our marches we collected contributions in pennies [0.5p], sixpences [2.5p] and shillings [5p], from the clerks and City workers, who were touched perhaps to the point of sacrifice by the emblem of poverty and starvation carried in our procession. By these means, with the aid of the Press, money poured into our **coffers** from Trade Unions and public alike. Large sums came from abroad, especially from the British dominions [empire], whose contributions alone amounted to over £30,000. Contributions from the public sent direct by letter or collected on our marches totalled nearly £12,000; more than £1000 came in from our street box collections, and substantial amounts were obtained through the help of the Star, the Pall Mall Gazette, the Labour Elector, and other papers.

A weekly newspaper gave its readers vivid illustrations of London's 1889 Dock Strike (above left) and its organizers at their headquarters (left).

Demon drink

Excessive drinking and drunkenness have been social problems throughout European history. By the Victorian era, the problem had become especially serious among members of the industrial working class. The repetitive work at factory machines and poor living conditions drove many to drink as a way of escaping the wretchedness of their daily lives. Though factory owners knew that workers were less efficient, and could even cause accidents if they were drunk, they did little to improve the lot of their workers. Children also suffered as some workers spent their wages on alcohol, plunging their families into poverty. Crime and violence were another result of excessive drinking. Sadly some workers lost their jobs, became seriously ill or died very young because of alcohol-related diseases.

The Chartists, the **trade unions** and religious groups such as the Salvation Army (founded in 1865) insisted that 'the demon drink' lay at the heart of many social problems. They believed that **temperance** was the key to battling this problem. Their temperance meetings, held in most cities, offered people the chance to have a decent meal and to be guided towards a life without drunkenness.

The journalist James Greenwood toured some of the poorer districts of London in 1867. He recorded the words of this song, which was performed at a temperance meeting organized by a Reverend Mookow.

Come, brothers, listen unto me, and a story I'll relate,
How I in time was rescued from a wretched
   drunkard's fate.
I used to swill my nightly fill of ale, and beer, and gin,
   Nor for my wife and family cared I a single pin.
My eyes were bleared, a razed beard, likewise a
   drunkard's nose;
My children bare and naked were, because I pawned
   their clothes;
My wife I bruised, and much ill-used, and, shameful
   thing to say, **Distrained** the bed from under her
   my tavern score to pay.
But, thanks to Mr. Mookow, now all that is set aside;
Upon my wife and family I now can look with pride.
The reason's plain, I now **abstain**, and mean to, never
   fear-
I never more intend to be a slave to gin and beer.

Behind the Bar, an 1866 painting by Herbert Marshall, shows a Victorian pub scene with an assortment of drinkers, including a mother rubbing her baby's gums with whisky to calm teething pain or to send it to sleep.

Rural life

The great changes taking place in Britain during the nineteenth century were not confined to towns and cities. Despite the dramatic rise of industry, more than a quarter of the British population still worked on the land at the end of the Victorian era. For them seed drills, threshing machines and steam-powered machinery changed methods of planting and harvesting. Many of the most powerful land-owning farmers adopted a policy of enclosure, increasing the size of their farms at the expense of small farmers and land held in common for communities. Enclosure hit Scotland especially hard, and thousands of Scots were forced off their land – and often out of their country. Many of them **emigrated** to Australia, Canada or the USA.

A crowd of spectators watch a steam plough display on a farm in 1850. Steam power had a dramatic effect on farming, reducing the time it took to plough, sow and harvest crops.

During the nineteenth century the **Acts** known as the Corn Laws were **repealed**. These Acts had controlled the flow of cheaper foreign grain entering Britain, keeping prices for British farm goods high. When Ireland (an important source of grain for Britain) suffered a disastrous **famine** in the 1840s, there were more calls for allowing imports of foreign grain. Despite the repeal of the Corn Laws, British farmers still prospered between the 1850s and 1870s because the booming population needed feeding. Farm labourers, however, saw few of these benefits. Throughout the century they were forced to move from farm to farm in search of work. The Warwickshire farm workers' **strike** of 1872 was crushed, but it showed that discontent was common among farm labourers.

This folksong records the misery caused by the Highland Clearances.

The 'Highland Clearances' emptied thousands of hectares of rural Scotland of its small farmers and their families, especially in the highlands and islands.

Hush, Hush

Once our valleys were ringing
with sounds of our children singing -
but now sheep bleat o'er the evenin'
and shielings [pastures] stand empty and open.

Chorus:
Hush, hush, time to be sleepin'
hush, hush, dreams come a creepin'
dreams of peace and of freedom
so smile in your sleep, bonnie dearie.

We stood, our heads bowed in prayer
while battles laid our cottages bare -
the flames, fire, the clear mountain air
and many were dead by the morning.

Chorus

Where was our good Highland mettle?
Our men once so fearless in battle?
They stand cowered, and huddled like cattle
and wait to be shipped o'er the ocean.

Chorus

No good pleading or praying
now gone, gone, all hope of staying -
hush, hush, the anchors are weighing
don't cry in your sleep, bonnie dearie.

Chorus

The Last of the Clan, **painted by Thomas Faed in 1865, shows a Highland Scot in traditional clothing leading his family away after losing his land during the Highland Clearances.**

Education

At the start of the Victorian era only the wealthy could afford to send their children to **public schools**. Vast numbers of working people were unable to read and write. Although many people felt it was important that people could read the Bible, others were worried that if working people began reading newspapers they might start calling for reform. **Trade unions** saw education as a way of releasing people from poverty. The Mechanics Institutes and special schools for adults helped teach working-class people to read and write.

All of these advances, however, were separate from each other and not part of a national plan for education. That changed with the Education **Act** of 1870, which provided that there should be a school within reach of every child. This resolve led to the building of hundreds of new schools in British villages and inner-city neighbourhoods.

Much of British education had been aimed only at boys, but girls and women began to benefit as well. The year 1872 saw the formation of the Girls' Public Day Schools Company, and Cambridge University pioneered the first two women's colleges – Girton College in 1869 and Newnham College in 1871.

Educational opportunities for women improved during Victoria's reign, although only a small number benefited. Here female students work in a laboratory at Girton College, Cambridge University in 1900.

Mrs Jones remembers her school days

Mrs Jones was born in Lancashire in 1887. In this extract she remembers her school days in the early 1890s.

I left school at the age of twelve ... Children went to school from the age of two and a half and they had to pay school money – a penny or two pence a week. They were sent so early in order to 'get from under the feet' ... If you passed an infants' school whilst lessons were on you could hear children's voices chanting C-A-T spells cat, D-O-G spells dog and so on ... Many teachers were never without a cane in their hands ... For good attendance one received a framed certificate. The walls of our house were covered with the things.

A group of very young school children with their teacher in 1898. Discipline and obedience were prized as highly as hard work in a Victorian classroom.

The Victorian woman

Women, even rich women, were not treated as the equals of men during Victoria's reign. A woman lost most of her property once she married. Divorces were difficult to obtain and women risked losing their children if they left their husbands. Educational opportunities were limited and there were few jobs open to poorly educated, single women apart from factory work, farming and **domestic service**. Educated women normally had to choose between writing and teaching.

Improvements did take place during Victoria's reign. The Infants Custody **Act** of 1839 gave mothers more legal rights, and the 1857 Marriage and Divorce Act gave women a better chance to divorce their husbands. A series of Married Women's Property Acts (1870, 1874, 1882, 1893) allowed women to own and inherit property and also gave them the right to enter into legal contracts and to start businesses. They did not win the right to vote in elections until 1918.

Despite the limits placed upon them, a number of women made their mark on Victorian society. Florence Nightingale made an important contribution to medical practices and the training of nurses. Dorothea Beale's tireless devotion advanced the causes of women's education and women's right to vote.

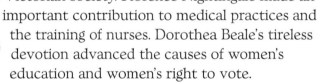

Annie Besant reports

In 1873 Annie Besant left her husband and became an **atheist**. In 1888 Besant, who was interested in the problems faced by poor working people, heard about the high dividends (share of the profits) paid to those who invested in the Bryant and May match factory, and compared these to the low wages paid to the labourers there. She wrote a series of articles that led to a public **boycott** and a **strike** of 1400, mainly women, match makers. This is an extract from one of her articles.

The hour for commencing work is 6.30 in summer and 8 in winter, work concludes at 6 p.m. ... The splendid salary of 4 shillings [20p] is subject to deductions in the shape of fines; if the feet are dirty, or the ground under the bench is left untidy, a fine of 3 pence [1.25p] is inflicted; for putting 'burnts' – matches that have caught fire during the work – on the bench 1 shilling [5p] has been forfeited, and one unhappy girl was once fined 2 shillings and 6 pence [12.5p] for some unknown crime. If a girl leaves four or five matches on her bench when she goes for a fresh 'frame' she is fined 3 pence, and in some departments a finc of 3 pence is inflicted for talking. If a girl is late she is shut out for 'half the day,' that is for the morning six hours, and 5 pence [2p] is deducted out of her day's 8 pence [3.5p]. One girl was fined 1 shilling for letting the web twist around a machine in the endeavor to save her fingers from being cut, and was sharply told to take care of the machine, 'never mind your fingers.' Another, who carried out the instructions and lost a finger thereby, was left unsupported while she was helpless. The wage covers the duty of submitting to an occasional blow from a foreman; one, who appears to be a gentleman of variable temper, 'clouts' them 'when he is mad.'

Annie Besant

Literature as a record

Much of what we know about Victorian life and values comes from the many **novels** written at that time. Great writers such as Anthony Trollope, George Eliot, Charlotte and Emily Bronte, and Charles Dickens cast an eye on life around them and drew thousands of readers into their worlds. Their novels described the life of all sorts of people – rich and poor, educated and **illiterate**, noble and evil. Many of the best-known characters in world literature – including Ebenezer Scrooge, Sherlock Holmes, Jane Eyre and Lewis Carroll's Alice – were created by Victorian authors.

The works of Charles Dickens provide a vivid picture of Victorian life. In this 1843 illustration from *A Christmas Carol*, the miser Ebenezer Scrooge meets the ghost of his former partner Jacob Marley.

The Victorian period was recorded in writing like no previous era in British history. Novels were written that described the new ideas of the time and how people reacted to them. One of the most famous authors of the period, Charles Dickens, wrote books that shocked people into thinking about the injustices that existed in Victorian society.

As more schools were teaching children to read and write, so there were more people who could enjoy this pastime. The first public libraries were opened during this era.

George Eliot writes

This passage comes from the novel *Middlemarch* (published 1871–2), written by George Eliot. Her real name was Marian Evans, but like other women writers, she found it easier to have her books published if it looked as if they had been written by a man. Eliot's novel describes the life of a small town, and the efforts made by Dorothea, who has inherited a large estate, to improve conditions for the local poor. In this exchange, her future brother-in-law, Sir James Chettham, asks her about her plan to build new cottages for farm labourers.

'Do you know, Lovegood was telling me yesterday that you had the best notion in the world of a plan for cottages – quite wonderful for a young lady, he thought. You had a real "genus", to use his expression. He said you wanted Mr Brooke to build a new set of cottages, but he seemed to think it hardly probable that your uncle would consent. Do you know, that is one of the things I wish to do – I mean, on my own estate? I should be so glad to carry out that plan of yours, if you would let me see it. Of course, it is sinking money; that is why people object to it. Labourers can never pay rent to make it answer. But, after all, it is worth doing.'

'Worth doing! yes, indeed,' said Dorothea, energetically, forgetting her previous small **vexations**. 'I think we deserve to be beaten out of our beautiful houses with a **scourge** of small cords – all of us who let tenants live in such sties as we see round us. Life in cottages might be happier than ours, if they were real houses fit for human beings from whom we expect duties and affections.'

Entertainment

At the beginning of Victoria's reign in 1837, entertainment – like so much else in Britain – was divided. The rich had a wide choice of banquets and balls, concerts and plays. Pageants and religious fetes offered amusement in country areas. Poorer people in cities, though, had little to amuse themselves in what free time they had. But, like so much else in Britain at the time, things did improve. The working week was shortened for many factory workers, giving them half of Saturday as well as Sunday to enjoy. Behind these changes were a series of new laws driven by the 'Ten Hours' movement to limit the working day. **Acts** passed in 1847 and strengthened in an 1850 act paved the way for later laws that opened up leisure time by limiting the hours of work.

Theatres and similar venues began offering entertainment for ordinary working people. The first music halls, providing songs, sketches and comedy routines, opened in 1843. Similar entertainment

– circus acts, operettas, magic performances and pantomime – all became part of everyday life by the late nineteenth century. The increasing range of entertainment also provided new work for people – as actors, singers, stage workers and advertising people.

A photograph from 1900 shows the crowded gallery of a music hall where people would enjoy a mixed programme of drama, comic sketches and music.

Entertainment advertisement of 1879
Posters promising exciting or comical entertainment competed with each other to attract people's attention in Victorian Britain. This advertisement appeared in London in 1879.

An 1889 programme for London's Empire Theatre shows the variety of entertainment in a single evening, ranging from comic acts to ballet perfomances.

MASKELYNE & COOKE
BRITAIN'S HOME OF
MYSTERY EGYPTIAN HALL

Every Evening at 8. Tuesday, Thursday and Saturday at 3.
Seven years in London of unparalleled success.

A MAN'S HEAD CUT OFF WITHOUT LOSS OF LIFE

A strange statement, but no more strange than true.
In addition to the important discovery of a means of playing a brass band by mechanism, the same inventor, Mr. J. N. MASKELYNE, is showing the public, at the Egyptian Hall, London, how easy and pleasant it is to cut off Mr. Cooke's head. The clever illusion is introduced in such a manner as to provoke unrestrained laughter. No visitors to the great City should return home before witnessing Maskelyne and Cooke's Entertainment. It is one of the principal sights of London.

Private Boxes from 21s. ; Stalls, 5s. and 3s. ; Admission, 2s. and 1s.
Boxes and Stalls can be secured at any of the Agents in
the City or West End, or at the Hall.
W. Morten, Manager.

Sports and pastimes

One of the other areas of recreation that Victorians loved was sport. Working-class people, by the mid-nineteenth century, began to have some free time at weekends to take part in, or simply watch, sporting contests. A few Victorians saw sport as a way of earning extra money or – with the development of professional sports in the late nineteenth century – as a way of earning a living. Boxers had been fighting for money for more than a century, but football and rugby widened the choice of professional sports. Many of the football league teams that we know today were founded during the 1880s and 1890s.

The **public schools**, which were thriving because of all the new wealthier, middle-class students, stressed the importance of sport as a way of developing manly character. They taught sports, such as hockey, rowing and rugby. Many sports, such as rugby, badminton and lawn tennis, were invented in Victorian Britain. Others, such as football and cricket, developed the modern rules and regulations that still govern them today.

The Victorians did not simply love team sports. At home families entertained themselves with pastimes such as playing cards or reading aloud. Women and girls occupied their time with sewing and embroidery. The more adventurous pastime of cycling became popular from the 1880s onwards, and with travel made easier by the railways, families began taking trips to the seaside.

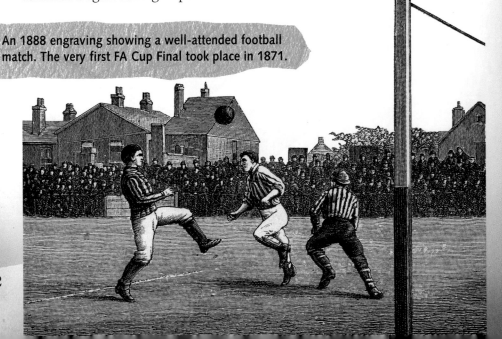

An 1888 engraving showing a well-attended football match. The very first FA Cup Final took place in 1871.

Police officer Edward Owen reports

Nineteenth-century Britain had colder winters than today, and ice-skating was a popular pastime for nearly everyone. This passage describes how people would flock to the Serpentine Lake, in London's Hyde Park, whenever the ice froze thick enough to support skaters. Policemen like Edward Owen were posted along the banks of the lake to make sure the skaters remained safe or to keep them off the ice if it began to thaw!

When the Serpentine or a portion of it is reported to be safe, all is plain sailing, and it is a fine sight to see the thousands of ladies and gentlemen, soldiers, boys and girls, all intermixed, enjoying their skating and sliding. The evenings on such occasions are novel sights, for probably there are then more people on the ice than in the daytime. The shops and other business places being closed, it becomes practically crowded. To stand on the Magazine Bridge and witness the moving mass of lights, made up of torches, **Chinese lanterns**, etc., carried by the skaters, presents a most fantastical scene. One thing I cannot understand; it seems to me to have such a fascination that some people don't care what money or property they risk in order to indulge in this recreation.

This 1900 tea advertisement shows a couple out on a cycle ride. Cycling became a popular pastime from the 1880s onwards.

Victorian art

Victorian artists responded in different ways to the changing world around them. Some tried to reflect people's sense of loss at the disappearance of the old ways of life. A group of artists known as the Pre-Raphaelites painted detailed works featuring shepherds, farmers and landscapes – without a railway line or factory chimney in sight. Photography, which was invented earlier in the century, was also used as an art form, and many of the photographs taken later in the century make valuable **primary sources** for historians studying Victorian life.

In the late 1840s and early 1850s the architects Sir Charles Barry and Augustus Pugin designed and rebuilt the Houses of Parliament in the fifteenth-century gothic style, since many Victorians believed that their own era was an echo of that 'golden age'.

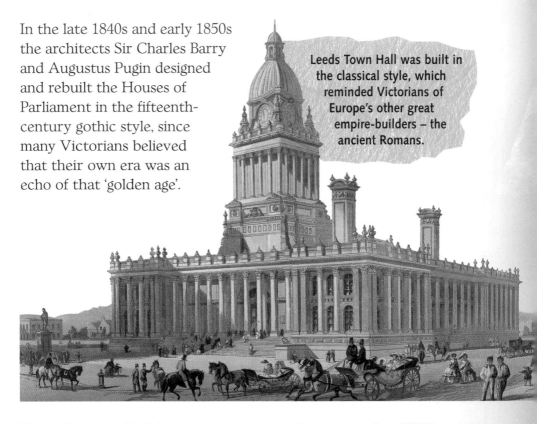

Leeds Town Hall was built in the classical style, which reminded Victorians of Europe's other great empire-builders – the ancient Romans.

Towards the end of the century artists and critics, such as William Morris and John Ruskin, claimed that mass-produced goods were destroying the livelihoods of craftsmen who had once taken a pride in their work. They also criticized many of the fussy, ornate styles in furniture and decoration that had become popular. Instead they called for styles and methods of production that depended on the imagination of the person making the goods. The works they created, though very beautiful, were too expensive for most ordinary people to buy.

Tapestry by William Morris

William Morris made this beautiful tapestry called *The Adoration of the Magi* in 1880. It was designed by the painter Sir Edward Burne-Jones and became one of Morris's most popular religious tapestries. William Morris was dedicated to reviving crafts such as weaving, stained-glass-window and furniture making. Morris wrote in an essay, 'Have nothing in your houses which you do not know to be useful or believe to be beautiful.'

William Morris was a man of many talents. He wrote poetry, painted pictures and was an excellent craftsman and businessman. Later in life he became a pioneering **socialist**.

The Golden Jubilee

Just as 1977 and 2002 were times for Jubilee celebrations in Britain, so the nineteenth century also had occasions for national pride. The Great Exhibition of 1851 was one event, Queen Victoria's Golden Jubilee, celebrating fifty years of her reign, in 1887 was another. Victoria had been proclaimed Empress of India ten years earlier and during her Golden Jubilee, India and the colonies played an important role in the state celebrations.

Overall, the economy was settled, although farming had been suffering from low prices for land and produce for more than fifteen years. Nevertheless British ships were still carrying British goods to the four corners of the world. The country felt secure, as British troops had not been involved in a major European war for more than thirty years, although they had been fighting in other areas of the world, especially in India and Africa.

The national mood in 1887 was confident and enthusiastic, and the celebrations reflected this. Special events in London, attended by Victoria herself, took place throughout the year, and the atmosphere outside the capital city was also jubilant. Towns and villages organized special events – reaching a peak on 22 June 1887, the date set aside for the celebrations.

Thousands of Londoners lined the streets to cheer Queen Victoria during her Jubilee procession in June 1887.

Reverend Jones records the Golden Jubilee celebrations

Reverend C. W. Jones, Vicar of Pakenham (Suffolk), kept detailed records of the important events in his village from 1864 to 1904. This extract describes how the people of Pakenham celebrated the Golden Jubilee in 1887.

On the 21st of June, which marked the completion of the mystic period of fifty years and a day in the reign of Queen Victoria, the village street was decorated with festoons of greenery from side to side, and a peal was rung before the daily ten o'clock service, to which a special service hymn and prayer were added.

At 3 p.m. the Village Church of Britain Temperance Society Fife and Drum Band, reinforced from Ixworth and Thurston, paraded the street from end to end and back again, and then up to the Church door. The choir then proceeded up the church singing the hymn

'King of kings Thy blessing shed
On our anointed Sovereign's head'

The elders amused themselves in the Vicarage gardens, and in the portion of Mr Green's park set apart for the sports till these began. They lasted till dark, and, indeed some had to be curtailed owing to want of light.

Then came the fireworks, which were many and excellent, and did not conclude till past eleven o'clock at night. They ended with an external illumination of the church by means of changing coloured lights, which served to guide the spectators towards their homes, while the village street was prettily decorated with **Chinese lanterns**.

Christian duty

Far more people attended church in Victorian Britain than they do today. Jews, Muslims and people of other faiths were free to practise their own religions. However, most British people were Christian. Many people believed that the Bible was the direct word of God, with strict commandments about how people should behave. One of the most important commandments for the Victorians was 'to keep holy the Sabbath (Sunday)', which was intended as a day of rest and worship. Many people, especially from the middle class, went to church or chapel two or even three times on a Sunday. Shops and places of entertainment remained closed.

Belief in God went far beyond observing Sundays, however. Many Christian groups, such as the Methodists, Quakers and Salvation Army, believed that all Christians had a duty to help improve the lives of others. William Booth, who founded the Salvation Army in 1865, wanted to help those people who did not go to church. He also campaigned against the drinking of alcohol. Booth's army, with its military style uniforms and its brass bands, soon spread around the world.

The Salvation Army was founded as a religious organization that aimed to improve living conditions in Britain and beyond. This chart from 1890 shows how the organization thought they could solve people's problems.

David Livingstone's speech

Other Christians, called **missionaries**, travelled abroad believing it was their duty to teach the Christian religion to those who had not heard about it. David Livingstone, the Scottish missionary and explorer, travelled across much of Africa between 1840 and 1873, spreading Christianity and recording the geography and customs of the African peoples. This extract comes from a speech he gave at Cambridge University in 1857.

My object in going into the country south of the desert was to instruct the natives in a knowledge of Christianity, but many circumstances prevented my living amongst them more than seven years, amongst which were considerations arising out of the slave system carried on by the Dutch Boers. I resolved to go into the country beyond, and soon found that, for the purposes of commerce, it was necessary to have a path to the sea. I might have gone on instructing the natives in religion, but as civilization and Christianity must go on together, I was obliged to find a path to the sea, in order that I should not sink to the level of the natives. The chief was overjoyed at the suggestion, and furnished me with twenty-seven men, and canoes, and provisions, and presents for the tribes through whose country we had to pass.

What have we learnt from the Victorians?

In looking through the **primary sources** in this book, we can see the range of opinion and outlook that marked Victorian society. There is plenty of evidence of the terrible living and working conditions that people suffered. At the same time we can hear the voices of those who worked hard to change those conditions, as on pages 13 and 37. It is their belief in progress which chiefly distinguishes the Victorians from people of other ages, though of course some Victorians did not want to see change at all. Generally, however, most were pleased with their achievements, their literature, their scientific discoveries and inventions, their missionary and charitable efforts; but they also thought that they could do better, and that subsequent generations would do better still. They took it for granted that there would be 'progress'.

In nearly every aspect of daily life, from medicine, science and transport, to entertainment, we reap the benefits of the progress that the Victorians made. We also face many of the same conflicts that they did: industrial disputes, debates about education and health, science versus religion and so on. Only time will tell if we are any better or worse at solving these problems than the Victorians.

A newspaper journalist reflects on the end of an era
The following extract appeared in *The Times* on 23 January 1901, the day after Queen Victoria died. The writer is worried about the state of Britain at the end of an era. In fact, as the writer suggests, 'others', probably meaning the USA and Germany, were catching up with Britain in terms of industrial growth and trade. Britain's position as the wealthiest country in the world was under threat.

The Times

23 January 1901

At the close of the reign we are finding ourselves somewhat less secure of our position than we could desire, and somewhat less abreast of the problems of the age than we ought to be, considering the initial advantages we secured … Others have learned our lessons and bettered our instructions while we have been too easily content to rely upon the methods which were effective a generation or two ago. In this way is the Victorian age defined at its end as well as at its beginning.

The end of an era. Mourners watch the gun carriage carrying Queen Victoria's coffin making its stately way through London during her funeral in 1901.

Timeline

1815	Corn Laws enacted to prevent entry of cheap grain and keep farm wages low and bread prices high.
1819	Birth of Victoria.
1820	Death of King George III. The Prince Regent becomes George IV.
1830	Death of George IV. William IV becomes king.
1837	William IV dies and Victoria becomes queen.
1840	Victoria marries Albert of Saxe-Coburg-Gotha, who becomes known as the Prince Consort.
	The Penny Post is established.
1842	The Mines **Act** bans employment of boys younger than ten and all girls and women from working in underground mines.
1843	Charles Dickens writes *A Christmas Carol*. Music halls and Christmas cards begin to appear.
1846	Corn Laws **repealed**.
	First operation in Britain performed under **anaesthesia**.
1847	Potato **famine** in Ireland; millions either starve or **emigrate** to Great Britain, Australia and the USA.
	Britain's new Ten Hours Bill limits the working day to ten hours.
1848	First Public Health Act passed.
1851	The Great Exhibition opens in London in the Crystal Palace.
1854	Great Britain enters the Crimean War which started in 1853. Great Britain, France and Turkey fight against Russia; Florence Nightingale achieves fame there and founds the nursing profession.
1857	Transatlantic telegraph cable laid between Britain and the USA.
1859	Charles Darwin publishes *On the Origin of Species*.
1861	Prince Albert dies; Victoria mourns until her death in 1901.
1865	The Salvation Army founded.
1869	First bicycle factory established.
1867	The Reform Bill extends voting rights to most working-class men.
1870	The Education Act provides free education for all children up to the age of eleven.
1875	The Employers and Workmen Act guarantees the right of **trade unions** to call **strikes**.
	Public Health Act passed.
1877	Victoria crowned Empress of India; the British Empire is at its peak.
1887	Victoria's Golden Jubilee celebrated.
1889	The Great Dock Strike ends with the first major trade-union victory.
1901	Victoria dies.

Find out more

Books & websites

Life and World of Queen Victoria, Brian Williams, (Heinemann Library, 2002)
People in the Past, Victorian Children, Brenda Williams, (Heinemann Library, 2003)
The Victorians in Britain, Peter Chrisp, (Franklin Watts, 1999)
Turning Points: The Steam Engine, Richard Tames, (Heinemann Library, 2000)
Victorian Village Life, Neil Philip, (Idbury, Village Press), 1993

Go Exploring! Log on to Heinemann's online history resource.
www.heinemannexplore.co.uk

www.historyteacher.net/APEuroCourse/APEuro_Main_Weblinks_Page.html
This site has a variety of primary sources and also has several sound files for
downloading.

www.spartacus.schoolnet.co.uk
The Spartacus site contains a wealth of information about many aspects of Victorian
Britain, with a useful search engine for finding specific information.

www.victorianlondon.org
This site has a wide variety of documents and informative articles about life in
nineteenth-century London.

www.victorianstation.com
This site is devoted to Victorian Britain, with special emphasis on Queen Victoria
herself. There is a fascinating section on quotes by Victoria, recorded throughout
her reign.

List of primary sources

The author and publisher gratefully acknowledge the following publications and websites from which written sources in the book are drawn. In some cases the wording or sentence structure has been simplified to make the material more appropriate for a school readership.

P.9 *The Aylesbury News: News from the English Countryside 1750–1850*, Clifford Morsley, (Harrap, 1979)

P.11 http://members.tripod.com/~midgley/rowlandhill.html from extract from *The Life of Sir Rowland Hill and the Penny Postage*, R. and G. Birkbeck Hill, 1880

P.13 Hector Gavin: www.victorianlondon.org/index1.htm

P.15 Charles Dickens: www.victorianlondon.org/index1.htm

P.17 Charles Darwin: quoted in *For Country and Queen: Britain in the Victorian Age*, Margaret Drabble, (Andre Deutsch, 1978)

P.19 *Art Journal* http://www.speel.demon.co.uk/other/grtexhib.htm
The *Sun* www.channel4.com/learning/main/netnotes/dsp_series.cfm?sectionid=349

P.21 quoted in *For Country and Queen: Britain in the Victorian Age*, Margaret Drabble, (Andre Deutsch, 1978)

P.23 Samuel Smiles:
edweb.tusd.k12.az.us/UHS/WebSite/courses/WC/Historiography/industrialization_and_social.htm

P.25 http://learningcurve.pro.gov.uk/victorianbritain/divided/default.htm

P.27 Isabella Beeton: www.fandom.net/~daeron/Beeton/beeton1.html.

P.29 Ben Tillett: www.spartacus.schoolnet.co.uk/TUdockers.html

P.31 James Greenwood: www.victorianlondon.org/index1.htm

P.33 http://site.yahoo.net/np/versesong.html

P.35 'Old People's Reminiscences', Lancashire Record Office, DDX.9783/3/13

P.37 Annie Besant: 'White Slavery in London' reprinted on:
http://www.wwnorton.com/nael/nto/victorian/industrial/besantfrm.htm

P.39 George Eliot, *Middlemarch*, (Penguin Classics, 1994 p.31)

P.41 www.victorianlondon.org/

P.43 Edward Owen:www.victorianlondon.org/

P.45 *The Adoration of the Magi* tapestry made by William Morris and Co. 1890

P.47 Reverend C.W. Jones:www.pakenham-village.co.uk/History/PakRJ1887.htm

P.49 David Livingstone: http://www.cooper.edu/humanities/classes/coreclasses/hss3/d_livingstone.html

P.51 *The Victorian Scene: 1837–1901*, by Nicolas Bentley, (Weidenfeld & Nicolson, 1968)

Glossary

abstain   hold back from doing something

act   (of parliament) law passed by parliament

anaesthesia   deadening of pain, usually caused by drugs, so the patient doesn't feel pain during an operation

antiseptic   substance that stops the spread of germs

atheist   someone who does not believe in the existence of God

bias   judgement that is based on personal opinion

boycott   refuse to use or have anything to do with something, usually as a form of protest

Chinese lantern   collapsible lantern made of thin paper, often used as a decoration

cholera   disease, often fatal, which causes acute stomach pain, vomiting and diarrhoea and which can easily be passed on to others

coffers   funds held in reserve for a group or institution

colony   group of people separated from, but governed by, another country

coming out   event, usually a ball, where wealthy young women first join adults at social occasions

distrain   seize property from someone until that person can repay a debt

domestic service   working as a servant in wealthier people's houses

draper   someone who sells cloth

emigrate   leave one country and settle in another

epidemic   widespread outbreak of disease that spreads quickly

evolution   change in a type of plant or animal over generations, suggesting that the strongest in one generation are likelier to reproduce and pass on their characteristics to later generations

famine   terrible, and often prolonged, shortage of food

festoon   string or chain of flowers or ribbons, hanging in a curve as a decoration

gentry   class of people in Britain below the nobility, but still owning large amounts of land and other property

gibbet   wooden frame on which convicted criminals were hanged

hygiene   attention to cleanliness and the avoidance of spreading germs

illiterate   unable to read or write

Industrial Revolution   period, beginning in Britain in the 1700s, during which new inventions and methods of working brought about rapid changes in industry

manufacture   making a large number of goods using machines

missionary   person sent to another country specially to spread the Christian religion

naturalist   scientist who studies the natural world

novel   work of literature, usually much longer than a short story, in which invented characters are involved in a series of events

primary source   original account or image describing a historical event or era

Providence   the protective care of God

public school   school that charges fees. Typically only children of the wealthy would attend such schools.

repeal   annul or overturn an act of law

Royal Commission   organization given royal approval to suggest government action

scourge   whip or lash used to punish people

secondary source   historical account recorded some time after the events and by someone who was not there at the time

socialist   someone who believes wealth should be shared equally and that the main industries should be controlled by the government

species   specific category of plant or animal; members of the same species share many similar characteristics

strike   stop work until some improvement to working conditions is made; usually done by a group of workers in the same type of work or employed at the same business

temperance   deliberate choice not to drink alcohol

trade union   organization of workers, usually in the same type of trade or work, which aims to improve the working conditions of its members

transported   sent by force to another country as a punishment. Criminals were often transported to Australia and were forced to stay there for a long time, even for minor offences.

tuberculosis   infectious disease that leads to small swellings in many parts of the body, especially the lungs

turbine   type of engine

typhus   infectious disease, transmitted by lice and fleas and causing fatigue, violent headaches and reddish spots on the body

vexation   something that annoys or is a nuisance

workhouse   institution for the very poor where they would receive food and shelter in return for work

55

Index

Titles in the *Witness To History* series include:

Hardback   0 431 17044 4

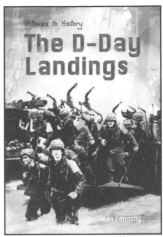

Hardback   0 431 17043 6

Hardback   0 431 17042 8

Hardback   0 431 17034 7

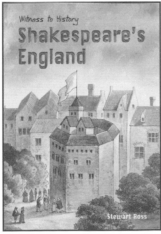

Hardback   0 431 17046 0

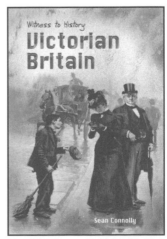

Hardback   0 431 17045 2

Find out about the other titles in this series on our website www.heinemann.co.uk/library